THE TREE THROUGH

Book One of the Panagea Tales

McKenzie Austin

Chapter One

The natural world had died. Mankind had stripped the land of its trees, its creatures, and its essence. People had claimed the rocks, the rubble, and all the structures upon it. Old world gods had disappeared from memory. Machines of iron and steam had lain waste to inefficiency. The inhabitants of Panagea had massacred the organic, undomesticated wild. But the cruel touch of humanity could only stretch so far. They had killed the land, but the sea did not relent to their selfish desires.

The sea remained alive.

The storm outside rocked the ocean vessel, bucking it over the waves, like a wild stallion. Lightning split the sky in two, illuminating the ebbs and flows of the violent water.

The liveliness of the elements outside was a stark contrast to the lifelessness of the body slumped over a table within one of the ship's many cabins. A scarlet liquid seeped from beneath the fallen maiden's head, down the imperfect table, and oozed until it teetered on the edge. Lightning flashes through a small window illuminated the gruesome scene, highlighting

A knock sounded at the do(
screams of old wood creaking un(
sea.

The body remained motionle
Another knock, more forcefu
ilar response. Silence.

With
found it.
It took a
words. Once his

Additional beads of red liquid trickled to the edge of the table. They formed a larger puddle that slipped over, dangling, until another chaotic wave shifted the ship. The droplet plummeted from the ledge, struck the floor and splattered.

The woman's eyes shot open. She blinked several times to banish the fatigue from her body as she sat upright. Angry pops from her spine voiced their disapproval for passing out in an uncomfortable position.

"Gods be damned," she hissed, wiping the blood-red stain of wine from her cheek. Her gaze lowered when she realized she not only had spilled it all over the table but had passed out in the puddle. The captain would not be pleased that the last of his natural wine flowed more through the cracks in the floorboards than through her veins.

A third knock cleared the haze from her brain. She stood, boots clicking on the floor as she approached the door, and pulled it open. "Evening, Captain," she grumbled, pushing a chunk of hair glued together by wine from her eyes. "Awfully late to be running around all willy-nilly in a lady's quarters, don't you think?"

It was hard to gauge his facial expression as a well-timed crack of lighting silhouetted his form. The dark figure crept into her room, staggering in height. "I hate to get your hopes up, Bermuda," he muttered sarcastically, "but this isn't a late-night booty call."

"Well, shucks." Bermuda feigned disappointment as she stretched, trying to get blood flowing into her fingertips. "Then to what do I owe this pleasure?"

The captain faced her, his eyes unable to contain his thrill. the passion of a madman, he whispered through a grin, "We

moment for her fuzzy mind to catch up with his message settled over her, the adrenaline fueling her body disbanded any lingering aches. "The well?" Her eyes narrowed in disbelief. "You found the well?"

"*Mimir's* well." He laughed, slamming an open palm on her table in excitement. "We should arrive in seven days."

Bermuda eyed the captain, her jaw slack. Gods, could it truly be? Mimir's well promised to be their biggest score, better than all the other fairytales and myths of old they had hunted prior. The well's guardian was a prize more valuable than the loot they had salvaged from Gargan's wreckage, more esteemed than the fabled Book of Plythius they had plundered from the coves, more lusted after than any mythological treasure they had ever tracked from the tales passed down by ancient orators.

Several versions of the story floated around the world, but the bottom line was the same—with a sacrifice to Mimir, water from his well ensured one's deepest fantasy shifted from hopeless want into reality.

Bermuda's gaze hit the floor as she tried to absorb the confession. Mimir's well. It was a rare find. Panagea and the dried husks of land surrounding it did not have many of the old-world wonders left. Gods and goddesses, brought to life through mankind's imagination, had been replaced long ago when men found they could answer their own prayers. They did not need to appease the gods to grow their crops when they could mass produce their own food-like products. They did not need to beg for their favor when they fell ill if they could manufacture their own medicines. Without sacrifice and prayer to sustain them, the gods and goddesses faded from existence.

It was not just the deities who remained in short supply; all legends of old were difficult to come by. The crew had shared limited successes in myth hunting, often supplementing their time by plundering more literal treasures instead. But, even in the trying times, where years separated them between one mythological prize and the next, moments like these made the wait of those years disappear into nothingness.

"Kazuaki Hidataka ..." Bermuda smiled at the man, having no shame in dropping the formality of addressing her captain by his name instead of his rank. "It's moments like this that make serving with you bearable."

Kazuaki slicked his hands through his damp mass of long black hair. A slow smirk crept across his face as he stared at his quartermaster. "I'll drink to that."

Bermuda's face fell as Kazuaki reached for the dusty bottle atop the table. His aura of enthusiasm faded into one of irritation. "Bermuda ..." He raised the bottle and tipped it upside down to draw attention to its glaring emptiness. "I can't help but notice you sullied the table with my Meritage Bordeaux."

"Not before it sullied my liver," she quipped, trying to downplay the offense. She knew the bottles were precious to him and tried to respect the fact, but some nights were longer than others. Sometimes man-made alcohol just didn't fill the hole. She bent over, using her sleeve to soak up some of the mess. "How many bottles do you have left from those ruins anyway?"

"Not enough," Kazuaki murmured, staring at the red liquid that seeped into the wooden table. "In the future, I would prefer you not drown your sorrows with irreplaceable harvests."

Though he tempered the heat in his words, she felt his disdain like a physical force. Bermuda understood his frustration. These were not the days of old where grapes grew with the loving influence of a tender vineyard keeper. Grapes were only a memory now. Bermuda had read many accounts. They seemed to be a popular delicacy, their praises sung of in the memoirs of olden days.

Though she'd never admit it out loud, she adored reading those ancient transcripts. They transported her to a time where her own troubles could not follow, to an imaginary land where philosophy and hands-on work reigned supreme. Those journal entries painted a simpler life, where oxygen flowed like rivers over the world. Though the authors of those texts were long dead, their words brought that time to life. Funny how several hundred years changed a landscape so much.

"This still deserves a toast," Bermuda said, breaking the silence. "How about something from the storage cellar as opposed to the private stash?"

Kazuaki spit on the floor and scowled. "Mass-produced rubbish. If I wanted to blacken my tongue with that toxic sludge, I'd have brought a bottle with me."

Bermuda crossed her arms, a knowing look on her face. She waited with patience.

The captain elongated the long pause between them before he sighed. She knew him too well. He pulled a flask from his long jacket's pocket. "To the well," he toasted and sipped from the container before handing it to his comrade.

Bermuda smiled, raising the flask. "To the well." She took a swig of her own.

The two stood in the cabin, absorbing the impact of the moment. If all went well, their lives would be very different by next week.

Bermuda grinned, delighting in the fantasy of an existence free from her biggest flaw. It wasn't until she thought of what the captain would ask for that her glee shifted into a weak frown. She glanced at him and thought how he seldom mentioned his condition, but alcohol had pulled it out of him more than a few times in their adventures. Bermuda knew Kazuaki lamented his circumstances, despite how comforting she found them to be.

"Will you ask him for it then?" she wondered out loud, unwilling to wait seven days to discover for herself. "Mortality?"

The captain pressed his lips together as he stood in the shadowed room. He had many long years to experience the pros and cons of an unending life. There existed no shortage of men or women who would have thought him crazy for trying to rid himself of his affliction, but only those who walked his path knew the crushing weight eternal life had on a man. On a soul. Individuals clamored for immortality. Ancient texts highlighted it as a glamorous boon, never having to worry about the prospect of death. Kazuaki Hidataka knew better. He did not choose eternal life. He was cursed with it.

"Yes." He stroked his beard, unable to look at her. "I believe I will."

Bermuda's gaze fell to the floor. It seemed the years her captain and comrade had chased after freedom from his pestilence would finally pay off. She struggled to understand why he wanted to invite the opportunity for death into his life, but Bermuda suspected the captain knew a great deal more about the nightmares of an everlasting existence than she did.

The quartermaster's frown grew more potent. Accepting the loss of a loved one had never come easy to her. Contrary to Kazuaki's desires, Bermuda loved that no risk existed of losing him. It provided her with a permanent sense of relief.

As the silence between them grew, her gaze flitted to him. He wanted this. She knew he had hunted it for many hundreds of years. Perhaps she could cling to a small hope he might change his mind. "Well"—she hitched her shoulder, forcing a smirk—"just don't go rushing into any suicide missions after it's done."

Kazuaki caught her stare, noticing her lingering anxiety. "I have no desire to rush toward the afterlife, Bermuda." One side of his lips tugged into a half-grin. "Only the desire to see it one day. With any luck, before the world sees it first."

The captain turned away and pulled back his shoulders. He was not blind to the struggles of their realm; Panagea was suffering. It was the land's obvious cries for help that had prompted him to find the cure to immortality sooner rather than later. He shuddered to think of what madness awaited him if the world and everything in it withered into nothingness while he remained left to endure it.

Kazuaki glanced at Bermuda to survey her reaction. She seemed to have accepted his response, at least as much as he expected her to. "So ..." The immortal cleared his throat. "What will *you* ask of him?"

Bermuda's warm face iced over.

Kazuaki flinched. He held fast to their unmoving eye contact, though he regretted asking after the shift in her demeanor.

The quartermaster focused on the empty flask as if willing it to refill itself. "You know damn well what I'd ask of him."

Kazuaki's shoulders tightened. "Yes." He tucked his hands behind his back and stepped away from her. "I suppose I do."

Damn it all. Awkward moments rarely existed between the two, but he had walked straight into this one. He should have known how she'd react. Kazuaki had mastered the art of tempering his feelings, particularly those involving his quartermaster, but Bermuda ... she wore her heart on her sleeve. In the susceptible position in which she left it, it was her heart that caused her the most trouble.

Kazuaki stole a glimpse of her in the dark. He saw the invisible burdens she carried with her. Even in her rare moments of vulnerability, he still witnessed her fierceness, her loyalty—irreplaceable, enigmatic, and one of the best things to happen to him in his multitude of lives. Bermuda may have despised her heart, but Kazuaki adored it. It was the greatest shame that his condition prevented him from claiming a piece for himself.

The captain's eardrums pulsed, homing in on the crew's up-roarious laughter in the dining hall. He had not shed the light of the good news to them yet. It had been more pressing to relay it to Bermuda first. He was dutiful to those he employed. Each one was handpicked for possessing one positive quality or another, but Kazuaki admitted to playing favorites. Some were just more trust-worthy than others. It was a hard lesson he had learned throughout the countless years spent with people. The generation they hailed from made no difference; bad apples who suffered from irreparable character flaws always hid amongst the masses.

He should tell them, he thought and cringed at the reality of it. It would be a long seven days sailing with a ship full of men and women who were about to have their deepest wishes granted. He hoped his crew's dynamic wouldn't change much when they found out. It did not surprise him anymore how quick a man turned ugly, given the right conditions—even trusted ones.

Pacing the room, the captain's thoughts drifted to earlier days. Since man had first gathered around prehistoric fires, stories spread of their evil and greed. Kazuaki had witnessed plenty instances for himself. He once had seen a man murder his own brother over ownership of a prize as small as an animal's carcass. He had beheld another man mutilate a farmer over a handful of pumpkin seeds. A woman had drowned her own child at the docks where he had worked hundreds of years ago, before the art of seafaring had died. Her action had been bred from nothing more than sheer spite that her child's father had chosen a life at sea rather than a life with his own family.

Realizing how much tension invaded his shoulders, Kazuaki forced his muscles to relax. He had to remind himself that the un-flattering characters of his memory were nothing like his present-day crew. He knew what psychological characteristics to look for in someone he gave his trust to. Of course, it remained wise to always inject a healthy amount of caution into each situation. Many books and tales of betrayal regarding mankind's hideousness spread through his ship. Kazuaki never surmised why men recorded as much of their history as they did, being that most of it was unflattering.

His eyes widened, and he patted his jacket. The musings put him in mind of the contents in his other pocket. "I almost forgot," he muttered, reaching to pull the small leather-bound book from its hiding place. "While Bartholomew and I were sifting through ancient texts for documents on Mimir, I found this." Kazuaki handed the dilapidated book to Bermuda. "I know how much you enjoy peering into the eyes of the past."

Bermuda accepted the gift, cradling it in her open palm. Her fingers ran over the cover, though not too hard, as the book was in such a state it seemed a soft breeze could destroy it. A peaceful smile fell over her. "Thank you." She flipped open the cover and turned to a random entry. "Join me in a listen?"

The captain became locked in eye contact that would betray his feelings of disinterest had he not perfected the ability to contain his emotions. Kazuaki cared little about the contents of that journal. He had already lived everything the pages ever contained and more. He had skimmed the book for any mention of mythological sites they could plunder, but he'd only made it through the first couple entries before deeming it a tedious record of daily activity belonging to a man long dead. It didn't matter that an important man had penned this journal—one of the Time Fathers of the Northern division from many years prior. Even important men were irrelevant to Kazuaki Hidataka. "Of course," he found himself saying. At least it would be a short opportunity to enjoy Bermuda's company.

The corner of her lips formed half a smile as her eyes flitted to the page. "*The push to modernize comes strongly from the Time Fa-*

thers of individual divisions." Her finger slid beneath the words as she spoke. "*But to what end? Can the convenience provided by the cold touch of metal and steel ever outweigh the romance of natural products? A metal pole can plunge through the earth with more strength than a wooden stake, for sure, but at the end of the day, with proper structure, each still holds the cow in the pasture ...*" She wrinkled her nose. "What the feck is a cow?"

Kazuaki watched the storm through her cabin's small window. "A large beast fit for eating, milking, shitting, and not much else."

Bermuda chortled and skipped to a different entry. "*There never was so perfect a thing than the burst of those cherry tomatoes on my tongue, small spheres of scarlet sweetness that exploded and melted over my buds ...*" Bermuda's soft laughter from before grew louder as she peered at Kazuaki. "Paints himself as a bit of a dandy, aye?"

The captain scoffed then joined her in a chuckle, still watching the lightning compete with the sea. "Comes as no surprise to me. All the Time Fathers I've ever encountered were self-righteous jackasses."

"You'd almost have to be to think you're important enough to control an entire division's time." Bermuda turned page after page. "This journal *must* be old. He talks an awful lot about the natural elements here—flowers, herbs, vegetables, and the like. Here, listen to this." She ran her finger to a specific entry. "*I have filled my lungs with the generous oxygen these lush trees provide, but never has any organ inside me been so close to bursting with fullness as my heart when it fills at the mere sight of her ...*"

Kazuaki, about to make a crude joke about full and bursting organs, stiffened as the enthusiasm in Bermuda's voice waned. No greater annoyance existed than a love-struck man with a pen. The atmosphere in the room shifted as the words she read settled over the two.

His eyes pinched shut, and he stifled a groan. Dammit. He should have known better than to gift her the book. The subject of love had found its way into every snippet of scribing since man first developed the written word. Given the circumstances, he preferred to spare Bermuda any reminders of its existence. "It's true," he interjected, trying to change the subject. "Can you believe there once was a time when oxygen was free and plentiful? We didn't need supplementation in its various forms." He slid his hands into his pockets to thumb the syringe hiding inside.

Bermuda didn't listen. Her eyes remained glued to the thin, age-soaked sheets of parchment and ink. "*She was a vision*," she continued, her words now marinated in venom instead of whimsy. "*She coated the world with existence everywhere she went. She breathed life into this place, much as she breathed life into my soul.*" Bermuda cleared her throat and slammed the book shut, tossing it onto the table. Several fragile papers flew from the binding, turning pink as they soaked the wine that still sat on the tabletop.

Kazuaki regarded the book to give his eyes a focal point that wasn't Bermuda's face. Every instinct screamed at him to say something, do something, anything that would bring her some shred of comfort. Perhaps a well-timed hand placed on her shoulder or a thought-out platitude would ease her torment. Instead, indecision claimed him, and he did nothing.

"I'm getting tired," Bermuda whispered, turning her back to her superior as she approached the door. "If we're through here, Captain ..."

Kazuaki frowned. It was disheartening to watch. Of all the horrors he had seen in his long lifetime, witnessing Bermuda's emotional fall was the most traumatizing. It was like watching a great warrior, who had bathed in the blood of many to win countless battles and wars, fall to their death from the common cold. Too often the only one alive strong enough to destroy Bermuda was herself.

"I should see that Brack is staying on course." Kazuaki straightened his rain-soaked long jacket as he approached the door. "So easily distracted, gods know that man could find an old mop attractive if he was left alone with it long enough."

"Right." Bermuda opened the door to see him out. "Goodnight, Captain."

Before he mustered a reply, he felt the door close behind him. The rain poured without mercy, weighing down his clothing and matting his untamed hair to his bearded jaw. He cursed himself for not further delving into the contents of the book before he had handed Bermuda's glaring weakness to her on a silver platter—or rather, on aging paper. But she would bounce back. She always did.

The captain started toward the ship's wheel, concerned now that Brack "The Rabbit" Joney might well be caught with his pants down if he did not relieve him of his duties soon enough. He trusted the man with everything he had in him. He trusted each one of his crewmembers to a similar degree. But Brack, he was an odd sort. He was a man who would take a bullet for a comrade but then try to feck the hole it left behind.

"Cappy!" The shrill voice cut through the storm like a knife through a manufactured butter substitute. Brack held the wheel steady, though one could see it was no easy feat. "Quite a storm, eh?"

Kazuaki approached Brack with his usual sense of authority and commandeered the ship's wheel. He made it look effortless despite the wheel's desire to spin out of control like a wild animal. After years of practice and muscle memory, there was no storm yet Kazuaki Hidataka could not tame.

"It's *Captain*, Brack, and so it is!" he shouted over the whipping winds and water the sea spat onto his face. "You're relieved, Rabbit. Return below deck, if you please."

"Aye, Captain." Brack used his calloused hands to wipe an hour's worth of rainwater from his sun-damaged face. "You and Bartholomew find what you was looking for in them old books?" he yelled back, accustomed to loud conversations held in apocalyptic weather.

Kazuaki grinned, allowing the thrill of their next adventure to replace the guilt of Bermuda's anguish. "We did, my good man." He held the ship's wheel steady with one hand and patted Brack's shoulder with the other. "We're well on our way to Mimir's well."

"You sing a sweet song, Captain!" Brack laughed, pumping his fist and spinning on his heels. His primitive jig showed only a fraction of his excitement. "When do we hit land? I need to count the hours between now and eternal happiness."

"I struggle to believe you could count so high." Kazuaki smirked. "Eternal happiness, is it? That's what you'll ask Mimir for?"

Brack exploded into riotous laughter. "Go on. We all know what I'll be asking that little lesser god for now, don't we?" He flashed a toothy smile, and Kazuaki found himself grateful the winds were strong, as they spared him from the off-putting smell of Brack's breath.

Kazuaki furrowed his brow and tried to stop his imagination from thinking too hard. "I shudder at the very idea, Rabbit. We'll be there in seven days. Go on, grab some bottles from the storage below deck and tell the rest of the crew the good news."

"Bottles?" Brack howled with more laughter. "I'm sure you mean bottles of the *good* stuff, aye?"

Kazuaki shot the man a glare. All it took was one look to know nobody was to put a hand on his personal supply. The captain was hard but fair; he had distributed a specific amount of the valuable goods to the crew when they had raised that old-world wine from its resting place. Why should he suffer simply because he was better at rationing them than they had been? Since the grapes' disappearance, quality wines were impossible to come by. The bottles were far too precious to Kazuaki to chug. The taste brought him back several lifetimes ago, before he had seen as many horrors as he had. To Kazuaki, that wine was invaluable. It tasted like better memories.

Brack withdrew his jubilance, but it was hard to make it vanish altogether. He was just too happy a man. "The regular stuff it is, Captain." He slipped into the belly of the ship to deliver the news to his mates.

Kazuaki breathed deeply and refocused on the raging sea. Though the air was much thinner than he remembered it being in decades past, the glorious chaos of the waves were always enough to oxygenate his blood. Tempests such as these were soothing. When one traveled the world for as long as he had, it was easy to develop an algorithm for occurrences, but storms were unpredictable. They held an element of surprise. He *loved* the feeling. It felt like the thrill of mortality again, if only for a moment.

He had made his home on the ocean. It provided him with things the land could not, such as freedom from prosecution. A thieving history and unwillingness to bend to social expectations had banished him from the mainland of Panagea long ago. While a part of Kazuaki Hidataka missed having a stable place to plant his feet, the sea melted into him. They may have been forced into cohabitation, but saltwater ran through his veins.

With both hands planted on the wheel, Kazuaki's thoughts returned to Bermuda. They often did, despite his best efforts. How could he have so carelessly handed her that ticking time bomb of words? The man shook his head. Soon it wouldn't matter. In a week, their anchors would drop into the sands of Mimir's hiding place. If the legend held any truth—and there was always a fraction that did—the lesser god would fulfill her heart's greatest desire. Then she could be free of what ailed her.

Though seeing Bermuda enter a stage of newfound peace was a top priority on his agenda, Kazuaki couldn't help but feel the tingle of anticipation in seeing his own desire come to fruition—to no longer be doomed to see civilizations rise and fall, to be free from the shackles of watching each new dawn begin and end the same as it had during the course of what seemed like forever, to feel surprise again and not just in the eye of a storm, to feel like even the most meaningless interactions between loved ones were memories to hold onto, knowing one day they would have an expiration date. To know *he* would have an expiration date.

If not a soul in the world thought it made sense, it made sense to him.

Kazuaki leaned into the ship's wheel. Though he had lived more lifetimes than he cared to remember, he recalled the instance when he'd spent eleven years shackled to a dungeon's rusting chains before he had freed himself from that place where time stood still. He had endured days so monotonous they almost drove him mad. He would have to channel that mental experience now. Out of everything he'd been through, with his anxiousness as high as it was now, the trip to Mimir's well would be the longest seven days of his life.

Chapter Two

A hand flew up from its haven under soft blankets and crashed onto an end table. A vase filled with faux flowers forged from copper toppled and fell to the floor. Writhing fingers searched the tabletop until they curled around a syringe-like device. Skin and fingertips teetered on the edge of turning an off-putting blue before the hand jammed the tip of the needle into the chest of its owner.

There was no graceful way to gasp for air. Nicholai jolted upright as the shot delivered much-needed oxygen to his blood. His heart, thundering like the gears of an overworked engine, slowed to its normal rate. He dropped the now empty syringe to the floor and pressed his palms over his face. After sweeping beads of sweat from his forehead, he focused on returning his breathing to normalcy.

As the man rehearsed a calming mantra in his mind, an alarm clock sounded from his opposite side. A clumsy, mechanical bird fashioned from aluminum popped from its brass cage. The man-made creature sounded seven grinding warbles before retreating into its prison. Nicholai peered at it from behind his fingers.

"A day late and a coin short on that one, old friend," he muttered, coaxing his legs off the edge of the bed. An alarm clock seemed pointless when a little oxygen dip supplied enough adrenaline to start the day.

The industrial advancements of mankind ushered in many great things, but generations of thinning air weren't one of them. Hypoxia became a frequent occurrence—enough that oxygenated vials were never far out of reach. Nicholai scratched at an itch on his scalp, ruffling his dark hair until the irritation disappeared. He stretched his arms and yawned, preparing his mind for the duties of another day.

"Are you okay?" a lovely woman's concerned voice called into Nicholai's room from the hallway. Her red curls continued to bounce though her body had stopped moving. They softened the distressed look on her face.

Nicholai smiled from his place on the bed. "Perfect." His gaze trailed from the young woman to the decorative flowers on the floor. "Your flowers probably wouldn't say the same, but ..."

The woman sighed and smiled back, swooping down to scoop the metal artwork from the floor. She returned the flowers to their rightful place on the table. "It's all right." She arranged them as if it mattered. "It's not as though you can kill them."

Nicholai placed a hand over his heart. The warmth of his sternum was a stark contrast to the cold pocket watch dangling around his neck. "Then I envy their existence." He chuckled, choosing to find amusement in his rude awakening.

Lilac rolled her eyes and sat beside him on the bed. She threw a heap of blankets onto her lap to warm her legs chilled from running around the sharpness of early morning in a flowing skirt. Her gaze zeroed in on the mark left by the syringe. She frowned. "I can swing by Papa's today and get an ointment for that." She motioned to the tiny hole.

Nicholai arched a brow, trying to assess the damage by looking down. "Don't worry about it." He wiped at the injection site with his index finger. It was small and little need for an ointment, but Lilac was a worrier. "Not as though that's the worst thing that'll happen to me today."

"Oh?" Lilac laughed, her voice a bandage for all that ailed him. "Big day today?"

"I'm afraid so," Nicholai muttered, grabbing the clock that dangled around his neck. Guided by muscle memory, he winded the top, ensuring the hour, minute, and second hands would rotate for another day. "But at least I have a very important date with an incredibly beautiful individual to look forward to."

Lilac's laughter interrupted his corny charade. "Nicholai Addihein"—she smacked his arm—"you can beg all you want to, but I have a very busy day myself." She threw the blankets from her lap and stood from the bed.

Nicholai grabbed a crumpled white shirt left on the floor from the evening prior. "Someone's got a big head. What makes you think I'm talking about you?"

The redhead rolled her eyes a second time and put a hand on her hip. "Who else would possibly have you?"

The same hand that had forced oxygen into his deprived bloodstream not several minutes prior seized Lilac's hand. With unbridled affection, he laced his fingers together with hers. Nicholai gazed at her from his place on the bed and smiled. "Wouldn't matter. There's nobody else I'd possibly want." He tugged her into his lap as he wrapped his arms around her waist.

Lilac smirked, straddling her legs around him and placing her hands on his chest. "Honeyed words," she accused and kissed him regardless.

The two fell backward onto the bed and enjoyed one another's embrace. In a world of metal, the touch of a lover's skin remained one of the only soft, organic luxuries left.

Nicholai lingered on her lips for as long as he could, gliding his hands up her bare back from beneath her shirt. His heart raced again, for reasons much different than oxygen deprivation. The moment was short lived however, as Lilac slid off him. Though her body had left, her gaze lingered on her lover. Much as she wished to lose herself to him, there was far too much to do today.

He wished to escape the world with her under the sheets, but he understood the need for her departure. Nicholai's gaze met with Lilac's, and he grinned. "Though," he mused with sarcasm, finding a paisley vest on the floor to throw over his shirt, "I am meeting with Nordjan today. If he treats me to a fancy dinner, you may have a little competition."

Lilac scoffed with a playful smile. She threw up her hands in false defeat while Nicholai buttoned his vest. "How could I compete with the bottomless pockets of the Northern Time Father?" She sauntered to the edge of the room but tossed her head over her shoulder before exiting. "If he treats you to a free meal, I'll take something to go."

Nicholai chuckled, standing to throw his legs into a pair of dark-colored pants. "Anything specific?"

"Doesn't matter." Lilac unabashedly watched him get dressed. "Everything tastes the same anyway."

Nicholai smirked. Her great exaggerations were adorable. Although there remained a limit to the number of flavors today's chefs manufactured from the materials available, there still existed a veritable smorgasbord of options. Having come from a long line of individuals who romanticized all things natural, Lilac Finn was a tough critic of everything synthetic. Nicholai beheld her in adoration. Yes. A beautiful creature born in the wrong era. She wasn't afraid to be vocal about her disinterest in the Time Fathers' push for an all-metal world of efficiency.

So it was ironic, he found, that she was sleeping with one.

"I'll meet you back here, say, five tonight?" Nicholai approached a mirror to slick product through his loosely curled hair. He tempered the craziness of each strand until they settled atop his head. He placed his hat atop his head with little concern to his appearance. Goggles balanced on the hat's brim, ready for use should he need eye protection against any sweeping bursts of coal dust.

"Five-ish." Lilac smiled with whimsy. Never one to bind herself to the suffocating restrictions of hours or minutes, she walked farther down the hallway and into the kitchen they shared. She raised her voice to ensure he heard her through the distance that separated them. "Ointment or no, I'll be stopping by Papa's anyway. I must bring him more water. He also promised me a snippet of microgreens. They're big enough to share now."

Nicholai nodded as he continued to get ready.

Malcolm Finn, Lilac's father, remained the only man in the entire Southeastern division who still grew plants. More impressive still, he was one of the few left in Panagea's entirety who dedicated his life to raising living vegetation. Despite its rarity, his shop was not suffering. Though the majority appreciated the ease of today's modern meal, a handful of die-hard naturalists remained who enjoyed the fascination of watching something grow.

Limited space and desire for efficiency aside, the water rations kept most residents from growing in the confines of their own property, but Malcolm made it work. While it was fine for hobbyists, the efforts were abandoned on a large scale. Growing food became an inefficient way to feed an exploding population. People did not wish to suffer through a three-month wait to grow corn when a factory made a suitable substitute within a matter of minutes.

"A soft five o'clock it is." Nicholai double checked his reflection in the mirror before he crossed the distance to find Lilac in the kitchen. He watched as she packed her things—water jugs and a microscopic sample of jam she had made from a single blackberry plant in their impossibly small back yard. Gods, she was perfection. "I love you, Lilac."

The woman gazed up from her collection of containers. Her focus landed on Nicholai with the softness of silk. She tilted her head and smiled. "I love you too."

Her words were the gears to his inner clock. She wound him up every day with the sound of her voice, sustaining him through the hours until he returned to her at night.

After their exchange of farewells, Nicholai slipped out the front door. Checking the time displayed on the Chronometer around his neck, Nicholai cringed. He was cutting it close to his meeting with Nordjan. The elder was obsessed with efficiency. Thirty seconds too late would almost guarantee Nicholai an outlandish tirade about how Time Fathers were the least of all men who should be unpunctual.

The rhythmic booms of busy cylinders and pistons greeted Nicholai as he walked deeper into the town. He straightened his off-white shirt's collar and readjusted his hat, chastising himself for not having set his alarm earlier. Nordjan would notice he had taken no steps to iron his clothing. Useless formalities to Nicholai were critical steps to the Northern Time Father. A small part of him felt guilty for neglecting his duties, but cutting the little things from his daily routine gave him more time to focus on the important things, and a Time Father's days held plenty of those.

Thick coatings of coal dust clung to the air. The wind blew microscopic specs of black debris onto his shirt, and, while small, their presence looked obvious on the white rayon. It was a common visual irritant. Despite the vexation, Nicholai rarely adjusted his goggles over his eyes. The coal did not bother him much. It seemed more off-putting to wander down the sidewalk with goggles drawn over his face, though that was the norm of most inhabitants. The more affluent people who could afford the hats with attached tubes that led to concealed oxygen tanks looked even more ridiculous, he thought. Then there were those who could not afford the luxurious oxygen-tubed hats. They opted for a grotesque face mask to ward off the air pollution instead. Though their fashion choices came from necessity, they still looked ludicrous.

The hiss of steam sounded in the distance as Nicholai halted at a cobblestone intersection. Though his destination resided only blocks away, it took time to get there. The man had to make frequent stops to allow industry to flourish in the form of passing steam cars. They were in no short supply in Panagea. Ever a tool of efficiency, even the lower-middle class stretched their budget if it meant they could incorporate one into their arsenal.

After enough space cleared in the road, Nicholai crossed the street. He made his typical waves and acknowledgments to those who recognized him. He enjoyed the people of the Southeastern division, especially those in his hometown of Nenada. They knew his routine and went out of their way to say hello.

The monthly meetings with Nordjan had been carrying on for so long, the process of leaving his house and appearing at the café was a subconscious habit by now. Much like the machinery that surrounded him, he felt robotic in his current task. It made all the difference when the residents engaged him. It helped him feel human.

"Dammit all!"

Nicholai's ears perked. A frustrated voice cut through the monotony of gyrating gears and unoiled wheels of passing cars. He narrowed his eyes, peering through the thickness of coal dust to see an elderly man struggling with the hand crank on his vehicle's engine. They were difficult enough to use when manipulated by young bones; he couldn't imagine how hard it was to operate with the pains of old age.

Nicholai pursed his lips. He already expected to hear an earful from Nordjan for the carelessness of his physical appearance. Stopping to assist this man would bring no more of a verbal onslaught than he already had coming.

Cutting across the road, Nicholai approached the man. Upon closer inspection, he recognized him as Edwent, one of the region's many mail couriers.

"Can I lend a hand, Edwent?" Nicholai grinned, placing his hand on the crank before he received an answer. He knew Edwent to be a prideful man who would decline help if he gave him a chance. Seeing how erroneous cranking could cause a backfire capable of breaking a man's arm, he did not wish to give him the opportunity.

"Nicholai ..." Edwent acknowledged him with a hoarse voice, wiping sweat from his brow. His irritation at having to rely on someone for help eased into a prominent look of relief. He slid his clammy palms on the legs of his pants while he watched the Time Father crank his vehicle. "Thank you, young man."

"My pleasure." Nicholai patted his shoulder. To kill time as they waited for the car's burner to achieve the proper temperature, Nicholai engaged the man in conversation. "Long route today?"

Edwent shrugged and hoisted his body into the high seat of his automobile. "They all feel long when you get to be my age," he muttered through a quiet chuckle.

Nicholai grinned. "You don't look a day over thirty, my friend. I'm likely to be mistaken for your older brother if I linger here much longer."

Edwent's small chuckle grew into a prominent laugh. "You're either too kind or you're in dire need of some eyeglasses." The courier tapped the spectacles that sat on his bulbous nose. "I've seen thirty a lot in my lifetime, though the numbers mean less and less the older you get."

"Come now." Nicholai raised his voice as the clamoring of Edwent's combustion engine rattled from the car. "You're only as old as you feel."

"Yeah, yeah." Edwent snorted, waving off Nicholai with wrinkled hands. "Go on now. You have more important things to do than chat with an old man."

"And those letters won't deliver themselves, I'm sure." Nicholai smirked and stepped backward to allow Edwent to continue down the street. With a quick turn of the heel, he started back toward the café.

Two brass bells above the café door rattled as Nicholai pushed it open. He spotted Nordjan immediately, and the man appeared as irritated as he suspected.

Though the Northern Time Father was almost twice Nicholai's age, he had a powerful reverence about him as he sat, stooping over his beverage. "You're—"

"Late. I'm afraid so." Nicholai smeared coal dust and filth from Edwent's car onto his shirt as he wiped it to smooth any wrinkles. "My apologies, Nordjan."

The Northern Father scowled. He watched Nicholai slip into the chair across from him. "You've been Time Father of the Southeastern division for almost a decade now, Nicholai. You would think, at some point, you could conduct yourself with an air of professionalism."

Nicholai donned his best look of playful remorse and shrugged. "I don't know what else to say, Nordjan. I'm sorry."

Disgust emanated from Nordjan's eyes as they settled upon the insulting condition of Nicholai's appearance. He released his grip from his copper mug and rubbed his temples with disdain. "The Western Father may be your flesh and blood, Nicholai, but his title does not guarantee your immunity. Your power here is in its infancy when compared to all the other ruling divisions."

Nicholai raised his hands in defense. "I never asked Edvard for this position—"

Nordjan pursed his lips, his voice like venom as he narrowed his eyes. "Then perhaps you shouldn't have accepted his offer. It's a great deal of responsibility being accountable for an entire region's time. The stakes are higher now than they've ever been."

"Nordjan—" Nicholai stopped himself. He had a thousand and one sarcastic remarks stored in the back of his mind, but he battled his instincts and pushed them to the side. Despite himself, he tried to be a better, more productive leader. It was difficult competing with the experience of the other Time Fathers. He had a lot to prove, and while Southeastern boasted higher than normal morale, Nicholai often struggled to make the more difficult decisions required of his title. He cleared his throat, trying to regain the air of diplomacy. "If the stakes are higher than they were previously"—he interlocked his fingers before resting them on the table—"we should discuss our options."

"Agreed." Nordjan straightened his posture. "More of Eastern's coast has separated from the mainland and fallen into the sea."

Nicholai raised a brow. "Another? We already lost several acres last month."

"Precisely. The land is dying, like diseased parasites falling from the flesh of a sick host. The more land we lose, the less remains for us. For industry. For progression."

Nordjan lifted his mug to his lips and took a small drink before setting it back down.

"I've sanctioned land for more research facilities in Northern. Vadim commissioned more factories to be built in Northwestern to manufacture materials for the buildings we've lost to the sea. We'll make strides to combat these issues. In the meantime, your division is to build additional settling tanks. Water purification on a large scale is becoming more critical by the day."

"Sure," Nicholai agreed, his previous disregard for the importance of Nordjan's visit vanishing at the news.

Panagea had been crumbling for some time now, but the rate at which large pieces withered, dried up, and detached from the mainland to disappear into the ocean caused sleepless nights. Industry flourished, and families flourished with it. The higher the population climbed, the more land was needed for homesteads, but they competed with the need for more facilities, more factories, and more purification plants.

Acreage remained as important for the townsfolk as it did for the businesses. Nicholai knew if the two had to compete over shrinking land, it was the families who would suffer. The blue bloods of Panagea owned the companies that manufactured the food and the corporations that produced the pharmaceuticals; they always held the upper hand in the grand scheme of things. To the masses, business was vital. If it came down to a small family of four needing land for their residence or a multi-million-dollar corporation needing land for expansion, that family would be homeless.

Nordjan seemed pleased by Nicholai's devastated look. "I'm glad to see you're taking this seriously," he whispered, trying to keep his voice down. He did not wish to risk prying public ears to cause widespread panic.

Nicholai blinked, bringing himself down from the height of his imagination and into the café with Nordjan. "Right." He shook his head. "But space is limited here as it is. I'd have to instruct established businesses to tear down shop to make space for building settling tanks." The opinion was not a poplar one, but he'd sacrifice the companies before he demolished a home.

"Then start with the most useless ones and go from there." Nordjan slid his now empty cup to the center of the table. "I'd start with that ridiculous plant shop if I were you."

Nicholai felt his stomach sink. "With all due respect, Nordjan, a good handful of people here really appreciate Finn's Greenhouse. The nursery is small, but—"

"Pointless. A hobby like that does not feed and clothe the world. Peoples' lives are at stake here." He placed his palms on the table and leaned forward, his face inches from his colleague. "You start making some hard decisions, or by the next decennial gathering of the Time Fathers, we will find someone else who will."

Nicholai glared at Nordjan, unflinching. He inclined his chin, grinding his teeth to save himself from saying something he'd regret. "Yes, sir."

Nordjan slid back and straightened himself. "Good man. Now, if you'll excuse me." He pulled the silver pocket watch from beneath his pristine suit. "I only have six hours and thirty-seven minutes to return to the Northern division before I must wind."

Nicholai said nothing. It wouldn't have mattered if he did. The most critical part of a Time Father's duties was to be within his realm to *wind the watch*, as they called it—the one, sole task that kept time in their assigned division moving forward. It was so heinous a crime for a Time Father to stop his realm's time that he knew an uptight conformist like Nordjan would never miss the opportunity.

Though he wished to debate further which businesses he would have to shut down, Nicholai did not wish to delay Nordjan's return. Stopping time in one realm while others continued onward damaged the world's infrastructure. It was fragile enough as is.

"Until next month," Nordjan grumbled, tossing money on the table to cover the cost of his beverage. Before he left, he turned, lingering in the doorway. "We are the ones burdened from overseeing time, Nicholai, and we are running out of it. Do your part to ensure Panagea keeps ticking."

Nicholai watched in silence as Nordjan slipped out the door. He forgave the irritating play on words. The once jovial ringing of the bells seemed more ominous with Nordjan's exit. He spied from the window as the Northern Father climbed into the personal flying machine he had parked in a designated space outside. The ornithopter was a rather clumsy looking device by any standards and a wasteful way to travel. Still, it remained the only way to make a quick return to his wintery division in time.

Nicholai sat back in his chair, defeated by their hurried conversation. How would he explain to Malcolm Finn why he had to destroy his storefront? Perhaps more pressing on his thoughts was how he would explain it to Lilac.

A waitress saved him from dwelling on those concerns when she swooped over with a smile. "Can I get you anything, Nicholai?"

The Southeastern Father donned his best face. It was a gift and a necessity to spare the locals from political anxieties. "Not today, Marta, but thank you."

Marta returned his kind smile with a nod and cleared Nordjan's copper mug from the table. "Well, I'll be at the front if you change your mind. I'm sorry, I would have come over to ask you sooner, but you know that man makes my skin crawl."

"Yes," Nicholai agreed with her, sparing Marta any regret at having said an unflattering thing about the Northern Father. While it was expected the public treat the eight Fathers with respect, no love was lost regarding the more abrasive superiors. "Let's just say I wouldn't hurry to invite him to any parties either," Nicholai added with a gentle smile.

Marta's cheeks reddened as she tried to contain her laughter. "Oh, you. Well, I'd better go make myself useful," she said between tiny giggles.

Nicholai watched as she scurried to her duties. Without the waitress to distract him with chitchat, he once again found himself in the unenviable spot he was before. Malcolm Finn's entire life weaved through that greenhouse. He and his wife had devoted their souls to the place. After Mrs. Finn's passing, Malcolm's obsession with plant life only grew. Having grown up in that environment, Lilac had inherited her parents' love of nurturing the little seedlings. To sentence Malcolm to abandon his store ... Nicholai had no clue who would hate him more: Malcolm Finn or his daughter.

The defeated man buried his face into his hands and released an exasperated sigh. He sat in silence until the sound of glass setting onto the table caused him to look up.

Marta stood over him again with a soft smile. "Here you go, love. This one's on the house. I'm not sure what you and that pompous lout talked about, but you look like you could use this." She slid the offering toward him.

Nicholai eyed the small shot glass and smirked. The distinctive smell of alcohol rose from the gift with potency. "You're too kind, Marta, but I don't drink."

The waitress stared him down, dissecting the truth in his words. "Forgive me for saying, but, by the looks of you, sweetheart, maybe you should start."

She drew a laugh from him, though Nicholai regretted the obviousness of his anguish. In normal circumstances, he was good at concealing it, but the weight of Nordjan's news was heavier than usual. Not wanting to insult her generous offer, Nicholai grabbed the small glass between his fingers and lifted it in a toast. "Cheers," he said with a feigned appreciation before he tilted back his head and banished the drink down his throat.

"There you are." Marta smiled, taking the now empty glass from his hands. "Wasn't so hard now, was it?"

The man felt a fire rise from his guts. His eyes watered at the corners, and he exhaled to expel the taste. "Tell me. Is it supposed to burn all the way down?" he uttered between pounding his chest with a fist.

"'Tis." Marta patted his back. "The more burn in your body, the less burn in your thoughts—that's what I always say."

"Charming." Nicholai coughed and laughed at the same time. "Thank you for your mercy drink, Marta, but I really should be off now." He stood to his feet and reached into his pocket. "Are you sure I can't pay you?"

"I'd consider it a personal insult if you did." Marta wiped the table with a damp rag after he stood. "See you next time, Nicholai."

He nodded a formal goodbye and excused himself out the door. He surveyed the hustle and bustle of the townspeople naïve to the fact their world was crumbling. Most would take the news of establishing more settling tanks well. When worded with the right finesse, it would appear to be a positive thing—more work for the jobless, more money flowing into the pockets of individuals who could disperse through businesses for goods and services, and more purified water for those who otherwise had to ration it. Yes, painted in the right way, the public would rejoice. At least ... those who didn't have to close their businesses to make room.

The burn of the alcohol had a lingering influence on Nicholai's body. He rubbed his tongue along the roof of his mouth as if that would help. While his brain told him to move, to make haste with the preparations, his body remained paralyzed in its place. He wondered how long he could avoid telling Lilac. He wondered how long it would take to build new tanks or how many more pieces of Panagea would decay and crumble from the continent. He wondered if another shot would make any of it better or worse. Making difficult decisions was never his forte. He had fumbled his way through ruling an entire division for almost ten years, but the rapid decline of the world's health was something he had never expected. The Time Fathers had always led him to believe everything was progressing as it should, with nothing more than minor bumps along the way.

Nicholai also wondered how many other things they had neglected to mention to him before his father had nominated him for this position. He contemplated seeking council from Edvard, but the two weren't close. The last time Nicholai had seen his father was at the decennial anniversary, his induction day to govern the Southeastern division. It was hard to believe he had maintained Southeastern's time for almost ten years. The next decennial would be upon them in a handful of months. It would be the first time he ventured to the central point of separation for each division as a Time Father instead of an inductee. Though the meetings were traditionally reserved for nominating potential new Time Fathers in the event someone lived in failing health or wished to retire, he could still discuss things with his father then.

It remained the only place on Earth where each superior traveled to be within talking distance of every Time Father and remain within his own division. It took a great deal of planning to arrange, and, being the typical term a Time Father served was upward of fifty years, the meetings weren't a frequent occurrence. Nicholai preferred it that way. He already knew enough about the other Time Fathers based on statistic reports and the occasional biography.

Nicholai cleared his mind of such things. It was with fortune he had several tasks today that would keep him busy. At the end of the day, he'd have to engage in a very difficult discussion with Malcolm and Lilac Finn.

Chapter Three

There was no sound more beautiful than anchors dropping into the waters below. The chain's rattling clamored with an intensity that almost matched the ship's captain. Kazuaki stood at the bow and watched his small band of men and women prepare to disembark. Energy had run high since announcing the discovery of Mimir's hiding place.

After everyone finished readying the ship and themselves, the captain prepared himself to tell half the crew they needed to stay behind. It was an unenviable position, but Captain Kazuaki Hidataka was a leader before everything else. There was no way, not even for a moment, he would leave his beloved ship unattended.

"Everything is set, Captain," a voice called from below deck. Elowyn Saveign, the only other female member of Kazuaki's crew, signaled to her superior. She ran her hands through her short black hair to remove any sweat that had formed on her forehead. "The ship is stationary, and supplies are bagged." Though she was a petite thing, Elowyn's voice carried tempered violence befitting her character. She embodied a small hurricane, the right balance of intelligence and muscle Kazuaki required of his team.

"Everyone gather 'round!" The captain's words bellowed like a cannon, summoning the entire band of ten to the forefront, including Granite's excitable mutt.

The dog yipped and wagged his tail but quieted when the behemoth Granite laid a huge yet gentle hand on the canine's head.

Kazuaki put his hands behind his back and stood tall, ensuring everyone was present before he continued. "The first band of us will start our course to track Mimir. Five of you will stay here with the ship. I'll return for you once we find the little bastard and take you to him after, so you might get your go with him too."

The crew exchanged uncomfortable glances. His orders came as no shock; they knew Kazuaki never left his ship in a vulnerable state. They had waited a long time, ever since they had joined Kazuaki's crew and learned of Mimir and the supernatural spoils he afforded to those who found him. The last seven days had been unending torture waiting to dock. They all wanted to be the first to leave.

Kazuaki continued, "Bermuda, Elowyn, Brack, Revi, Granite, you'll all come with me. Bartholomew, Iani, Rennington, Penn, Jirin, you'll all watch the ship until we return." Though his every instinct thought it would be better to leave the trustworthy Quartermaster Bermuda on the ship, he couldn't. The two had searched for Mimir for years. Even though time had worn away most of his weaknesses, Bermuda remained the chink in his armor. He couldn't deny himself her company.

Bartholomew was a close second in rank of those he most trusted. The scholar served as a fine guardian for his beloved ship in the rare event something went wrong.

"Ready yourselves. We head out soon," Kazuaki added, descending the stairs that led to the main deck.

"Belay that!" A disgruntled Jirin stepped in Kazuaki's path. He shot out his arm to stop the captain from walking farther.

With a speed that matched lightning, Kazuaki caught Jirin's forearm in a vicelike grip. Jirin had only been a crewmember for the last month, a hasty replacement for a good man who had died in one of their supply trips to the mainland. It was difficult to keep everyone out of harm's way. Their activities were illegal—stealing supplies and plundering various parts of Panagea in their search for legendary treasure. This often solicited backlash from the footmen on Panagea's divisions. In the event a footman captured a crewmember, their choices were a cell or a bullet. Anyone under Kazuaki's employment earned the latter. The militia knew the captain's tactics. If one of his men were thrown in a cell, come firestorm or high water, he would get them out. It became much easier for the footmen to put them down.

Jirin's tenacious spirit earned him a spot on the ship, but he suffered from being a loose cannon. Kazuaki did not shy away from commandeering Panagea's castaways; his entire crew was comprised of those the divisions had shunned. But, while there was room for Jirin's temper in Panagea, there was no room for it on Kazuaki's ship.

The dog barked as the tension grew.

"Disapproval, Jirin?" The captain lowered his voice, eyes locked with his challenger as he tightened his hold.

Jirin scowled. He tried to jerk away his arm with no success. His fingertips tingled from lack of blood flow, but, in his discomfort, he still hissed, "We've already been waiting too long! We deserve this!"

"I'll tell you what you deserve, mate." Kazuaki withdrew his machete from his hip and rested it on Jirin's underarm. He tapped it on the man's exposed skin. It was easy to do physical damage, but that was not his intention.

Jirin's efforts to free his arm became more panicked. "C-Captain ..." Jirin's attempt to avoid showing fear fell flat. But, even in his apprehension, he remained angry. "This is shit. I ain't waiting here like a feckin' idiot while you go off getting the rewards for yourselves."

Kazuaki arched a brow. He had experienced his fair share of disobedience, but that was years ago, long before he had made a name for himself. Now whispers of the great Captain Kazuaki Hidataka were enough to put a man or woman in his or her place. Jirin's tenacity won him no favors. Kazuaki applied more pressure with the machete.

Jirin's skin split where it met the blade.

"You'll wait," he ordered as a small trickle of blood dribbled from Jirin's fresh wound. "Or you'll wait armless."

Silence blanketed the crew during the showdown, save for the barking of Granite's dog. Nobody stood up for Jirin. Not only was it unwise to cross the captain, but the crew did not like Jirin. It was a long process for newbies to gain acceptance from the crew after the death of a trusted friend, and he did not put much effort into gaining their respect.

Jirin gritted his teeth, knowing the captain would cut off his arm without a second thought if he delayed him from leaving much longer. "I'll wait," he muttered through a clenched jaw.

Kazuaki stared at Jirin long enough to allow him to wonder if he had submitted in time to keep his limb. After a suitable amount of tension passed, he let the man's arm fall to his side. The flesh wound, though not deep, would scar. It would serve as a reminder to stay in his place. "Move out!" Kazuaki eyed those he had assigned to take the first trip.

The five men left behind watched the first team depart. A stillness overshadowed the crew. Discovering the location of Mimir's well still settled over them.

Jirin showed less captivation, rubbing at his wound with little thought to the bacteria that might live on his fingertips. Though the cut bled, the injury to his ego was far more severe.

"Do you think he'll do it?" Rennington asked, staring in the direction the captain took the others. "Do away with eternal life, I mean?"

"Not sure why anyone would," Penn replied, shielding his eyes from the blinding sun with his hand. "Who the feck wouldn't want to live forever?"

All the men who served under him had grown up with the tales of Kazuaki Hidataka's exploits. Though the captain had never announced his condition to the crew, his legacy implied immortality. Not only had his stories floated around in the minds of their great-great-grandparents, but they'd all witnessed him suffer several injuries that would kill a normal man. Death did not come to him. Whispers of his desire to end his contract with immortality had filtered through the ship's walls over the years, but none of the men thought he'd find himself in a situation where he could end it. But here, with Mimir, anything was possible.

"If he's stupid enough to give up immortality, then he deserves to die, if you ask me," Jirin seethed, still fiddling with his injury.

"Bite your tongue," Bartholomew scowled. The scholar glared at Jirin with equal parts hostility and restraint. "Your opinion is as worthless as your temper, Jirin. If another unflattering word about the captain escapes those lips of yours, I'll cut out that insolent tongue and use it to scrub the shit off the deck."

Iani and Rennington snickered, not even trying to stifle their amusement. It was not uncommon to haze a newer member until he fell into submission—sometimes it happened quicker than others. Poor Jirin took a long time. He was a great fighter, but his off-putting personality added roadblocks for him. He struggled with earning the crewmembers' acceptance, but their acceptance didn't seem important to him.

Jirin scoffed and flipped off Bartholomew before skulking away, uninterested in remaining the topic of their harassment.

Iani and Rennington Platts still chuckled amongst themselves, finding great humor in how Bartholomew dealt with Jirin. As a learned man of philosophy, it was out of character to see him engaged in verbal attacks. It made the sight of it much more enjoyable when it occurred.

Penn still stared into the direction where the others had disappeared, uninterested in Jirin's dramatic display. "The man's a feckin' legend. Can you imagine a world without Kazuaki Hidataka?" he asked, focused on the strange topic of a man wanting to rid himself of immortality.

Bartholomew followed Penn's gaze. He held great respect for the captain—the legend and the actual man, as the two suffered from obvious differences. "While I suspect the divisions might delight in his absence"—he crossed his arms—"I'd hate to imagine a world without him."

THEIR DESCENT INTO the barren wasteland was quiet. Wildlife was nonexistent in this day and age. Not even the comforting chirps of birds existed. Kazuaki reflected on adventures past where the sounds of nature had joined him. It used to be a nice reminder he wasn't alone. He didn't need such luxuries anymore. Time beat the need out of him.

"Pretty ballsy, aye?" Bermuda approached Kazuaki and joined him at his side. She motioned back toward the ship with her head. "Surprised you let him keep the arm."

"Yes." Kazuaki removed an aging book from an old leather pouch at his side. "I'm surprised too." He opened the journal and skimmed through its interior. He was too eager to find Mimir; in any other circumstance, Jirin would have been down one arm.

Bermuda waited while the captain studied the journal's contents. She glanced over her shoulder to Elowyn, Brack, Revi, and Granite, to be sure they kept pace.

Granite's dog ran circles around him while he took measured steps forward.

Bermuda smirked. The two were a comical contrast to one another—the silent, stoic giant and his lanky, high-energy dog. Though it was a pain in the ass to ensure they had extra supplies for the mutt, he remained a welcomed addition on the ship. Granite, too, was helpful to have around, and one did not get Granite without the dog.

Revi also kept pace with the others. Much like Granite, he did not carry much facial expressions. Bermuda approved of Kazuaki's team picks. Revi was an asset. He loathed himself so much he did not value his own life. It was a depressing assessment, but it made him a fearless fighter. He was a madman with a gun and a sword in his hands. Aside from Kazuaki, Bermuda lived in certainty Revi had slaughtered more assailants than any other crewmen on the ship. It was easy to battle when one did not fear death.

With Granite and Revi in check, Bermuda shifted her gaze to Elowyn. They formed a natural bond, being the only two women to set foot on Kazuaki's ship, except for the trollops Brack snuck on board when he could afford their company. Bermuda appreciated Elowyn's tenacity, and both united over their shared contempt for the Northern division's military.

"What'll be your request, Elowyn?" Bermuda asked, making small talk to pass the time.

The lithe woman gazed toward Bermuda with a look of absence. She pursed her lips in thought. "You know, I've had years to decide. There are so many things. I can honestly say I don't know what I'll ask the little bugger for when we find him."

Silence stemmed from Granite and Revi as they walked alongside the two women.

Bermuda thought strategy was involved with Kazuaki's choices, and it became increasingly obvious with the minutes of stillness that passed. He chose those who kept their mouths shut. Silence was a better environment in which to concentrate.

"Here we are," Kazuaki said from the front of the pack. His gaze flitted to the page in the journal.

Bermuda peered over his shoulder, skimming the words as the captain read to himself. *"T'was the two hundred thirty-second day of travel when I first laid eyes on the well through the trees. I kneweth first hand t'was an enchanted thing. The aura that sprung forth from those bricks, unnatural and alluring ... it called to me."*

"Ominous," Bermuda muttered, watching Kazuaki cradle the book. "One problem, Captain. There are no trees here." There hadn't been any trees anywhere for as far back as she remembered.

"We're still close to the coast." Kazuaki kicked at the sand beneath his boots. "We'll climb that hill there." He motioned to a steep incline ahead. "A lot of time has passed since the author penned these words. If we're lucky, all the fungi died the same time as the trees. That would slow the decomposition." He closed the book and started for the incline. "If nothing else, we should find indicators to where trees once were."

The team followed Kazuaki to the steep slope. At the top, a wall of rocks awaited them, a straight formation the height of two grown men.

Revi dug his boots into the crumbling rubble of the wall and hoisted his body without hesitation. He was in good shape and made short work of it, finding stable rocks that held his weight as he climbed. As soon as he reached the top, he pulled himself onto solid ground.

"Revi," Granite's baritone voice sounded from below.

Revi stuck his head over the ledge, looking down at Granite.

Granite grabbed his dog, looked up at Revi and, without warning, said, "Catch." He hurled the dog upward with his incredible strength.

It was just low enough that a panicked Revi reached forward and seized the wiggling animal. He collapsed backward with the mutt, who then pinned him to the ground.

The beast wagged its tail and licked his face.

"Damn, Granite!" Revi pushed the jovial dog off him and wiped at his saliva-covered face. He glared at the mutt's owner, who pulled his body over the ledge. "A little more of a warning next time would be great, eh?"

Granite ignored Revi, looming down to stare at Elowyn and Bermuda as they climbed. "Need an assist?" he offered, though he knew full well they did not require his help.

Bermuda and Elowyn exchanged glances, shrugged as best as they could while clinging to the ledge and looked up at Granite.

"I'll take a free ride." Elowyn extended her arm over her head.

Granite grasped a single hand from each woman. He lifted their small bodies with little effort and sat them on the ground above.

By then, Kazuaki had made it to the top and already trekked forward.

Bermuda gazed at the back of the captain.

He halted about thirty feet ahead. His long jacket blew around his legs with the strong coastal wind.

"Captain?"

Kazuaki stared forward as his team joined him to see what captured his attention.

They saw more barren land. Large stones and pebbles surrounded the area. Too much time had passed to leave much evidence of tree trunks, but black gnarled roots sprang forth from the cracking earth. They looked ethereal, like supernatural fingers reaching from their dried-up graves. The roots' chilling presence was not as eerie as the out-of-place structure sitting in the middle of the wasteland, an inanimate object surrounded by oblivion. Smack dab in the outstretched realm of nothingness sat a decrepit, run-down well.

"Is ... that it?" Elowyn asked, unimpressed and thinking it looked more like an abandoned piece of junk than the homestead of the lesser god, Mimir.

Kazuaki narrowed his eyes and started toward the well. He was not ready to relinquish the dream. In his many experiences, chasing legends and myths was never a guarantee. Some had proved to be nothing more than fairy tales, written for the entertainment of a storyteller's audience. But most enough were true accounts. Even if the storytellers had embellished them over time, a shred of truth always remained.

The journal that had led him here painted a strong picture of its author. Kazuaki took the writer for a man of genuine curiosity, a treasure hunter who'd had wealthy acquaintances finance his voyage. He checked his sources. The financiers proved to be real people, long dead. He felt in his soul that this was an authentic account. Time had a way of changing a landscape, but he did not believe it would change the outcome he had hunted for so long.

Still, the situation looked grim. The well was here, but the land surrounding it looked dry; it seemed to be a stretch for it to contain any of the supernatural water described in the accounts. And, even if it did, Mimir was nowhere to be found to grant any requests.

"At least Jirin will be pleased he got to stay on the ship now," Elowyn joked. "Saved himself a big waste of time."

"No," Kazuaki interjected, approaching and placing his hands on the well's cold stones. He leaned over, staring into the structure's shadowed contents. He could decipher nothing, just a gaping circle of darkness that somehow remained unilluminated despite the sun shining overhead. It mocked him.

Bermuda placed a hand over her eyes to shield her vision from the sun's rays, searching for any sign a lesser god lived here. She felt disheartened with each passing moment. If it wasn't for Granite's dog grunting as it spun in circles chasing its tail, it would have been quiet as a cemetery.

Though he wasn't eager to abandon the dream, Revi remained a realist. He did not want to spend all day wishing for something that didn't exist; he spent enough time doing that already. "I think it's a bust, Captain."

"No," Kazuaki repeated, still staring into the jeering darkness that lingered in the well. He relied on this. He *needed* this. For centuries, he had been doomed to the nightmare that was immortality, watching the lifetimes of others peak and fall. This was the only shred of hope he had to rid himself of his curse. They could plunder all the riches from all the legends in all the world, but those prizes paled in comparison to the reward this would have been. "No!" he shouted, frustration mounting as the realization settled in. He struck the bricks with a clenched fist. The blows harnessed such intensity the structure cracked under the force, along with the skin on his knuckles. A series of cursing followed as the captain used the well as a personal punching bag, despite the havoc it wreaked on his hands.

Everyone, even Bermuda, looked alarmed at the sight. Captain Kazuaki Hidataka was always the picture of composure. Even in the heat of battle, Kazuaki's rage was methodical and calculated. This unhinged madman was a side of the captain none of them had witnessed.

Kazuaki accosted the well with such unforgiving intensity it looked even worse than it had before. The condition of his hands matched the state of the well, and, after unleashing his frustration, he rested his bloody palms on the ledge one last time. The man leaned over the structure, jaw clenched, his brain trying to calculate his next move. Something that came so naturally to the captain was now difficult to tap into.

The crew exchanged glances that asked one another if they should head back, but nobody moved, each too afraid to upset the captain further.

Kazuaki tightened his grip on the well wall. A slither of blood trickled from his broken skin and winded down the well's interior before disappearing into the darkness. "I was so sure," he growled, more disappointed in himself than anything else. Before he had discovered the legend of Mimir's well, he had always kept a healthy level of skepticism between his ego and any myth. He knew full well the risk it might not exist. He had let himself want this one too much to believe for a moment it wasn't true.

Kazuaki pulled the book from his pack. The longer it loitered in his palm, the more saturated with blood it became. And the longer Kazuaki stared at it, the angrier he became. "Useless drivel," he snarled, throwing the soiled book into the well.

More silence. It was a recurring theme since they set foot in this place. Though a rage consumed him that would distract a lesser man, Kazuaki straightened his posture as the book fell into the well. He heard no sound of it bouncing off the walls. He heard no indication it ever hit the ground.

Bermuda approached him from behind, having drawn the imaginary short straw as to who would try to convince the captain not to linger. "Kazuaki," she started, voice low, "Do you think we should—"

The captain raised a bloody hand to silence her. "*Shh* ... Listen." His eyes were drawn to the well.

Bermuda rubbed the back of her neck but obeyed. She stood in the quiet for a moment before admitting defeat. "I hear nothing."

As Bermuda finished her sentence, the darkness inside the well stretched out and over.

Kazuaki shoved an arm in front of Bermuda's body and forced her behind him.

The onyx-colored shape resembled one of the gnarled roots as it crawled forth from the ground. It took them a moment to realize it was a hand, black as night and clutching the blood-stained journal Kazuaki had hurled into the well. A creature pulled itself to the surface—a gangly, humanoid beast with eyes that burned like red coals. It sat hunched over, perching clawed feet on the edge of the well.

Granite's dog barked with great fury as the creature flashed a toothy grin, the sharp daggers of white a stark contrast to the blackness of its body.

"I hope you don't think this counts as your sacrifice," the creature's voice echoed as it stroked the bloody book.

The crew stared, dumbfounded.

The fur on the back of the dog's neck stood on end as its warning barks shifted to protective snarls.

Fueled by instinct, Revi drew his knife with one hand and his gun with the other.

The creature chuckled. "Save your bullets, young man." It readjusted as it sat on the well's ledge. "I am no sooner able to issue you unrequested harm as you are able to issue harm unto me."

Kazuaki had witnessed limitless things in his lifetime. He had developed an innate ability to remain composed in even the strangest of scenarios, save for his explosive episode a moment ago. But even ten more lifetimes of experiences could not keep the captain from gazing at the creature with an open jaw and a thundering heart. He had waited for this for so long. The reality of the moment gripped him and did not let him go. "Mimir ..." he uttered, giving a name to the creature.

Mimir's grin broadened as he lowered his crouch. "I see that no matter how much time passes, my reputation precedes me." His red eyes darted back and forth, like a lizard's, eyeballing the barren surroundings. His face shifted into one of surprise. "And indeed, much time has passed since I last laid eyes on the surface."

"You must know why we're here," Kazuaki interrupted. Though the genuine surprise of Mimir's emergence from the well still seized him, the captain shoved those feelings aside. He had waited for so long. He did not wish to let another minute pass.

"The same reason anyone ever comes knocking," Mimir said as he snorted. He set down the journal and motioned Kazuaki forward with a curled finger. "There's a certain air about you, Captain. I should *very* much enjoy making a deal with you." He grinned.

"You'll be making a deal with all of us," Bermuda interjected. She was just as eager as Kazuaki to rid herself of her demons.

Mimir faced her, unimpressed. "I see." He sighed. "What can I do for you, fair maiden?"

"I need you to ..." Her voice lowered as she remembered her audience. Kazuaki, Elowyn, Granite, and Revi seemed much closer than she realized. While the captain had familiarized himself with her past, the others had not. She hesitated, aware of how weak her problem made her look. Bermuda preferred being seen as the fearless quartermaster; she was not eager to vocalize her vulnerabilities for all to hear.

Mimir wrapped his thin black fingers around Bermuda's nearby wrist. It happened so quickly neither she nor Kazuaki had much time to react. The touch granted Mimir supernatural cognizance to her plight. "I see." He reacted as if she had alluded to her desires aloud. "I should have known. I needn't a touch to know matters of the heart are the second-most common reason people seek my well."

Bermuda stared at the creature's crimson eyes, too mesmerized to pull free from his grasp. She wasn't sure how he knew, but she didn't care enough to delve into the *whys* of the lesser god's abilities. "What's the most common?" she whispered.

Mimir smirked. With his free arm, he cranked the lever to his well, lowering a sorry-looking bucket into the darkness. "Power," he said through the squeaks of the rusty crank, "Always power."

His answer sent a shiver into her bones. Perhaps it was the way he had said it. Bermuda cleared her throat, still finding herself in the god's grasp. "So, can you help me?"

"I have plucked worse things from the hearts of men and women than misery. When I'm through, not only will thoughts of Ty Aldon no longer plague you, but the sentiment known as love will no longer affect you at all."

Bermuda inhaled, as terrified as she was eager. "Well ..." She hesitated for only a moment. "Go about it then."

"Ah ..." Mimir withdrew his hand around Bermuda's wrist. The bucket he had lowered returned to the surface, dark water sloshing back and forth within it. "But these things come at a cost, you must know. A reciprocation is necessary to feed my existence. Gods are great, but we love our trinkets. What do you offer for an analogous exchange, young lady?"

Kazuaki stiffened, spying the stunned faces of his crew. Something in his gut didn't feel right. An acid bubbled from deep within, beckoning him to interject. But he could not. In the battle of instinct versus desire, desire won. It had been winning for years.

Bermuda gave little thought to what she would offer. There wasn't much she wouldn't give to rid herself of the pain in her heart. "I-I don't know," she stuttered, finding it uncomfortable to lock eyes with the god for too long.

Mimir kept his unwavering gaze upon her. "Well"—he grabbed her left hand—"since there will be no room for romance in the heart, you'll have no need to wear the prison that is a matrimonial band. As such, I doubt you'd miss this much."

In all the time she had tried to forget the weak heart that dwelled within her, Bermuda could not ignore it now. The prospect of losing her hand made it beat with enormous protest, pounding inside her with such force it was almost as if it tried to escape its fate.

Kazuaki interjected before she could reply. "She's not going to give you her—"

"I'll do it." Bermuda stepped in front of Kazuaki to put herself between him and Mimir. "Make it quick." It was a large sacrifice, but, to her, the reward was greater than the loss.

"Bermuda ..." Kazuaki reached to pull her toward him, but Mimir pulled her forward first.

In the blink of an eye, with Bermuda's arm outstretched, the blackness of his body grew an extra limb and sliced the hand free from the wrist. It was a clean cut, over in milliseconds.

In addition to a heaviness Bermuda felt leave her chest, she felt her blood leave her wrist just as quick. Though a surge of adrenaline pumped through her, she fell to her knees, and her face paled.

"Shit!" Elowyn lunged forward and threw open her pack. She withdrew supplies and placed a tourniquet on the arm. After forcing the injured woman to elevate her arm, she removed a blood-clotting powder from her pouch and applied it. It was a useful tool to have handy when one participated in as many showdowns as the criminals aboard Kazuaki's ship did. But even with her medical background, Elowyn's supplies out here were limited. There was only so much she could do.

Kazuaki snarled and seized the creature by what he guessed was its chest. His fingers sank into the material that comprised Mimir's body as if it were a gelatinous substance. "Fix it!" With all the anger inside him, it was all he could say.

Mimir regarded Kazuaki's hands, watching his body ooze over the captain's skin and stain them a dark color. The creature dipped his hands into the bucket of water and splashed several droplets onto Bermuda's body as Elowyn tended to her medical needs. He then met the captain's eyes with a delightful grin. "There now, I already did." He chuckled as he held Bermuda's hand. "When the well water absorbs into her skin, she will have a heart free from the burdens of love, just as she requested."

Granite's dog whimpered but still approached the blood Bermuda spilled and licked it up.

Mimir looked to the mutt with interest then to Granite. "I have a lot of human and human-related accessories in my collection." He eyed the gnarled black roots that surrounded them. "But I have not yet added a canine. Would you care to trade him to fulfill your bargain?"

Granite remained steadfast. His expression did not betray his true emotion of concern for Bermuda's condition, but it illuminated his icy hostility at Mimir's suggestion. "I do not know how to kill a god, but, if you touch the dog, I'll figure it out." The last man who had tried to bring harm to the animal was Granite's own brother. He found himself at the very unforgiving hand of the family's butcher knife.

"Silence, creature," Kazuaki hissed as Revi and Elowyn pulled Bermuda to her feet, draping her arms over each of their shoulders while keeping her severed wrist elevated. There was so much he wanted to say, to do, but he knew he was powerless in this situation. It was an unfamiliar feeling to Kazuaki Hidataka. Powerlessness. He did not enjoy it. Bermuda had entered a verbal contractual obligation with Mimir. She was severely wounded but by her own say. He found himself frozen.

"Why do your eyes cast such hatred upon me, Captain?" The lesser god cocked his head. "I fulfilled her most pressing wish. She is free from the weakness that is the human heart. Now, wouldn't you like to be free from something that haunts you as well?"

Kazuaki had to get Bermuda to the ship. Mimir's offer hung over him like a thick cloud, but he released the lesser god from his grasp. He wiped his hands on his long jacket to remove the residue Mimir's body left on his skin. He was a captain and comrade to Bermuda first and foremost. She needed to be taken somewhere safe. "Get Bermuda to the ship," he ordered Granite, Revi, and Elowyn.

While the three had their own bargains they wished to make, witnessing Bermuda's experience diluted their desires to proceed. Even if it hadn't, one did not disobey a direct order from Kazuaki Hidataka.

Granite plucked the woman from Revi's and Elowyn's arms and carried her in the direction they had come.

Elowyn and Revi followed, along with the dog who finished cleaning the spilled blood from the rocks.

Revi only walked twenty feet before he turned, realizing the captain remained locked in a staring contest with Mimir. "Captain?"

"Go on, Revi. I'll be along," he said without turning, knowing Bermuda resided in capable hands.

"With all due respect, Captain—"

"I said, *go!*"

Revi lingered for a moment before he relented to the captain's orders. It did not sit right with him to leave the man alone with a god who had just severed his crewmate's hand. But Revi Houton was no stranger to leaving those who needed him. With a tinge of regret that opened his old, mental wounds, he left the man behind.

"Let's make this quick," Kazuaki hissed. "Thanks to you, I have pressing matters that need my attention."

"No matter proves so pressing than that of your lifelong problem, Captain. As a lesser god, I am intimately familiar with the problems of immortality. Your life is but a fetus compared to the years I have lived. All that time ... it's enough to drive someone mad." He smirked, fiddling with the fingers on Bermuda's detached hand. "Especially when you've fallen from the memories of the men who made you. But, you, you're still remembered, aren't you, Captain? They've sung songs of you. They haven't done as much for me in many, many years."

Kazuaki growled. "Get on with it, demon. I'm growing tired of your pointless banter."

Mimir sighed. "Yes, yes, eager to rid yourself of that cursed immortality, I know. The ego of man is too great to fully understand how terrible it is unless they've endured it themselves. But you know, to wander through the horrors of this place with no known end in sight, it is a troubling curse, is it not?"

Kazuaki tried not to look at the severed chunk of flesh that once had been attached to his comrade. Mimir's babbling was incessant. The captain suspected it was a tactic to infuriate him, to dull his intelligence by clouding it with rage. "Just tell me what you want to rid me of it!"

Mimir grinned. "There was an old saying I've always liked. 'An eye for an eye leaves the whole world blind.' I think, in this circumstance, Captain, an eye is a very fitting trade—one of the very eyes that had seen one too many decades of existence, yes?" Mimir prattled like a mad man, ignorant of Kazuaki's request for urgency. "Man covets immortality, and yet all you see with everlasting eyes is everlasting nightmares."

"You're stalling! Cure me, demon, and be gone with you!"

"Temper, temper." Mimir sighed, throwing the detached hand in the air and catching it in a twisted little game. "Perhaps *that's* what you should rid yourself of instead of your immortality, Captain."

Kazuaki inhaled a measured breath. He knew Mimir was playing mind games with him. He needed to clear his head, but something was maddening about the creature's presence that eliminated his wits. The ethereal aura the lesser god emitted was vexatious. "I do not wish to remove my temper. Take the eye, whatever you want, just release me from the nightmare that binds me to this Earth."

Mimir leaned back, satisfied with Kazuaki's word choice. "As you wish, Captain."

Another appendage sprang forth from Mimir's body and plucked the sphere straight from its socket.

Kazuaki's hand shot to his face to cover the injury sight, but he gave the god no satisfaction by damming his sounds of agony. A snarl was all that left the captain's mouth as blood seeped from between his clenched fingers and trickled down his forearm. The pain caused him to take to one knee, but he righted himself to standing. "That's it then," he muttered, trying to disguise the pain in his words. "A deal's a deal."

"It most assuredly is." Mimir dipped his hands into the well water. He flicked the droplets onto Kazuaki's face but frowned when, instead of being absorbed into the skin, they sizzled at the touch of his body. "Hold up now." His face twisted into a look of displeasure. "It seems someone else has beaten me to the punch, Captain. You didn't tell me you have already suffered from a curse."

Kazuaki snarled, his hand still firm over his bleeding eye as if it tempered the blinding pain. "How the feck do you think I became an immortal to begin with?"

Mimir frowned. "No matter." He dropped the eye into his well. "Just an extra step. As soon as you cleanse your soul from your current curse, you can accept the conditions of mine."

The captain squared his shoulders. He'd had it with Mimir's rigmarole. "And how do I accomplish that?"

"Move your hand."

Hesitation was his first instinct—he did not wish to remove the hand holding in a socket's worth of blood—but he needed to expedite the process. With all the mental strength he could muster,

Kazuaki slid his hand down his face, exposing the open hole to Mimir.

The creature scooped water into his palm and poured it into the socket.

Kazuaki winced as the liquid sizzled inside his skull. It bubbled and felt as if something formed in the open wound. Had that done it? Had Mimir *cleansed his soul*? He remained uncertain. With so much confusion, Kazuaki found himself lost in the madness of it all.

"There we are. You'll be right as rain soon. Now go forth and finish your time on Panagea. I'll be waiting for you when you're done."

"Only if I go to the Underworld when I die," Kazuaki muttered with bitterness and too consumed by concern for Bermuda and the seething pain of losing an eye to pay much attention to what Mimir said.

Propelled by the need to return to the ship and Bermuda, Kazuaki forced his legs to move despite the overwhelming sting in his brain. He did not creep too far before his last words to Mimir settled into him like the well water had. Kazuaki halted, feeling Mimir's gaze burning into his back as the unsettling, acidic nausea in his gut returned. He faced the lesser god again. Mimir's stare shifted into a gradual, maniacal grin. Then he knew. "You're a conman."

"Not in the least. You'll get your wish, Captain. By your own decree, when you die, I will release you from the nightmare that binds you to this Earth."

Kazuaki stood, unmoving. "And what nightmare awaits me after?"

Mimir smirked. He hurled Bermuda's severed hand into the well.

As it disappeared into the darkness, Kazuaki felt a small rumble beneath his feet. He stepped backward, and five withered, blackened fingerlike roots pierced through the surface. Though they looked fresh from the earth, they appeared as deadened as the graveyard of roots that surrounded him—another piece added to Mimir's eternal collection.

"All in due time, Captain. Let's just say, I'm very excited to finally have a friend."

Kazuaki glared at the lesser god. The creature had already tarnished his collected state. The lesser god's presence had deadened the captain's wits since he had first arrived at the well's doorstep. By supernatural forces or not, Kazuaki had chosen his own words. His fate was sealed. The captain would not allow Mimir to cause one more undignified action in him. He would not sacrifice another moment of merit or respectability.

With a clenched jaw, Kazuaki nodded, accepting his outcome. He turned and headed for the ship. It would not be easy breaking the bad news to the crew; not of his condition but, after Bermuda's and his experience with Mimir, he wouldn't allow any of them to leave the ship. He may have traded one eternal nightmare for another, but he could spare his comrades from making the same mistake.

Mimir watched him exit and eyed his well, his prison, his penitentiary until the next fool stumbled across the legend of the lesser god and his well of promises. He lingered atop the well's decaying brick edging for as long as he could, soaking in the sight of freedom.

Before long, otherworldly arms from the darkness reached up and pulled him down. As he fell into the shadows below, he hoped Kazuaki cleansed his soul sooner rather than later. After lifetimes of sitting around his collection of silent body parts traded from men and women of all time periods, Mimir looked forward to the company.

THE STRUGGLE OF CARRYING a body did not slow the three crew members. Granite's brute strength offset any inconvenience caused. They reached the ship in good time. It did not take long for those who had stayed behind to spring to life at the sight of Bermuda's bleeding form.

"What happened?" Bartholomew barked, eyes wide as Granite carried Bermuda to the deck below.

Elowyn ignored his inquiries, following Granite to further assist Bermuda.

The loyal mutt also disappeared into the deck below, pursuing Bermuda's blood trail.

Revi panted from the brisk pace Granite had kept the entire time they had trekked back. He glanced at Bartholomew as brothers Iani and Rennington Platts joined the crowd. "I-I don't even know how to explain it."

"Was there an ambush? A trap?" Iani inquired. Before he received an answer, he shook his head. "I knew this whole thing was too bloody good to be true."

"Where's the captain?" Bartholomew looked past Revi's shoulder to see if he was close behind.

Penn emerged from below deck with confusion and panic. "I just saw Granite covered in Bermuda's blood. What's happened?"

Questions barraged Revi like cannonballs from an enemy ship. He raised his hands and tried to answer as best he could under the current conditions. "We found the well. She ... She traded her hand, willingly. Something to do with her heart." Even Revi did not understand why Bermuda had made such a bargain. He was not familiar with the intricacies of her reasoning. "She brought it on herself,

I-I think." Confusion crippled the man. He had heard Bermuda make the deal; he knew she was cognizant when she had accepted Mimir's terms. But none of them wished for her to endure the consequences of what had happened to her. Elowyn was a capable medical professional, but he wasn't sure if Bermuda would survive long enough to enjoy whatever reward she had gained from the lesser god. "Where is Jirin?"

The four men left aboard the ship exchanged glances, trying to make sense of what they heard.

"Sulking about after the captain yelled at him. Haven't seen him since you all left," Rennington answered.

Bartholomew's attention shifted to the distance when he saw a figure appear. A tall individual lurched forward after sliding down the faraway hill, lumbering across the sand as he advanced toward the ship. "The captain," he breathed, relief in his voice. "At least *he's* all in one piece."

Kazuaki continued, hand still clamped over the hole where his eye used to be. He walked with necessity as his fuel. He regretted letting Bermuda go first. If he had been more persistent, he could have saved her from making a huge mistake.

"Captain!" Bartholomew called out from the distance separating them, waving his hand above his head. "Are you all right?"

Kazuaki raised his hand, a silent indication he was fine. It seemed like a small eternity to return to the ship's ramp. It was nothing short of a miracle the waters were deep enough near the island's shore for the vessel to float safely nearby. He didn't want to deal with a bumpy ride in a cockboat right now.

Finally placing a single foot on the ramp leading to the deck, Kazuaki paused at the base of the shoreline. Footsteps rattled through the boards from above. Fearing the consequences of drawing attention to his bleeding face, Kazuaki didn't look to identify who descended from the main deck above. He felt certain it Bartholomew. The scholar could be a worrier.

"I know it looks bad," he muttered to the approaching shadow, silhouetted by the sun, "but I'll live."

"Not for long," the voice replied, followed by the deafening shots of a pistol.

Jirin. Kazuaki felt the bullets enter his chest. It wasn't an unfamiliar feeling. There wasn't much immediate pain with bullet wounds, but the area burned with an outward irritation that consumed his torso and radiated to his limbs. He had been shot countless times. It came with the territory of being a criminal in Panagea's eyes. But this time differed from the rest. He felt the panic creep in, the panic that only belonged to those who feared death.

For years, he had craved that panic. But it was only one of many emotions that ran through him now—determination to ensure Bermuda was okay, regret that he only tasted the thrill of mortality for mere minutes, rage that Jirin dared to betray him, apprehension of what awaited him in Mimir's afterlife. When he had fantasized about his death, this was not what he'd had in mind. Mimir had stripped all the excitement from it. The strength of each emotion caused a stir of turmoil within the captain's already suffering head.

Kazuaki's hand slipped from his empty eye socket as he listened to his blood flow through his veins. He waited for his body to realize something fatal had pierced its lung. He'd only been struck in the lungs once or twice before. It was not a pleasant experience. Immortality did not excuse him from feeling the pains of gunshot wounds and stabbings. The intensity seized him and took control over his body. While he felt every cell inside him scream, his mind went numb, too ravaged by the chaos in his brain.

Jirin's sadistic smirk faded into a look of horror. His eyes locked on the captain's gaping socket.

Kazuaki could not tell what was transpiring as he stood waiting to die, but the man looked as if he saw an apparition.

"No," he whispered, taking several steps backward. "No!" Jirin shrieked a blood-curdling scream. He dropped the smoking gun and raised his hands, though nothing attacked him. He swatted at the sky like a lunatic.

The captain heard another gunshot.

The back of Jirin's head exploded upon the bullet's impact.

Kazuaki dropped to one knee, bewildered. While Jirin's body crumpled to the ramp, the captain felt as if the veins in his empty eye socket buried themselves deep into his brain tissue. He had experienced the same sizzling sensation when Mimir had poured the well water into his socket, a feeling more horrid than any gunshot wound he'd had endured. The captain thought he heard Bartholomew call out as several of his men ran down the ramp to retrieve him, but he couldn't decipher what they said. An ear-shattering sound reverberated in his skull that drowned out every other sound.

"Captain!" Bartholomew hit the sand, skidded in front of Kazuaki and put both hands around the fallen man's arms to steady him.

They'd seen him get shot many times before, but, regardless of the pain, he had never fallen. In any other circumstance, Kazuaki would have made short work of Jirin's betrayal, but something gripped him.

Bartholomew narrowed his eyes. He must have done it; the captain must have ended his contract with immortality. Bartholomew surveyed the bullet wounds and then Kazuaki's eyes.

In the same fashion as Jirin, Bartholomew's face twisted into one of horror as soon as his gaze met Kazuaki's. He fell backward and skidded away, swatting and screaming at ghosts nobody saw.

Kazuaki felt the veins plunge deeper into his brain once more. He closed his eye, forcing his palms over his face to stop the onslaught of agony. Several of Bartholomew's horrified cries pierced through. The captain collapsed.

"Bart!" Rennington tried to jostle the scholar to lucidity, but he continued his delusional panic. He looked at Iani, exasperated. "What the feck is wrong with him?"

"Let's get him inside." Iani grabbed one flailing arm while Rennington wrestled the other. They struggled to drag him back up.

Bartholomew's paranoid kicks rattled the ramp as they pulled him along as best as they could.

Revi leaned over the captain, whose hands remained clenched over his face, and jostled his torso. "Cap, what do you need? What's going on?"

Kazuaki laid there, feeling the rise and fall of his chest with each attempted breath. His damaged lung made traditional breathing difficult. His mind rattled a mile a minute, bouncing between surprise he was still alive, to Bermuda, to Mimir and his cryptic ritual, to trying to make sense of Jirin and Bartholomew's meltdowns, to the pain that occurred in his brain after each man looked at his socket. He guessed the latter had something to do with that rat of a lesser god. He'd have to ask him when he accompanied him in the afterlife.

"Get me back on the ship," he muttered to Revi, his voice muffled through the hands that covered his face. He didn't know if he would die, but, if he did, it would be on his own vessel, not this damnable island.

Kazuaki felt strange. Something was amiss, aside from the bullets Jirin had lodged into his lungs. The fear subsided, taking the feeling of relief with it. Through the cacophony of other thoughts that ravaged his mind, one leaped forward, something Mimir had said. He hadn't paid much attention to it in the heat of the moment. But now, with more questions than answers, the captain couldn't help but wonder what Mimir had meant by *cleansing his soul.*

Chapter Four

The reprieve of entering Malcolm Finn's store was a harmonious gift known only to some. Once one stepped into the warm walls of his establishment, all the insidious metallic scents of the outside melted away. Instead of being greeted by the cold smell of iron, a person enjoyed the gentle embrace of lavender, the savory grip of thyme, or the herbal calm of sage. It was like entering a small world within a world. The aura beamed off the walls with the same warmth of the lights that loomed over the plants, mimicking the sun.

Lilac loved this place. It was her paradise. The second she entered her papa's greenhouse, the healing power of the plants sucked the toxins in her blood dry and replaced it with peace. She anticipated the feeling as she slid into the door and closed it behind her, maneuvering four large water jugs and the sample of jam with her. To ease the heaviness they created in her arms, she set them in a corner on the ground, trying not to cause a ruckus.

Malcolm was in the middle of instructing a class. He did not look his age when he stood before his plants and the admiring eyes of four eager students. As a child, Lilac remembered when he had taught more than thirty at a time. The numbers had dwindled as the industries flourished. The want for efficient synthetics had replaced man's desire to get his hands dirty. Nobody wanted to watch nature grow in exchange for hard work anymore. But whether thirty students or four were present, those who sought to learn from Malcolm Finn possessed dedication, often traveling outside their respective divisions to find him. He operated one of only two greenhouses left in Panagea's entirety.

His operation seemed small to some, housing only a handful of various fruiting plants and herbs. The countless species she read about in books as a child had gone extinct long ago. They were the stuff of myths and legends now.

Lilac beamed with pride as her father explained the peppermint plant's medicinal qualities to his students. "It's a world wonder. Peppermint can soothe an ailing stomach, provide relief for headaches, boost your energy, and perhaps, most important of all"—he popped a single leaf off the plant and ripped it into quarters—"it can freshen awful breath." He placed a quarter of the leaf into his mouth and chewed then handed the other pieces to the students to sample.

The students let out small obligatory chuckles as they tried the little offering.

Malcolm wished he could've allowed them to try a larger sample, but it was his only peppermint plant at the time; growing another had been a struggle, and he wanted to conserve as much of it as he could.

Everyone whispered to one another about the depth of flavor and the uniqueness of the taste on their palates.

Malcolm delighted in their hushed banter as the students exchanged ideas on what peppermint might pair well within a culinary setting. "I'm sorry I can't give you anything at the moment which would help you reproduce your own peppermint plant." Malcolm crossed the warmed room to a different table. "But I'll give each of you a cutting from one of these thyme plants. Ensure your soil is well drained and upward of seventy degrees. Then you'll have thyme in no time."

The students' laughter was more genuine this time. They huddled in a circle and sniffed the thyme, breathing in the richness of its scent.

Malcolm drew his focus from the students when he caught Lilac's shadow from across the room. "Ahh ..." He extended a welcoming arm her way. "And here comes the most beautiful flower of all."

The students looked up, all smiles. "Hello, Miss Finn," one of the younger women greeted. A series of *hellos* and *how are you*s followed from the rest. They were all familiar with Lilac's presence. She was almost as much a staple in Malcolm Finn's store as the plants.

"Hello, all." Lilac smiled. "I trust Papa isn't boring you too terribly, is he?"

"Nonsense!" Malcolm wiped his soil-covered hands on an old rag. "If I were boring them, they wouldn't be doing so well. They're thriving just as well as these carrots they planted at the start of the semester." He motioned to the back of the room with pride, where the students had cultivated a small carrot crop. Although they were one of the easiest vegetables to grow, he showed how impressed he was with the level of love his students had poured into the process. It was a rare thing to encounter youth who exchanged hard work for a slow reward.

Lilac raised her brows and did a slow clap. "Congratulations! Not an easy feat, what with all the oil leaking into the soil these days."

The woman did not exaggerate. The ground had become so contaminated over time, Malcolm had made a special trip to the Southern division several years ago. Though it was illegal to transport soil from one division to another, he had done so without raising alarms. Away from the prying eyes of the public, he had found a miniature piece of land that had remained relatively untouched by industry. Less than a year after, he had shipped in a carload of the soil, and the Southern Time Father had claimed the virgin land. A church now stood where he had dug up that dirt. Darjal Wessex loved his symbols of righteousness, especially when the coffers poured wealth into his pockets. Even in its separation from underground chemical leaks, the soil was not perfect. Pollution caused the rainwater to act as an enemy to the ground.

Had it not been for Nicholai's access to purified water—a luxury afforded to him from being the Southeastern Time Father—it would have been difficult for Malcolm to raise his plants with success. The act of purifying water was a difficult process; the public only had access to whatever clean water rations their Time Fathers issued them. Malcolm often assumed the only reason his greenhouse remained one of the two left in Panagea was due to his access to purified water through Lilac. It was a blessing to him that his daughter had fallen in love with a man of affluence and generosity, even better that he treated her like a goddess.

"Yes," Malcolm agreed, eyeing the carrots. "I think it's cause for a small celebration. A toast?" He surveyed his students to gauge their reaction to his suggestion.

The students radiated from his praise and exchanged nods and agreements.

Malcolm disappeared into a back room and returned several minutes later with six small glasses of cucumber-infused water. "After your carrot harvest"—he distributed the drinks—"I'll teach you how to grow cucumbers. They're a delightful creeping vine that's not too challenging to nurture. Then you can make your own cucumber water."

Lilac smiled, swirling her cucumber water around in the glass before she took a sip. "It's a shame we can't toast traditionally, with good, old-fashioned wine."

Malcolm laughed, nursing his water while the students gulped theirs. "You know as well as I do no one has found a grape in decades. Though, what a time to be alive, that would have been. Legend has it, the wine festivals of some cultures lasted for weeks, a no-holds-barred approach in honoring the gods and goddesses who shined favor on the harvest."

One student lowered his glass, swallowing a mouthful of the infused beverage. "I heard Kazuaki Hidataka discovered authentic wine kegs a few years back. It happened in the Southwestern division, just before I moved here. The papers didn't report anything about it, but the Southwestern military surrounded a cavern on the coast for days. My friend said that's where he pulled it from. Could you imagine?"

"Imagining is about all you can do when you speak of that old pirate." Malcolm chuckled, setting down his empty glass. "My grandparents used to tell me stories of the great Captain Kazuaki Hidataka and his hunts for the legends of old. Occasionally, I'll catch wind of a story involving someone who saw him." He shook his head. "But I take none of it for a fact. If Kazuaki existed, there would be hard evidence. I suspect, if he ever existed, he's long dead now. A shame if that cavern full of wine existed though. It would be a waste for it to go untasted ..." Malcolm's eyes glazed over as he tried to imagine what it would be like to experience a full-bodied wine. He'd never seen a grape in all his life, let alone witnessed them turned into the alcoholic beverage. As far as he knew, and ever would know, it was a drink that only existed for the tongues of the gods.

Lilac returned her empty glass to her father. "I'll get going. You know how I hate to interrupt class." She tucked a strand of red hair behind her ear. "Thanks for the water, Papa. I put your jugs by the door, as well as a little treat I cooked up with my blackberries."

Malcolm glanced over his daughter's shoulder to see the purified water she had snuck from the house she and Nicholai shared. His smile was great as he squeezed her hand. He knew the other Time Fathers could reprimand Nicholai if they discovered he supplied Malcom and Lilac with twice the water rations they should have been getting. But for his boldness, Malcolm was grateful. "And these"—he pulled a small wrapped package from his back pocket and stuffed it into her palm—"are for you. Enjoy."

Lilac held the microgreens to her chest and kissed his cheek. "Thank you, Papa. Enjoy the rest of the class, everybody." She waved to the students and slipped out the door, inspired to go home and see what kind of dish she could concoct with the microgreens. Even if she had to combine the natural ingredients with manufactured food-like products to create a more filling meal, the greens would bring a freshness to her palate the artificial food could not.

The woman's feet didn't carry her too far from the store before she heard a man shout her name. "Lilac! Lilac Finn!" She turned in time to see a middle-aged man running toward her.

When he closed the distance, he seized her arm with unintended aggression. "I need to see Nicholai. It's imperative!"

Lilac jerked away her arm in a show of disapproval. "Excuse me!" She sized up the stranger with her eyes. She was a small woman, but the size difference between the two would not stop her from trying to drop him if need be. "Do I know you?"

"I need to see the Time Father!" He tried, without success, to grab her arm again. "I know you two are of a together sort, married or unmarried, it matters not to me. It's my daughter. She's in dire need. She's gravely ill. Please. I need to see Nicholai."

The anxiety in his face was easy to detect. It illuminated tenfold by the panic in his voice. After the initial shock of his less-than-gentlemanly approach, her heart went out to him. Lilac was nothing if not a caring sort. On the rare occasion an animal found its way into the iron city, Lilac gave it her all to be sure they were well before reintroducing them to a safer space in the outside world. She extended the same gratitude to people. But, even still, she did not understand his request. "I'm sorry to hear it, but I don't know how he could help. Nicholai is not a medical doctor."

"Please! I *need* to see him. I must. She's running out of time."

Something about his request did not feel right in her gut. But his persistence and obvious love for his daughter compelled her. It reminded her of her relationship with her papa and how he would move the stars in the sky to bring her a small shred of comfort. "I ... suppose I can take you to the house." Her soft heart was both her most positive and negative attribute. "We can wait for him there."

"Thank you." The man put his hands together in prayer. "That's all I ask."

A churning lived in her stomach. Lilac questioned his motives as the two started toward her house. She was not sure if her indecision rose from within herself or if it was a side effect of this desperate man's chaotic energy. But it was not about him; it was about his child. There wasn't much Lilac wouldn't do for a child in need.

"So," she started as they walked, "tell me about your daughter."

NICHOLAI'S HOME WAS often a refuge for him. He looked forward to returning there after every long day he endured. But today was different. He dragged his feet more the closer he got to the door. Each step meant putting himself closer to telling Lilac about the expiration date on Malcolm's store. It had burned at him all day. He had drudged through every possible scenario to avoid it, trying to find creative alternatives to the inevitable, but it all deducted to two outcomes: either he defied Nordjan and opened himself to the horrid aftermath that would bring or he metaphorically stabbed Lilac and her father in the heart. Either scenario would kill him, one way or another.

The sun was setting. The lamplighters of Nenada had lit each streetlight one by one. It was beautiful, the way they came to life at night. His modest home came into view. Due to his prestigious position, he possessed the largest house in the Southeastern division, but it was still only five small rooms of less than eight hundred square feet. Other Time Fathers chose lavish buildings as their residence, but Nicholai did not need such luxuries. Furthering industry had always been valued above the comforts of the people. The residential areas made the necessary sacrifices to business. He felt if his people had to suffer in small spaces, then he would too.

Nicholai furrowed his brow. Every evening prior, he would see a comforting glow of light coming from the front window. But the house was dark. Lilac sat on a bench outside the front door, talking to a man he did not immediately recognize.

Lilac spotted him in the distance and jumped to her feet. It was clear she was glad to see him, relieved to have a buffer between herself and the man's thick desperation. "Nicholai!" She waved, beckoning him over with haste.

Nicholai was no stranger to those who wanted to consult with the Time Father after hours. He was a little relieved himself to have something to help him further delay his unpleasant conversation with Lilac. As he drew closer, he recognized the man to be Rodgie, a mechanic belonging to the steam car factory half a mile away.

They hadn't spent much time together—a seminar here and there, at mechanical repair conferences. Rodgie attended them to further his knowledge in fixing automobile-related issues. Nicholai attended them too. It was required all Time Fathers remained well versed in maintaining the integrity of their Chronometers. Though his attendance was forced, Nicholai loved the inner workings of various machines and was a savant regarding the subject. He and

Rodgie had shared small conversations at the seminars, bonding over their mutual enjoyment of working with cogs and gears to create a functioning item, but he never expected to see him outside a convention.

"Rodgie ..." He extended a diplomatic hand to shake. "To what do I owe the pleasure?"

"Nicholai, it's my daughter." Rodgie bypassed the hand as he stood to his feet, too consumed by his task to focus on formalities. "I need your help, please."

"She's quite ill," Lilac added, having absorbed the details during the time she had spent with Rodgie. "She's contracted black lung disease, I'm afraid."

Nicholai frowned, though he remained empathetic. Black lung became a common diagnosis. With the number of air pollutants increasing and the amount of fresh oxygen depleting, the number of people afflicted had grown to epidemic proportions. Competent medical professionals were harder and harder to come by. Most of the higher-paying jobs belonged to trained mechanics or those who entered manufacturing jobs. Few young adults wanted to put in the years of effort and energy required to earn a medical degree when they could make more money joining the blue-collar workforce with little to no effort at all.

"I'm so sorry, Rodgie ..." Nicholai trailed off. Black lung disease was a death sentence, and the tone of his voice showed as much.

Rodgie bristled at his words. "Please, I do not need your condolences, just your help. Word on the wind is Aggi Normandy of the Northeastern division is working on an experimental treatment. Evvy needs it, posthaste."

Nicholai opened his mouth to speak but stopped. "Rodgie ..." He tried to find the right words. "My sympathies know no bounds for you, friend, but I fail to see how I can help. Could you not just request it be sent through the post?"

"No!" Rodgie yelled but calmed himself soon after. "I'm sorry. No. It would take weeks for my proposal to reach Northeastern, another week to process my request, and then several more weeks before the medicine reached my doorstep. Nicholai ..." His face was beseeching. He looked tired. "She has but hours. A day at most. Please."

The Time Father shifted in discomfort. Rodgie had occasionally spoken of his daughter at the conferences. She must have been seven or eight years old now. He tried to push the image of the dying girl from his head as it was too painful to imagine. He'd seen those who lingered at the end stages of black lung before—their chest almost collapsing in on itself, their eye sockets dark and sunken, skin pale and thin. It must have been a nightmare for her father to see her like that.

"Rodgie, you know I cannot leave the Southeastern division for more than twenty-four hours without dire consequences." Direr than he cared to admit. If he were not in his division to wind his watch, time here stopped. If time in one division stopped, the tectonic plates in every other division met resistance at Southeastern's borders. Nothing could move, not an inch. It did not seem like much, but the natural mechanics of Panagea's underbelly would turn into utter chaos. "I don't have access to a flying machine as Nordjan has. There's just no way I could make it there and back in time conventionally."

"Conventionally, no." Rodgie's voice hinted at something Nicholai did not care for.

The Time Father glanced at Lilac. It was clear from her expression she did not understand what he was insinuating. Nicholai returned his attention to the desperate man. He thought he knew, but he asked anyway. "What are you implying, Rodgie?"

Rodgie paused, understanding the severity of what he was about to ask. "You ... could stop time here. Just for long enough to reach the Northeastern division and return with the medicine. I'm sure it wouldn't be more than three days to jump through the hoops of securing it. Two days if you—"

"Absolutely not!" On any other day, he might have considered it. But Nicholai Addihein teetered on the edge of Nordjan's watchful eye. He needed to step up and be a leader. It was unfortunate leadership required making difficult decisions. Stopping time was, without a doubt, the biggest taboo any Time Father could commit. Even without the political consequences, the physical ramifications to Panagea were too great. She was already so fragile. "I can help in any other way, friend, but that, I simply cannot do."

Lilac's face fell as the two men spoke. She knew in her heart Nicholai could do nothing for Rodgie's daughter, but she hoped, for the little girl's sake. She put a sympathetic hand on the poor man's shoulder. "I'm so sorry, Rodgie."

He forced his shoulder from beneath her touch. "Your pity means nothing. I need action. *She* needs action!"

"You know I care for each of Southeastern's people like my family, Rodgie." Nicholai lowered his voice to return calm to the situation. "But I can't—"

"You can," Rodgie corrected with a frustrated growl, "but you refuse! Were it your own flesh and blood, or Lilac"—he motioned to the woman beside him—"you would do so without blinking an eye. Whispers abound you give them more than their fair share of fresh water!"

"I ..." Nicholai stopped, unable to deny the accusation. He frowned, knowing his playing favorites was unfair, but he did not think about the long-term consequences returning to haunt him. In every other way, he tried his best to be a fair leader to his division. "I would never stop time for personal gain. But that's neither here nor there, Rodgie. This is not like you. You're a man sick with love for his daughter, and understandably so. I would give my arm to help her if I could, but I can't stop time. If I can do *anything* else, name it, and I'll do it."

"We both will," Lilac added, joining Nicholai in his efforts to ease the embittered man's suffering.

Rodgie glared at them both with hatred and anguish.

Nicholai saw the glassy orbs glaze over with wetness as the man fought away burning tears.

He shook his head and backpedaled to create distance between them. "You *can* stop time," he whispered, clenching his fists. "You *choose* not to!"

Nicholai stepped forward, holding up his hands. "Rodgie, calm down. We'll take you home. Lilac can make Evvy a nice tea to soothe her pain. Lilac, do you still have that ginger root or peppermint from Malcolm?"

The woman nodded, glancing to the unhinged Rodgie. "I do. I can make her some straight away—"

"No!" Rodgie yelled, finding himself at the mercy of his heartache. "You will stop time, Nicholai." He reached into his vest and brandished an old pistol. The weapon's metallic sheen glistened in the lamplight above. His hands shook as he aimed it at Lilac. "I'm sorry." Tears escaped from his eyes and streamed down his cheeks. "I'm so sorry, but I love her too much."

Nicholai's eyes widened as he glanced at Lilac.

She stepped backward and instinct lifted her hand to protect herself, though the flesh was a poor shield.

Instinct overtook Nicholai too. He didn't even realize he'd done it. In the time it took Rodgie's quivering finger to squeeze the trigger, the Time Father's thumbnail dug into the crown of the Chronometer and popped it up. But it was too late. He heard the discharge.

The world around him stopped in every way. It took a moment for Nicholai to collect himself. The deafening silence of nothingness surrounded him, adding more fuel to the fire of his panic. His heart thrashed from inside as the weight of everything crashed down.

The bullet paused inches from Lilac's horrified face. The curls of her red hair defied gravity as they suspended in the air. Like everything else around them, they were frozen.

Nicholai closed his eyes. Perhaps the darkness would keep him from screaming. But even a scream may have been welcomed. He had never stopped time before; the silence was maddening. He pushed aside the panic bubbling inside him and slowly approached Lilac. He outreached a hand, trembling as much as Rodgie's had been moments earlier. Her face, though rife with fear, was soft and warm beneath his fingertips. He stared at her for what felt like hours though it was likely only minutes. It was hard to tell when no time passed.

It took everything he had to tear himself away from Lilac and step toward Rodgie. His expression was a cocktail of hopelessness and regret. His love had twisted him into a demon capable of monstrous action. Though as Nicholai surveyed the land where time stood still, his own questionable actions came under intense scrutiny. He ran to Lilac, cupping her face in his hands. He closed his eyes, wanting very much to rest his forehead against hers as he had countless times before, but he could not move the bullet that stood in his way. Or her arm. He was incapable of manipulating anything while his division's time remained paralyzed.

There was a way out of this. There had to be. A creative solution existed for this circumstance; just because he had failed to invent one to save Malcolm's greenhouse, he could still find one that saved the love of his life. He needed time to think. But it was a luxury he didn't have if he lingered here. At any moment, his betrayal would surface. The Time Fathers would know.

Laws. That's what he needed now. He had to find a loophole, a way to manipulate the frozen things here. If he could move that bullet five inches to the right, it would bypass Lilac. Nicholai reached and, though he knew it would result in utter failure, tried to move the fragment.

As expected, despite how much force he applied, the bullet remained unmoved. Time ticked—not here but in his head. The mocking sounds of each passing second in his brain tortured him. He needed a library. He would pour himself over every personal recording from every Time Father who ever existed if it meant finding the solution to this problem. But he could not do it here; not only were the books frozen in their places, but the militaries of individual divisions would descend on him soon. While only a Time Father could enter Southeastern's borders while it remained frozen, they could still surround him until he surrendered or starved to death. He was a criminal now, at least as far as the other Time Fathers were concerned.

Nicholai ran his hands through his hair as he paced. They would strip him of his Chronometer and murder him for his betrayal against the divisions without so much as batting an eye. His atrocity was unforgivable, even with his father on the council of existing Time Fathers. If they killed him and retrieved his Chronometer, they would initiate a new Time Father. He would reboot time in the Southeastern division. Lilac would be dead.

Nicholai's ears perked as he heard a distant boom. It was soft, but he knew what it was. Where the borders of the other divisions met Southeastern, the tectonic plates in the earth's crust shifted. The immovable southeast met the force of the other moving divisions underground. Though he could not see it with his eyes, that boom would be the first of many. He didn't have much time.

With the sounds of the dying earth dissipating, the only noise surrounding him was his thudding heart. He didn't know where he was going, but he had to go. Nicholai eyed Lilac, trying to remember a time when her expression was more comforting than the one she held now. He leaned his cheek against the side of hers and whispered, "I will fix this, Lilac. I will. I promise." Nicholai kissed his muse's cheek.

He did not know where to begin. They would hunt him in every division. In a world where most of the land was colonized, there were not many places to hide. He could not even gather any supplies to accompany him, with all the foodstuffs frozen in place. Eating was necessary; he'd have to enter a division. He could navigate south, where Darjal Wessex reigned supreme, or east, where Avital York was in charge.

Avital was the eldest of all eight existing Time Fathers. It showed in his face. His division was the most industrialized of all, resulting in many health problems for the townsfolk. The population was so high that traveling to Eastern would be suicide. It would be impossible to hide from everyone's watchful eyes in that district.

Darjal of the Southern division was a religious man; his passion did not rest so much in industrialization as it did in cleansing the world of its sins. He forced his people to attend the churches daily and considered it a betrayal against the division and a slight to his self-imposed godliness if their attendance slipped. That would be his best bet. The more people in attendance at the churches, the less roamed the streets to spot him.

Nicholai beheld the scene before him—Lilac locked in fear, Rodgie frozen in bitterness; he had gotten what he had wanted. His daughter would not die today. Not unless Nicholai pressed the crown on his Chronometer.

He could start time again, tell the Time Fathers it was an accidental occurrence. They might buy it. But it also bought Lilac's certain death. He preferred to gamble with his own life than hers. If he held the Chronometer for the Southeastern division, she would remain living. With a heavy heart and little other choices, Nicholai departed. It would be a long journey on foot, with only his regrets to keep him company. With the pressure of finding a solution gnawing at him the entire time, it would be a painful journey as well.

Chapter Five

Churches smelled weird. The stale stench of people deferring through monotony, Iani Platts thought. He watched the men and women of the Southern division pour into the gothic building in droves for the evening service. The citizens of Avadon would be prisoners there for the next hour. Most, anyway. Those who attended the morning service would skip the afternoon and evening ones, already at home in their beds. As early risers, they liked their rest. Iani and Rennington knew the town's routine well, as they used to be part of the military protecting it. Not many pedestrians traversed the streets at this hour. It was the perfect time to commit a crime.

"I don't miss going to church," Iani admitted to Rennington, "and not just because of the smell."

The two stood in the shadows of a narrow alleyway, watching and waiting for the church doors to swallow up the patrons and keep their prying eyes off the streets.

"Come on now," Rennington replied, arms crossed as he leaned against the alleyway wall. "That church is doing us a good bit of favor right now."

Iani spat and shook his head. "Nah. Nothing good ever came from Southern."

"On the contrary, little brother." Rennington watched the last person enter; the large metal doors squealed as they closed behind them, sealing them within the church's guts. He looked over his shoulder and flashed a cocky grin. "*We* came from Southern."

Their experience here had led Captain Kazuaki Hidataka to send them on the supply run. Ever the strategist, the captain knew they could get in and out with efficiency, raising the least alarms. They'd done it before, and they could do it again. Though the town of Avadon hadn't been their home base when they lived in the Southern division, they had been dispatched to patrol here often enough when the military was shorthanded.

Iani and Rennington exited the alley and walked along the street, blending in plain sight. As expected, it was barren, save for a handful of townsfolk and the occasional footman. The brothers slipped into the marketplace where vendors peddled their wares, morning into night. The dawns here were always abuzz with the clamoring of people, but it was quiet now.

A Southern footman marched down an aisle of tightly packed businesses. Some had already closed for the night, iron bars keeping the contents of the small trade shops safe. But there were always a few—the greedier, or perhaps more desperate—men and women who kept their doors open. Open doors meant more opportunities to make money. In the competitive world of Avadon's marketplace, a shopkeeper who stayed open at all hours stood a much better chance at achieving financial success.

Rennington pulled a harmonica from his back pocket and glanced at Iani.

His little brother nodded and adjusted the large camping backpack he carried over his shoulder.

The two went their separate ways. They knew the routine like the backs of their hands.

The eldest brother approached the widest aisle of the marketplace, the area with the most foot traffic. He pulled an empty crate into the center of the road and stood upon it, holding up his hands. "Ladies and gentlemen, let me regale you with a tale. A tale of a man ..." He played his harmonica, providing a musical serenade to accompany his story before he paused and started again. "A man who met a lady—a siren, a vixen of seduction and delight!" Rennington played more, the music getting increasingly magnetic. His sound painted a picture of captivating desire until he stopped playing. "Indeed, his thoughts drifted to her porcelain skin, her milky thighs, her heaving breasts, and his impure thoughts angered the gods." The harmonica music shifted to a deeper tone, more ominous and unforgiving.

Iani did not make eye contact with his brother while he drew what little crowd there was toward him. He rolled his eyes when he heard the repertoire Rennington chose. "Went with *the gods* one again," he muttered to himself, careful as he came behind a merchant.

Avadon's residents were suckers for god-infused stories, and Rennington's performance captivated the merchant too much for him to notice Iani's stealthy movements from behind. Exposed on all sides to allow airflow and prevent heatstroke, Iani had no problem reaching under the counter and seizing a box of rations before retreating undetected.

The case only contained fifty individual ration meals. This would have to be one of many they loaded onto the cockboat that hid on the shore. He was lucky the merchants weren't guarding their supplies more diligently. In those instances, Iani changed tactics, stealing money from those too distracted by Rennington to notice. The pilfered currency purchased the needed supplies. While it raised less red flags than stealing entire crates of goods, it was also a gamble.

As deserters of the Southern division military, they always ran the risk people existed who still recognized their faces from the wanted posters. But that had been almost a decade ago. Their desertion was no longer fresh in the minds of the townsfolk. The Platts brothers had not encountered any trouble when they pulled the same stunt in Avadon six years ago, but Iani did not want prior success to make him cocky. Cocky men made mistakes. He didn't have time for mistakes. Especially when they had to collect ten or more crates to bring back to the ship by dawn if they wanted enough supplies to make it to the next port.

Iani took the box into the alley and hid it under an old, discarded blanket. He turned to fetch another unattended container. He looted as much as he could from the unwatched booth before he employed his other tactics. With fluid, efficient movements, he acted fast. The ability wasn't just a perk but a necessity. Rennington was a solid harmonica player, one of the best Iani had ever heard, but even his brother could not captivate the audience forever.

Iani Platts hid three boxes in the alley. He did not wish to press his luck by going for a fourth. The businesses commanded small spaces. They would notice multiple crates of missing supplies if he got too greedy. As he was about to alter his tactics and pluck money from unsuspecting satchels, he heard someone shout, "Thief!"

Iani froze. He never thought for a moment he would be caught. The Platts brothers *never* got caught.

Rennington's music stopped.

The small crowd, once lost in his talent, gasped at the declaration. They patted their pockets to be sure their own money was safe.

Rennington scanned the area for his little brother, assuming the alarm bells were raised due to his actions. He tried to pinpoint him, ready to jump in if things escalated. If this town unleashed a mob on Iani Platts, they had to get through Rennington first. He was not afraid to police these people; the townsfolk of the Southern division were weak and timid. He learned that after spending many years with them when he and Iani had belonged to the Southern military. To him, they were spineless. They'd have to be, to witness the horrors the Southern military executed and not riot in protest.

The movement of two footmen caught Rennington's eyes. He thought for sure he spotted Iani in the distance, though it was hard to tell. The sun set, and darkness moved in. His eyesight was not immaculate. Though Elowyn had a great deal of medical training, she could do much for those who suffered from night blindness. He squinted to see better, but all he witnessed was the shadow of a man running in a direction opposite the footmen.

"Guards!" a merchant shouted, waving his arms. "He went that way!"

Iani watched the thief flee. His heart raced, having figured for certain he was the one under the heat of the footmen's attention. They chased after the stranger without giving Iani so much as a glance. A wave of relief washed over him until he saw Rennington shove through the small crowd and chase after the footman and the thief.

"Bloody shit," Iani hissed, panicked as he ran his hands through his hair. What would have been an amazing opportunity to plunder the marketplace with the footmen distracted by another thief had turned into a shit show. Rennington must have mistaken the thief for himself. Iani was humbled that Rennington had abandoned all fear to save him, but he also realized what an idiot his brother was for not recognizing the thief wasn't him. "Gods damn it all, Renn. You'll get us killed," he breathed to himself, sprinting after the elder Platts brother.

Two nearby patrolmen joined the two footmen chasing the thief.

The stranger, shrouded by a hooded cloth, was quick on his feet. Shadows whipped and fell from his body as he dashed under streetlamps with haste. He was fortunate to have a lead on the footmen as he darted into an alley flanked by the walls of the church and a steam engine repair shop.

The four footmen stopped before they turned into the alley. They did not want to charge in blind and risk getting shot. After exchanging glances with one another and issuing several hand gestures, they motioned to one another for all to draw their weapons.

"You're surrounded!" one footman shouted, his back pressed against the repair shop's exterior. "Exit peacefully and we will not shoot!"

Silence followed.

Frustrated it would not be an easy takedown, the footmen readied themselves. All eyes were on their superior as he silently counted down with his fingers—three, two, one. The four men charged into the alley, handguns and falchions positioned in front.

"What in the feck?" One footman narrowed his eyes, bewildered they were all staring at an empty alleyway.

The soft glow from the street lanterns illuminated the nothingness. It was a dead end, no logical way for anyone to exit. They crept into the alley, each moment that passed leaving them more puzzled than before.

"He didn't just disappear into thin air," one said, lowering his gun.

They looked up, thinking perhaps he had somehow scaled the church's textured walls.

Rennington appeared at the mouth of the alleyway. Believing Iani to be in the hands of the footmen, he fired with little hesitation. The bullet struck a soldier's throat. The gurgling sound that escaped his lips would have haunted anyone who hadn't witnessed such horrors before, but the eldest Platts brother was unaffected. He didn't bat an eye as the soldier fell to his knees. Rennington fired another round, striking another guard in the arm.

THE SOUND OF BULLETS ricocheting off the alley walls echoed through the thief's ears as he watched from his safe space. Narrow slits in a hidden grate attached to the lowest point of the church wall allowed him to see all the goings-on without drawing attention. He lowered his hood, feeling safer within the underground catacombs of the church. Nicholai was fortunate enough to know all about the secret tunnels that wove through each of the divisions. These catacombs weaved to Seacaster, the hometown of the Southern division's Time Father, Darjal Wessex.

Though each division had a series of underground passageways leading from every Time Father's hometown to the nearest piece of coast in the event of an emergency evacuation, Darjal's was the most elaborate. He was a paranoid man, securing many exits for himself should the necessity arrive. His fundamentalist views on religion made him an unpopular Time Father and the most common target of assassination attempts.

Nicholai watched with confusion as the fight outside ensued. Who was this man who assaulted four footmen without a second thought? Was he trying to save Nicholai from falling into the unforgiving hands of the lawmen? He couldn't understand why; the Southeastern Time Father had been careful as he had weaved through Avadon. He'd been here for over a week now, pillaging food and any useful information he could. In all the time Nicholai had spent sneaking through the shadows of this town, he had never seen that man before.

"IANI!" RENNINGTON SHOUTED, trying to locate his brother in the alley's darkness and the unrelenting chaos of the three remaining footmen. He squeezed off another shot at his attackers but missed. His cautious aim was his downfall; he didn't want to fire without consideration for fear he might hit his brother.

But when no response followed his call, Rennington realized the grave mistake he had made. Iani was nowhere in sight.

He only took a second to scan the area for his brother. But when one was up against the competent aim of the Southern military, one second was all it took. Rennington's upper shoulder felt the familiar sting of a bullet, painless at first then radiating with agony. The sudden shock caused him to drop his gun, and he cursed. There was no time to stop and pick it up; the footmen already realized they had disarmed him and drew closer, weapons ready.

"You'll come quietly, or you'll come in pieces," one footman ordered as Rennington clutched his bleeding arm. The soldier approached the wounded man, who knew better than to move. He did not wish to be shot down.

Rennington guessed they wanted him to run. They enjoyed gunning down a target. At least they had when he had served alongside them.

The footman sneered and punched him hard in the gut before unclipping his restraining device.

NICHOLAI WATCHED FROM his safe space beneath the church. He had an unexpected attack of conscience. Clearly, the man had mistaken him for somebody else, but his actions were still noble. Though the Southeastern Time Father did not approve of his slaughtering methods, it was hard to watch the footmen drag away the man who would have been his savior. He contemplated assisting. It was ingrained deep into Nicholai's character to help when a person needed it, but it was a big risk to blow his cover for a stranger.

RENNINGTON WAS TOO proud to groan from the punch; though between the stomach assault and his bullet-ridden shoulder, his body screamed in one too many places. He waited to feel the icy touch and unforgiving weight of the iron shackles on his wrists, but they never came, only the sound of another gun discharging.

The shackles rattled in the alley as they landed beside the footman Iani had shot in the forehead. He fired another round at one of the other two militiamen, but they were quick on their feet and dodged his aggressive advances. Both teams had the darkness to contend with. Only the dim light of the main road lanterns offered help in seeing their opponents.

The two remaining footmen scattered; one took shelter behind a large metal dumpster while the other propped up his dead comrade to use as a human shield.

"You could've killed me!" Rennington backed away from the corpse Iani had left behind. It was a close shot, and his little brother wasn't exactly an expert marksman. Luck had been on his side to pull off that hit.

"We all gotta die of something." Iani fired rounds into the metal dumpster. His words were callous. Rage consumed him. He was overwhelmed with the insult that these men would dare harm his sibling. *Nobody* spilled the blood of a Platts brother and lived to tell the tale.

Iani was so focused on the footman behind the dumpster that his consideration for the rest of his surroundings abandoned him. Rennington caught the weak shimmer of a lantern light as it reflected off the metal barrel of the second footman's gun. He seized his little brother. The adrenaline coursing through him allowed him enough strength to push Iani's body behind his own as the gun fired.

Two shots and one brutal punch was enough to bring Rennington Platts to his knees. He wasn't even sure where the second bullet
had struck him, but his body felt the effects of his injuries.

"Renn!" Iani panicked and fired round after round at the man
who had brought down his brother. Soon, the only sound in the
alley was the mocking *click, click, click* of an empty chamber. Iani
cursed and dropped his weapon, falling to the ground and grasping
his brother by the shoulders to keep him upright.

"I knew it." The footman who had shot Rennington smirked,
satisfied with the sound of Iani's empty weapon. In any other circumstance, he would've gunned them both down then and there.
But the name Rennington had shouted earlier during his initial assault and the name Iani had uttered rang a bell in his brain. "Rennington and Iani Platts. Jernal, these are the feckin' deserters!" he
called to his comrade.

Jernal emerged from behind the bullet-riddled dumpster,
weapon still drawn in the event they continued to resist. "No kid-
ding." He sneered, then a grin spread across his face. It had been
many years since the two brothers had deserted the Southern division's army, but they remained a common subject amongst the men
in its military. No greater act of treason existed than to abandon
a post. "Darjal would *very* much like to make an example of you
two."

NICHOLAI'S MORAL COMPASS spun. He watched the two
footmen force the man to his feet despite his injuries. He couldn't
hold himself up. Each time he collapsed to the ground, they raised
a knee to his stomach or pistol whipped his skull. The other man
looked like a demon as they laid into the wounded man. The footmen had to let the man fall to the ground, as it took both men to

subdue the fiery other one and his insurmountable fury. After a relentless struggle, they restrained him.

"I SEE A PROMOTION COMING our way," Jernal said to his partner, his voice coated with pride. "But I'm mostly curious to see what Darjal will do when he sees these two."

The men walked Rennington and Iani out of the alley and toward the confinement center. They'd detain the outlaws there until they could send word to Darjal in the next town over.

NICHOLAI DID NOT HAVE to wonder what Darjal would do to a military deserter. He had only met the other Time Fathers face to face once during their ten-year meeting at Panagea's center, but he took it upon himself to become familiar with the type of men they were through biographies and the public statistics of their divisions.

Darjal Wessex was an unforgiving sort. He believed in old-world punishment as brutal as it was effective. While his tactics were off putting to most, Darjal had no qualms in his unrelenting behavior. He stood behind the claim that his people would revere him as a god. An omnipotent being couldn't commit murder, only cleanse the world of sinners. It was a dangerous thought process Nicholai never agreed with, but the Time Fathers allowed him to have his delusions. Until this moment, he never assumed it would be an issue he'd have to deal with.

Deserters. If they were guilty of their crime, rules dictated they should accept the consequences. More critical still, they had killed two men. It went against everything Nicholai believed in, but something called to him to help. As if a supernatural force drove him, he creaked open the hidden grate and pulled his thinning, hungry body from the darkness of the catacombs. Most of him already regretted his actions. But the one part of him that did not was the one that resonated the loudest; Lilac would have done it. He saw the sadness in her eyes when he announced to Rodgie he could not help his daughter. Ever the voice for the underdog, she would have freed these men or died trying.

Nicholai bent near the body of a fallen soldier. He cringed in the darkness, a squeamish feeling rising inside him as he rolled the body to grab the weapon trapped underneath it. The skin was still warm. He pulled up his hood to conceal himself. Nicholai had seen dead bodies before, but he had never watched a man get murdered before his eyes. It was ... unsettling. More so because he harbored a suspicion he'd see a lot more in his future. A man on the run from the seven most powerful leaders in Panagea would see rivers of blood before he reached his goal, if he reached it at all.

The Time Father gripped the gun. It felt awkward. Though Nicholai held experience in all things mechanical, the gun was never one of his favorite machines. Metal could create many other more useful things. Without further stalling, he quickened his pace, exiting the alley and following the blood trail the wounded man had left behind.

Soon he walked behind the two footmen. He wasn't without fear. He knew this was the most foolish thing a man in hiding could do. But a man in love was a fool, and knowing Lilac would want it was all the fuel he needed.

"Release the men," he instructed, cocking the revolver's hammer.

THE SOLDIERS DID NOT have much time to react. They each had holstered their sidearms, as they needed their arms to carry the injured Rennington and did not want to risk a boisterous Iani stealing them. Their expressions were equal parts confusion and surprise.

"The thief," Jernal whispered, recalling the original suspect of their chase. He narrowed his eyes. The man looked familiar, but he could not place him. "You're affiliated with these rats?"

"No questions, gentlemen. Just release them."

They had little choice as they stared down the pilfered revolver's barrel. They could drop the two men and draw their guns, but the man could shoot one or both of them in the time it took to do so, and releasing Iani was a gamble in and of itself. Even handcuffed, the man was a cannonball. The two footmen hesitated before releasing Iani and Rennington.

Iani tried to catch his brother as he fell to the ground, but he could do little while restrained.

"Keep your hands high, gentlemen, and point me toward the keys which unlock these shackles."

Jernal clenched his teeth as frustration boiled inside him. "There." He motioned to the set which dangled around his waist.

Nicholai frowned. He did not want to get *that* close to the footmen. That was a pair of dice he had no intention of rolling. But he also didn't want to encourage any of them to lower their hands. With no other choice, he said, "Unbind these men ... very, very slowly."

Jernal's mind raced. Nicholai saw it in his eyes. He calculated the risk of whether he should make a move. He determined it too dangerous to chance. Acting on instruction, he stuck the skeleton key into Rennington's cuffs first. The heavy chains rattled as Jernal pulled them from the wounded man's wrists.

Iani offered his wrists; it was the first time since Nicholai saw him restrained that he did not try to unhinge himself.

Jernal unlocked his restraints next, and, before they even fell to the ground, Iani reached for his older brother.

"Make no mention of this to Darjal." Nicholai backed farther from the two footmen. "He would not be pleased with your failure."

Jernal scowled along with his partner.

Refusing to turn his back on the two men, Nicholai backpedaled, gun still drawn.

Rennington grimaced as Iani adjusted him over his shoulder. He was difficult to hold. Rennington had five inches in height and fifty pounds of muscle on his little brother.

"Who the feck are you?" Iani backed away in the same direction. Though the Platts brothers did not enjoy being the subjects of rescue missions, Iani's ego was not so big that he would walk away from their best chance of survival.

"Does it matter?" Nicholai replied without taking his gaze off Jernal.

Iani arched a brow, surveying the situation the stranger had freed them from. "S'pose not."

Nicholai's eyes narrowed as he regarded Jernal, though he suspected the hood obscured his face. "Now, turn around and run. Send condolences to the families of the men you lost tonight." Though he tried to sound direct, his last sentence appeared sincere.

The soldiers nodded.

"Right," Jernal said, stepping backward.

Neither felt brave nor stupid enough to turn their backs on an armed man. They backpedaled until enough of a distance separated them that Jernal's partner felt comfortable turning and running. Jernal could not help but loiter and tried to study the cloaked man's face. He knew him from somewhere. It vexed him.

"What are you waiting for?" Iani muttered, eyeballing Nicholai with a judgmental stare. "Shoot him."

"I won't shoot him." Though his response was instinctual, as he never intended to take another man's life, he regretted saying it.

Jernal's keen insight sensed his weakness, and he withdrew his weapon.

"Run!" Nicholai shouted, grabbing Rennington's other arm and hauling the body off with Iani.

The youngest Platts brother looked delirious as the two men carried Rennington toward the alley. One of Jernal's bullets whizzed past his head as he yelled, "What in the— Feckin' shoot him, mate!"

Nicholai did not respond. He focused on moving Rennington and not getting shot.

Iani cursed and reached to rip the gun from Nicholai's hands. He spun on his heels, leaving Rennington's entire weight for Nicholai to support as he fired round after round at Jernal. It bought Nicholai enough time to reach the darkened alley between the church and the repair shop. The ominous chords of choir voices reverberated through the large building's walls as he set down Rennington and opened the hidden grate once more.

It was difficult stuffing a grown man's body in a small hole. Rennington scowled at Nicholai's forceful touch. "I can do it, mate, gods be damned," he muttered through a clenched jaw, painfully shifting his body and sliding into the hole. Though he wriggled in, he still could not find the strength to stand and collapsed once his feet hit the ground of the catacombs below.

Nicholai waited for Iani to emerge around the corner. The sound of bullets being exchanged made it seem like hours, but it had been mere seconds.

Iani rounded the corner, eyes falling on Nicholai as he motioned to the secret grate. "Charming disappearing act," Iani said, running and sliding into the grate with a grace Nicholai did not know the wild, young man possessed.

The Time Father followed and sealed the grate after him with haste. He did not know if Jernal had followed Iani, but he did not want to take any chances by dawdling.

"So, *this* is how you pulled off that little vanishing performance earlier," Rennington murmured from his place on the ground. He seethed and tightened his grip on his arm where the first bullet had entered. The second hole appeared to be around his hip.

"Too right. The feck is this place?" Iani whispered, trying to keep his voice low.

The church choir's haunting crescendos echoed through the catacombs.

Nicholai knelt next to Rennington. It was impossible to see his injuries in the darkness. "These catacombs run to the coast. We'll need to find some light if we've any chance at all of extracting those bullet fragments."

"You some sort of doctor?" Rennington asked, trying to maintain his composure in his current state.

Nicholai paused. "No. To be honest, I don't even know how to get bullet fragments from a man's body."

Rennington cursed and eyed his brother. "If these run all the way to the coast, we can get back to the cockboat and—"

"I'll get you back to Elowyn," Iani finished, bending to help his brother by pulling him to his feet. "Just try not to die between now and then."

Rennington muttered something under his breath.

Nicholai flanked the injured man's opposite side and helped him move.

As they crept farther into the belly of the catacombs, Iani spoke to break the silence. "And to whom do the Platts brothers owe a debt of gratitude?" His voice was agitated, but the sentiment behind his statement was sincere.

Nicholai frowned in the darkness. He wasn't sure who he could trust. He was a well-known character in all the eight cardinal directions. Revealing his name while he remained on the run would not be the wisest decision. Then again, neither was exposing himself to save the lives of two strangers.

"Nico," he replied, bridging the gap between their current spot and the coast with each passing step. "Just Nico."

Chapter Six

Darkness bowed out. It's time ended, and it offered the lead role to light. It crept into eyesight with a slow linger, an expected crescendo of glory that tucked away the blacks and indigos of the sea and sky. The blinding colors of fire spread across the horizon. The way the sun climbed and cast its net of rays over the rippling waves of the water was poetry in motion. A new dawn was one of the world's natural wonders, a reliable and beautiful thing one counted on every day. The sun always rose.

The beauty was lost on Kazuaki. He stared at the day with detachment. The ship anchored in the harbor as far from the prying eyes of land dwellers as they could muster. Rennington and Iani's cockboat was nowhere in sight. Kazuaki squinted as he caught a bright ripple of light off a wave. Turning his back to the climbing sun, he leaned against the quarterdeck and touched the bandage wrapped around the hole of his empty eye socket.

Years. Several *long* years had passed since he had traded it to Mimir. He felt the thin sheet of metal underneath the synthetic-leather cover strapped to his head. The captain remembered the pain of cauterizing the protective piece of titanium to his face like it was yesterday. But it had been a necessity. He did not want to take any chances. Not with Mimir's little *gift*. Not until he reached Bermuda.

"They should've been here by now."

Kazuaki perked at the sound of her voice. Though it held no emotion, her pitch still had a way of rousing him from his deepest thoughts. As Bermuda approached, the captain cleared his throat. "I'm sure they'll be here in a moment's notice. Best prepare for departure. Ensure all hands are on deck. The outgoing tide is favorable, as is the wind. Should be an easy exit, given Rennington and Iani arrive on time."

"Too right, Captain." Bermuda nodded and turned on her heels to instruct the rest of the crew.

Kazuaki's gaze fell to her missing hand as she walked away. The guilt only attacked him at the forefront for a moment before he buried it deep within his subconscious, but it lingered like a dull toothache.

Her handicap did not slow her. She was as useful as before. With her heart freed from the burden of mourning, Bermuda channeled her focus into becoming a better fighter, a more skillful deckhand. Perhaps she was a better quartermaster in her current state than before. But she was no longer Bermuda.

Kazuaki gazed into the farthest reaches of the world and found nothing as valuable to him. She was a flawless creature, a woman of passion and wit. Though the oppressive thumb of Panagea's patriarchal society crushed most women into submission, Bermuda spat in the face of any man who stifled her. She was a breath of fresh air in his stagnant lungs. She always was, from the moment he had seen her punch a man square in the jaw for grabbing her ass in a pub. Kazuaki berated himself often; he had taken this perfectly imperfect thing straight to the creature who stole everything she was. Mimir did not just take her hand or her heart. He took her whole self and left a hollow, robotic shell in her place.

Kazuaki knew his thought process was selfish. Bermuda had gotten everything she wanted in that trade. But he could not walk into the nightmare that was his afterlife without knowing he righted his egregious error. He could not rest until every cell that comprised her body no longer suffered from the touch of that conniving demon. Matters of the heart, while all-consuming and gut-wrenching, were mandatory steps on the path of being human. He had robbed her of that. She had robbed herself of that. Had she given herself more time, he knew she could've overcome it. Bermuda could overcome anything.

The captain's eardrums homed in on the sound of far off rowing. The splashes of the oars sinking into the water and propelling the small craft forward were subtle but distinct. He spied the approaching cockboat but bristled with caution when he saw not two but three passengers. Though it was hard to tell from the distance, one seemed hunched over. Wounded, he guessed. Had it become necessary for the Platts brothers to take a prisoner?

The captain clenched his jaw and headed to the main deck. Bartholomew, Penn, Granite, and his dog were already there, preparing the vessel for departure.

"Looks like we have a visitor, boys," Kazuaki announced to the men as they scurried about. "Let's be sure we treat our *guest* with behavior most becoming of gentlemen, aye?"

Penn smirked at the captain's sarcasm as he approached the foremast. "None more gentlemanly than us, Captain."

Kazuaki was a patient man. He waited on the main deck until the cockboat was abreast of the ship. While it was no surprise to hear Iani's voice call from below, he did not expect the words that followed. "Captain! Man down, immediate assistance, if you please!"

The captain peered over the ship's railing, narrowing his eye as he saw Iani and a stranger holding a haggard-looking Rennington. "Granite," Kazuaki ordered, motioning the giant of a man to the cockboat below, "they'll be needing an assist."

Granite's dog jumped up with excitement at the mention of his master's name.

The man grabbed a large rope and tied it around the main mast, fashioning a quick harness around his waist. He repelled down the side of the ship and landed in the cockboat with a thud.

Nicholai gripped the sides of the small boat, fearing the sheer weight of Granite's body would sink the vessel.

Without making eye contact, the giant man threw Rennington over his shoulder.

The injured Platts brother groaned though he tried his best to muffle it. "No need to be gentle," Rennington uttered with cynicism. "Not as if it's painful being riddled with bullets."

Granite said nothing as he pulled Rennington and himself up the rope, keeping the man balanced on his broad shoulder. His boots scraped against the ship's barnacles and old boards, but he made short work of the effort, dumping Rennington onto the main deck above. He removed the rope from his waist and threw it over the side, so Iani could join them.

"Where's EP?" Rennington asked through his agony, clutching the area where the bullet had entered his hip.

"Here," Elowyn answered as she ran from the deckhouse to kneel beside him. Her brows furrowed as she noticed the two bullet holes. "Gods, Renn, what the shit happened to you?"

"Feckin' Southern footmen is what," Iani called out, having heard Elowyn's inquiry while he climbed the rope. He hoisted himself over, breathing hard as he ran his hands through his hair. "Damn near threw both of us in the cellars to rot too. Probably three days away from Darjal putting our heads on a godsdamned pike."

Kazuaki frowned. He motioned for Granite to help Elowyn get Rennington to her cabin where she could further assist in his medical recovery.

Rennington swatted at Granite's dog as it tried to shove its muzzle into his pelvis, tongue lolling out to lick the wound. "Get your feckin' bilge water mouth away from me, beast. That tongue will give me sepsis!"

"Down," Granite said to the dog.

It obediently abandoned its mission.

Kazuaki ignored the tomfoolery and fixated on Iani. "And how did the Platts brothers manage to evade death?" he asked, putting the wonder of whether someone had followed them in the back of his head until he received more details to the story.

As if on cue, Nicholai finished climbing the rope. Hunger and thirst dulled his ability to perform any physical task with ease. It was obvious from his performance in Avadon's marketplace he was not a successful thief. Lacking in this skill left him famished most nights since he left the Southeastern division. He loitered on the railing, staring with caution at the men and women who stood on the main deck.

"This bugger here"—Iani thumbed toward Nicholai—"can't fire a gun worth a damn but was slick enough to get those military dogs to let us go. Took us to these catacombs that run throughout the underground. The mouth opens right at the shoreline, hidden beneath some rubble. So, fear not, Cap, we weren't followed."

The captain squared his shoulders and approached Nicholai as he leaned over the rail for support. His gaze was skeptical. "I suppose you think I owe you a debt of gratitude for assisting my men." That was as close as a *thank you* Nicholai would get from Kazuaki Hidataka. The captain grabbed the Southeastern Time Father's shoulders and pulled him onto the main deck where he fell to his knees from the force.

Nicholai shifted his weight to help himself sit, eyeing the captain through his hood. "I'd hate to see how you'd handle me had I had let them die."

"Yes," the captain agreed, scrutinizing Nicholai as he placed his arms behind his back, "you would."

Granite, Elowyn, and Rennington disappeared into the cabin. With his brother out of sight, Iani's face showed his concern for Rennington's well-being. "Think he'll be okay, Cap?"

Kazuaki glanced over his shoulder in the direction they'd gone. He had taken a few shots to the hip before. He did not doubt Rennington lived in a great deal of pain. The bullet to the arm was only a flesh wound, but, depending on where he had been hit in the pelvis, he could suffer long-term consequences. Rennington seemed to move well despite his injuries, then again, the elder Platts brother wouldn't show weakness in front of his sibling. "He's in very good hands."

Iani accepted this as the most reassuring answer the captain would provide.

Brack and Revi joined the others on the main deck, each man eyeing Nicholai with skepticism.

"Who's the newbie?" Brack asked with curiosity, unaware of what had transpired earlier.

"Calls himself *Nico*," Iani answered before Nicholai spoke. "Got me and Renn out of a jam on the mainland."

The ground rumbled. They were unaffected in the harbor. The ripples from the force cascaded outward, sloshing against the ship's side.

Kazuaki expected to see another chunk of land fall into the sea. But, if a detachment had taken place, it was out of eyesight. It happened often, pieces of the land vanishing into the sea. He couldn't blame Panagea for disintegrating. Man ravaged her daily. Though it was an alarming trend, it was not one he concerned himself with. Panagea had chewed him up and spat him out long ago. While a part of him missed having stable ground to call home, he was a man of the sea. Kazuaki convinced himself the unwelcoming jaggedness of rocks and earth meant little to him.

As the reverberations settled, the captain turned a blind eye to the aftermath. Instead, he knelt to be eye level with Nicholai, who still hadn't pulled himself up from his place on the ship's sole. "Tell me more about these catacombs."

Nicholai peered at the captain from underneath his hood. He hesitated. It seemed wrong to relent his information, but he valued living. Nicholai suspected he wouldn't live much longer if he didn't offer the truth. "They run through the undergrounds, serving as escape routes for Time Fathers should a situation arise their military can't handle. Each division has them. The older tunnels all feed into neighboring cities, but, when it became clear the mainland was crumbling"—he gestured toward the sound they'd heard moments ago—"they commissioned additions. Now they also run to the nearest coast. Typically, an aquatic vessel is hidden somewhere near the exit, stocked with enough non-perishables to reach the next division and then some."

Without taking his gaze off the stranger, Kazuaki said, "Penn. Brack. Join Iani, and take the cockboat to the tunnel's exit. See if you can't find those non-perishable items Mr. Nico mentioned."

"Yes, Captain." Penn approached the railing and repelled with ease into the cockboat.

"You got it, Cappy!" Brack followed Penn but paused when Kazuaki addressed him.

"Brack. It's *Captain*."

"Too right, *Captain*." The Rabbit laughed, ego none the injured as he disappeared to the cockboat.

Iani lingered, his gaze in the direction where Elowyn had taken his brother. He lamented leaving his side while injured.

"He'll be here when you get back," Kazuaki said knowingly, dismissing Iani with his hand.

The man cleared his throat and nodded. "Yes, Captain." With that, he joined his comrades to find the hidden boat and supplies.

Kazuaki's attention returned to Nicholai. He saw the man's hunger. His thirst. Even through the shadows of his hood, he witnessed the man's sunken eyes and chapped lips. "I'm not an unfair man, Nico. You appear to be an individual of certain knowledge. Pray tell, how did you learn about these catacombs? Perhaps an exchange of information for a meal and a drink?" It was a mercy deal. Kazuaki would have gotten the information one way or another, by means of torture if need be. But he extended a proverbial lifeline to Nico, a reward for his efforts in helping Rennington and Iani.

Bartholomew approached. As a scholar, Nicholai's knowledge of the catacombs intrigued him. He seemed to know their history a great deal. Curiosity caused him to loom behind the captain, his hands behind his back as he listened.

Nicholai hesitated again. The allure of a meal was tempting, but he was not ready to reveal that he was a Time Father. He still wasn't certain who he could trust. It was obvious he had fallen into the company of outlaws—though he was technically one of them now after the atrocity he had committed in Southeastern. Once they discovered his identity, they might hand him in to the military of any division for a quick reward.

"I ... discovered records ... while searching for the library Darjal hides beneath the church in Avadon." It was only a partial lie. Nicholai had crawled through the catacombs to find easy access to the library since he arrived in Southern. It would at least be believable he might stumble across literature in his search.

"A library?" Bartholomew's eyes widened. The scholar did not even try to stifle his interest. He was a philosopher, an academic ever on the search for knowledge. His hunger for information had only grown since he had left the Northwestern division many years ago. The Time Father there, Vadim Canmore, had destroyed every learning institution available in Northwestern, paving the way for industry to thrive and funnel more money into his own pockets.

Unlike the rest, Bartholomew was no criminal. Panagea did not shun him; he shunned her. Vadim's greed had driven the scholar to Kazuaki's ship, where he had discovered more of an opportunity to learn than he had in Northwestern. But, in all his adventures with Kazuaki since then, Bartholomew had never been more excited than right now. They had stumbled across occasional pieces of literature in their hunts for legends and proved enough to satisfy his lust for learning. But an entire library, hidden from the public knowledge, blew his mind.

Kazuaki's intrigue rose also, though he hid it well. "And what particular piece of literature were you hunting for in this ... underground library?"

The Time Father shifted. This captain was a prying and clever sort. He did not know how long he could get away with withholding information. "Rumor has it, Darjal hides all pertinent literature there—old records, accounts of the way things used to be, old fairytales that might ... contradict his religious efforts." Nicholai hoped his answer was enough to satisfy the captain but vague enough not to betray his intentions. "Anything you could think of you wouldn't want the public eye to fall on, especially if you were trying to sustain an environment where you're to be revered as a god."

"I see." Kazuaki leaned back but kept his kneeling position beside Nico. Old fairytales locked away in the catacombs beneath a church—it had Kazuaki Hidataka written all over it. "Revi,"—the captain shifted to his feet—"head to Penn's galley. Perhaps he's left something edible for our visitor. See he's well fed. He'll need his strength, if he's to lead us to that library later."

"Yes, sir." Revi approached Nicholai and pulled him to his feet. "Come on, you. Follow me."

Nicholai followed Revi, casting a cautious glance over his shoulder at the captain.

Kazuaki glared at him the whole time, keeping an ever-watchful eye on Nicholai until he disappeared toward the galley with Revi.

"An entire library, Captain." Bartholomew ran his dark hands over his head, trying to take in the anticipation of the moment. "Do you think it's true?"

Kazuaki stared at the door where Nicholai had vanished with Revi. "I think our so-called friend knows more than he's letting on, but I also suspect he's a reliable source indeed."

"We'll find out," Bartholomew offered, looking toward the mainland. "If the boys return with the supplies on that hidden boat, that's a keen indication he knows a thing or two more than we do about the goings-on here."

"Too right." Kazuaki tore his gaze from the door and connected with his comrade. He trusted Revi to keep a watchful eye on their visitor. He wanted to make a quick check on Rennington and assess his condition. If things went the way he intended, he'd have to leave the injured man on the ship while they stowed away to the catacombs. Rennington's condition would tell him how many men he needed to leave behind to man the vessel in their absence. He felt the rare thrill of excitement bubble inside him for the first time in years. With any luck, Nico falling into their laps would be a great boon. "Only time will tell, mate," he said to Bartholomew, waiting with patience alongside his trusted friend. "Only time will tell."

IT WAS INCREDIBLE HOW many non-perishable food items fit in a getaway boat for a Time Father. Iani, Penn, and Brack returned several hours later, having found the vessel hidden amongst the rubble, as Nicholai had said. Kazuaki watched his crew unload the crates from the small stolen boat and place it into the storage hold of their own ship. It was enough food to keep them at sea for months if they rationed it well. Though the food was by and far the most critical prize, the hygiene products and entertainment—decks of playing cards and dice—were also valued. They left nothing behind.

"She's empty, Captain," Penn announced as they removed the last crate. "You'll be wanting us to be rid of the evidence?"

"Aye. Have Revi follow you out with the cockboat. Return quickly. We'll be tending to business soon."

Penn and Revi nodded, setting out to sink the stolen ship farther into the sea.

The captain recounted the numerous crates commandeered from the small vessel. He wanted to wait until the dead hours to return to the catacombs when the likelihood of anyone being present in the church was nil. The day had provided an unexpected fortune. If what Nico said was true about all the Time Fathers hiding vessels by their hometown's nearest coast, they could raid the remaining seven and never risk capture by dropping anchor near a major port for a long time. But that journey needed to wait. A much more pressing one awaited them. By validating the hidden boat's existence, Nico's talk of underground libraries sounded promising.

Kazuaki adjusted his long jacket. "Bermuda, get everything ready for tonight."

"Yes, Captain." The woman moved forward, guided by programmed thinking.

Kazuaki watched her depart before heading toward Elowyn's room. Though he knocked on the open door, he did not wait for a response before entering. It was a modest space—a bed for the patient and a bed for Elowyn that allowed her to monitor. Though the woman was absent to assist the others in preparing for departure, it was not Elowyn Saveign the captain came to see. "How do you fare, Rennington?"

Rennington opened his eyes and blinked away his fatigue. "Aye, Captain. I'm right as rain." He tried to slide himself upright in the makeshift bed.

Kazuaki saw the bottom of a bandage peeking from beneath Rennington's shirt sleeve. Elowyn had removed the bullet from the shoulder and bound the wound. He assumed she had extracted the bullet from his hip, but Kazuaki did not plan on removing Rennington's bed sheets to verify. He felt someone behind him.

Iani had returned from dropping off the stolen supplies in Penn's galley. He cleared his throat from behind the captain. "Can I ...?" He motioned to his brother.

Kazuaki stepped aside.

Iani smiled, relieved to see his older brother sitting up and alert. "You look like shit."

"Feck off," Rennington rebutted, trying not to chuckle for fear he'd exacerbate his wounds.

Kazuaki observed the brothers for a moment. "We're heading to the catacombs to look for that library that Nico fellow mentioned I'll leave Elowyn with you for medical circumstances, should you need her. Penn will be here, should you need a meal. Granite, should you need any muscle."

"Gods, take his dog with you." Rennington flopped his head onto the pillow. "Beast has been clawing at the door all day. Damn creature wants my blood more than Darjal Wessex does."

Kazuaki allowed him to complain before he finished his earlier statement. "And Iani ..." He regarded the youngest Platts brother. "You'll be staying as well."

Iani looked surprised. He assumed he'd be returning, since, aside from his brother, he was the most familiar with Southern and its happenings. But he nodded without arguing. "Yes, Captain. Thank you."

"Right," Kazuaki muttered and took a deep breath as he backed toward the door. "Get well, Rennington."

"Captain?" Rennington sat upright again, propping himself on his elbows. "If I may, though it kills me to say, that guy really did save our asses."

Kazuaki nodded. "I've heard."

Rennington frowned, seeming unsure for a moment. "Forgive me for bringing up old garbage, Cap, but we never did replace Jirin. It's been years. I think this guy could be a good addition."

Kazuaki glanced at Iani, his expression revealing nothing. "Did he suffer head trauma when he got shot?"

Iani blinked, uncertain whether the captain was serious or joking.

"I'm just saying, keep an open mind. For what it's worth, I like him. More than I ever liked that piece of shit, Jirin."

"Duly noted," Kazuaki retorted, lingering in the doorway. "Until we return, then. Keep an eye on the ship."

The captain's boots thundered as he ran up the small flight of stairs to the main deck. He beheld his surroundings and cracked his knuckles, ready to start. "Brack, Revi, Bermuda, Bartholomew, you're with me!"

The crewmembers grabbed their supplies and empty satchels as they heard their names and headed for the cockboat.

"And you." He plucked Nicholai from the bench where they had left him while they unloaded the boat.

"I've got legs," Nicholai interjected as the captain forced him to his feet.

"You'll discover quickly that insolence is not welcome aboard my ship, Nico." Kazuaki's words were straightforward, like the calm before a storm Nicholai had no desire to endure.

They boarded the cockboat and headed for the catacombs, waiting to light their lanterns until they drew closer to the mouth of the secret tunnel. They did not want to raise any alarms should anyone see lights pouring into the mainland. Once inside the protective arms of the tunnel, everyone pulled a lantern from their packs, save for Nicholai.

Kazuaki removed his flint and steel and sparked a kerosene-soaked wick to light each device. The flint and steel was an older method of achieving fire, but Kazuaki'd had lifetimes of practice and had mastered the art. With their shadows flickering across the the catacombs interior, the team crept deeper into the darkness.

Nicholai listened to the sounds of their marching feet echo through the narrow corridor. Their shadows followed them like ominous demons. How did he find himself here in the company of a band of outlaws? Who were these strangers who clung to the ocean? Seafaring was a dead art. The whole thing was strange.

Nicholai lamented his predicament. Not several weeks ago, he had been Time Father to an entire division, overseeing the water purification industry's expansion and furthering the growth of technology by making more-advanced machines. He'd always had water and food available and wanted for nothing. Now, he crawled through dusty catacombs to steal literature meant to be buried by a fellow Time Father. If he lived a thousand years, he never would have predicted this.

"You sure we're just here for books?" Brack asked, his lantern illuminating the mild disappointment in his face as they walked. "No myths, no legends—just paper and ink?"

"*Just* paper and ink?" Bartholomew's deep voice boomed louder than usual in the narrow tunnel. "These documents probably hold the knowledge of countless lifetimes. Secrets long forgotten and cast away from the public. These books are sure to be priceless."

Brack shrugged. "Forgive me for not finding old parchment as exciting as heaps of gold."

Bartholomew muttered something.

Kazuaki held his lantern high, casting his light deep into the tunnel. "The goal is not so much the books themselves, Brack. Knowledge brings us opportunities. The opportunities are what bring us the real prize."

Brack blinked, familiar with Kazuaki's insightful rants but never absorbing the full impact. "That's why you're the cap, Captain," was all he said, knowing it was better to soothe Kazuaki's ego than enter a full-on philosophical debate. That was far more up Bartholomew's alley than his own.

Nicholai walked ahead of the crowd, motioning toward several places he had hacked at with a chisel and hammer. "These were some locations I scouted already, but I had little success."

Joining his side, the captain inspected Nicholai's former efforts. "Were you digging mindlessly, or do you have evidence-based assumptions as to the library's location?" he asked, half-insulting, half-inquisitive.

With a mild irritation, Nicholai replied, "All I know is it's beneath the church. And the catacombs are beneath the church."

"We should've brought Iani," Bermuda mentioned, looking bored as she glanced around. "He was forced to attend services here. Without the blueprints to the church, he would've been our next best asset in terms of where to look."

"Iani was not needed here," Kazuaki said. "He's too concerned with his brother to focus. That makes him useless right now. It's more likely the library will be some place easily accessible from the church interior. It's more practical to seal off an existing room than make an entire new one to house banned books. Do you know the approximate location of the church basement?"

The inquiry grabbed Nicholai's attention. The captain's observation made sense; it irked him he had not thought of it before. "Of course. I thought I found the room earlier when I removed some brick work, but it just led to the church basement." He stood before a brick wall with some obvious foundation flaws. The occasional shifting of the Earth's plates below had weakened the walls. "I replaced them, as not to draw attention, but they should slide out easily enough." He gripped the edges of a brick with his fingertips and slid it out.

Bermuda, Brack, Bartholomew, and Kazuaki helped Nicholai remove more bricks. The hole he made earlier was barely big enough for a child to fit through.

"Chisel more in the mortar joints," Kazuaki instructed the crew, "as quietly as you can. I realize the irony in asking you to demolish a wall in silence, but it's still likely there are footmen outside, even at this hour."

"Especially since your men left two bodies behind in our escape," Nicholai muttered. He did not enjoy being a participant in any man's death, even when others deemed it a necessity.

"Only two?" Kazuaki's brow rose as he watched Brack remove more bricks. He sounded disinterested and showed no emotion to indicate otherwise, though the news came as an alarm. The death of two footmen guaranteed increased surveillance. They would have to exercise caution if this was to be a successful trip.

Bermuda could not operate a chisel and hammer with one hand and therefore stood by, annoyed at her own inability. Once they had set aside enough fallen bricks, they crept into the church basement one by one. Greeted by ghoulish-looking figures and carvings of various religious deities, it almost looked as if an ambush awaited them inside the basement walls. All were inanimate but eerie. The room was a glorified storage facility for all the decorative overflow. Religious paraphernalia piled in every corner of the small space, but none were the books they sought.

"Room seems small for a church of this size," Bermuda observed as they walked farther into the space. She approached a wall with a bookshelf covering it. A small portion of the original wall behind it remained visible. Lifting her lantern to get a better view, she squinted. "Captain, these bricks differ from the walls of the others."

Kazuaki closed the distance between them and leaned over her to get a better look. The brick's reddish hues on the obscured wall were much lighter than the others. "This looks like a great place to start."

Nicholai's heart raced as he approached the wall.

Bartholomew, Bermuda, and Brack grabbed the bookshelf and slid it across the floor to remove the obstruction. With little delay, the men started with their chisels and hammers again. No conversation ensued.

Anticipation emanated from Kazuaki, Bartholomew, and Nicholai. Each man held a different reason for craving the contents of the library, but the level of excitement was the same.

"Captain!" Bartholomew panted, holding his lantern to the small hole they had created. "Look ..."

Kazuaki peered into the hollow room that waited on the other side. There, stored away from the eyesight of mankind for many years, was a veritable treasure trove of reading material. It was everything Nicholai had said it would be. Lingering on the other side of the wall was torture.

"Dig," the captain ordered, a broad grin spreading across his face. "My gods, men, dig!"

Chapter Seven

The dust was unwelcomed. It attacked their lungs like an invisible army, inviting a series of coughs from each person as they entered the darkness of the hidden room. It was a sight to behold—an entire space filled top to bottom with literature dating back hundreds of years.

Brack continued coughing as they entered the room, pounding his chest. His fit escalated. His face paled. He appeared more panicked as breathlessness consumed him.

Nicholai recognized the look, the sound. He pulled a syringe from his pocket and regarded Brack for consent.

The man nodded, and Nicholai jammed the syringe into his chest. As the solution flowed through him and the tight grip on his lungs faded, Brack patted a hand on Nicholai's shoulder. "Thanks, mate. I knew by the look on Bart's face it'd be breathtaking but I thought more of a metaphorical sense, you know?" He coughed several more times, grinning all the while. It seemed nothing dampened the man's mood, not even oxygen deficiency.

Nicholai glanced at Brack's hand on his shoulder and forced a smile. "Couldn't very well let you suffer," he said before easing out from under the man's touch.

Each person scattered to a different area of the room to increase their search's effectiveness. It was chaos. Subjects lumped together in thoughtless piles. This deterred no one from diving in.

Kazuaki set his lantern on a tall stack of books to provide illumination as he sifted through the oldest tomes. Fairytales, myths, legends—those were the subjects that called to him.

Bartholomew drifted to philosophical texts and journals from men of science and thought.

Nicholai found himself in the political documents, rummaging through to find any references to Time Fathers, searching for the elusive loophole that could carry him back to Southeastern to spare Lilac's life.

Bermuda drifted without direction, only there to act as another hand to help steal and carry books back in her satchel.

Though his focus first laid with the books, Kazuaki's attention slipped. His gaze followed Bermuda as she stood in the surrounding black. Literature put him in mind of the woman she was years prior, before Mimir. The Bermuda he knew would have been nose deep in the old journals, enjoying the trip the authors long gone painted. She used to love throwing herself into the days of old. She loved nothing now, doomed to live a life robbed of every pleasure.

"Oi!" Brack's boisterous voice made everyone in the room jump. "Here I thought this would be a boring trip. I guess there really is something for everyone!" He shoved a medical book in Bartholomew's face with a laugh. "Check it out, Bart." He pointed at the anatomical illustrations that showed a nude adult woman. "Wench's tits are as big as cannonballs, aye?"

Bartholomew glanced at the page and rolled his eyes before looking away. "Gods alive, Rabbit. You're awful."

"Too right. I forgot she's not your type." He smirked and turned the book back toward him to admire the drawings again.

Bartholomew bristled. "Sexual preferences aside, it's a medical journal. Show a *little* respect for the work its author and artist put into it."

Brack tilted his head, squinting his eyes so he could read some text. "Right-o, Bart. Forgive me. What I meant to say was, check out this young *female*. Her *breasts* are as big as cannonballs."

Bermuda knocked the book from his hands to cease his relentless laughing.

Brack was unaffected, chuckling as he shoved books into his pack. "At least one of these smut books is coming home with me."

Bartholomew shook his head and walked away, choosing to get lost in his environment and not Brack's behavior. "This place is stunning. All these writings, hidden from the public eye. All this knowledge, wasting away in a tomb. It's criminal."

"So's stealing it, but we're still doing that." Brack continued to pile books Kazuaki handed to him into his bags.

Nicholai sifted through the texts like a madman, trying to find anything that might be helpful. Most of it was catalogs of Time Fathers dating as far back as the written word, but nothing that seemed useful.

Kazuaki observed his fiendish pilfering through the political documents. The captain kept a watchful eye on him between his search through the books of folklores. It was amazing what a religious fanatic considered a threat to his cause. There were fairytales hidden away even Kazuaki had not heard of before—all banished before they spread, in hopes they would remain forgotten, unable to contradict the details of Darjal's religion.

As Kazuaki combed over the books in his section, he gravitated toward Nicholai.

As Nicholai's texts thinned out, he unknowingly edged closer to Kazuaki.

The pile of fairytales and political texts intersected as the two met in the middle, each setting their hands on the cover of the same book. Kazuaki eyed Nicholai, undeterred, until Nicholai submitted to his intense stare and moved his hand.

"*The Balance of the Earth Mother*," Kazuaki read the title aloud, eyeing Nicholai with a quizzical brow raised. "Is this political or myth?"

Nicholai cleared his throat, uncertain. "I've never heard of an Earth Mother, so my guess is a fairytale," he murmured, still on the search for the Time Fathers' code. He was paranoid by Kazuaki's awareness but tried not to let it bother him.

Kazuaki shrugged and handed it to Bermuda.

"We're almost full up, Captain," the quartermaster noted as she stored the book with the rest. She looked comical with her large bag of books dangling on her back. One would doubt a small woman could holster so much weight, but she didn't break a sweat.

"Mine too, Cappy," Brack mentioned, repositioning the weight of the full satchels on his shoulders.

Kazuaki scoffed at the unflattering moniker. "Just as well. We best be getting out of here before—"

"It came from over here," a voice sounded from the basement, causing the crew to straighten upright. From their place in the hidden room, they saw the beams of lanterns bounce off the basement walls.

"Gods dammit all," Kazuaki hissed, drawing his weapons when he realized the weight of the books encumbered his men. "I'll clear the way." He cocked the hammers on his revolvers. "Get back to the cockboat. I'll meet you there." The captain lunged through hole they had made earlier, drawing attention away from the hidden room before the intruders plucked them off like fish in a barrel.

The intensity of the gunfire increased tenfold when the surprised footmen returned fire.

Though Bermuda, Brack, and Bartholomew were at ease, having been exposed to these kinds of fights repeatedly, Nicholai panicked. This was only his second firefight. To add insult to injury, he didn't find the information he sought.

Bermuda and Bartholomew lingered near the room's entrance, waiting until Kazuaki obliterated the threat, surprise splayed across their faces as they realized how many military men were dispatched. Nicholai was right; leaving two footmen's bodies behind during Rennington and Iani's rescue was a sure-fire way to garner a lot of unwanted attention from Southern's military.

Kazuaki stood behind the statue of a prophet, firing at whatever body parts came across the revolvers' front sights.

One marksman got a lucky shot. The statue's head shattered into pieces.

The captain cursed as the dust from the old clay got into his eye. Even with the inconvenience, his rain of dual revolver fire pushed the footmen to the basement entrance. "Fast and away!" he called to the others.

Bermuda and Bartholomew slipped from their hiding places in the hidden room and darted into the mouth of the catacombs.

Several brave military men turned from the safety of the wall to shoot, but their bullets only found a place in the book-packed satchels.

The thick paper protected their flesh, and they made it without injury into the protection of the crypts.

Brack lingered in the door, staring as Nicholai feverishly moved a stack of books aside. "You comin', mate?"

Nicholai ignored him as his search intensified.

Brack shrugged. "Aye, it's your ass." He turned to follow Bermuda and Bartholomew.

Nicholai found his best chance—a decrepit, rotting rectangle with the words *Fundamental Principles of Behavior and Precepts for Time Fathers and His Chronometer*. Most of the lettering was sloughed off on the front. It was a dry title but, with any luck, his salvation. He seized it with force and exited the room, though jolted back into the security of it when he realized the danger waiting on the other side was still in full force.

Kazuaki stood in the manmade entrance to the catacombs. Having emptied one revolver, he hurled it onto the ground and pulled a third gun from inside his boot. He did not appear to be waiting for Nicholai.

"You're leaving without me?" Nicholai shouted over the gunfire.

The guttural sound of a dying man pierced the captain's ears.

The soldier fell into the pile of bodies that had accumulated at the basement entrance.

Kazuaki flinched when a bullet lodged into his thigh, but he recovered with haste. "A useful man needs no help, Nico," the captain replied through clenched teeth. His shots were quick. It didn't even appear as if he aimed, but the amount of damage he did to the mob left no doubt strategy was involved.

"Are you serious? A platitude?" Nicholai grabbed a broken piece of a tabletop to act as a primitive shield. He took a deep breath, held it and hurled his body at the catacomb's entrance. He felt the puncture of bullets into the old wood, each one coursing his adrenaline faster through his veins. Though rattled, by a miracle he arrived at the entrance unscathed.

Kazuaki stepped aside to allow him passage then sprinted for the coast.

"They'll follow. The catacombs will lead them right to the ship!" Nicholai said through breathless lips as the two men ran down the corridor, trying to catch up with the other three.

"We'll be long gone before then," Kazuaki said and stopped to rifle through his pack.

"You're—you're stopping!" Nicholai halted his running. Though the captain had nearly left him behind seconds ago, it was not in Nicholai's nature to do the same.

"You're an observant young man, Nico." Kazuaki pulled a hollow clay device from his pack resembling a large acorn with a wick sticking out the end. The liquid inside sloshed as Kazuaki set it on the ground and removed his flint and steel.

Nicholai felt the sting of a bullet whiz past his cheek. His touched his face and felt the warmth of blood beneath his fingertips. Though it was just a scratch, it bled. "Come on, come on," he tried to prod Kazuaki to move faster as the footmen ran toward them down the corridor.

A spark ignited as the flint met the steel. The slow, satisfying burn trickled down the wick. Kazuaki stood, holding the little grenade as he stared at the approaching footmen.

"He's got a bomb!" one yelled.

They all skidded to an immediate halt.

Nico's gaze met a familiar face.

Jernal locked stares with him, recognizing his dark-hooded shroud. "You," he growled, clenching his jaw.

"Best run quick, mate," the captain said to Nicholai and rolled the makeshift device at the crowd of men.

Nicholai followed the captain's orders without hesitation.

Both men did not have much time to run before a powerful blast ignited from behind them. The explosion's force threw their bodies forward with great speed, causing Kazuaki and Nicholai to roll across the tunnel grounds like rag dolls.

The captain pushed himself up with a swiftness. His eye darted to Nicholai to see if he had survived.

He was engaged in a coughing fit but alive. A glistening object fell from the cut of his shirt, dangling back and forth around his neck as he tried to catch his breath.

Kazuaki narrowed his eye, watching through the dust and debris as Nicholai shoved his Chronometer into the confines of his clothing. The captain knew now why their guide showed so much interest in the political texts.

As if the uncertainty of whether the grenade had killed all the soldiers wasn't motivation enough to keep moving, the rattling of the fragile catacomb walls was. Nicholai and Kazuaki pushed themselves to their feet and quickened their pace as the tunnel threatened to collapse. They heard Bermuda shout something from in front. The light of her lantern shimmered like a star in the sky, guiding them from the danger of the collapsing catacombs. Neither man looked back as they fled the disintegrating tunnel.

"Get on with it then," Kazuaki ordered, throwing his satchel of collected books into the cockboat with a thud.

They all piled into the small vessel, and the captain took up two oars, paddling with the rest of the crew to create as much distance between their boat and the tunnel mouth as possible. Though the pain of multiple bullet holes shrieked at him with each stroke, he knew they were not fatal and pushed through the bite of the misplaced metal.

They moved forward with surprising speed. The desire to live was an excellent motivator.

Nicholai turned to stare at the catacomb entrance he had come to know well throughout the week. He squinted as he saw several shadows emerge—the footmen who had survived the blast.

The cockboat was too far for their weapons to have much chance of hitting their target, but the soldiers still fired. One lucky shooter hit the stern, but it did little to slow them.

"This will get back to Darjal," Nicholai said between plunging his oars into the water. His voice was distant, lost; the magnitude of the situation sank into his mind.

"Yes." Kazuaki looked over his shoulder to see how far the cockboat remained from the ship. "But we'll be gone by then." The captain knew this was not Nico's primary concern. He would place money on it that the man's apprehension stemmed more in the fact that he, himself, was a Time Father—a Time Father on the run, by the looks of things. But he said nothing. Not yet.

"Too right we will." Brack laughed, the moonlight highlighting his infectious grin. "No military has captured the infamous Captain Kazuaki Hidataka yet, aye, Cap?" He released one oar long enough to punch the captain's shoulder.

Kazuaki winced as Brack's impeccable accuracy punched one of his bullet wounds. "Just keep rowing, Rabbit."

Nicholai glanced the captain's way. Perhaps the explosion had deafened his ears, and he had misheard. "Did ... Did you say, Kazuaki Hidataka?"

The cockboat moved along, not far from the ship with the force of five bodies propelling it.

"Aye." Brack nodded. "The one and only!"

The Time Father stopped rowing due to the unadulterated feeling of disbelief that overtook him. "That's impossible ..." His eyes flitted between Brack and the captain. "Kazuaki Hidataka is, is a fairytale. A myth. He's just a story to tell children to keep them from staying out too late at night—"

"Oi, yeah, did you hear the chant about him the wee kids sing when they're playin' around the streets?" Brack laughed as the boat bumped into the hull of Kazuaki's ship. He stood, grabbing the satchel of books as he tried to remember it. "I think it goes something like, *Captain Hidataka, at your door he'll knock-a / Though you may beg, he'll chop off your leg, and you'll no longer walk-a.*"

Nicholai stared at Brack as he sang the children's rhyme in a singsong tune. His jaw fell open, and he struggled to find words. "That's ... That's—"

"Hold it. There's more," Brack interrupted, continuing with the song. "*On the captain's deck, a rope tied 'round your neck, if you try to run, he'll fire his gun, and sink you like a shipwreck.*"

The Time Father remained slack-jawed. "I ... I don't believe it." He ran a hand through his hair as if it would help contain the throbbing of disbelief in his skull.

"I know, right? Children's rhymes are feckin' twisted as all shit." Brack tied the satchel to the rope dangling off the ship's side. He pulled on it twice, indicating to Revi above to hoist the cargo.

As the crew moved the stolen books to the main deck and everyone exited the cockboat, Nicholai returned to the bench they had placed him on earlier. He sat, mentally and physically exhausted as he tried to make sense of the new world he found himself in. The organized chaos of the crew running around him seemed like blurs in his line of vision; their voices distorted sounds his brain did not register as discernable language. He leaned back, soaking in the overwhelming number of things he had endured in the last several weeks as they readied the ship to sail. They were quick; they needed to exit before the military stood a chance at following.

He was in the presence of a legend. Nicholai had struggled prior with the morality of staying in the company of these men and women. They batted no eyes at taking a man's life. But now he remained stuck with one of the most ruthless bandits known across time—Kazuaki Hidataka, the man mothers and fathers warned their children about to twist their behavior. *Don't wander far from home,* he remembered his grandmother saying when he was a boy, *or Kazuaki Hidataka will carry you aboard his ship and cut out your eyes.*

Nicholai Addihein was nothing if not a law-abiding man. At least, he tried to be. He bent the rules to suit Lilac and Malcolm, but his efforts were always for the citizens' betterment. His entire world was one good deed after another—nothing but scrupulous, forthright action. He went from furthering the world's industrious efforts and helping old men start their steam cars, to accompanying murderers and thieves and thieving himself. Though Nicholai considered himself adaptable, this new environment seemed staggering even to him. He spied the captain. Out of everything he had encountered, being in the presence of and at the mercy of Captain Kazuaki Hidataka was the strangest of all.

The crew readied the sails. They raised the anchors. They secured the cargo and cockboat into their places.

Kazuaki climbed to the foremast, peering across the horizon line. It was still dark; he couldn't have asked for better accommodations to slip unseen into the night. He felt a favorable breeze and shouted, "Carry on!" to the crew below.

They hoisted every piece of canvas the yard could carry, and the ship nudged forward, beginning its slow crawl into the depths of the sea.

Kazuaki observed his crew, each exchanging stories of what had occurred. He watched Brack imitate the explosion with his hands then break into riotous laughter. Everything seemed as it should. He spied Nicholai sitting on the bench, sequestered from the rest of the crew. He had made himself useful, both with Rennington and Iani and now with the library. But Time Fathers were men of law. They weren't found outside their division, especially for this length of time. Kazuaki was well versed in the knowledge of Nico's kind. It meant one thing; if Nico was here, he wasn't present to secure the goings-on of time in his division. If he wasn't present to maintain the time, it stopped ticking. Kazuaki knew within an inch of certainty the man before him was the Southeastern Time Father, Nicholai Addihein. Once he discovered he was a Time Father, it didn't take long for the captain's intelligence to put the puzzle pieces together. The only question at the forefront of his thoughts was, why? What was his story? Kazuaki intended to find out.

The captain considered himself a man immune to most of the world's surprises. But here he was, surprised. As the ship rolled into the sea's welcoming waves, he let the rare feeling wash over him.

Out of everything he had encountered—gods, curses, legends, immortality—finding himself in the presence of a rouge Time Father was the strangest of all.

Chapter Eight

Darjal sat on the cushions of his elaborate throne. The furniture was exquisite, matching everything else in the grand room. Bronze legs belonging to the regal chair wrapped upward, looming high above the cushion. The sides flanked out, forging a masterful interpretation of religious iconography shaped by precious metals. It was an admirable piece commissioned by a monumental man. Though the church coffers paid for its construction, they replenished every day the constituents of Southern attended the daily services.

Twin fireplaces provided the room with light and warmth. The embers danced from the fuel of gas. Flames whipped back and forth in their metal prison. Its presence was superfluous; the room remained warm and well-lit without it, but it fit with the common theme of the space. Everything here was excessive.

The room held a strange beauty, though a thick aura of vexation tainted it. It emanated from Darjal as he stared at the formal parchment in his hands. Crumbles of red wax once used to seal the paper from mail couriers' wondering eyes sat in Darjal's lap. In any other circumstance, he would have swatted the wax chunks, preferring not to let their appearance tarnish him. But his mind was too busy obsessing over the letter's contents.

Nicholai Addihein had frozen time in the Southeastern division.

In all his years reigning over Southern, Darjal Wessex had never encountered a Time Father who committed the ultimate taboo.

He had read tales of such things happening in the distant past but had never seen this atrocity implemented with his own eyes. Darjal knew the boy was too green to run a division. He thought it from the moment Edvard Addihein of Western had suggested Nicholai take over Southeastern. He wagered the other Time Fathers wished they had heeded his suggestion now.

The paper requested all Time Fathers to part with a fraction of their military. The borders of Southeastern required them, should Nicholai try to exit it, or return, if he had already left. Though the young Addihein boy's betrayal was a shock, Darjal doubted he had roamed far. With sections of seven different militaries bearing down on him, he had nowhere to run. Doomed to walk on foot, with all the vehicles in his division frozen in time, Nicholai couldn't travel with speed. If he still lingered in the safety of his division, hunger would drive him to the border soon enough. Even if he already had entered a neighboring division, he wouldn't live long. They'd capture or kill him on sight.

Once they stripped Nicholai of his Chronometer, they could find a suitable replacement and carry on. Keeping this knowledge from the public would be an irritation, however. If word spread about Southeastern's state, the citizens would panic. To prevent chaos from exploding across the divisions, the Time Fathers would have to sever all ties with Southeastern—no traded exports and imports, no exchange of civilian mail. Concocting a convincing reason without revealing the truth would be annoying, but the public was easy to sway. If the time taken to subdue Nicholai and restore time in Southeastern didn't turn into a long stretch, it could happen. The only concern that lingered in the back of Darjal's mind was whether Nicholai's father, Edvard Addihein, would fuss at his son's assassination.

The sound of the door knocker striking the room's iron entryway echoed through the cavernous room, interrupting the Southern Time Father's thoughts. He set down the parchment and looked up with frustration. "Come in." His voice boomed, forceful for a man of his age.

With a slow grind, the door slid open. Moving the heavy entrance aside was a feat, achieved with a series of cranks that footmen posted outside the entryway operated.

When the opening was wide enough to accommodate a man, Jernal and several other officers entered with the structure and grace expected from an organized military. "We have a matter of importance to discuss, Lord Wessex, if you have the time. Though I must enhance the gravity of the matter," Jernal said with calculation.

Darjal stood, his hands moving behind his back as he approached the men.

They stood all rigid, their posture respectful for a man of the Time Father's rank.

He regarded each one, mentally noting the efficiency in which the men presented themselves. Satisfied each soldier conducted himself with an appropriate amount of dignity, he turned to Jernal. "I have a matter of importance I am already dealing with, Jernal." He cast aside the formality of addressing the man by his rank.

If the lack of respect bothered Jernal, he did not let it show. "I understand, Your Grace. But I suspect you'd be interested—"

"Your suspicions had best be accurate." Darjal tapped a bored finger against the side of his wrinkled cheek. "Much like a man's lifeforce, my time is irreplaceable."

Jernal knew better than to allow formalities to slide, despite how much he wanted to blurt the reason for his appearance. He allowed Darjal to finish his self-serving monologue before clearing his throat. "With your permission, My Lord, I would like to tell you."

Darjal stared at the man as if he had inspected the value of his words before speaking them. After several torturous seconds, he raised his hand. "Go on then."

"Two soldiers were killed outside the Avadon church three nights ago."

Darjal sighed and turned his back on Jernal. "My boy, you know a soldier accepts his fate as soon as he signs away his life. If you're here to request the finances to hire additional recruits, I believe I should assess whether you can hire competent footmen before we proceed." Darjal postured. He could not spare additional men. Not after sacrificing the amount he needed to deploy to Southeastern's border.

Though Jernal's expression did not betray his irritation, he clenched his jaw tighter. "Rennington and Iani Platts killed them, My Lord."

Darjal's dull eyes widened, and he turned around. "Those names ..." His voice shifted from diplomatic to heated "The deserters."

"Precisely."

Darjal's face twisted into one of annoyance. "Precisely, what?"

Jernal pursed his lips. He didn't pause long, as the repercussions for disobedience were high. Tempered with the fact he took his position in Southern's military seriously, he responded, "Precisely, *My Lord.*"

Satisfied, Darjal nodded and looked away. "Bold is he who returns to the place of his biggest disgrace," he muttered, rubbing his hands together. "And are they in your custody now?"

The soldier felt his nerves choke him. "No, Your Grace. We had them subdued. The elder brother, Rennington, was shot twice. Both were in shackles, but—"

"All I'm hearing is your failure, Jernal!" He craved vengeance on those two the minute word of their betrayal reached his ears.

Rennington and Iani had the pleasure of living for far too many years. They needed to cleanse themselves of their sins. Panagea needed to cleanse itself of them.

"A strange man we had detained for thieving stopped us. We mistook him for a common rat, but he managed to secure the freedom of Rennington and Iani Platts."

Darjal's rage grew, consuming him.

It did not surprise Jernal; he acquainted himself with the Southern Time Father's temper. It made him a cold and unforgiving ruler, but Jernal could not deny the advances Darjal made for churches across the Southern division. As a religious man himself, he respected the efforts the Time Father provided. It made it easier to bite his tongue.

After pacing in the large room, Darjal lifted his head. "Identify this man. He will suffer the same fate as the deserters upon capture. I don't give a damn about the cost, Jernal." The Time Father's veins in his forehead and throat throbbed with rage. "Find them, and alert me immediately when they're in your custody. Now go, you've already wasted enough time traveling outside Avadon."

Jernal cleared his throat again. It was a risk not immediately obeying Darjal's commands, but he couldn't leave without relaying the whole message. "There's more, My Lord."

The Time Father's eyes twitched as little red veins split from the sides of his corneas. He drew in a creeping, considerate breath. "Do tell."

The soldier glanced over his shoulder at his men, as if looking into Darjal's gaze was physically painful. After a moment, he forced his attention to his superior. "We caught some thieves in the Avadon church's basement the night following my men's deaths. Rennington and Iani were not present, but the man who freed them was there. He was under Captain Kazuaki Hidataka's command."

The Time Father's rage bubbled over.

Jernal feared he might suffer an aneurysm, but the mention of the church basement switched Darjal's expression to one of concern.

"What were they doing in the church basement?" he whispered with a hint of panic.

Confused by the tonal shift, Jernal's expression changed to one of perplexity. "They were raiding an old room. A hidden one. We spoke with the priest. He was the only member of the Avadon church who seemed to know of its existence. They made off with some books, nothing more."

"Some books?" Darjal wheezed, trying not to succumb to his unforgiving emotions. He straightened his posture and adjusted his Chronometer's chain around his neck. "Do you know which titles?"

"Ah ..." Jernal rifled through the interior pockets of his uniform. "Yes. The priest cataloged the library's contents. He said you'd want to know. Various titles from the myths and folklore sections, some philosophical journals, one medical text, and ... it appears they pilfered some of the political pieces as well, relating to Time Father's and such."

Darjal tried to make sense of it all. "Kazuaki Hidataka has been a thorn in Panagea's side for years."

Between the various thefts and murders of anyone who stood in his way, Kazuaki had helped himself to treasures that should have been the property of the divisions. Worse yet, he had risked exposing these myths as a truth to the public. He had stolen criminals from Panagea and had spared them from their necessary prosecutions for hundreds of years. As hard as it was to keep the captain's existence from the people, it was harder still to catch him. The Time Fathers preferred the public see Kazuaki as a myth. Whatever black magic or archaic god crafted the immortal captain, the

Time Fathers wished to conceal it. Old-world expectations had finally dissipated. Technology had finally replaced omnipotent beings. The power to grant wishes had fallen into the hands of the people, not the whims of the gods. They didn't need the public trying to resurrect temperamental deities to the surface. Man had outlived his need for false gods, and they intended to keep it that way. It had made it that much easier for Darjal to convince the Southern division they should revere him as the only god they needed. But silencing Kazuaki's actions had proved difficult. Since the supercontinent of Panagea connected all divisions, traveling by sea was not a necessity. It was more fruitful modernizing the whole of Pangaea's roadways and perfecting air travel than engaging in seafaring. They needed nothing from the ocean. The Time Fathers knew of only a small handful of nearby islands, and they served their purposes well, but maritime exploration was a low priority. Because of this, they hadn't crafted a vessel that could compete with Captain Hidataka's ship, let alone know a man experienced enough to operate it. The knowledge of the sea had died long ago, for everyone except Kazuaki Hidataka.

"I have a list of the exact titles," Jernal said, holding a piece of parchment to Darjal.

He snatched it from the soldier and scanned it. "The Earth Mother," he muttered, lowering the list from his sight. If anybody possessed the wherewithal and the equipment to find her, it was Captain Hidataka. And now he knew of her existence too.

Jernal stood, patient and apprehensive. The meeting hadn't gone as he had envisioned it. The Time Father was not telling him something, but he didn't dare ask what.

Darjal took a deep breath, stopping to feel his lungs expand. He released it, trying to collect his thoughts. "Jernal ..." He closed his eyes. "You've mentioned this man's appearance twice, the one who ruined your efforts at capturing the deserters. Surely, you did not let him escape twice."

Standing tall, he accepted his fate. "He managed to escape, My Lord. He and Hidataka's men exited to the coast through a series of catacombs running underneath the church."

Darjal's eyes snapped open. The catacombs. The only ones who knew of their existence were the Time Fathers. His brain clicked. Things fell into place. With an eerie craning of his neck, he looked in Jernal's direction. "Did you identify this man?"

Jernal fluctuated in his impeccable posture from the vehemence of Darjal's stare "Ah ... I-I believe I heard the captain reference him once. It was difficult to hear in the firefight, but I think he referred to him as *Nico.*"

The Time Father's eyes glazed over. "Nicholai Addihein," he mumbled. He thought if the sinner had tried to leave Southeastern, he'd take refuge in his own father's division. Edvard Addihein would've been Nicholai's best bet at living longer, though Darjal hoped the Western Time Father would have sacrificed his son, as his duty dictated. But no, the devil had crept to his doorway. A demon roamed through his perfect land, and his blood boiled at the thought. His flawless world's cement grounds had no room for impurities. He needed to cleanse the entire city of Avadon now. It was a shame he couldn't do it with the blood of the damned. Nicholai was long gone if he had fled with the captain at sea.

"My Lord?" Jernal asked, unable to stand the crushing weight of the silence. "What are your orders?"

Darjal Wessex seethed. The Southern Time Father spied the parchment sitting on his throne. He needed Jernal; he had to make him cognizant of the situation. "A universal decision has been made instructing us to dispatch men to Southeastern's borders. Nicholai Addihein has frozen his division's time. It is my belief he and your *Nico* are the same man."

The news came as a shock. Jernal never thought he'd see the day when a Time Father froze his division's time. It was reprehensible. The crime not only robbed men and women of their freewill but affected Panagea as a whole. Though Jernal was not privy to the Time Father's knowledge of the world's affairs, he was not an unintelligent man. Anyone with enough mental capacity could feel the gravity of the situation. He did not know the specifics, but he ventured a guess Nicholai's actions had caused the increase in tremors and earthquakes. Chunks of land had disappeared into the sea at an unprecedented rate—the unnatural state of a huge portion of land, frozen and immobile. It wasn't just a crime against the Time Father's code, it was a crime against all Panagea. He couldn't believe he had let him escape. Twice. "I'll send my best men."

"No." Darjal raised a hand, garnering confusion from Jernal. "Nordjan may think he knows what's best, but the lamb will rarely approach the wolf. We must go to him. Send competent men to Southeastern, but save your best. I'll commission a warship. We will hunt Nicholai Addihein at sea if we must. The capture of Kazuaki Hidataka will merely be a bonus."

Jernal shifted uneasily. "A vessel of that size would take months to build, and the cost alone—"

"Will be covered in full." He had no qualms in depleting his division's finances dry if it meant the capture of Nicholai Addihein. "You do not have months, Jernal. You have weeks. I don't care if you pluck every engineer and capable hand from all the factories in Panagea, you will get it done, and you will get it done on schedule."

The soldier felt doomed to Darjal's merciless behavior before the project even begun. "A large ship is difficult to hide, Your Grace. If the public sees us crafting an ironclad, they will suspect something is amiss."

"Tell them they're doing their god's work! Go, Jernal! Let my will be done!"

The soundwaves diminished around the men. Jernal knew when to call it quits and nodded. "Yes, sir." With that, he motioned his men to follow and set off to perform his futile orders.

Once Darjal was the only one who remained in the stillness of his cavernous room, he approached his throne. His fingers curled around the parchment, taking no care when it wrinkled under the force of his grip. He walked to the fireplace and stood before it as the orange light flickered over his facial features. Nicholai threatened the world Darjal built for himself, for his people. Though the other Time Fathers' desires rested in manufacturing and advancing the abilities of mankind, they did not understand the vital importance of religion or the power that accompanied it. But it didn't matter. His people already revered him as a god. Darjal needed no help in growing his immaculate, uncontaminated world. At their leisure, they would soon see that land without purity, advanced and industrious or not, was still land that was an insult to him—the man who rose to omnipotence and became their one true god.

But it wasn't just Darjal's perfect world Nicholai threatened.

With the knowledge of the Earth Mother's existence, Kazuaki and Nicholai could upset everything the past Time Fathers had worked to achieve. The destructive forces of nature and the gods who had accompanied it had always been a hindrance. It had taken many years, but long gone were the days where merciless root systems had plunged into and destroyed the sewage pipes running below ground. No longer did trees as tall as towers fall onto nearby houses, businesses, and facilities in storms. No more forests dominated entire portions of land that could be used for more purposeful efforts. The annoying creatures that dwelled in the environment had almost died out too, eliminating all the issues that accompanied them. No more diseases spread through vile vermin; no more poisonous creatures prepared to attack. Most important of all, the lesser gods and goddesses of mankind's creation had disappeared.

No longer did they have to bend to the whims of false deities for help. No more unanswered prayers from fickle idols existed. Man oversaw his destiny now, and his destiny belonged to technology and the true god—Darjal Wessex.

They had eliminated every inconvenience of nature, save for one. Though Earth Mother was less of an inconvenience and more of a necessity, kept alive only to serve in creating oxygen through her trees in an oxygen-starved world, she had her purpose, and she had her place, and it was not on Pangaea.

Darjal needed to find them. He had not dedicated his life to his religion to see it fall to the wayside. He wouldn't let his people dabble in the sinful ways of the past. Those gods would not starve him of the attention he deserved. The thought of purposeless orgies, of wine and debauchery replacing the dignified effort of honoring *him* in a church was infuriating. He would not allow his sheep to stray from his flock. Their souls depended on it.

Darjal stared at the flames as they reflected in his eyes. "My wrath is revealed, and every sin brings its punishment with it. You can hide from the eyes of the world for as long as you can, Nicholai Addihein ..." He hurled the crumpled parchment into the fire. The edges curled in on themselves and withered into nothing but blackness and ash. A small puff of smoke billowed from the fireplace, creeping around Darjal's body like an ethereal, translucent snake. "For I am the eyes of god, and you cannot run from me."

Chapter Nine

L ife onboard a ship did not come easy. When one lived on land their entire life, adjusting to the wind and the waves took time. Seasickness was a common affliction of ocean life, coming on violent and unexpected, like a storm. Nicholai missed the little things, like the earth not moving beneath his feet with every step. Or the absence of crippling cabin fever. Or not dwelling every day in the company of murderers and thieves. Yes, the little things.

He had tried to keep his head down for the last two days, holing up in the small room Kazuaki had gifted to him. He used the term *gift* loosely. His roommates were an old, metal bucket and a sorry-looking mop that should've been thrown overboard. It was less of a small room and more of a large supply closet with a cot. But the Time Father couldn't complain. Not out loud. It was a lot better than a prison cell in Avadon or a gravesite where the other Time Fathers dumped his body should they catch him after his treachery.

After using the last of the candle he had found in his room, Nicholai ventured with caution toward the main deck. He needed a light source to study the political text he had taken from the library. The sun was as good as any—the oldest light source of all. It lingered high at this hour, providing ample brightness.

It felt good to stretch his legs. Save for slinking into the galley half a dozen times to take scraps of food from Penn, the ship cook, Nicholai did not leave his room at all. He became a man obsessed with scouring the transcripts for anything he could use to save Lilac from her unfortunate fate.

A plank of wood creaked under the weight of his boot as he traversed the narrow corridor that led to the stairs.

A familiar voice came from an open door to his right. "EP? That you?" Rennington called from inside the room.

Nicholai hesitated, unsure whether he should ignore the man. It wasn't in his nature. Even still, he remained curious about how Rennington faired after suffering from the footmen's onslaught several days ago. "I-I'm afraid not." He peered into the open doorway to see Rennington still bound to the bed due to his injuries and without a tunic. He surveyed the bandage around his arm and shoulder, along with many scars scattered across his entire torso. Old battle wounds, he suspected. "Just me. I could try to find EP for you, but I don't know who that is."

"Good man." Rennington grinned and sat upright in bed. "You haven't met Elowyn yet? Haven't you been on board here a few days now?"

Nicholai looked over his shoulder, feeling awkward for blocking the hallway; though nobody was behind him. He crept into the room, rubbing the back of his neck. "Yes, a few days, but I ... I haven't left my room much."

"A fearful sort we are, aye?" Rennington chuckled but regretted his display of jubilance, and he grabbed his hip with a wince. "Captain Hidataka gave you a room? He offered you a position on board then?"

"No," Nicholai retorted quicker than he should have. "I don't think I—*he*—would enjoy that much," he said with a small, forced laugh.

Rennington shrugged the shoulder without a bullet hole. "EP is Elowyn. Elowyn Saveign, but she's practically a sister, so Iani and I, we made her an honorary Platts. You'd like her. I mean, not at first but over time, if she's not being a total wench. That's her there." He pointed to an old, framed photograph hanging on the wall above her bed.

Nicholai tilted his head when he saw the image of the young woman flashing a huge smile and donning the traditional garb of the Northern military's medical unit. "Oh, her. She's the medic in your crew then?" The Time Father squinted, noting the woman's arms wrapped around the shoulders of two smiling men wearing Northern military uniforms. The photo quality wasn't great. Nicholai had a hard time discerning their faces but assumed they were Rennington and Iani. "Forgive me for prying, but I thought you and your brother had belonged to Southern's military."

Rennington's expression altered to one of concern. "Yeah, mate. Iani and I, we're Southern born and raised. That ain't us in the photo. That's EP's blood brothers. The three of them served Northern a good handful of years back."

"I see." Nicholai wondered how three upstanding-looking individuals had fallen from the grace of a powerful military and onto the rotting decks of a criminal sea vessel, but he did not ask. "Are they on board the ship as well?"

Rennington paused. "I suspect they are," he uttered, staring at the photograph. "On board and alive in EP's heart at least, but they've been dead a good long while now."

Nicholai's face fell. He had engaged in a conversation all of three minutes and had already put his foot in his mouth. "I'm sorry to hear that," he offered with sincerity. Criminal or otherwise, nobody deserved to lose a sibling.

"Sorries make no sense in death, mate." Rennington stretched in the bed that held him captive. "Might as well apologize for getting wet after it rains. It's just a part of life. Speaking of, I owe a debt of gratitude to you for saving mine and my brother's."

Nicholai stepped backward and raised his hands. "Please, it was no trouble. It's—" It's what Lilac would have wanted, he wished to say. But the words didn't come out. "It's no big deal."

"It is to a Platts brother." Rennington grinned. "I don't often trust newbies, Nico, but I happen to think I'm a pretty good judge of character. I'll make it up to you."

Nicholai shook his head. "That's not necessary, really."

Rennington maintained his grin. "Well, I won't keep you here any longer. No sense in two of us having to hole up here in the land where time stands still."

Though he made a joke, his choice of words caused Nicholai to adjust his stance. If only Rennington knew the irony in his statement. Nicholai eyed the door, feeling the book's weight in his hands. It called him to go resume his task: scouring for loopholes that could help Lilac.

He appreciated Rennington's candor. Save for Brack and Iani, he remained the only one aboard the ship who made any effort in welcoming him. "If you need anything, just let me know. A book to pass the time perhaps? You guys have quite a bit on board now after that library raid."

"Yes." Rennington laughed but tempered it as not to cause himself pain. "That one Brack found might hold my attention."

Nicholai chuckled despite himself. It was the first time he had heard his laughter in a long while. "I'll see what I can do." He stopped in the doorway. "Thanks."

Rennington grinned from the bed. "Off you go then, mate. That big ole book of smut won't find itself."

Nicholai smiled and shook his head. He exited to ascend the stairs to the main deck but stopped as a shadow loomed down on him from above deck. He squinted, trying to decipher the face of the tall figure silhouetted by the sun.

"I see you finally ventured beyond the galley." Kazuaki kept his dominating spot above Nicholai at the top of the stairs. His spotted the book in the Time Father's hand. "I'm afraid you won't have much time for reading. Now that you've had several days to rest, you'll make yourself useful as a deckhand. We're down a man, with Rennington in recovery."

Nicholai knew it wasn't a question. He didn't know how to respond. He wanted nothing more than to expedite the process of saving Lilac, but he understood the logic behind Kazuaki's order. Whether he liked it or not, he belonged to these outlaws until they reached land again, and, with all the non-perishables he had helped them unearth in Avadon, it could be a long wait. On a positive note, the sea kept him safe from the Time Fathers' wrath. It gave him enough of an opportunity to formulate a solution to Southeastern.

"Typically, when I give an order, the proper response is an acknowledgment," Kazuaki said, not missing a chance to establish the ship's hierarchy. "Since you're so familiar with the galley, you can head down there. Go dump your belongings in your room and get on with it. Help Penn clean the dishes, scour the area, sort through all the foodstuffs we gained, and whatever else the man tells you."

Nicholai increased his grip around the book and inhaled. Yes. He would play Kazuaki's game. Not only would he play it, but he'd also excel at it. Though he gave the orders in Southeastern, he needed to learn how to take them. It was his only chance at survival. He swallowed his pride. For Lilac.

"Yes, sir," he replied, turning and heading to his room to dispose of his things before going to the galley.

Kazuaki arched a brow, taken aback by Nicholai's quick submission. He shrugged it off and turned around, coming face to face with Bermuda. He wasn't aware she stood behind him. The woman was so close he felt the heat coming off her body. "Bermuda," he said with a start, feeling the usual quickening of his blood at being near her. "I didn't see you there."

She seemed unaffected by his proximity and took a logical step backward as not to crowd him. "You're pawning him off on Penn?" She looked over the captain's shoulder in the direction Nicholai had disappeared.

"For now. Penn could use the help. He's been letting the galley's condition slide for a while now."

"For how long do you intend to keep him? I mean, what are your long-term plans? Do you intend to bring him on as a new crewmember?"

Kazuaki shoved his hands into the pockets of his long jacket as a breeze blew his unkempt hair. "I plan on running him ragged. We'll work him so hard he won't know which way is up. I don't want to give him many opportunities for anything else." Kazuaki did not divulge his plans in their entirety, but he knew he did not want to allow Nicholai time to find whatever he looked for in that book of his. The sooner Nicholai discovered whatever it was he was looking for, the sooner he'd abandon the captain's ship. Kazuaki was not ready to part with the Time Father yet. On top of their need for an extra deckhand, he proved to be a useful pawn in his endeavors. The captain suspected their *friend* held more value than they realized.

The books they had stolen from the library provided a fountain of knowledge. Kazuaki delved into fairytales he had never heard of before. Their list of new leads was a mile long. Ancient, mythological treasures of all sorts waited for someone to unearth them. He and Bartholomew had perused through most of the texts, cataloging each lead in order of importance and likelihood of their truth. They now had an overwhelming amount of opportunities at their fingertips. With any luck, one of them led to a solution for

Bermuda. Seeping the toxic touch of that demon Mimir's influence from her heart remained his top priority.

"If I can think of any tasks to give him, I'll assist where I can," Bermuda said.

Kazuaki's exterior remained stoic, but her mechanical tone tore his insides to pieces. He missed their banter, the sarcasm, the thrill of certain moments. Though he knew better than to pursue her affection before her affliction, those little moments he fantasized about the what-ifs sustained him. Those were long gone now.

"That's why you're my right hand," he forced himself to say.

Bermuda shrugged a single shoulder, eying the stump of her wrist. She gave him a quick salute and excused herself to command the crew to keep it running smoothly. There was no rest for the quartermaster.

The captain watched her depart. He would save her. It was taking longer than he had wanted, but he would hunt the rest of his countless lives. With Nicholai occupied, he returned to his cabin. With any luck, the books held her salvation. Come firestorm or high water, he would fix that woman's heart.

NICHOLAI PEERED INTO the small galley, finding Penn. The man loomed over the crates they had plucked from the escape boat, shoving food into the already chaotic cabinets high above his head. Cast iron pots and pans rattled and clanked together with each bounce the ship made on larger waves, creating a cacophony of primitive music enjoyed by the ship's cook and cooper.

Without looking up from his duties, Penn said, "There's food on the counter for you." He knew Nicholai was there, despite his effort not to come across as a nuisance.

"The captain suggested I come lend you a hand." Nicholai entered the cramped quarters that made up the ship's kitchen. He looked left, beholding a stack of unwashed dishes that hadn't seen soap and water in weeks.

"Suggested?" Penn asked, still refusing to make eye contact as he shoved another handful of rations in a cabinet.

Nicholai pursed his lips, approached the sink and donned a brave face. "Well, suggested, ordered ... semantics, you know."

Penn walked to a metal bucket full of water that sloshed about on the galley floor. With the efficiency of a man who held many years of experience, he placed the bucket on the heating surface of the fire hearth. He maneuvered around Nicholai to another cabinet and removed a scrubbing brush before shoving it into the Time Father's hands. He bent near a low cupboard and rifled through, removed an old hunk of soap and tossed it in Nicholai's direction. "Once the water's heated through, combine it with the soap and scrub," was all he said before resuming his original task.

Nicholai fumbled before he caught the soap, finding it difficult to grab while also holding the scrubbing brush. He knew Penn did not share Rennington's interest in chitchat. He cleared his throat, waiting in long, awkward silence for the water to heat. When he was certain the temperature had climbed high enough, he plugged the sink and loaded it with the first of what promised to be many sets of dirty dishes.

The two men worked in silence for some time. The tension was thick. A man could cut it with any of the filthy knives Nicholai scrubbed with his brush. Even with the hot water and soap, the filth was difficult to remove. It baffled Nicholai, only because he suspected Penn did a limited amount of actual cooking. All the meals they had pilfered from the boat were ready-to-eat rations. At most, all they needed was for someone to heat them. He suspected their meals prior were the same, since non-perishable goods made the most sense to carry on long journeys.

"So," he started, trying to kill the silence, "have you been working for Kazuaki long?"

Penn said nothing at first.

Nicholai's only response was the sound of his brush scrubbing at cooked-on food.

After Penn finished his task of emptying the last crate, he said, "My entire adult life."

Surprised the man of few words had answered him, Nicholai tried to keep the momentum going. It was easier than sitting in the quiet, with only his thoughts to amuse him. Most of his thoughts had bordered on the dark side during the last several weeks; breaking away from that and gaining more knowledge about the people he'd be spending a good portion of his time with seemed like a logical thing to do.

"What did you do before you met him?" he asked, remembering Elowyn's time she had served as a medic for the Northern military and Rennington and Iani's lives as Southern footmen.

Penn looked annoyed. All of Nicholai's hopes of having an easy conversation sank when he responded with, "What did *you* do before you met him?"

The Time Father paused scraping a cast iron pot with his soapy brush, not expecting a heated reply. "Point taken."

"The feck are you doing?" Penn rushed over and removed the cooking vessel from Nicholai's hands. "You'll scour off the seasoning!"

Nicholai rubbed the back of his neck with no care to the fact his hands remained covered in soap and water. "And with any luck, the bacteria too."

The cook muttered something and set the cast iron atop the fire hearth. "Salt and water to make a paste—*that's* how you clean cast iron. Not sure what rock heap the captain pulled you out of, but he normally makes good decisions on who he brings aboard. You're feckin' useless in the galley, can't even clean a pot right."

The insult didn't bother him. Penn was right; he was useless in a kitchen. Lilac prepared most of their meals, save for the occasional time when he purchased a dinner elsewhere and brought it home to her. If he stood any chance at all of thriving in this environment, he needed to rise above these tests.

He stepped aside and gestured to the sink. "Show me."

Penn arched a skeptical brow. Though he seemed surprised at first, his temperament shifted to a blend of skepticism and irritation. "You trying to pawn off your dirty work on me then?"

It wasn't easy to win with this guy. Nicholai shook his head. "Just tell me how to do it. One time. That's all I need. Take a break if you'd like. When you come back, this place will be spotless. To *your* liking."

The cook narrowed his eyes. His chin inclined as he mulled over Nicholai's offer. "All right, newbie." If he wanted to work, Penn would give him work, as merciless as it was unrelenting. "Here's how it's done ..."

KAZUAKI HIDATAKA WALTZED without shame into the sorry quarters he had issued to Nicholai during his unexpected stay. After hours of bending over books, he needed a break and had no qualms about rummaging through the man's belongings, scarce as they were. The captain lifted old clothing, inspecting the pockets for anything that hid inside. He raised the cot, feeling around the thin material for any unusual lumps where Nicholai might have stashed his things. He found nothing that aroused suspicion.

The room was so small it was easy to perform a thorough sweep in a short time. Kazuaki knew all the hiding places a man might hoard something of importance, but Nicholai utilized none. His search for hidden objects initially made him overlook the book at the foot of the cot. Hidden in plain sight, as soon as his gaze fell on it, he recognized it as the book Nicholai had been carrying earlier, the one he had lingered long enough in the catacombs to find, despite the onslaught of gunfire.

The captain grabbed the book, analyzing the cover. "*Fundamental Principles of Behavior and Precepts for Time Fathers and His Chronometer*," he read aloud, bored halfway through the title. It did not make much sense to him why Nicholai obsessed over this book. As a Time Father, he should've already known everything this piece of literature held.

Flipping the tome open to a dog-eared page, he scanned the contents. He guessed this was as far as Nicholai had gotten. The words were as dry as the book's title—a series of laws and regulations relating to everything expected of a Time Father. One chapter discussed Chronometer maintenance. Another chapter detailed how to initiate a new Time Father by lubricating the Chronometer first with an established member's blood, followed by the blood of the recruit. Tragic stuff, just one stifling demand after another. Why anyone wanted to sign themselves up for this life, Kazuaki Hidataka never knew.

He skipped ahead several chapters, scanning the pages. Boredom almost propelled him to set down the book when his gaze fell upon a phrase. "The Earth Mother," he whispered aloud, recalling a time where he had heard those words before. It was the catacombs, the library, the book he was uncertain on whether it was political or legend. As the captain scanned the short article dedicated to the Earth Mother, his interest grew. Nicholai had said he knew nothing about the topic.

The book's covers met with force as Kazuaki slammed it shut. He placed it back on the bed. With haste, he ushered himself to his cabin where he kept the other books. The information he gained reignited his desire to research. He needed to return to the other book they had found, *The Balance of the Earth Mother*. If the small amount of information he had absorbed from Nicholai's book held true, he may well be onto something big.

One thing remained certain. As the captain strode toward his cabin remembering how the Time Father had told him he knew nothing of the Earth Mother, Nicholai would rue the day he dared to lie to Captain Kazuaki Hidataka.

PENN SAT ON THE MAIN deck, his legs draped over the rails of the ship as he teetered on the edge. Though he drank large swigs of alcohol from a soiled copper mug, his balance remained in tune with the dips and rises of the ship at sea. It had been a long while since he took time to enjoy the sunset and the delicious feeling of liquor coursing through his veins. As the cook and cooper, his duties aboard Kazuaki's ship were limitless. Though not as skilled with a weapon as most of the others, his abilities complimented things the crew experienced on a day-to-day basis rather than the occasional occurrence. Penn Elmbroke was a busy man. But now, all he busied himself with was killing his mug of booze.

His reprieve did not last long. The quartermaster's forceful bark almost caused him to drop his mug into the ocean. It would've been a shame too, as it was his favorite.

"Penn Elmbroke!" Bermuda shouted from behind him, putting a hand on his shoulder and forcing him to turn and face her. "Where's Nico? You were supposed to be watching him!"

"I was," Penn replied without alarm, swinging his legs over the rails and positioning himself onto the boards of the deck. "I put him to work in the galley."

"Alone?" Bermuda narrowed her eyes into slits. "For how long?"

Penn shrugged, aloof. "I don't know. A good few hours, I'd say." He did not recall the precise time when he left the man down there, but it was long enough to gain a good buzz from the alcohol.

The quartermaster seethed at his indignant response and motioned him to follow her. "Gods only know what he's doing down there."

Penn followed. He did not enjoy bowing down to authority, but he respected Bermuda and the captain, even after she lost herself to Mimir's influence. That respect alone drew him to follow her. Stubbornness lived inside his every bone, but they had his loyalty on lockdown. Though his bullheaded actions and rebellious behavior led some to think otherwise, Penn loved the captain and the quartermaster with a fierceness. They weren't his blood, but they were certainly his family.

The woman burst open the galley door and stopped, blinking at the sight before her. Copper pots hung in their place glistening with a brightness she never recalled seeing on them before. Nicholai had cleaned all the dishes, once a common fixture in the galley sink, and had placed them in their locked cabinets. He had scrubbed the bricks to the fire hearth with a nylon bristle brush and had wiped it down, restoring it to its former glory. The clutter that clung to the limited counter space found a home out of sight. From the ceiling to the floor, the ship's galley had never looked so pristine.

Nicholai just finished reorganizing the rations Penn had stored earlier. He turned over his shoulder to see the two and motioned toward the cabinets. "I hope you don't mind." He pulled open the doors to allow them a better look. "I categorized the non-perishables into breakfasts, lunches, suppers, that sort of thing. It should be easier to find what you're looking for now, Mr. Elmbroke."

Penn surveyed the room. He scarcely recognized it as his galley. He eyed Nicholai and blinked, unsure whether he was seeing things due to the amount of alcohol he had consumed or if what stood before his eyes was a reality. "Penn." Though his tone still held a hint of irritation, he relented to Nicholai's efforts to formally address him. "You can call me *Penn*."

Bermuda straightened her posture, scrutinizing the room. "You accomplished all this? By yourself?"

Nicholai nodded, rubbing at his exhausted face with both hands. "Yes, well ... with Penn's instruction, of course."

Penn showed no sign of gratitude for his acknowledgment, but his demeanor softened.

Bermuda glanced once at Penn then back at Nicholai. She caught the Time Father staring at her wrist where a hand should've been. The woman frowned. "Well, if you're finished here, see if Elowyn needs any assistance. She's been caring for Rennington 'round the clock. She could use help."

Nicholai closed his weary eyes, feeling the fatigue wash over his eyelids and brain. Exhaustion would not deter him. "Yes, ma'am." He nodded to Penn before he squeezed between the two and headed toward Elowyn's room.

Bermuda watched him go then faced Penn, who wore a smug look on his face. "Get to work. He may have cleaned this cesspool, but you've still got casks to make. We'll need more places to store our dry goods if Captain plunders those other escape boats."

Perhaps it was the liquor or his arrogant demeanor, but Penn could not temper the vainglorious undertone in his reply. He smirked at Bermuda, a rare expression for the cook and cooper. "Yes, Quartermaster."

The woman regarded once more the cleanliness of the galley. It was almost as immaculate as it must have appeared in its heyday. She did not allow herself to linger any longer and slipped out of the room. Even with the setting sun, a quartermaster scarcely slept.

FATIGUE HAUNTED HIM as he trudged down the hallway to Elowyn's room. Nicholai rubbed at his face again, hoping to jostle life back into himself. Tending the galley had taken a lot out of him, but he could not show any weakness, not in front of these heathens. The first sign of debility or any shortcoming on his part could lead to an unpleasant experience. He didn't know what, but he tried to keep his imagination from running too wild. If he remained useful to these outlaws, he would stay safe.

As if on cue, he felt the full force of what he imagined was a steam engine plow him into the corridor wall. Nicholai winced as the crushing weight of two hands pinned his exhausted body to the hard surface. A face lingered so near to his that he smelled his assailant's breath. The Time Father's heart thudded from the adrenaline rush, and his eyes met the captain's scowl.

"You told me you knew nothing of the Earth Mother," Kazuaki whispered. Though his body language suggested an incredible rage, an eerie calm lingered in his message.

It took a moment for the Time Father to find his ability to speak. The assault had caught him so off guard his mind had trouble catching up with his mouth. "I— What?" He shook his head. "Earth Mother? I don't know what you're—"

"Belay that!" Kazuaki gripped Nicholai's shirt and tugging him forward enough so he could slam him back into the wall. "Now, I'd get to talking before I find other ways of *encouraging* you."

Nicholai remained slack-jawed as a state of confusion and panic consumed him. He thought he had assured himself another day of safety with his performance in cleaning the galley, but it seemed he had made a mistake. "Captain, I assure you, I do not understand what you're talking about—"

Kazuaki narrowed his eye. He stared into Nicholai's soul for what felt like an eternity, inspecting the validity of his words. Many interrogations had occurred aboard his ship over the years. He always got the answers he looked for. The captain came to learn a thing or two about reading a man. While a part of him detected the sincerity in Nicholai's voice, he was not ready to relinquish the hunt for information. "I've been around longer than I care to admit, Nico." Kazuaki eased the pressure on the Time Father's shoulders until he lowered his arms altogether. "I have a lifetime of experience on my side. If you're hiding something, I will find out."

Nicholai inhaled, having forgotten to breathe the entire time Kazuaki's hands were on him. He rubbed the sore spot on his shoulder, knowing full well it would bruise the next day. "I suspected as much." He cleared his throat, hoping to ease the captain's wrath by appealing to his ego. "Yes, I've heard of you my whole life. Your exploits speak for themselves. Tell me ..." Nicholai straightened his posture, trying not to appear weak. "How does a man become a legend?"

Kazuaki's eye shifted. He paused before drawing in a deep breath. "Legendary men and women are birthed in single acts. They perform a feat so grand it's forever embedded in the memories of the people. It spreads like wildfire, spilling from the mouths of orators for generations. The only thing that truly matters, though, is if your momentous act is born from greatness." He pressed his index finger onto the Chronometer hidden underneath the Time Father's clothing. "Or stupidity."

Though the heat of his skin warmed the metal, it suddenly seemed cold under the weight of Kazuaki's finger. Nicholai felt it pressing into his sternum, the vibration of his thundering heartbeat reverberating through his Chronometer. When he gathered enough wherewithal to speak, he said, "How long have you known?"

The captain's finger withdrew from the cloth that covered the Chronometer. He removed *The Balance of the Earth Mother* from a deep pocket lined in his long jacket's interior. "Long enough to know that, because of what you are, you should possess at least some knowledge of this." He shoved the book into Nicholai's hands. "This book states an Earth Mother should reside in every Time Father's division. That book *you've* been reading also contains a small section about it."

Nicholai tilted his head. It was obvious the captain had rummaged through his belongings, but he remained confused. The Time Father did not yet arrive at any chapters that mentioned an Earth Mother. He lifted Kazuaki's book to his face and sifted through its contents. His expression gathered more perplexity as he delved deeper into the writing. A look of concern overtook him. "I've heard nothing of an Earth Mother for as long as I've overseen Southeastern. Not even my father mentioned such a creature, and he's ruled over Western since I was a child."

"There are coordinates." Kazuaki seized the book from Nicholai and flipped to the last page. He pointed to the handwritten scrawling without taking his eye off Nicholai. "What do these mean?"

The Time Father studied the coordinates before he shook his head, dumbfounded. "I don't know."

"These coordinates touch no known edges of Panagea." Kazuaki slammed the book shut and returned it to his pocket. "They're in the middle of the ocean insofar as I know."

"That's ... I'm not sure what to say."

The captain smirked. It was the first time Nicholai saw his expression shift to one of jubilance, however macabre it was. "No need to say anything, *Nico*. Just ready yourself for whatever awaits us at these coordinates." The man stopped, glancing over his shoulder at the baffled man. "Unless you have more pressing matters to attend."

It felt like a trick question. Nicholai did not wish to continue living on this vessel of thieves, but he didn't expect the captain would let him walk away either, especially now that Kazuaki shared his plans. The Time Father's face fell. It all clicked. The captain was sending a message. Kazuaki's openness to discuss his strategy was a silent indication Nicholai would go nowhere.

Dwelling with the thieves had one advantage. The ship remained the safest place he could be while attempting to devise a solution for Lilac, for Southeastern. But, if they planned to run him ragged the entire time, he did not know if he'd have any opportunities to further his research. It didn't matter either way. His options were severely limited.

"I don't," he finally said, eyes hard on the captain.

"Very well then. Carry on." Kazuaki vanished up a flight of stairs to the main deck, leaving as quickly as he had appeared.

The Time Father's heart pounded. He laid a hand on his Chronometer, silent, as it still held Southeastern frozen in time. The man had lived outside Southeastern for weeks now and was no closer to a solution. And the farther they crept toward those coordinates, it seemed the further from a solution he became. Though they were far from Panagea's coast, and therefore unable to experience the rapid deterioration of land breaking off into the seas, he still felt the people and the divisions suffering in his entire body. Nordjan had instilled in him at their last meeting that things were getting worse. Nicholai sighed.

He hoped Panagea could hold out just a little while longer.

Chapter Ten

Western had grown a lot in the forty years Edvard Addihein served as its Time Father. He took over for the previous keeper at the tender age of seventeen, making him the youngest Time Father in all of Panagea's history. People raised questions about the young man's capability, but most of Western did not fuss at his initiation. Even as a boy, Edvard Addihein had possessed intelligence, calculating skills, and ambition. The people of Western knew it too. While they had mourned their previous ruler's passing, a lot of anticipation existed over what Edvard could do for their division. He didn't let them down. He poured his heart and soul into the growth of Western for his entire adult life. Unfortunately, that did not leave him much time for other endeavors, like raising children.

Edvard had harbored a lot of plans for himself and his division during his youth. His plans had kept him busy. He knew they would. Because of this, he had never wanted children. He knew he couldn't give a child the attention they deserved. But his wife, Enita, had pressed him on the topic often.

In his earlier years as Western's ruler, Enita had dwelled in their homestead, left alone for days and weeks while he carried on with his overwhelming duties. Her loneliness crippled her. She had begged Edvard to give her a companion, someone she could pour all her love into, and Enita had plenty to spare. It was her compassion that had drawn Edvard to her. He had wanted to be the one to help her unburden her overflowing heart, but his duties had often kept him from her for long stretches. Eventually, her sadness had broken him, and he had relented to her desire. Their child, Nicholai, had become the primary focus of her attention.

Edvard's face fell as he recalled those memories. He had accomplished many great things, but they had come at a cost. He had served Western well. Edvard was a great ruler but a terrible husband. And, perhaps, an even worse father.

It was a realization Edvard had lived with for some time. He had accepted it years ago, but it had been too late to remedy the circumstances. Too much time had passed. The best he could do was remain true to what he knew best: manage his division with efficiency, as he always had. He excelled at it. That alone eased the guilt he harbored for failing in other aspects of his life.

Despite his best efforts, even when he threw his entire self into his work, the guilt had a way of breaking to the surface. That same guilt had caused him to suggest to the other Time Fathers that Nicholai should become the Time Father of the Southeastern division. The current ruler in Southeastern had aged beyond common political leaders. His age, combined with the evidence he suffered from a black lung diagnosis, showcased the fact he ruled on borrowed time. A pressure had already existed to initiate a new Time Father within twenty-four hours of the man's impending death. Because of this, the other Time Fathers had agreed with reluctance that Edvard's son would take over the Southeastern division.

At least they'd have one thing in common then, Edvard thought.

The aging man's ears perked at the sound of Nordjan's flying machine in the air. The ornithopter looked clumsy as it flapped its wings. It appeared even more ridiculous with the bulbous hot air balloon providing the vehicle with an additional lift. Though the technology had grown since its first introduction, it still looked awkward in flight. Lack of perfection on the machine kept it from most of the public and other Time Fathers. The art of flight exploration and technology was new and untrusted by many. Transportation by steam train remained Panagea's preference.

Nordjan and those in the snowy Northern division required the ornithopters and other flying machines. Frequent blizzards hindered the steam trains' entry into Nordjan's territory. Edvard understood their necessity there, but whenever they traveled outside Northern, they garnered some snickers from Panagea's citizens. They called them *flappies*. It was not a term of endearment.

As the bulky invention settled on the ground, Edvard approached. He waited in patience for Nordjan to collect himself. The Northern Time Father did not waste much time; they only had an hour and thirteen minutes before Nordjan needed to return to his division if he wished to make it back to maintain his area's time.

"Edvard," the looming man addressed the Western Time Father, adjusting his posture as he dusted off his attire. "I appreciate you meeting with me on such short notice."

Edvard nodded. He had written Nordjan an immediate reply after receiving word the Northern Time Father wished to schedule a get-together. Though he did not know the exact intention for Nordjan's visit, he speculated it had something to do with the *other* letters he'd received: one instructing each division to send militiamen to Southeastern's borders, and a second from Darjal, detailing what he knew of the events that transpired in Southern.

"Of course," he replied.

"I suspect you know why I'm here." Nordjan's voice remained neutral. "It's approaching a month now since Nicholai left Southeastern in a sorry state. Things are getting critical. If we do not restart time in his division soon ..." Nordjan cleared his throat. "I need any information you might have about Nicholai, and I need it now. It couldn't be done by letter. As you know, time is of the essence, Mr. Addihein."

"I understand," Edvard said with a dim nod. He had a hard time maintaining eye contact with the Northern Father. He commanded so much attention. Edvard couldn't escape the shame he felt at his son betraying the divisions. "I'll help however I can."

"Excellent. Do you have any idea where he might have gone?" He knew it was a long shot, but, if anyone possessed insight into Nicholai's mind, their best bet was his father.

Edvard hesitated. He did not have a direct answer. "I received word from Darjal. It's my understanding he's traveling with Kazuaki Hidataka. With the sea at his disposal, I'm afraid his reach is limitless now. He could be anywhere."

A frown crossed Nordjan's face. As he feared, Edvard's reply was not helpful. "Do you know why he might have done it? We had one of our monthly meetings the morning of the day he froze Southeastern. It was straightforward as far as I was concerned. Though he showed the same level of unprofessionalism as always, he did not appear in a damaged state of mind."

Edvard's gaze turned to the horizon as he drew in a deep breath. "I fear I won't be a great asset to you, Nordjan. I know little about Nicholai's dealings. He wrote to me once, to tell me of the woman he intended to marry. Lilac Finn, I believe her name was. But we have not seen each other since the last decennial anniversary at Panagea's center."

"*Anything* would be of use. Something from his childhood perhaps? Did he suffer from any bouts of judgment lapses before? Any brushes with the law?"

Edvard shook his head. "None so far as I know. The only thing Nicholai suffered from as a child was inheriting his mother's bleeding heart."

Nordjan inclined his chin. "And we all know how far that got her."

A low blow. Edvard's stomach tightened. His fingernails dug into his palm to steady himself. "In any case, I have no information that will lead to his coordinates, Nordjan."

Once again, Edvard's recounts of Nicholai's childhood left Nordjan no closer to finding him than when he had first arrived. Nordjan knew of Nicholai's inherited bleeding-heart syndrome. It caused many of his late arrivals when the Northern Time Father had visited him in Southeastern to keep the inexperienced man abreast of what he needed to do. Nicholai had always needed an extra push. Nordjan had chalked it up to his inability to disappoint people but assumed that, as time went on, he would fall into his role with much the same success as his father before him. He just needed Nordjan's influence.

Nicholai's abandonment of Southeastern was not the only reason for Nordjan's visit to Western. "Edvard"—he scrutinized the man's face—"how much did you tell Nicholai about the Earth Mothers?"

Edvard clenched his jaw. His eyes looked lost, and he shook his head. "I told him nothing of them. Of her. Nicholai should not even know she exists." He knew where Nordjan planned to take the conversation. "Darjal explained in his letters. I know the titles that were stolen from the library."

Nordjan knit his brows together. Nicholai would have been the first Time Father who wasn't exposed to the complete history of their title. Traditionally, each initiation came with the knowledge of the Time Father and Earth Mother pairings. It cemented the necessity of their annihilation six-hundred years ago, save for the one they spared. He studied Edvard. "I cannot surmise why those titles would be amongst the collection he stole if he knew nothing about her."

Edvard's eyes focused again, and he turned his attention to Nordjan. "Perhaps it was not Nicholai but the company he was with. Hidataka has a penchant for hunting myths. Enough time has passed since the Earth Mothers' cleansing. Their history may well be considered a legend by now." He paused. "Nordjan ..." Edvard's voice lost its usual authority. "If they find her, if they bring her back, what effect would that have on Panagea?"

The man inclined his chin. "I have not even considered it. I hoped we would have found him by now."

"I doubt we can. He travels by sea." Edvard scanned the horizon. "A limitless ocean stretches before him. With the art of seafaring lost, we've no men alive who possess the skills to find him, much less a vessel for them to operate. Her return strikes me as an issue we may need to ready ourselves to deal with."

"Darjal has commissioned a vessel. The fool thinks I know nothing, but I have eyes and ears in every division, and he's made little effort to disguise his undertaking. No doubt using ill-gotten finances from his churches or the division's treasury, but I've chosen to turn a blind eye to his indiscretion due to its necessity. My only concern is causing a public panic. We can handle Darjal's ego, but a mass riot would be unquestionably harder to maintain."

"Forgive me, Nordjan, but if it *is* the Earth Mother they seek, they have everything they need to find her before Darjal completes his ship. If she returns, the Time Fathers' sordid history will come to light. The people will know what our forefathers have done."

"They did what they thought was right for Panagea. The Earth Mothers stood in the way of blooming technology. They held back mankind from their true potential. We've made incredible strides since their removal. We've utilized nearly the entire landmass to its ultimate potential."

It sounded as though he recited a book, Edvard thought. "At what cost?" he mumbled. "We've come so far now. If word got out that our forefathers had slaughtered women to achieve their goal of advancement ..." Edvard shook his head. "I fear the primitive ways of how men had conducted themselves may appear vulgar in the eyes of the modern public. If we thought they would panic at the knowledge that a rogue Time Father has frozen Southeastern—well, I fear news that murdering a critical part of Panagea's history would not look favorable either. There are only eight—seven—of us and millions of them."

"Some would see the sense in the elders' actions. The blue bloods—those who own the research facilities, the factories, everything that pushes us forward—they understand the importance of technology. They would agree with our forefathers. Indeed, their actions were not without consequences, I'll admit, but, if we keep moving forward, we'll find the cure to what ails Panagea. There's nothing technology can't cure. We just need to discover that next breakthrough. Soon, this crumbling world will be a problem of the past, just as the Earth Mothers are."

A sense of duty made Edvard nod. Nordjan was right; the world existed in a sorry state. He was unsure what issues other divisions had experienced, but one of their top ten largest factories on the coast of Western had suffered irreparable damage when an earthquake of incredible magnitude had ripped it apart like paper. Two thousand people had died that day, including the countless commercial and residential damages it had caused. Edvard had run himself ragged sending as much help as he could to the area, but commanding an entire cardinal direction was a big space to control. Edvard had already depleted most of his brainpower with the Nicholai fiasco. Many sleepless nights had plagued the Western Time Father these last four weeks.

Nordjan dusted off his sleeve though there wasn't any dust to remove. He studied his haggard-looking comrade. "Why didn't you tell him, Edvard? About the Earth Mothers? If you had simply outlined the importance of why the forefathers did what they had—"

"It wouldn't have mattered. I cannot claim to know my son well, but what little knowledge of him I possess points to his idealism. He's a fantasist. A wishful thinker. He never would've seen the necessity of killing them." Edvard took several steps away from Nordjan, rubbing his face. "I wanted him to respect the Time Fathers and everything they stood for. I wanted us to at least have *that*. The knowledge of the past would have destroyed that ... even if it was hundreds of years ago."

Nordjan frowned, though he seemed to accept Edvard's explanation as a reasonable answer. He had never fathered children of his own, too focused on his duties as Northern's Time Father. But he knew it was not an uncommon desire for a father to want to share a bond with his child. Unfortunately, his journey here had been a waste of time. Edvard knew nothing about Nicholai, and the little he did proved useless.

One more topic burned on the Northern Time Father's mind, and he needed an answer before he continued his efforts to track Nicholai. "Edvard ... I know you've proven your loyalty in the past. You know when he's found, he'll be killed on sight."

The Western Time Father's face betrayed little of whatever emotions he felt. Whether it was due to his exhaustion or his incredible skill at hiding it, Nordjan wasn't sure. "I suspected as much."

Nordjan narrowed his eyes. He remained unsure of what to make of the man's behavior. "Given Nicholai's ability to traverse the sea, it would not surprise me if he washed up on Western's shores at some point."

Edvard pursed his lips. "The thought had crossed my mind," he admitted, surprised his son had gone to Southern first instead of seeking shelter under the arms of his family in Western. Surprised, but relieved. He didn't know what he'd do if Nicholai approached him. Perhaps that's why he had steered clear of Western. Nicholai knew Edvard better than Edvard knew Nicholai. Throughout his entire childhood, all Edvard ever showed Nicholai was that he valued his duties above everything else.

"I need to know ..." Nordjan approached Edvard and placed both hands on the man's shoulders. "I need to know what you would do if you or your men were to find him first."

Edvard felt the pressure of Nordjan's hands on his shoulders. They seemed heavier than the weight he put on himself. He understood Nordjan's question and its necessity and therefore took no offense. He drew in a slow, deep breath. "I would do what needs to be done, for the good of the divisions, for the good of Panagea."

Nordjan searched his face as if it might hold a small shred of insight into whether the man spoke the truth. He always trusted Edvard; he was a lawful man of his word. But blood was often thicker than water, and the Northern Time Father needed to be sure what to expect should the moment arise. "Good man." He patting him once on the shoulder before he stepped backward. "That's all I needed to know."

Edvard accompanied Nordjan as he returned to his flying machine. He hesitated, waiting until the Northern Time Father finished buckling himself in to ensure his safety before he asked, "Were we wrong, Nordjan? Were they wrong? Our forefathers ... cleansing Panagea of them? It's been on my mind."

A slow, skeptical look crept across Nordjan's face as he took a moment to answer. "Too much time has passed. It's too late to remedy it now. All we can do is put our faith in them and continue forward with the path they set in motion for us."

Edvard nodded and stepped backward as the ornithopter's wings flapped.

Nordjan operated the burner, filling the balloon with hot air to assist in the rise.

The Western Time Father watched for longer than he should have as the flying machine disappeared from his field of vision, returning to its home in Northern. He let Nordjan's words settle over him, though it didn't take long for him to accept it as an answer. He was already familiar with those words. They had been his mantra for a while.

It was too difficult to remedy things when too much time had passed.

Chapter Eleven

The crew ran him hard. Only fleeting moments of free time existed. At the day's end, Nicholai held the options of sleeping or studying his book. His mind and heart always gravitated to the book, for Lilac's sake, but his body only granted him minutes with it before it forced him to sleep. Every morning, he discovered he had collapsed in exhaustion over the text, and, before he had the chance to dive back into it, a crew member knocked on his closet door and put him to work.

He never complained. Not in front of the outlaws. No weakness. No failure. Morning after continuous morning, he pressed on.

Today, Brack drew the short straw and came to wake him, though Nicholai suspected the man didn't mind. He didn't seem to mind much of anything. Nicholai had familiarized himself with the rest of the crew. The Rabbit remained the only person on the ship the Time Father never saw in dull spirits.

"Good mornin', sunshine!" Brack beamed when Nicholai opened the door to his room. He held a plate of breakfast—a metal bowl containing a heat-and-eat porridge. It looked gray, lumpy, and entirely unappetizing, but Nicholai accepted it with graciousness as Brack handed it to him. "I told Penn I had to rise you today. He made sure I brought this with me. Seems he's taken a shine to you, mate—not easy to do with Mr. Elmbroke, that!"

Nicholai forced a smile as he shoved a spoonful of the mush into his mouth and swallowed. His tongue protested the taste, but his empty stomach didn't mind. "He's one of the few, I'm afraid, which makes your kindness even more appreciated."

"Come now. I know Iani and Rennington took a liking to you when you plucked 'em from the hands of those footmen. Everyone else on board is as merciful. You just need 'em in the right setting."

Nicholai smirked. Their entire lives had played out on board the ship. The scenery had never changed, but he still asked, "What setting would that be?"

"Tell you what. You join me tonight as my honored guest in the dining hall, aye? No more wolfing down meals by yourself in whatever corner of the ship you find. We'll put a few drinks in 'em, and you'll see they're right as rain."

The Time Father hesitated. Though he held compassion for all people, he wasn't sure he wanted to get to know *these* people on an intimate scale. Even Rennington and Iani, who were generous to him in their attention compared to everyone else, still shot men in Avadon without remorse. Their pendulum of ethics swung in the opposite direction of his own. Rubbing elbows with murderers and thieves, much less introducing alcohol into the situation, seemed like a bad idea.

Then again, gaining their trust could be a worthy investment. If he connected with these people, the likelihood of them killing him when he ran his course of usefulness lowered. Nicholai needed to approach this with the same level of dedication he approached the jobs they had given him so far; he'd have to exceed their expectations. If he earned their trust, they might ease up on him. Then he'd have more time for his studies.

Nicholai donned his best smile. "I accept your offer, Mr. Joney. Thank you."

"Oi, Mr. Joney was my dad's name." He pointed a faux stern finger at Nicholai's face. His ability to hold a concerned expression did not last long, and it twisted into a smile before he cracked into full-on laughter. "Least, I think it was. Never knew the fecker!" He laughed at his joke for longer than he should have before taking Nicholai's empty bowl. "But no, mate. You can call me *Brack*. Or *Rabbit*, most everyone here does."

Nicholai thanked Brack with a nod for taking his dirty dish. "That's a curious nickname. Can I ask how you acquired it?"

A devilish grin crept across the man's face. He motioned Nicholai to follow him toward the galley to dispose of the bowl. "Courtesy of Captain Hidataka. I never seen one with me own eyes, but he says my habits put him in mind of a rabbit. Something to do with them having a healthy appetite for—"

"Food?"

Brack grinned. "Nah, mate."

Nicholai blinked. He picked up the subtleties. "Everyone needs a hobby, I suppose."

Brack burst into laughter again. He slipped into the galley and tossed the bowl in the sink. "Too right, that!" He motioned Nicholai to follow. "You're with Granite and Revi today. They're our boatswain and carpenter." He turned toward the main deck. "Just follow them 'round, get a feel for things. They keep the ship pretty tiptop. You'll probably only be doing minor repairs on wood and canvas, maybe some tinkering in the engine room. Pay mind, they'll make you swab the deck if you piss them off."

Nicholai nodded as he joined Brack on the main deck and crossed the distance to Granite and Revi.

They stopped when they saw the others approach, appearing irritated at having to babysit Nicholai.

Granite's dog did not share their annoyance. It scurried about the deck, pleased with the new company. He ran to Brack and Nicholai and weaved between the men's legs, yipping with excitement and wagging his tail.

"Mornin', beasty!" Brack seized the flopping mutt's face. He ruffled the animal's cheeks and cooed at it.

The dog wriggled with great force, trying to lick Brack's face, but he kept out of reach.

"Oh, I love you too, you filthy animal!" He laughed and pet the dog before he looked to Revi. "He's with you today, boys. Be gentle now. He's good people."

Revi sniffed and hocked a mouthful of mucus over the side of the ship. "Right. We just finished rigging maintenance. We were about to head below deck to survey the boiler and the engine room."

"Good luck, mate." Brack patted Nicholai's shoulder before he abandoned him with the two men. The jester had his own duties to perform, and though he came across as an unkempt mess like everyone else on the ship, Brack existed to work hard.

Nicholai couldn't believe how much he missed Brack's presence in the moments that followed his exit. Granite was an intimidating man, a huge behemoth who held a permanent look of displeasure. The dog did not match its master. It jumped onto Nicholai and stood on its hindquarters while it struggled to reach his face with its tongue.

"Friendly little sort," Nicholai said with a smirk, petting the creature atop its head. "What's his name?"

"Ain't got one," Revi answered for Granite and raised his hands to his face to shield his vision from the blinding sun. "You of any use around an engine?"

Nicholai perked at the mention of an engine. The engine existed as the most critical component of a ship; he didn't think they would've trusted him near it. "Yes, I could be of use," he offered, neglecting to mention all the experience he had with the inner workings of most mechanized items. "Though I must admit, I'm not too familiar with sea vessels. If you have access to engines, what need have you for the sails?"

"It combines two useful techniques," Revi said as he motioned for Nicholai to follow. The three men and the canine entered the belly of the ship. "Captain Hidataka may be old, but he kept up with current tech. Two propellers below the hull power the ship. She uses sloped surfaces to transition rotational motion created by the steam engines into an axial force that moves the ship forward. The sails are just added power if the winds are favorable."

Nicholai blinked, surprised. He did not peg Revi for a well-educated sort and regretted stereotyping the man. It was clear he knew his stuff. Nicholai also knew his stuff; with any luck, he'd leave them with a good impression. Thanks in part to his natural curiosity and all the classes he had attended in Southeastern, Nicholai spoke the language of mechanics. He hoped that would be enough to earn Granite and Revi's favor.

"You got your syringes then?" Revi asked as they approached the boiler room. "Gets hot in there. It's ventilated, but it's triggered oxygen deprivation before."

Nicholai reached into his pockets and thumbed the familiar device while staring at the boiler room's entryway. "I'm good."

"Not much use for those down here." Revi pointed to the goggles Nicholai wore around his hat. "They'll keep the coal out of your eyes, but the heat will fog them. You'll be of no use if you're working blind." Revi entered, feeling the intense temperature shift punch him in the face. He waltzed to one of the several boilers, opened a hatch and grabbed a shovel to shovel coal into the opening. "We only need a couple running to maintain cruising speed."

Granite joined him. He made short work of the chore, able to shovel loads twice as heavy as Revi.

Nicholai removed his hat and felt the beads of sweat collect on his forehead. He tucked it under his arm and scanned the boiler room, immersed by the ship's inner workings. The surroundings reflected what he imagined life would be like inside a giant clock. He watched every piece of metal and fuel interact with one another in a way that kept things moving with efficiency. It captivated him.

"Don't just stand there, Nico. Get your hands dirty," Revi muttered, barely audible through the noise.

Nicholai cleared his throat, finding Revi's caution about the constricting heat affecting his lungs correct. He set down his hat, grabbed a shovel and helped.

"Cruising speed is the most efficient rate for coal consumption. Burned coal heats the steam and drives it to the engine room. Should we ever need to go slower, never let a boiler go out. Reigniting it is a pain in the ass."

As the men worked in silence, Revi noted Nicholai held up surprisingly well in the conditions. Though time and a lack of grooming gave the man a haggard look, Revi did not peg him for a useful sort. It pleased him that he was wrong. Three working sets of arms cut down the time a lot. They efficiently completed their work in the boiler room.

"That's it for the boiler room. Off to the ER." Revi carefully closed the grates and exited the sauna-like environment. "The engine room is aft. Follow me." He pushed passed Nicholai and continued his mission.

Nicholai eyed Granite. "You both come across as quite skillful in this element. Have you been at this a while then?"

Granite regarded him with an irritated expression. He said nothing and walked ahead.

His jovial dog ran a circle around Nicholai before it followed its master.

Nicholai rubbed the sweat that had accumulated on his face with his hands, smearing coal across his skin as he followed. Once he reached the engine room, he waited for Revi to enter first before he trailed after him.

It was a veritable trove of gears and mechanics churning in a rhythmic tune. It consumed Nicholai with a comfort he missed—the familiar sound of metal as it clanked and turned. He liked it even more than the boiler room. He knew it well and felt more at ease in this environment than anywhere else he had explored on the ship.

"Steam turbine, fuel pumps, feed pumps." Revi rattled off the names of things as he pointed at them. "All the necessities to move a ship."

"Impressive." Nicholai breathed deep as he lost himself in the beauty of the functioning gears. "It sounds as though this area here may need lubricant." He motioned to an area on his right. "Should anything ever need a tune-up, just let me know. The mechanics of machines, well ... They're a hobby of mine, you could say."

"I should hope so." Revi tilted his head to pop a stiff spot in his neck. "Wouldn't pay to have a Time Father who couldn't keep his Chronometer in check."

Nicholai spun and met Revi's gaze with haste. The man's words surprised him; though, after a moment, he wasn't sure why. It made sense word would spread once Kazuaki figured it out. "I see the captain told you."

"He told the whole crew." Revi crossed the distance of the engine room and grabbed lubricant to bring to the spot Nicholai had pointed out earlier. "That's one thing we like about the captain, no secrets between crewmembers. So, why did you do it?"

Puzzlement crossed Nicholai's face. "Do what? Join the Time Fathers?"

"No, mate." Revi lubricated the gears and handed the canister to Granite after he finished. "Why'd you freeze time in Southeastern?"

Nicholai grimaced. Even though they no longer lived in Panagea, everyone familiarized themselves with the politics of Time Fathers. "I ... I needed to buy myself more time."

Revi glared at him across the engine room, silent while seeming to contemplate something. The man grabbed a rag from the floor and cleaned his hands. "Speaking from experience, mate, time rarely ever solves your problems, no matter how much of it you have."

It was an ominous message, but it held a sincere undertone. Nicholai studied Revi's face. "From experience, you say?"

For a moment, it appeared Revi had regretted saying anything. But his gaze lingered on the various gears Nicholai had suggested they lubricate. "Just be sure if you abandon something, you're ready to let it go. No sense in letting things linger in limbo. It's a coward's way out." Hate tinged his voice. Nicholai felt the hatred belonged more to Revi than it did to his situation with Southeastern. "You think you need time, but then you give yourself too much of it. Then it's too late to go back."

The somber words struck the Time Father. He felt a heaviness in Revi's words. It wasn't just because they related to his situation, but because, for whatever reason, Revi knew the truth behind them; he knew it *entirely* too well. The man harbored demons, without a doubt. It appeared they were demons created by his own actions. Those were the hardest ones to get rid of.

"Thank you, Revi. That's sound advice."

"Yeah, well ..." His eyes glazed over before he rubbed his face and shook his head. "Look, if you ever need a hand in these rooms, come look for Granite or me. We're here if you need an assist." Revi thumbed to the man beside him who, for a giant, existed in such quiet it was easy to forget he was there. His dog, however, maintained a steadfast presence for such a small creature.

Its ears perked up with excitement as it heard someone down the hallway. The canine was the only one who detected the approach.

"Everything good in here?" The quartermaster appeared from nowhere and loomed in the doorway, her posture alert and rigid.

Revi startled at her appearance. When he realized it was only Bermuda, he waved his hand at her in a polite dismissal. "Yes, yes, Bermuda. Just showing Nico the ropes here."

Granite's dog jumped on her then jumped off then jumped on her again.

Bermuda didn't acknowledge the creature. She caught Nicholai staring at the stump of her wrist again and frowned before returning her attention to Revi. "Be sure you teach him well. No need for a useless mouth to feed." Her eyes shifted to Nicholai with skepticism before she turned on her heels and exited with the same quickness in which she had appeared.

"She's like a feckin' ghost, the way she sneaks up on you," Revi muttered after waiting until she was out of earshot. He checked the gauges to ensure the levels remained satisfactory.

"Revi ..." Nicholai trailed off before he faced the man. "May I be so bold as to ask, do you have a room with spare parts for the engine and boiler room? Pieces you may need in the event of a repair?"

Revi arched a brow and rubbed the back of his neck. "Sure. It'd be suicide if we didn't. They're all in the adjacent room, but it's cluttered with extra garbage from some of Captain Hidataka's plunders or just shit on the ship that breaks. Why?"

"Oh ..." Nicholai inhaled and shrugged. He smiled at the man to ease his questioning. "You know, just looking to ... make myself useful."

OF ALL THE PLACES ON the ship, the captain's quarters were the quietest. Bartholomew gravitated here often. Kazuaki did not always permit him, but he was fair in sharing his space. Bartholomew appreciated the captain's generosity. The library raid had brought in a slew of new books, and they called to him, begging for a set of eyes to read them, to explore them. He divided his time well, remaining useful as the ship's navigator, but his true passion was in the analysis and dissection of language as it related to the content in the books.

He stretched his dark arms to ease the stiffness he had gained during hours spent at the table. His appetite for knowledge consumed him. He remained immune to the aches and pains until he completed his obsession. Satisfied after he regained feeling in his body again, he lowered an additional lens over his existing pair, magnifying the small letters to help his tired eyes read them. "It's amazing," he said to the captain behind him. "The Earth Mothers' duties and capabilities are outlined so well. It's more specific than any other text I've come across. It leads me to believe this is based on actual events, or our author had an incredibly vivid imagination."

"I'm leaning toward the former." Kazuaki placed his hands behind his back and loomed over Bartholomew's shoulder to examine the book. "I've cross-referenced their existence in a book Nico was carrying around with him—a political text of sorts, relating to the Time Fathers."

Bartholomew pushed his glasses farther up his nose to aid his focus without removing his gaze from the page. "You're aware that with the Time Father of Southeastern in our company as long as he's been, his division is frozen. The other seven divisions will hunt him without mercy."

Kazuaki scratched at an annoying itch on his scalp. "It's crossed my mind. They've desired our capture for years and have failed.

They may be the law of the land, but maritime law is lost on them. I'm not concerned. Not yet."

"It is a wise man who leaves room for doubt," Bartholomew added as he moved the book closer. "The medicinal qualities these women retain is unprecedented. They could give Elowyn a run for her money, and she's the most talented medic I've come across."

The captain arched a brow and slid an old, wooden chair across the floorboards next to Bartholomew. "What kind of medicinal qualities?"

"They can convert and exchange energy within themselves to grow various plants." He licked his finger and turned the page. "Plants with antioxidant capabilities, fever reducers, natural pain relievers—it's all quite fascinating, really."

"Really," Kazuaki repeated. He narrowed his eye as his brain fired off possibilities. He wondered what had happened to the women detailed so well in the book. The text was an intricate account of their existence. He did not doubt the authenticity, but, if they existed, where did they go? The more he learned, the more his desire grew to find one, if any remained at all. The mysteries of the world pulled all of him in and didn't let go. He hoped the coordinates in the back of the book somehow led them in the right direction. "Tell me more about these healing properties, Bartholomew. I have a vested interest in their limits."

Bartholomew looked up from his book and removed the glasses from his face. He regarded the captain with minor concern. "You can't blame yourself for what happened to Bermuda, Captain."

It was not an easy feat, but Bartholomew caused the great Kazuaki Hidataka to flinch. He knew better than to deny it, and he would not insult Bartholomew's intelligence by doing so. "Once again, your perception knows no bounds, my friend."

Bartholomew frowned. "Come on, Captain. I've got eyes, don't I?" It didn't take long for him to realize his poor choice of words.

The scholar raised his hands in mock defense. "I'm sorry. I didn't mean to draw attention to the whole *eye* thing."

Kazuaki closed his eye—his original one. The other remained hidden under the protective layers of metal and synthetic leather. He scowled. Not a day passed he didn't dwell on his *gift* from Mimir. As if it knew it was the subject of his thoughts, the captain's false eye burned beneath its prison. "I take no offense." He waved his hand to dismiss the man's concern.

Bartholomew eased into his chair but still felt the stab of residual guilt. He knew the captain despised topics which gravitated around Mimir or anything that reminded him of that day. "Well, based on what these texts detail, it doesn't seem like there's much a plant *can't* do under the right circumstances."

"Indeed." Kazuaki laced his hands together and rested his index fingers on his chin. He remembered little of what plants could do. They had only bloomed for the first quarter of his long existence, each species dying out on Panagea one after another. He remembered them with fondness. Though he only had commingled with them for a short time, he had developed his preferences. Grapes remained among his favorite.

A familiar ringing bell interrupted the captain's reverie. Penn's dinner bell. An indication that a prepped and readied meal waited for them below deck.

Bartholomew did not want to tear himself away from the book. He could have spent the rest of his life here. His gaze flitted to the captain to realize Kazuaki's mind lived somewhere else, fantasizing about discovering an Earth Mother and finding the cure to Bermuda's heart, no doubt. Bartholomew worried about the man. His mind was a deep place; sometimes he lost himself in there for days, tortured by his obsessions. Kazuaki went days without eating. The scholar knew he wasn't in any danger of death, but it concerned him still. Kazuaki possessed immunity to physical deterioration, but mental collapse remained a threat.

Assuming the captain needed an extra umph to exit his quarters, Bartholomew pushed his chair from behind him and stood. "Shall we retire to the dining hall, Captain?"

Kazuaki glanced at the book. He hungered for more knowledge about the Earth Mothers, but Bartholomew's questioning stare prodded him. His mind whispered, *Just ten more minutes*, but Bartholomew's expression made Kazuaki knew he wouldn't relent. He forced a smile, and he lowered his chair to all four legs before he too stood and dusted himself off. "Well," he muttered, putting on his best face, "we can't very well focus on an empty stomach now, can we?"

A PRIMITIVE WOODEN table took up most of the room. Five chairs flanked each long side and single chairs seated at the short ends. Bermuda had already found a seat inside, filling one of the single chairs.

Elowyn sat beside her. The medic fidgeted in her chair, hoping like mad the others arrived soon. Though she had shared a tight-knit relationship with Bermuda before Mimir, Elowyn had suffered a loss of companionship when the quartermaster made her trade. The subtleties of intricate human emotions remained lost on her. There were no more sarcastic quips, no more empathetic moments. A bond remained the most critical thing a person shared on the lonely sea. In Bermuda's company, Elowyn never missed the human companionship of Panagea's people. But that had disappeared. She wasn't human anymore. She was a machine, calculating and cold.

Bermuda sat and stared straight ahead, focused on nothing.

Elowyn writhed in the silence, moving the silverware around the table to give her idle hands something to do. She almost jumped out of her chair when Iani entered, escorting his brother, who hobbled into the dining hall with the help of a crutch.

"Presenting the infamous, the fabulous, the impossible-to-kill, Rennington Platts, everybody!" Iani moved to his brother's side and motioned to him with both hands as if he showcased a priceless heirloom.

Elowyn smiled and nodded her approval. "So good to see you out of bed, Renn." She pulled out the chair beside her to make it easier for him to sit.

"Not as good as it feels to *be* out of bed." Rennington laughed, limped to the open chair and eased himself into it with the help of Elowyn and his little brother. "Gods, that mattress is a jail cell when you sit in it long enough."

"I never met a mattress I didn't like." Brack's familiar voice entered the dining hall with Granite, Revi, and Nicholai. "Especially if there was a dame layin' in it the same time as me, am I right?" He laughed, grabbing Nicholai's arm as he shoved him to the front of the crowd. "Look who finally joined us after a feckin' month, aye? About time this bugger eats with the crew, am I right?"

Rennington and Iani exchanged pleasantries with Nicholai while the women appeared less pleased.

Brack, Revi, and Granite sat next to Nicholai, opposite Elowyn and the Platts brothers.

Granite's dog leaped into the fifth available seat next to his master as he had done many times before. The beast knew how to balance on the small wooden seat, but his elegance remained in short supply. He placed his paws on the table and sniffed around for anything edible, but Penn had yet to serve the food.

Nicholai watched the dog. It was an easier place to rest his gaze than on the disgusted faces of Bermuda and Elowyn. Neither of the women warmed up to him, regardless of how hard he worked to prove himself. But the dog ... the dog liked him. He was easy to please.

Nicholai reached into his pocket and removed a cracker from the pack he kept on his person in the event his workload intruded on his ability to eat. "May I?" he asked Granite as he motioned to the dog.

Granite regarded the cracker then Nicholai, knowing full well the his animal companion would enjoy it. "He'd like that."

Nicholai tossed the cracker toward the excited animal, who leaped onto the table with the elegance of a drunk bison and inhaled it without grace. The dog jumped and spent the next several minutes poking its nose into Nicholai's vest, trying to locate any additional crackers.

Kazuaki and Bartholomew entered with little fanfare and found their seats. The captain appeared skeptical that Nicholai's face had found its way to their table, but he said nothing.

Penn pushed through the doors and set dishes on the wooden top. "Actual food tonight, ladies and gents." He placed a serving tray of fillets before the crew. "Finally pulled fish from the sea that wasn't mutated or doused in shit."

"Appetizing." Rennington stared at the flaky white fillets. "But if Penn says they're edible, they're all right by me." He sank his fork into a fillet and plopped it onto his plate.

Almost everyone fell into their comfort zone. The dining hall was their place of relief after a long day. Conversations amongst the crew filled the room; laughter and jokes smoothed over any stressful moments absorbed earlier.

The cook offered a fair share of other edibles, though most were the flavorless non-perishable food items the crew had become accustomed to over the years.

Nicholai suspected nobody minded the taste; the amount of alcohol they washed it down with likely tempered any foul aftertaste.

"Oi, Nico!" Brack's voice jumped from the crowd of boisterous conversation as he slid a mug in the Time Father's direction. "In need of a mead?" He laughed, taking too much joy in rhyming.

"No, no." Nicholai raised his hands with a light smile. "I don't drink."

Brack cocked his head. "You might as well be speakin' a foreign language, mate, because I don't understand a damn word you said."

"A toast!" Iani interrupted, paying no attention to Brack and Nicholai. "To my piece-of-shit brother, who has finally hauled his lazy arse out of bed to walk again! And to EP, the talented sonofabitch who got him there with her masterful talent!"

The majority raised their glasses, save for Nicholai and Bermuda. He didn't want to come off as rude, but he didn't have a glass to raise. It was with an awkwardness he raised an invisible glass, finding that a better alternative than risking insult to the others.

"To Renn and Elowyn!" the majority shouted, clanking various flagons and mugs together in a show of jubilance.

As the evening progressed, Nicholai paid close mind to the camaraderie shared between the band of misfits. The tales and laughter exchanged between them were intriguing and uplifting. More toasts followed the first, including some that detailed the lives of friends lost in battle or on more dangerous adventures. To his surprise, the Time Father found himself enthralled at the familial tie they shared. They appeared to care for one another with the same level of unity a traditional family would.

Bartholomew slid out his chair from the table and wiped his mouth with a cloth napkin. "Exquisite meal, Penn. You outdid yourself with the fish. Now, if you'll excuse me, I should go check our status." The navigator offered everyone a polite nod before he excused himself from the table and traipsed to the main deck.

"Since Renn's on the up and up, how's about a tune, eh?" Brack grinned, motioning Rennington to his feet. "Come on. It's been a quiet few weeks with you stuck in that old bed!"

Rennington choked down another mouthful of liquor and burst into laughter, the pain in his hip fading with each new swig from his cup. "I think I can handle that, but I'll need a little assistance. EP?" He stood from his chair with the help of his crutch and extended a hand to the petite woman beside him. "Join me on your cello?"

Elowyn smirked. The booze flowed in equal doses through her veins and banished any hesitation. She accepted his hand, though she used her strength to pull herself up, not wanting Rennington to apply any unnecessary pressure to his healing wound. The two crossed the distance to the front of the table as Elowyn pushed an old, dusty cloth off the body of her cello.

Rennington removed his trusty harmonica and balanced the crutch in the crook of his armpit while sporting a juvenile grin. "Ready when you are, m'lady."

Elowyn playfully rolled her eyes and placed the scroll on her shoulder, resting the bow on the strings. Though Nicholai thought the liquor would dull her movements, her fingers and arm moved with grace across the instrument.

Rennington joined with his harmonica, and the two played a haunting song in a minor key Nicholai hadn't heard before.

Her ethereal voice weaved through the crowd and silenced the other noises with its gentle caress. "*Though land be still and sea be wild, the two, they lovers be / The calm of earth, the rising wave, remind of you and me / Your heart, 'tis steady, yet mine, untamed, but I was ready to be reclaimed / Two opposites joining so perfectly, just as the land and the sea, just as the land and the sea.*"

Nicholai found himself stunned by Elowyn and Rennington. The two performed together with the skill of professionals, almost as though he were at an elaborate event. The blue bloods of Panagea—and even the other Time Fathers on occasion—sprang for extravagance of the like, ushering in the most talented musical performers in their divisions for a night of high-class elegance and entertainment. Nicholai never squandered his division's treasury on unnecessary luxuries. He admitted to wishing he could attend one, not just to sample the first-rate meals but to bask in the glory of the musicians' talents.

From the corner of his eye, Nicholai spotted another instrument hiding beneath the cloth Elowyn used to unveil her cello. He narrowed his gaze, believing it to be a clavichord. Before he knew it, the song finished, and most of the crew clapped and hooted their approval.

"That's what we've been missing!" Brack shouted, filled to the brim with booze and sentiment that only moving music brought. "Good ol' Rennington and Elowyn. Gods damn it all, I missed that sweet harmony!"

Elowyn tried not to blush while Rennington ate the praise as though it sustained his entire being. Everyone thrived in the environment, showcasing the best of themselves.

Even Nicholai found a smile on his face. Though he had spent the last month with these people, he had never seen them like this. The dining hall was a magical place. Barriers faded; apprehension melted away. It was one of the first times he had felt the companionship of man since leaving Southeastern. In his newfound sense of ease, he motioned to the instrument beneath the shroud. "Who does the clavichord belong to? I should love to hear it join in."

The boisterous laughter of the crew diminished to near silence. A sudden change in demeanor occurred; it caused Nicholai to cringe. The energy shift was sudden and abrupt, summoning discomfort in his stomach.

"I played the clavichord," Bermuda replied then took a mindless swig from her beverage.

Kazuaki bristled, and he turned to burden Nicholai with the weight of his gaze.

Soon, the Time Father felt the heaviness of everyone else's glare upon him. Their gazes shifted between him and Bermuda, as if waiting for her to react. Nicholai soon figured the reason she had retired the instrument; it was hard to play a clavichord one-handed.

The quartermaster took a long, calculating sip from her glass of liquor and placed it on the table, unfazed by the exchange of events.

Everyone seemed to breathe a collective sigh of relief. There would be no panic attack from the quartermaster today.

Nicholai no longer could handle the crushing weight of everyone's stares. His simple sentence had interrupted an entire evening of freedom amongst the crew. The dining hall, where they enjoyed their meals and a song or two if they were lucky, the place where they escaped the trials and tribulations of a long day's work, had shifted from a sanctuary of joy to a tomb of discomfort with six little words. He wasn't even sure why. He turned to Brack for an answer, but the Rabbit only offered a sympathetic shrug.

Nicholai was about to excuse himself, but Bartholomew burst into the dining hall with great haste. His eyes were wide as a look of pure excitement crossed his face. "Land ho! Captain! The coordinates—" He barely pulled himself together, trying to find the right words. "There's an island. It's straight ahead."

Kazuaki's chair flew from behind him and clattered to the floor. "Do *not* lie to me, Bartholomew."

"Land, indeed." Bartholomew clutched his chest. "And, Captain ... 'tis dark, but through the telescope ... be it the liquor or whatever else"—he drew much-needed air into his lungs before he made eye contact with Kazuaki again—"I'll be damned if I don't see a slew of trees."

Chapter Twelve

Tension clung to the air as the crew readied the ship in the moor. They approached the island as far as they could without the risk of running the ship aground. All anchors dropped the evening before to hold the ship in place. Though anxiousness vexed everyone, Kazuaki forced all to wait for the aid of daylight before they departed. Charging into unknown terrain in blindness from the night was a rookie move. Dawn cast new rays over the scenery and illuminated the foreign land before them in great detail.

Huge, towering trees climbed high into the sky with lush green leaves clinging to their branches. The sounds they made as the wind rustled them was unlike anything the crew had heard before, almost like a downpour of rain without a storm cloud. Various species of flowers sprinkled across the grasses in hues of lavender, sapphire, ruby, gold—not one color remained untouched from the palette of whoever had created this place. A fresh scent carried through the air. Their eardrums perked at the strange noises coming from the hidden creatures who dwelled on the shores. All their senses spiked from the ship. Life hurled toward them across the distance, more than had ever emanated from Panagea. It awakened a sense of prodigiousness in everyone, minus the unimpressed quartermaster.

"Gentlemen, ladies," Kazuaki addressed the crew, all on deck for the event. Though he knew they all craved a new adventure and the excitement it brought, the best interest of the ship came first.

"While my instincts tell me we're safe this far off Panagea, I'd be a fool to leave the ship unattended. Rennington, you'll be staying."

Rennington appeared deflated by the captain's announcement but understood the logic behind it. He still hadn't recovered from his injury in Avadon; his presence would only slow the team. "Understood, Captain," he replied with a morose sense of duty.

"Penn, Brack, you two stay behind. Rennington will need help to watch over the ship," Kazuaki stated as he shoved supplies into a pack.

Penn did not mind hanging back. Fighting and socializing weren't his forte. He had stabbed a man or two in self-defense, but he wasn't a brawler. He preferred the company of the ship.

Brack, however, did not appear pleased. Ever the social creature, the Rabbit craved adventure and any opportunities to delight in potential danger. "Aw, Cap, you're breakin' me heart!" He put his hands together in mock prayer. "I beg you to reconsider."

Kazuaki shook his head. He knew he could've left any of the other crewmen behind as a replacement, but he wasn't in the mood to tolerate Brack's off-handed banter. He had a way of turning a serious situation into a mockery, which Kazuaki enjoyed once in a while but not today, not with something this big. "Rabbit, you'll be of far more use here, in the event something goes astray." He patted Brack's shoulder before he faced the crew. Kazuaki would take a bullet for Brack, but his pleas did not compel him. The ship needed to be watched. "Alright, let's move out."

THE COCKBOAT AND ITS passengers approached the shore in silence, except for Granite's excited dog. It barked with an untamed wildness and tried to chase each seagull that flew overhead. The boat possessed limited room to run; the beast jostled all the travelers as he tripped over their laps. When the boat neared the shore, the dog jumped out and swam the rest of the way, too enamored by all the available things to chase to stay put.

What the dog soaked in without hesitation remained overwhelming for everyone else. Even Kazuaki found the sight exquisite. While the captain had memories of wildlife and trees burned into his mind from hundreds of years ago, he had not seen a forest *this* lush in his existence.

Everyone exited the cockboat, splashing into the clear water. Granite hauled the small vessel onto the sands of the shore and wiped sweat from his brow before he turned to watch his dog chase a displeased crab into the waves.

"Hidden in the back of a book all this time," Bartholomew said with a deep exhale.

The air smelled of salt and floral tropics. How long had this place existed, this small slice of nirvana? It proved to be everything Panagea was not. It came as a shell shock to the majority, but the breathtaking view eased most of their anxieties. Their hunts for the world's legends opened them up to astonishments often, but finding a paradise hidden in the limitless ocean countered any phenomena they had witnessed so far.

Nicholai inhaled a deep breath. His chest felt fuller. No longer did the crippling presence of dissatisfaction linger in his lungs with each inhale. Instead, they felt a deep sense of satisfaction they had never experienced before. The oxygen seemed richer, cleaner, and the waters reflected a purity that matched the air. Little streams bubbled down rocky paths with crystal clarity. Even the water purification plants of Southeastern never provided water so wholesome, so uncontaminated. He couldn't get past it. The purity put him in mind of Lilac. She would have loved this place.

The group felt the watchful eyes of curious creatures staring at them from the safety of the dense forest. Kazuaki recognized some from personal experience, but most were faces he had seen in old encyclopedias. They did not appear scared in the humans' presence, only curious.

"Do you ... think we'll find them here?" Nicholai asked with a faintness. He directed his question at the captain, for he knew the object of Kazuaki's search. "The Earth Mothers?"

The captain motioned for the others to follow him into the forest without looking at Nicholai. "Based on what Bartholomew and I have read, let's say I'm feeling optimistic."

The others followed their captain in quiet. The emergence into the forest put Kazuaki in mind of the last time he left the ship on a quest such as this. This island held many glaring differences when compared to Mimir's. Birds chirped overhead, and the forest, while growing darker the farther they went, held no ominous undertones. Enough sunlight shined through the branches to bring warmth to them with every other step.

Nicholai pushed a low-hanging branch out of his way before he looked at Kazuaki again. He had pegged the man for a bloodthirsty sort, with all the tales of Captain Hidataka he and many others had grown up with. One thing struck Nicholai as odd as they traipsed deeper into the woods was no financial gain seemed to exist from this endeavor, no treasure to divide amongst the crew. He couldn't pinpoint Kazuaki's drive. It vexed him. "Can I ask, Captain, why do you wish to find the Earth Mothers so much?"

"Am I to believe we're looking for a literal woman? Or literal women?" Bermuda's asked from the back, stopping the captain from issuing a reply.

Strategy and irritation prompted Kazuaki to ignore Nicholai's inquiry. He nodded to Bermuda. "Aye, from my understanding, that's exactly what we're looking for."

"Hey, EP," Iani called out from behind the medic.

Elowyn spun on her heels in time to have a lizard flung at her. She shrieked and brushed the tiny creature off her body while Iani laughed without restraint, finding great amusement in his prank. "You little fecker!" she hissed and wiped at her clothing, though the minuscule creature had already ran off unharmed. "That thing could be poisonous, for all you know!"

In-between laughs, Iani wiped a tear that leaked from the corner of his eye. "I hope not." He chuckled, finally composing himself. "Little bugger bit my thumb when I picked him up."

"Next time, pick up something bigger"—she crossed her arms—"so you might bleed out if it bites you. See if I help you then."

Bartholomew, unaware of the others' shenanigans, lost himself in exploration. He knelt beside various plants and slid on a glove from his pocket before he touched, smelled, and cataloged different notes in a journal he brought with him. He sketched the various shapes of as many creatures as he could. The scholar thrived in his new environment. All other sounds drowned out as he immersed himself in his surroundings.

Revi and Granite stood beside one another. Each found amusement as they watched Granite's dog romp through the terrain without restraint. The creature zoomed in one direction and tried to stop itself but failed, due to the speed it had built, and crashed into a tree trunk. Unfazed by its actions, the dog continued its play, until it tired itself out and lapped a drink from a stream.

"The beast has the right idea." Revi motioned to the animal. "If we get a few casks down here, we could load up on fresh water."

Kazuaki nodded, cradling his chin in his hand. It was an excellent idea, but he was far too obsessed with trying to figure out where this group of women could be hiding. The life that surrounded the island coincided with what he learned from *The Balance of the Earth Mothers*. He remained confident they were here somewhere. Though the island was small, plenty of hiding places existed. It could take weeks to comb this place's contents. His anticipation did not wish to wait that long. A faster way had to exist. "We can break off into groups. That'll help us cover more ground. We should find something much more efficiently then. We'll meet at the shores near the ship before nightfall."

The crewmembers nodded. It seemed like a solid plan.

As they were about to separate themselves into thought-out groups, a voice sounded from above. "There'll be no need for that. I will not make you hunt me, for I am not prey." With elegance and grace, the woman who stood high in the limbs of the looming trees leaped downward from branch to branch. She chose only those that held the weight of her lean, limber frame. In the blink of an eye, she dropped from her high point and landed on the ground in a crouched position then straightened herself to stand. Though naked, she showed no evidence of embarrassment. Long silver-streaked hair covered her exposed breasts, but the occasional breeze uncovered her. "I will not beg. If you came to finish what you started, I only ask you do it quickly."

Everyone stared at her unceremoniously, shocked by her sudden appearance and brazen nudity.

"Suppose it's well you left the Rabbit at the ship, Captain," Revi muttered without moving. "He would've passed out from lack of blood flow to his brain right about now."

The woman tilted her head and blinked, confused but undeterred. Her eyes fixated on Nicholai, and she stepped forward. "I want you to know I forgive you." The woman closed her eyes and bowed her head to await her death.

"Forgive me?" Nicholai tried not to turn red from embarrassment at the naked woman.

"You know each other?" the captain growled.

"No!" Nicholai raised his hands in defense. "How could I?"

"Forgive you for what?" Bermuda asked, panning between Nicholai and the nude woman.

"For the gods' sake"—Elowyn shook her head, wriggling from her vest before she tossed it to the stranger—"cover yourself."

Revi and Iani mumbled quiet noises of disapproval toward Elowyn as the woman caught the vest with a great deal of perplexity. "I'm afraid I don't understand." Her voice possessed a delicate nature as her gaze fell to the Chronometer around Nicholai's neck. "Are you not here to kill me, Time Father?"

"*Kill* you?" Nicholai's eyes grew wide as saucers. He backpedaled and shook his head. "Gods alive, madam, I would do no such thing!"

"Yeah, he's pretty useless with a gun," Iani interjected.

"We're here to find the Earth Mothers," Kazuaki said, taking an authoritative step forward to cease the madness.

Still holding the vest in her arms, her face showed a gentle acceptance. "Earth Mother," she corrected. "I am the last among them, I'm afraid."

"Oh?" Elowyn approached the woman. "What of the rest?"

"Gone." She gestured a hand to Nicholai. "I apologize for my assumption. The last time I saw a Time Father, he was crushing the life from my companions with a slab of stone. I thought, perhaps, six hundred years later, you had manufactured a supplement for oxygen and came to finish the job." Though her words were horrid, her tone of voice held no malice.

Nicholai, however, remained horrified with a look of disgust on his face. "Crushed? Time Fathers ... *killed* the other Earth Mothers?"

She nodded. "A tragedy. Even after all this time, I can still hear their screams."

"Six hundred years ..." Kazuaki whispered, scrutinizing the woman. He had met no one who had seen more years pass than him. Fleeting thoughts of her possessing immortality surfaced, but she couldn't suffer from the same fate, not if she thought they could kill her moments before. But, if she wasn't immortal, how was it she had lived longer than even him?

The woman realized everyone gawked at her. She smiled. "I am so sorry. Where are my manners? My name is Umbriel. Umbriel Dasyra."

"Well, Umbriel"—Elowyn helped the woman into the vest—"my name is Elowyn Saveign. This here is Revi Houton, Granite, Iani Platts, Bermuda, Kazuaki Hidataka, and Nico. Let me be the first person in a long time to give you a gift." She buttoned the vest, shielding the woman's bosoms from the rest of the world. "You can just go ahead and keep that."

Umbriel inspected the vest as she ran her hands over the material. It felt strange beneath her fingertips; it had been so long since she had donned clothing, but she did not wish to insult Elowyn's generosity. "You are too kind." She smiled as she beheld the woman's face. She turned and noticed the horror still plastered to Nicholai. "Time Father Nico, are you all right?"

Nicholai paled. He had lived with stories of the Time Fathers for years—since boyhood. The rare nights his father had come home, he would regale him with the occasional tale of what it meant to be a Time Father: honor, courage, strength, adversity, creativity, mercy for your people; at no point in his history lessons did mass murder surface concerning those who shared his title. "You—surely you're mistaken."

Umbriel's expression became conscience-stricken. She wrapped her arms around her torso as she shifted her bare feet in the leaves. "I wish I were."

"What ... How ... Why?" Nicholai wanted to condemn her, tell her it wasn't true, but, in his heart of hearts, her sincerity punctured through any denial he mustered. How painful to fall so far from grace. To go from a man who represented something he revered—that he was plagued with guilt for betraying—to a man whose forefather's had desecrated an entire group of women.

Umbriel shrugged a single shoulder. "We no longer fit into their idea of a perfect world. We were an exquisite team. The Time Fathers and Earth Mothers created a beautiful place together. For countless years, we were the keepers of the only two things that existed since the beginning: nature and time. But perfection is an ideal environment for just about everything, including disagreements. Their actions were not bred in malice. The Time Fathers just wanted what they thought was best for mankind: more advancement, more opportunities. The larger man's reach extended, the more they wanted to reach farther and farther. We sacrificed nature in pieces, holding on to the idea that life in all its forms could coexist, but, as the bigger mankind's appetites grew, the less room they had in their hearts for any other life form, including nature. When we put our feet down to resist, to save the other remaining lives who shared man's world, we were silenced. We gave, and we gave, and, when we no longer gave willingly, they took."

The group lingered on her every word, save Bermuda. Even Granite stooped to pet his dog when Umbriel mentioned mankind possessed an inability to share their world with lesser creatures.

Bermuda eyed everyone, incapable of feeling the gravity behind Umbriel's recount.

Elowyn felt enough empathy for them both. "So, how did you end up here?"

"They decided to keep one of us alive. As obsessed with advancement as they were, no man existed yet who discovered a way to supply the world with enough oxygen to support a supercontinent of people. They chose me at random, condemned to this island several hundreds of years ago. My only purpose was to keep the trees alive." She smiled as she motioned to the living collection around her. "I did the best I could, but, even at this distance, I feel

Panagea dying beneath my feet. She can no longer sustain herself. I was almost excited by your arrival. I thought, perhaps, it meant you had discovered a way to save her and wouldn't need me anymore. Though it would mean the end of my life, I would gladly give it for Panagea."

"Several hundred years ..." Revi repeated, tilting his head and spying the captain from the corner of his eye. "Would that make you an ... immortal, of sorts?"

"Oh my, no." She chortled. "I have encountered misfortune but none so bad as all that. Earth Mothers are alchemists of sorts. We tap into the cells of living creatures, giving and exchanging energy, extruding toxins and such. The surrounding life has helped me replenish the lifeforce of my own cells all these years. I persisted, as not to let my late companions down. Though their spirits live outside their bodies now, I will continue to represent everything we stood for until my dying breath."

Kazuaki perked. She spoke of what he hoped for—replenishing cells, removing impurities, everything that might help Bermuda. He and Bartholomew exchanged silent glances. The scholar knew why the captain's interest was piqued, but he suspected he wouldn't bring it up now, not in front of Bermuda. The captain executed more diplomacy than that.

Nicholai still looked as if he teetered on the verge of vomiting.

Revi approached him and patted his back. "You all right, mate?"

The Time Father's eyes glazed over. His arm crept up his torso and his fingers wrapped around the cold metal of his Chronometer. "I ... I'm not sure." Did his father know about this atrocity? Did any of the existing Time Fathers? Was that why that book remained locked in Darjal's hidden library? It was too much for him to comprehend. To Nicholai, murder did not serve as a solution when things didn't go the way he wanted. Though he was exposed to it through the company he kept as of late, it remained a foreign, repulsive process to him. "I cannot believe they would do such a thing."

Umbriel nodded, her gaze falling to the ground. "It was a shame. Life ... it's so sacred."

The silent moment of reflection filled with the sound of Granite's dog crunching on something hard. "Beast?" Granite's deep voice echoed through the trees. "What do you have?"

The dog eyed him unapologetically as its teeth crunched a small lizard's bones. A limp tail dangled from the dog's mouth.

"Give it." Granite extended his hand as he approached the canine.

The dog ate the lizard quicker.

Granite knelt beside the mongrel with a frown as he pried its jaws open and looked inside. The lizard was gone; to the beast, life was as sacred as it was delicious.

Everyone regarded Umbriel awkwardly, who smiled and shrugged. "Oh, that's just nature, survival of the fittest."

"It wasn't poisonous, was it?" Granite arched a brow.

"No, no." She shook her head. "He'll be fine."

"I think the beast has the right idea again." Revi crossed his arms. He didn't know how long the captain planned to stay here or why he had sought out this woman, but Revi Houton wasn't about to let the resources surrounding them go to waste. "We found what we were looking for, *who* we were looking for. Now, how about we stock the ship with food and water? This place is a gods-damned treasure trove of supplies."

"You're all more than welcome to stay as long as you like," Umbriel said, as if the island existed as her home and not her prison. "Please, we'll have a feast on the beach. It would be my pleasure to show you the delights of the forest."

"Those won't be the only delights you're asked to show once we get Rabbit off the ship." Iani chuckled, nudging Elowyn.

The medic rolled her eyes and shoved him away from her. "Revi's right. Let's gather supplies. It would be rude to deny Umbriel her gracious hospitality."

"Yes," Kazuaki agreed. He wanted more time to find an opportunity to get the Earth Mother alone to discuss Bermuda's fate. "We have a chef onboard our ship." He straightened his posture. "Penn has the finest tools available at his disposal to assist you in your preparations."

"Oh, I appreciate the offer, but I needn't any tools, Kazuaki," she said, finding pleasure in addressing someone by their name for the first time in what felt like forever. "I have everything I need here."

"Well ..." The captain cleared his throat and stole a glance at Bermuda, who still appeared aloof to the situation. Even in her cold, solitary state, one look of her caused his insides to stir. *Hang in there. We're close now.* He returned his attention to Umbriel and donned his most charming grin. "How *can* I help?"

THEY DIVIDED THE DAY into a series of tasks. Granite and Revi hauled casks of fresh water from the streams in the cockboat to the ship. Though Rennington wished to accompany Iani and Brack on their descent into the forest to gather firewood, Kazuaki put him in charge of watching the ship from the shore. It took convincing, but Umbriel assured Kazuaki no ill would befall his beloved ship. Her words allowed the remaining crew onboard permission to come to land. Logic dictated she was right; they were far from the vengeful grasp of the Time Fathers and their military, and Kazuaki assumed if nobody else had stumbled across Umbriel on this island for centuries, the risk anyone would show up unattended was small.

Penn and Nicholai tried to catch fish in their nets from the brook. Nicholai remained numb to his revelation and proved to be a useless fisherman. Penn kept him in check by issuing constant commands.

Bartholomew knelt in a corner of the forest, a feeble, crumbling encyclopedia of edible plants in his hands. He gathered whatever edible pieces he found that matched his text before he cataloged and sketched them in his journal.

Though Kazuaki limited himself to issuing orders and surveying the completion of everyone's duties, even he partook in the goings-on, having gathered dry leaves and sticks to serve as kindling for the firewood Iani and Brack brought back. He leaned near the future campfire site and set down another handful.

Granite's dog barreled from the water, much to Penn and Nicholai's relief, as it scared away any fish they tried to catch. The beast seized a stick in its jaw Kazuaki had dropped, chomping down before it whipped its head back and threw the stick into the air. Though gravity caused the stick to hit the creature in the face, he picked it up again and approached the captain. His tail wagged like a propeller.

The captain eyed the dog and quirked a brow. "What?"

The mutt barked, though it sounded muffled with the stick still in its mouth. It tried shoving the branch into Kazuaki's hands.

Kazuaki frowned as he grabbed the stick, getting a slimy film of canine saliva on his palm. He regarded the object with disgust then noticed the creature was failing to contain its pure, unadulterated joy. The corner of the captain's lips tugged into a microscopic smile as he withdrew his arm and hurled the stick as far as he could. The sound of dog barks echoed through the open air as he chased it down the beach.

Umbriel chose Elowyn and Bermuda to accompany her on a hunt. Neither woman had ever hunted game before, but hunting appeared far more interesting than what the others had to do. Though the noise of dried leaves crunched under their boots, Umbriel's bare feet somehow moved without sound through the forest interior. She spied the tracks in the soft, fresh soil and motioned the women to follow her. Much to Elowyn's relief, Granite had brought back clothing from her room in one of his many return trips to the ship. It was easier following Umbriel without her nudity as a distraction.

Umbriel pulled back a low branch of leaves, revealing a large deer a short distance away. It grazed on the forest floor, its ear flicking behind it.

Bermuda lifted her gun and whispered, "Let's get this over with—"

An arrow's wooden shaft tapped onto her metal barrel. She frowned and shot a glance at Umbriel, who smiled and shook her head. "I appreciate your technique, Bermuda, but just a moment, please—"

The quartermaster appeared irritated but dropped her gun to her side. She gestured toward the deer with a silent *do what you must do*, figuring Umbriel planned to hunt the creature her own way.

The Earth Mother mouthed, *thank you*, before she closed her eyes and held a clenched fist to her heart. Her lips whispered words inaudible to Elowyn and Bermuda at first. After a while, it became clear she was thanking the gods for the offering and to please pardon her for taking a life, as its primary purpose was to sustain additional lives.

Elowyn tried to share a perplexed glance with Bermuda but found the woman indifferent. They allowed Umbriel to finish her ritual before she breathed deep and opened her eyes again. "There we are." She tucked a strand of her long hair behind her ear. "Please, I did not mean to interrupt your style of hunting." She motioned for Bermuda to continue. "I prefer the mercy of a bow and arrow, but I am always willing to learn new approaches."

Bermuda lifted her gun. "This approach is short and sweet." When she pushed through the leaves to get a better shot, the creature raised its head, its eyes meeting hers. In a moment of panic, the deer turned as Bermuda fired. The animal was quick on its feet; her bullet sank into its shoulder as it ran. It wasn't enough to drop the creature, and it disappeared into the trees.

Bermuda cursed, unaccustomed to missing her target. She wasn't used to relying on stealth. Just as the injured deer bolted into the safety of the brush, Umbriel gave chase. The two women left behind stared after her as she displayed a level of agility and aptitude. They didn't have her in their line of sight for too long, but, in the seconds they saw her, it appeared as if her feet knew every inch of the forest. She launched herself off a fallen log, her body somehow as quiet as it had been when she crept. It was as if she made herself as light as a feather but fast as a bullet. In a moment, she vanished into the forest.

"Shit, I hope she returns." Elowyn stood there dumbfounded. "Captain will kill us if we lose her."

"I hope she comes back too." Bermuda disarmed her weapon and returned it to her side. "Because I don't know how the feck to get back."

Elowyn shrugged. "I guess the captain can't kill us if he can't find us."

A statement Bermuda would have once found amusing washed over her without acknowledgment. A tinge of sadness crept into Elowyn's heart. She missed her friend.

The two women stood in silence for what felt like forever before they heard the rustling of leaves ahead. Umbriel emerged from the thick vegetation and waved at the women, smiling. She dropped the legs of the carcass she carried and yelled across the distance. A single arrow protruded from the creature's chest where its heart hid underneath its skin. "Could I ask for your help, please? I'm not used to hauling such large game. Eating for one had never required so much sustenance before."

"She's good," Elowyn whispered to Bermuda, astonished she not only had caught the beast but had landed a single, accurate shot while in pursuit.

"Yes." Bermuda narrowed her eyes. "She certainly is."

Chapter Thirteen

The day flew by faster than any other had in a long time. The crew forgot the last time they had all disembarked from the ship without fear of persecution. Apprehension melted from them in the paradise of Umbriel's island. The captain mentioned using the opportunity to clean the ship's hull of barnacles. The island's safety made it the perfect opportunity but didn't make the awful endeavor any easier. Relief fell over the crew when the sun sank too low to offer suitable lighting, and they could put it off for another day. Instead, they returned to their readied site on the beach to relax in Umbriel's company with the fire and meal she had promised earlier.

Kazuaki continued to check on his ship. He needed to reassure himself it remained safe in the moor.

Umbriel observed his apprehension, and her gentle hand found its way to his shoulder. "She will be fine, Kazuaki. You have my word."

Her touch startled him, and he faced her. For the briefest of moments, he thought her words referred to Bermuda. He had found no opportunity to discuss it at length without the quartermaster's presence. When he realized the Earth Mother spoke of his ship, he nodded. "Right, yes. I suppose she is."

Umbriel lowered her hand and tilted her head. She had grown perceptive in her many years. Not much existed that the Earth Mother didn't feel on an intuitive level. Her eyes gazed deep into his, reflecting nothing but a tender concern and curiosity. The transparency in which she presented herself made the captain uncomfortable. "Kazuaki, I can't help but think you wished to discuss something with me."

The captain cleared his throat and felt the hope in his heart rise at the opportunity for discussion. He looked around. Bermuda stood far off, out of earshot. He had to seize the moment.

As he opened his mouth to speak, he heard Brack shout, "Hot damn! You almost burnt off my eyebrows!"

Iani and Rennington laughed from their seats on a fallen log. Iani clutched a bottle of kerosene, having had doused the wood with too much while Brack had lit the fire. The flames had plumed with such speed, the Rabbit had no time to react as he stumbled backward into the sand.

"I forgot how awful you boys were when you were together," Brack said, though he laughed, still humored by their prank despite being its subject. "Keep it up, and I'll send you back to that bed of yours, Renn."

"I'm never going back to that shithole," he said as he found Elowyn's face in the crowd. "No offense, EP."

Elowyn's eyes were closed as she leaned back in the sand, her features aglow with the gentle warmth of the fire. "None taken." She sifted her fingers through the soft beach beneath her.

Penn busied himself by processing the deer, sectioning certain chunks of meat and removing the skin. Previous culinary challenges had not prepared him for such a task; fortunately, with Umbriel's instruction, he managed to clean the creature with some semblance of success.

Granite played fetch with his dog on the shoreline, but everyone else gathered around the allure of the flames.

Kazuaki shifted in discomfort when Bermuda closed the distance between them, once again within earshot of the captain's voice.

Umbriel smiled with a silent apology at Kazuaki. His change in demeanor told her he wanted to wait for a private moment before conversing. The Earth Mother approached the others and found a seat of her own.

Kazuaki joined with a mild irritation that his opportunity for discussion had to wait once again.

"I'm so pleased to have company," Umbriel addressed the crew with the same warmth and comfort as the fire before them. Her honeyed words held a sense of calm. The Earth Mother possessed an aura of kindness. It had a sedating effect. "Please, tell me, what led you all to a life at sea? Did the sweet song of the siren call you to her waters?"

"Wasn't exactly a siren," Brack interjected with a grin, "and the cap's voice ain't all that sweet, but he called to me, nonetheless!"

"Please, like you wouldn't try to seduce him if he put on a dress," Iani cracked, looking at Umbriel as he thumbed toward the Rabbit. "This fecker only joined the crew so he could bang broads in every division and leave before the sun rose."

"Oi!" Brack threw up his hands, feigning insult. They lingered there for a moment before he dropped them into his lap and smirked. "Nah, he's right on that." He winked at Umbriel.

She blinked at him once and smiled. "Fascinating. And you, Iani? Did you also join to 'bang broads'?"

The younger Platts brother turned a shade of beet red and shook his head. "No, no, no, I would never— I mean, I would, but that's not *why* I joined Kazuaki—"

Rennington doubled over in laughter at Iani's embarrassment and smacked his brother's back. Between laughs, he choked out, "Good gods, Iani, you always been this smooth with women?"

"Rennington and I were footmen in Southern," Iani blurted, desperate to change the subject and shake the mortification away. "We served under Darjal for years."

"Aye." Rennington chuckled again, joining in after he got his amusement under control. "We were damn good at it too, weren't we, brother?"

Iani grinned and nodded. "Damn good." Before long, his cocky expression faded. "*Too* good. We killed many people in the name of Darjal Wessex and his feckin' religion."

Nicholai raised his head, curious. He stared at the two brothers in the light of the fire. They appeared remorseful for their actions, which made little sense to him, as he had witnessed them kill several others and show no regret at all.

Umbriel sounded from her place, pity dripping in her voice. "Oh ... that's unfortunate. And how did you find Kazuaki when you belonged to Southern?"

Rennington stared at the ground; the embers reflected in his eyes as he pulled forward all the memories he had tried to bury long ago. "We just assassinated a small resistance, a group of townsfolk who no longer wished to be forced into church attendance. It was about twenty, twenty-five people. Darjal referred to them as *the sinners*. Many of them left children behind." He paused. His ears burned as he remembered the sounds of those children's shrieks, how they had begged not for their own lives but the lives of their mothers and fathers. The hair on his arms stood on end. The memory chilled him. He looked away, unable to continue.

Iani observed his brother and looked down; shame consumed him. "Darjal did not wish to drain the division's treasury by providing for the orphaned children." The words spewed from him as if they were poison on his tongue. "He ordered us to do away with them."

Nicholai's stomach sank at this revelation—another punch in the gut from an already merciless day. He knew Darjal practiced old-world tactics compared to the other rulers, but never in his life did he imagine the Southern Time Father would order the deaths of children. Nicholai had a hard time adjusting to the knowledge the Time Fathers of old had lived as murderers, but to learn that behavior still existed today made the Southeastern Time Father nauseated. He touched his Chronometer again as it dangled about his chest. It symbolized something once so revered to him. Now he could not picture it without it being covered in the blood of women and children.

Umbriel's gentle gaze landed on the Platts brothers. "Did you do it?"

"No," Rennington spoke up again, feeling guilty that his younger brother had to tell the ugliest part of their tale. "No, we did not pull our triggers, but we watched like feckin' cowards as the other soldiers did. We told them our guns had jammed, to avoid any whispers of impending betrayal. Iani and I left Southern that night and found Elowyn in a small coastal town." He grinned. "She was plundering supplies for the captain. She told us of Kazuaki Hidataka, and we haven't looked back since. Well ... unless we looked back to steal shit from that sorry sonofabitch Darjal."

A wave of commiseration washed over Umbriel as she watched the brothers bathe in old memories of regret. "People tend to forget it's their own choices which dictate how they spend the rest of their lives." She brushed hair out of her eyes. "Though you live in guilt for your past choices, you must rejoice that you made a new one better for your conscience. Not a man or woman among us has not made mistakes, but, as long as you breathe, you have an opportunity to do better. To *be* better. And so you have."

Rennington and Iani looked at Umbriel for some time before they bowed their heads. "Thanks, Umbriel," Rennington whispered then sipped from the mug of alcohol Granite had hauled out from the ship earlier. Her words did not make the weight of their sins disappear, but it lessened the sting.

"It isn't just Southern's military that's gone to shit," Elowyn murmured then took a long drink. She wiped the liquid that had spilled around her lips with her sleeve. "Northern's is just as bad."

"Is it?" Nicholai eyed Elowyn. Northern belonged to Nordjan. Of all the Time Fathers and their divisions—his father included—he thought he knew Nordjan the best. The man possessed a roughness and focused on success, but Nicholai always admired his drive. He didn't want to believe Nordjan was as callous as Darjal Wessex. He already suffered through enough unfortunate revelations today.

Elowyn scowled at Nicholai and spit. "Good men died trying to create Nordjan's vision of efficiency. He ran his footmen to the ground, subcontracting them to perform duties suited to engineers and general laborers just to save time and money. Then the war at the border with Northeastern broke out when Nordjan tried to claim some of Aggi Normandy's territory. He sent waves of overworked, exhausted soldiers into those battles, unfit for anything other than collapsing from the inhuman conditions." Her shoulders tensed with rage. "I couldn't do anything medically for them except administer more adrenaline. They were so brainwashed by him, so terrified to disappoint him, they would not allow themselves rest. We would have lost that war. The quality of Aggi's soldiers was far superior, but we had him beat in numbers and tech. Nordjan sent fleets of flying machines into battle, ornithopters filled with men ordered to fly into the mobs of Northeastern soldiers. They were suicide missions. So many lives lost ..."

Including her two brothers, Nicholai surmised. He remembered the short war between the Northern and Northeastern Division. It had only lasted a week. Nordjan had mentioned it at one of their meetings but did not go into detail, except to claim his victory and condemn Aggi's hostility. Nicholai never investigated it further. He should have. But it had ended as soon as it had begun and had faded from his memory long ago. Nicholai wondered if more existed to that story than he was privy to. There seemed to be more to a lot of things than he was privy to. "To think I've been working under a history of evil this entire time ..."

Kazuaki's eye found Nicholai through the smoke of the fire. He leaned forward, propping his forearm on his leg. "Is that what you believe? Good versus evil? Like life is some gods-damned epic poem or something?"

Nicholai raised his head and stared at the captain. He held surprise Kazuaki had addressed him, since he often ignored Nicholai unless to humiliate him or crush him into a wall. "The Time Fathers' history is one of murder and forceful submissions. Would you not call that *evil*?"

Kazuaki's look flattened. He drew a long, slow drink from his metal flask. He exhaled the sharp taste of the alcohol and set down the container. "Good and evil, they're abstract terms. There is no right or wrong, Nico. Only men and women doing what they think is right. Sometimes it's self-serving. Sometimes it's not. Pray tell, you see a man kill a woman, what's your initial thought?"

Nicholai's face twisted into one of disgust. "That he's a monster or a madman."

"Now, imagine that woman murdered their child. Imagine that woman then tried to murder him. Does it still make him a monster?"

Nicholai fell silent, but, after a moment, he shook his head. "You may justify away your actions for taking another's life, Captain. Forgive me for being unable to arrive at the same level of exoneration."

Umbriel sat up straighter and shifted on her log. "I am a believer in protecting life too, Nico. But I believe what Kazuaki is trying to say is a man does not set out to do evil for evil's sake."

"Precisely." The captain leaned back in his seat. "The sooner you let go of that, the sooner peoples' actions become far clearer to you. Human psychology is a tool. Get into their minds and you'll know everything you need to. Right and wrong, they don't exist. People are predictable. They do what helps them sleep at night. They do what's right for them. Just so happens that what's right for them is sometimes wrong for others."

Nicholai looked appalled. He stood to his feet, fighting the urge to shout. "Can you really sit there, hiding behind your ridiculous rationalizations, telling me it's *okay* for men, women, and children to be murdered simply because it aligns with someone else's vision of utopia? Is that how *you* sleep at night, Captain?" He regarded the crew. "Do you all hide behind the same rationale?"

Kazuaki ground his teeth then bit from the deer leg he clutched in his hand. "I'd choose your next words carefully, Nico, lest you find yourself without a tongue to speak these righteous thoughts of yours."

Umbriel rose from her place on the log; her face was not stern, but her energy projected an unyielding firmness. "Gentlemen, control yourselves. Nico had a difficult day." She extended her hands and lowered them as if it would somehow deescalate the growing contempt. "Let us all calm ourselves, be thankful for this bounty, and carry on with what has been a lovely evening until this moment."

She had a way about her. The Earth Mother's presence soothed the egos of those involved as if by a supernatural force. Nicholai inhaled and closed his eyes before he sat. It did not pay to further engage with the captain. His ideals were older than Nicholai himself. They were from two different worlds crafted with conflicting principles.

Kazuaki glared at Nicholai and took another swig of liquor. He glanced once at Umbriel, swallowed and eased himself into a less defensive position. It did not pay to further engage with the Time Father. His youth filled him with unrealistic ideals. All that, and Time Fathers were arrogant pricks.

Bermuda stared at Elowyn. The quartermaster didn't pay attention to the rage that rose between her captain and the Time Father. She dwelled too much on the medic's words from before, losing herself in them throughout Kazuaki and Nicholai's impassioned conversation. It wasn't until they had calmed down she announced, "I recall a strong dislike for Northern's military too." Her face appeared frenzied as she struggled to bring a memory forward.

Everyone turned to look at her, growing more alarmed with each second she sat in her confusion.

The quartermaster raised panicked eyes to Elowyn at first but shifted them to Kazuaki. "I don't remember why."

"You wouldn't be the first," Bartholomew interrupted, trying to stop Bermuda before she slipped further into her alarm. "None of the division militaries have much love from the public anymore."

The crew stared at her to see if Bartholomew's words would deescalate her impending mental collapse. Memories of the Northern military brought memories of Ty. They all tried to avoid it daily. Mimir's madness knew no limits; the lesser god had removed Ty Aldon's retention from Bermuda's heart, but pieces of him existed still in her brain. The two organs struggled to coexist when the woman's brain recalled Ty Aldon, but her heart made no sense of those memories. It caused her to collapse into an unfortunate state of confusion. It haunted her, how she felt a critical part of her existence but had no context on why it called to her; often, it caused a flustered meltdown. Her brain flooded her body with too many chemicals to handle. It always ended with two or three people holding her down and required sedation. Bartholomew and the rest of the crew wished to avoid it at all costs. A great pain existed, watching a comrade who forgot a huge part of herself struggling to make sense of why a piece of her wasn't there.

Bartholomew's words seemed to do the trick. Bermuda accepted his explanation and settled into her seat, much to everyone's relief.

When the scholar seemed certain she had stabilized, he returned his attention to Umbriel. "You must harbor a dislike for the divisions as well, after what they did to you. I'm not sure how things were six hundred years ago, but their popularity is suffering. For a long time, I thought they existed to serve their people, that politics required sacrifices. I lived in Northwestern, under Vadim Canmore's authority. It wasn't until he destroyed the division's learning institutions to make room for more financially profitable operations that I questioned his motives."

Umbriel tilted her head. She had observed Bartholomew's lust for knowledge in the short time she knew him. "Oh, is that why you left?"

"It is one reason." Bartholomew took a bite from his piece of deer meat. After chewing and swallowing, he eyed the captain with a smirk. "Northwestern possessed a certain level of intolerance for beings who did not conform to traditional expectations. But Kazuaki Hidataka harbors no prejudices. So long as you can swing a dagger and shoot a gun, he'd take you on board no matter what else."

Kazuaki matched Bartholomew's grin, recalling the day he had welcomed the scholar onto the boat. "You do well enough with a weapon, my friend, but your strength rests in your knowledge. I've never had a more skilled navigator." He raised his glass from across the distance in a silent salute.

The scholar raised his glass as well with a grin. "Thank you, Captain."

Umbriel smiled at the pleasant exchange, enamored by her company. Solitude had been good to her, but she delighted in human attendance again.

Granite's dog came from nowhere and pushed his nose into her hands to lick at the juices from the deer meat that still clung to her fingertips.

She laughed and stroked the animal's filthy fur. "And you, Granite? How did you come to find refuge with your companions?"

Granite ripped a chunk of meat off its bone, clearing away the flesh before tossing the remnants to his dog, who abandoned Umbriel and ran off with its prize. He watched as the dog created distance to protect its bone. "I'm wanted for killing my brother in Eastern. Poverty's high there. Not much food, not much housing. Even in adulthood, families all packed into small homes. I found the beast in a garbage pit about seven years back." He shrugged. "I took him home. My brother took him for food. I took his life."

The crew continued to eat. They knew of Granite's checkered past and therefore remained unfazed by the appalling nature of his tale. Nicholai and Umbriel appeared stunned, however, and exchanged questioning glances.

After a long pause and reflection, the Earth Mother shook her head and sat back. "You did what *you* thought was right." The woman gazed in the dog's direction. "He certainly loves you. I could see why you'd want to spare his life."

Granite nodded and continued eating, having never experienced a meal as rich as this one.

"You outdid yourself, Penn," Elowyn complimented the chef to ease the lull in the conversation before she popped a mushroom into her mouth. "And you, Umbriel. Thank you for the main course."

"Penn is, indeed, a talented cook," Umbriel agreed, smiling at the quiet man. "Where did you gain such skill?"

Penn looked up from his plate. His discomfort at having all eyes on him showed. "The home." He shoveled more food into his mouth to save him from further explanation.

"Curious word for *orphanage*." Iani snickered, trying to get a reaction from the chef.

Penn scowled and sank deeper into his spot, though it seemed impossible for him to fall any lower.

Rennington swatted his brother's arm, trying to silence his childish behavior. Though he typically enjoyed Iani's loutishness, he knew Penn harbored a lot of shame at his history.

"Orphanage?" Umbriel's brows rose in curiosity. "Is that not a place where children become wards of their town?"

Penn glared at Iani before he shifted his uncomfortable gaze to Umbriel. "Parents got the black lung. I'd been there since I was about three years old. They put me to work early. I did all the cooking. That's ... where I learned to cook."

Umbriel sensed his anxiety and shifted the energy from one of pity to one of celebration. "What a wonderful chef you've become. Kazuaki is lucky to have you on his staff."

The man, who looked painful in his discomfort moments earlier, cracked a small grin and nodded. "Aye, that he is."

And Penn was lucky to have them. Though he'd never admit it, they were just as much his family as all his peers in the home. He loved those kids like his own brothers and sisters. Penn gifted the crew with the same loyalty. While he was better equipped with a stove than a sword, he would die for any of them at any moment.

"If you'll excuse me"—Revi stood—"I'll be needing to take a piss." He walked away from the campsite and into the woods. He noticed the theme of the evening—one by one, everyone's stories came to light by the fire, brought forth by Umbriel's curiosity. He wasn't eager to share his. A swift exit proved to be the safest escape from having to answer the Earth Mother's questions.

His absence did not deter her. In her state of wonder, Umbriel remained eager to learn about her new visitors. A fascination existed in seeing how much people changed in several hundred years. "I hope he returns soon. I've enjoyed hearing all your tales. There's a magic to what makes a person who they are. Although you've all faced terrible adversities, I find you to be wonderful people."

"Oh, I doubt you'll get a story from Revi," Bartholomew said as he scooped up the empty plates from around the campfire.

"True that, love." Brack shifted to sit closer to Umbriel. "Man's ashamed on account'a having left his pregnant wife and six kids to rot in Western."

"Gods, Brack!" Bartholomew released the handful of plates with a forceful clank. "Do you ever take a feckin' breath to think about what you say before it spews from your mouth?"

"What?" He shrugged, unaffected by Bartholomew's tirade. "This lovely creature wanted to know. You don't expect me to just—"

"I *expect* you to honor Revi's privacy." Bartholomew pointed a stern finger at the man. He noticed the Rabbit edged closer to Umbriel, and the scholar frowned. "*And* I expect you to keep it in your pants."

Brack smirked without apology. "No promises, mate."

Bartholomew rolled his eyes and returned to his seat after condensing everyone's mess into a smaller pile. "It's rude and lacks chivalry."

"So's killing people and stealing their shit," Brack said, "but we do that too."

Revi returned after his exit and sat, happy to see the conversation had shifted into mindless banter and some argument between Brack and Bartholomew. The man took a drink and settled into his surroundings once again, relieved he had avoided having to discuss what actions had led him to the safety of Kazuaki's ship.

"So, we've answered all of your questions, Umbriel." Elowyn slicked her hands through her hair to bask in the strong scent of campfire each strand held. "Now tell us, how did you make this place?" She surveyed the forest filled with towering creations she had never seen before. "There hasn't been a tree around in a long time, from what I know. This place ... it defies all logic."

Umbriel beamed at the inquiry. "Logic has its place in the world." She leaned over to scoop old soil from the hollow log she sat on. "But I find logic often limits the mind to what it already knows." She cupped the dirt in one open palm and held her other hand over the small soil mound. As she raised her arm, the firelight illuminated a tiny green plant. It poked through the soil and reached skyward. It grew, centimeter by centimeter, until two little leaves sprouted from the sides. It twisted upward another couple of inches in seconds. Umbriel lowered her arm, sliding the seedling off her palm and atop the moss-covered log. "Logic gives us the tools, but emotion gives us boundlessness. The only thing that hinders a person is the limits within his or her mind."

The crew watched as the plant grew from nothing. Umbriel earned herself some open-mouthed stares, to which she blushed.

"Is it magic?" Brack dared to ask. He questioned his sanity and whether he had too much to drink. They had witnessed incredible feats before. It came with the territory when hunting legends. But nature had died so long ago; it held an added mysteriousness to it that ignited the Rabbit's curiosity.

"No," Bartholomew answered for Umbriel. He had learned a lot from the book, *The Balance of the Earth Mother*. He stared at Umbriel as he spoke and hoped she would correct him if he misrepresented her. "It's an exchange of energy. All a plant needs to grow is a power source and time. She channels her energy into the seed, with which it can flourish. But you lose the energy you give to the plant, is that correct?"

"Yes." Umbriel nodded. "An Earth Mother can only channel her energy into a plant so far before the needs of the plant outweigh the energy her body possesses." She eyed Nicholai. "It's at that point that time takes over to continue the nurturing process. They are the two most unstoppable forces when combined—nature and time."

Nicholai caught her gaze in his. Something about the way she had said it made the hair on his arms stand. The two shared a long look until Brack interrupted their connection.

"Time can't be too unstoppable, considering Nico shut down Southeastern with the click of a button."

Umbriel's eyes widened, and she gasped. She faced Nicholai after her hands flew to her mouth in surprise. "You stopped time in your division?"

Nicholai winced under the pressure. It seemed the captain made just about everyone privy to his crimes. "I did."

"For how long?"

The Time Father frowned and tried to recall. Since he had left Southeastern, life existed in a blur. Days melted into one another, and he had a hard time keeping track. "Um ... one month, two months? I'm sorry, I don't know exactly."

Umbriel's face assumed a grave tone. "I see." She drew in a quick breath and exhaled it just as fast. "Then she will disintegrate faster than I feared."

Her words were quiet, but Kazuaki heard them.

Nicholai grew uncomfortable. He found it odd to announce his crimes after chastising the crew for their own misdoings. He stood from his spot, feeling the weight of his Chronometer around his neck. It mocked him. "I think I'd like to get some rest."

"For once, Nico speaks sense," Kazuaki confirmed, praising and insulting the Time Father in the same breath. "Let us put this evening to rest. Tomorrow we careen the ship. You'll need all the sleep you can get."

A unanimous groan escaped from the crew. They had avoided it today and knew it awaited them, but the act of careening stood to be long and tedious. No excitement existed in removing barnacles from a hull. But they had been on the run for so long, finding a safe place to careen the ship remained a rare opportunity. They knew it was necessary while they had the chance.

One by one, crew members returned to the cockboats, favoring the comfort of their beds to that of a sandy mattress. Brack and Kazuaki loitered near the campfire. Bartholomew glared at Brack as Granite pushed the cockboat into the deeper waters, his dog swimming circles alongside him.

"Rabbit," Bartholomew said, his tone rough. "You coming?"

Brack waved his hand at Bartholomew to silence him as he leaned closer to Umbriel with a clever smirk. "Not if the lady thinks she needs an extra body to warm her bed."

"You are too sweet. But I needn't your body for warmth, Brack. I've had the forests' warmth to surround me for hundreds of years."

He sat there, slow to accept the rejection. It wasn't until Kazuaki scowled at him he knew it was time to leave. "Too right. I'll be off then." He slipped toward the cockboat. "Treat her well, Cappy!" He winked before he sat beside his comrades.

Kazuaki's expression fell flat. He ignored Brack and turned to Granite. "Go on then. I'll be setting up camp here tonight."

Granite nodded without question and rowed the boat to the ship. He didn't care what the captain did with his free time, though the rest of the crew speculated why Kazuaki stayed behind.

Bermuda watched the captain as the boat carried them to the ship. He never slept off the vessel.

Kazuaki made eye contact with her the entire time until she disappeared from his line of vision into the darkness of the horizon.

Umbriel adjusted the clothing Elowyn had gifted to her. "I apologize that it took so long, Kazuaki. But now, on to your questions."

Kazuaki shifted uneasily on his feet. The captain knew how to demand results, but he did not know how to ask for them. He sighed at the unfamiliarity but did his best to remain gallant. "Forgive me for being straightforward, Umbriel. I've been searching for a solution for so long, and I must know. Your gifts—your healing abilities, in particular—we've read about them, cataloged in an ancient text. You showed the wonders of your abilities this evening. I need to know their limits."

"Oh, Kazuaki, I wouldn't call them healing abilities. It's more so manipulation of the cells and the surrounding tissues—anything that houses its own energy can be influenced to do what you want with the right—"

"Umbriel ..." Kazuaki took her hands into his own. He held them close, ensuring her focus remained on him. "The source matters not. I don't care how it's done, just that it *can* be done."

Umbriel allowed him to collect her hands as she searched his eye for answers. "You're cursed."

"Yes." He checked to be sure the boat was out of sight before he turned back to her. "But my concern does not reside with my troubles. It resides with Bermuda."

Umbriel's expression of disquiet shifted to one of understanding. "Of course." She recalled the short time she had spent with Bermuda and Elowyn in the woods. A supernatural force plagued the quartermaster. "She's incomplete. Her heart holds an absence."

"Aye, stolen by a bastard lesser god named Mimir several years ago."

"Mimir, that unfortunate creature. I knew of him. Condemned to suffer a thousand-and-one lifetimes." Her gaze fell to the floor. "You and I know the difficulties of forcing an existence passed its expiration date, Kazuaki, but none so much as the old-world gods. That poor demon was a creation of prayer. The people wanted a god who granted their desires, so they made one. He served them well. But once mankind discovered technology could answer their prayers for them, they forgot about Mimir. They damned their own creation to loneliness and bound him to his well. While I'm certain he's wronged you, you can scarcely hold him accountable. Mimir is a remnant of a forgotten time. His actions are guided by betrayal. He feels mankind abandoned him, and so he punishes them when they find their way to his well. If he has punished Bermuda, it's only because it's all he knows. He is a lesser god, Kazuaki, supreme and powerful. But anything man has created is susceptible to their flaws."

Kazuaki's jaw clenched. The creature possessed Umbriel's pity and understanding, but the captain did not practice the art of forgiveness. Mimir had wronged him. More critical still, he had wronged Bermuda. "With all due respect, Earth Mother, the circumstances which bred his insolence is none of my concern. I only wish to do away with the damage he's caused to her heart."

Umbriel frowned for the first time since Kazuaki laid eyes on her. "Bermuda's heart suffered long before Mimir placed his poison there. You needn't even be observant to feel it. She wears it like a piece of armor, visible to all who have eyes."

Kazuaki closed his eye and tried to reign in his frustration. He knew it would get him nowhere with this woman. He sighed, his grip on her hand tightening. "Umbriel, this is of vital importance. I would not beg before my crew, but, if you are confident you can help her, ask of me what you will. I would do anything."

The Earth Mother's gaze softened as he surrendered his dignity. She felt his undying love for Bermuda. It compelled her. His sentiments were as tangible as anything she could touch. "I can draw out the poison Mimir left in her heart, but I cannot replace what he took. Once the toxins are gone, it'll be up to her brain to fill in those gaps. Results are not immediate. It'll take time. But, once the poison vanishes, she'll have to face the pain again ... and that is something only she can cure."

Kazuaki breathed a sigh of relief. He squeezed her hand and bowed his head. "Thank you. I'll take whatever hope I can."

The Earth Mother smiled, but it faded. "Kazuaki ..." Umbriel tilted her head to get a better look into his eye. "Mimir influences you as well, doesn't he?"

The captain hesitated. He lowered her hands and released them from his grasp. A look of burden crossed his face. "Yes. Perhaps you would understand more than most. I traded my eye for the ability to die. He granted it to me, I suppose ... in some way." He touched the metal plate that hid beneath the cloth wrapped around his head.

"He misled you."

Kazuaki nodded. "Yes. He could not claim my soul at that moment, as I suspect he wanted. Someone else had beat him to the punch. I didn't know it at the time, but he placed a condition on me. Past choices leading to my immortality made my soul ... heavy. I had to cleanse it, effectively removing my prior curse before he could claim it for himself. He left me with a little gift to make it easier—an eye where my old one used to be. Those who make the unfortunate mistake of looking into it are beseeched with nightmares they think are real. Their misfortune lasts for but an hour before they regain composure, but, each time I unleash darkness onto them, I feel my soul become lighter, as if I burden the onlookers with the nightmares I have endured." Kazuaki narrowed his eye. He felt the rage build inside him at the thought. "Every time I lighten my soul of its nightmares, I walk one step closer to becoming Mimir's property in the afterlife. He did as he said. He gave me the ability to die. But I'll be condemned to spend my afterlife in his well, exchanging one nightmare for another, I suppose. That's why we arranged for this little protection plan." He gestured to the metal plate and patch covering his cursed eye. "If I can't use the eye, I can't lighten the soul. If I can't lighten the soul ..."

"Mimir can't claim it." Umbriel nodded as she understood the severity of the captain's condition. Her expression shifted to one of relevance. "You must have come by your immortality in such a manner, Kazuaki, that even Mimir could not combat your curse's strength."

Kazuaki squared his shoulders, sat on the stump he had made his chair and lowered his arms to his lap. It had been a long time since he had relived the moment of his initial curse. The tale was as unflattering as it was unfortunate. "It is ... unbecoming."

Umbriel sat beside him. "As most curses are."

Kazuaki glanced at the woman, knowing full well she expected an explanation. He took a moment to remember. It had happened so long ago. "The sea always called me, even as a boy. I can't remember where I hailed from ... what my parents' names were ... but I remembered the sea. I reveled in it, in a time when the bounties of the water held value. Every day, I was on the ocean, dragging in fish to sell at the market. Our captain thrived on the income. Greed got the best of him, and, though the sky showed signs of an oncoming storm, he ordered us to sea." He closed his eye as if it helped him remember clearer. "The ship was cast ashore on a small piece of land not far off Panagea but too far to swim. Everyone on board drowned. Everyone but me. I must have sat on those shores for a week, awaiting rescue and drinking rainwater I had collected in leaves. A creature emerged from the waters one day." A frown crossed his face. "I thought I'd gone mad from hunger and dehydration. Half fish, half woman. Everything about her was supernatural. We even spoke the same language. She lamented my misfortune.

I should have honored her presence, should have treated her with kindness."

Umbriel tilted her head as she leaned closer to the captain. "But you did not?"

"No," Kazuaki muttered, hatred in his voice. "I killed her. And I ate her, to survive."

Umbriel did not move. She only listened.

"Cursed with immortality for eating a mermaid. A fitting punishment, I suppose. She tried to help me, but I valued my life over hers, so I was cursed to live more life than any man should ever have to. That's why I started hunting legends and myths. I hoped, in the beginning, I might stumble across another mermaid one day, to beg for their forgiveness. I don't know. I've seen a lot of mythical treasures since that day. But never another mermaid."

Umbriel saw the regret inside him and placed a gentle hand on his arm. "I'm sorry."

"It matters not. I put this burden on myself."

"So, you did." Umbriel slid her hand off the captain's arm and into her lap. "An unnaturally long life is not without its difficulties. Watching loved ones die, knowing you'll never get to accompany them. It's almost unbearable. As is an afterlife with Mimir, I imagine."

Kazuaki craned his neck backward to stargaze. "I imagine the same. He took everything from me, even the fantasy of a peaceful afterlife. Now I don't know what I fear more: dying or living long enough to watch the world die, knowing full well I can't go with it. Most of all, I fear succumbing to one or the other without restoring Bermuda's heart."

"Oh, Kazuaki ..." The Earth Mother smiled and matched his posture, leaning backward to see the sky. "Change takes time. So long as there are no short cuts, I can restore Bermuda's heart ... just as I can restore Panagea."

Her words were so nonchalant, so confident, he almost missed the gravity of her statement. The captain stared at her, intense. "You can?"

"Restoring her heart is only a matter of drawing out Mimir's poison through a series of treatments. Adjusting Bermuda's condition is well within my realm of capability. And Panagea, yes. She is wounded, she is bleeding, but she is not dead. If I could return to her"—Umbriel laid her hands on the soil beneath her—"I am certain I could save her."

Kazuaki blinked, taken aback by her level of certainty. Panagea edged closer to death with each passing day. He did not wish to outlive her. Wandering around a crumbled land of isolation matched the horror of sharing an afterlife with Mimir. If Umbriel could save Panagea, that would be a far better alternative than his other options. But the most glorious sound to the captain's ears was her confession she could assist Bermuda.

With confidence in the Earth Mother's abilities, he took her hand once again and flashed a smile broader than any he issued before. "Umbriel," he said, showcasing all the charisma he could summon, "would you care to join me, in saving the world?"

Chapter Fourteen

The ironclad beamed with a majesty, a commanding symbol of supremacy in Panagea's metal world. Darjal stood in the vessel's shadow as it sat in Southern's harbor. A strong wind rippled the Time Father's hair while he observed the ship from his place on land. Construction should have taken months, if not a year. Dedication fueled by vengeance had built the warship in three short weeks. The men of Southern and surrounding divisions had worked around the clock, day after day, and into the night, with lamplight to aid them.

The undertaking had claimed the lives of many. Most had died from exhaustion and heatstroke. Some men had lost their footing and fell to their deaths off the ship's ledge. Others had suffered when struck by fallen steel beams. The cannons had experienced accidental discharges, taking several lives. The working conditions had caused men to overdose on various drugs used to keep them awake. Darjal thought the sacrifices were necessary. One couldn't gaze upon the monumental metal creation and not feel the deaths weren't in vain. Their creation was far superior to Kazuaki's substandard wooden craft.

Engineers crafted the vessel to be smaller; they wanted to be sure it would still be swift in the waters. The size also helped lessened construction time. It wasted no space, outfitted with enough cannons to claim Kazuaki's ship on all sides.

The Southern division had relinquished much of its metal to outfit the ironclad; many of the footmen's guns had been melted down, leaving them with only their falchions for protection. Businesses ravaged by natural disasters did not receive insurance money to rebuild. Instead, they had been issued IOUs—slips that dictated Darjal had claimed their money as the property of the Southern division. The metal and supplies were all to be used in their efforts to hunt Nicholai and Kazuaki. Darjal had spared no expense. He craved Nicholai Addihein's destruction. The hunger to end his betrayal grew larger every day.

Their best chance at capturing the rouge Time Father and the legendary captain laid with the ironclad. Darjal had drafted more than enough men from the Southern division to operate it. Everything had fallen into place. Only one loose end existed. He needed a captain.

"You wanted to see me, My Lord?" Jernal's voice called from behind Darjal.

The Southern Time Father spun on his heels to face the footman. By order of Darjal, Jernal had returned from his endeavor in Southeastern, where he patrolled the border. The soldier reveled in being useful to his division, but returning to Southern ignited an admitted relief in him. No signs of Nicholai existed in Southeastern since he left, and the soldiers sent to keep watch over the border experienced crippling morale loss. Staring at a piece of land where time stood still damaged their psyche. The edges of Southeastern experienced most of Panagea's natural disasters. Though they hadn't seen a moment of battle, Jernal had lost several men under his command to rockslides and flash flooding. His heart went out to his comrades left behind, but he didn't miss the depressing environment.

"Ah, yes, Jernal." Darjal weaved his fingers together and approached the footman with a devious smirk. "As you can see, the ironclad's complete."

"I see." Jernal regarded the incredible vessel with a noted lack of expression. He had heard it neared completion before he returned to Southern. The wind was thick with the outcries of the indignities suffered by the builders. The soldier had heard about all the lives lost, not just from Darjal's division but those funneled in from neighboring divisions to complete the ship's construction on the Southern Time Father's inhumane schedule. "It's impressive. I understand you had help."

"Not as much as I would have liked. Avital York sent Eastern's most-talented engineers. Vadim Canmore gave us Northwestern's most-brilliant machinists, and Carlo Angevin sent Southwestern's best help."

"It seems like it was enough," Jernal noted as he gazed again at the ship. He knew Darjal dwelled on his obsession. The Southern Time Father had money, power, and focus at his disposal. Even with all that, the soldier still marveled at how fast the builders had constructed the ship. It seemed like an impossible feat.

"It is not the *need* for extra hands that irks me so, Jernal. Their lack of action is an affront. I thought Aggi Normandy would have jumped at the opportunity to earn back trust amongst the Fathers after he started that battle with Northern."

Jernal crossed his arms. To his recollection, it had been Nordjan who initiated the violence, but he didn't correct Darjal. "Yes, I remember the war between Northern and Northeastern."

Darjal scoffed. "I would hardly call a short week of slaughter a *war*—more like a petty squabble between divisions. But it's the principle. Neither Aggi nor Nordjan issued any help from their divisions, claiming to have sent all their extra hands to Southeastern's borders. I thought if anybody would have lent help to the cause it would have been Nordjan, seeing as how Nicholai was his little pet project."

"Perhaps they did not wish to cause further alarm amongst the public. There have been so many riots. I can't imagine it's easy to keep the peace in an entire division when so many people have questions."

"No." Darjal grunted as he straightened his vest collar. "I expected more from Nordjan, but Aggi Normandy's behavior comes as no surprise. He has grown soft in his age. A shame to see a once-powerful man submit to the weaknesses of pity. These people do not need pity, they need leadership. It is the only way they will stay on the path of righteousness."

Jernal cleared his throat and tried to change the subject. "And what of Edvard? Has he been cooperative?"

Darjal's face flattened. "Edvard has been treading the line of bare-minimum effort. It is unlike him. It's normal for him to throw his entire self into his duties. He's performing adequately but has not surpassed my expectations. He, too, claimed to have placed all his extra hands at Southeastern's borders, having no men left to send to Southern's aid. The man expects me to believe he can't lend a hand, because he's busy tending to the public outcries in Western. He should try harder than any of us. All of this is his flesh and blood's fault."

The footman concentrated on his breathing to keep his calm. The more Darjal talked, the more it seemed the process turned into everything Jernal had feared it would. In the beginning, nobody had questioned the motives of the ship's construction. Darjal had issued a public statement saying they had used all of Panagea's land to its greatest potential and needed to commission a vessel to search for other landmass candidates to spread their influence to, but the people were not as blind as Darjal had assumed. Even the least inquisitive of civilians knew something wasn't right about Darjal's statement when they saw how many cannons clung to the vessel.

Waves of public tumults demanding the truth pounded on every Time Father's door across Panagea. Rumors spread like wildfire that Southeastern had been frozen. Letters to families in Southeastern went unanswered to those who lived in neighboring divisions. They noticed the exportation and importation of goods from Southeastern had come to a standstill. The more signs of something wrong, the more the people questioned. Too much time had passed to correct it. Jernal guessed those were the reasons three of the Time Fathers refused to issue assistance. The divisions remained divided on what was more important: dispatching every possible effort to find Nicholai or maintain as much public peace as they could muster.

"In any case, we have every possible need checked off our list. She is ready to sail," Darjal explained, beaming with pride at the speed in which the engineers had fashioned the ship. "There's just one more thing. The ironclad needs a captain."

Jernal followed Darjal's gaze to the ship then returned his focus to the Southern Time Father. He stiffened, apprehensive at what words followed.

"You, Jernal"—Darjal positioned his hands on the man's shoulders and grinned with confidence—"*you* will operate this vessel. Find Nicholai and Kazuaki. The deserters too."

Jernal frowned but corrected his look of disapproval. "My Lord, I do not know the first thing about operating a sea vessel."

Darjal's look of confidence shifted to one of irritation. "I thought you'd be more eager to receive an opportunity to correct your failures in Avadon." His grip on Jernal's shoulder intensified as his frustration mounted.

The footman cleared his throat and tried not to show any signs of discomfort at Darjal's increased grip. "Forgive me, Your Grace." He dug deep to muster saying, "I'm honored to be chosen."

"Good." Darjal released Jernal and stepped backward. "You needn't fear a thing. Just keep the boat afloat and give the men direction. Plenty will be at your disposal. I took a cue from Nordjan on how he handled Northeastern. More men will be at your command than ever before. If we cannot beat Hidataka's crew in skill, we will beat them in numbers."

"With all due respect, My Lord, it is not Hidataka's crew which puts me at unease but the rumored immortality of the captain himself. It's hard to kill a man who cannot die."

The Southern Time Father glowered. Darjal held the knowledge of Kazuaki's condition, but he did not suspect the soldier knew. Jernal was right to be apprehensive. Subduing Kazuaki would be a difficult feat, but Darjal wasn't about to lose his potential captain. "It's likely a myth. I say with certainty that immortality is a ruse. It's more likely that it's either a series of men who have laid claim to the Kazuaki Hidataka namesake over the years or it's a parlor trick. No man can escape death."

Jernal tried to accept Darjal's explanation with poise. "Suppose he *found* the secret to immortality, Lord Wessex?"

Darjal laughed. It was a strange sound. Jernal had never heard it from the Southern Time Father, and, though it was a sound of amusement, he hoped never to hear it again. "No man would be blessed with such a gift." If any man were to find that favor, Darjal Wessex suspected it would belong to a more fitting character—himself.

Jernal lowered his gaze and accepted that as the best answer he would receive from the Southern Time Father. He had witnessed Kazuaki Hidataka's abilities in the basement of Avadon's church. Through the thickness of gunfire smoke, he was certain he had seen the bullets pierce the captain's body more than any human being should have taken without succumbing to his demise. Jernal wanted nothing more than to serve his division, to protect his family and those who lived there, but a second standoff with Kazuaki Hidataka had him apprehensive. Duty called him. He had no other choice. "To where will I be sailing this vessel? Has there been any indication where he'll surface?"

Darjal scowled. "I'm afraid not. The best we surmised is they'll be returning to Panagea at some point. They have stolen many supplies from Southern's escape boat, but the sea cannot sustain them forever. You'll take this time to patrol the waters. Travel counterclockwise around Panagea. Keep close to the coastal towns, and check in often, should I send mail for you. Familiarize yourself with the ship and how to operate it until news comes of where we can intercept them."

It seemed like a sorry plan, though Jernal would never admit it out loud. But he still needed to familiarize himself with seafaring and accepted any extra time he received to do so. "As you wish, My Lord."

"I grant you a short handful of hours with your family. I understand you hadn't seen them since they posted you at Southeastern." Darjal thought his short allowance to be a grand, merciful gesture. "Say your hellos, and say your goodbyes. The ship departs tonight."

The soldier nodded, though Darjal's orders gutted him. He wanted to hug his wife, play with his kids. Those luxuries would be a short pleasure before duty called to him again. He would hug them all extra tight today; if he were to face off again with the captain, he was unsure whether he'd return. With the same level of professionalism he always conducted himself with, Jernal replied, "Yes, My Lord. I'll meet you back here with haste."

Darjal watched as Jernal departed and smoothed his hands through his hair. He returned his attention to the ship. A slow smile crept onto his face. Soon, he would correct this egregious injustice. Favor would shine down upon the great Lord Wessex again. His skin tingled with anticipation. Soon, the blood of the sinners would wash away their indignities, leaving nothing but a clear vision of righteousness for those who bore witness.

AVITAL YORK LOOMED over the ledge of his gothic mansion's balcony, surveying the state of the division sprawled below him. He had grown accustomed to the swells of industrious smoke billowing from the countless factory stacks. They brought promises of advancement in mankind's continuous quest for growth. Avital had lived with that smoke for a long time, finding it more of a symbol than an inconvenience. His division was the most dedicated to the flourishing industries. More water purification plants, factories, automotive advancement industries, and research facilities were packed into each square mile than any other division possessed. It was with some misfortune it created unrivaled pollution. Avital showed its effects on his face like a badge of honor. Wrinkled, nutrient-deprived skin clung to his old skull, but what some found repulsive, he considered a mark of wisdom.

It was not just the industrious smoke that filled his skies. Though the man's face often twisted into a permanent look of displeasure, the new plumes of smoke that infected his division vexed him more—those caused by the flames of arson from his people's violent protests as they demanded answers. Wives and mothers remonstrated, their husbands and sons sent to other divisions with no knowledge of why other than their Time Father had chosen them for a *glorious new undertaking*. None of the men deployed weeks ago returned, and the families were no closer to getting any answers.

Avital's military made any necessary arrests, but his prison overfilled. He made unpopular decisions on how to make room. With some fortune, a large earthquake had formed a deep canyon not far from his hometown. It served as an appropriate place to dump the bodies of the disobedient and the bodies of those who perished in the onslaught of natural disasters. Other towns and cities under his rule were not so lucky; they struggled with places to put their dead, and, from what he heard, the smell caused chaos amongst the public.

The rioters were a nuisance, but they did not bother the Eastern Time Father. He knew the public was often blind to what was best for them in the long term. They attached themselves to individual family members, mourning and acting out should any ill befall them, but they failed to see they paved the way for a better life for future generations. Avital did not need their praise. He was not as egocentric as Darjal Wessex. Knowing in his head and heart he did the right thing was all the praise he needed. It was hard to see in the whips and lashes of flames, the suffocating walls of smoke, and the ear-piercing screams of protest, but what served as a temporary tantrum from his people would soon shift into gracious understanding once Nicholai was dead, Southeastern restarted, and everything returned to normal.

His people lived in contentedness then. Before Nicholai's betrayal.

The eldest Time Father watched from his perch as the small shape of a footman forced a rioter into submission below. It looked as though a group of people were trying to pull a brass statue of Avital York from its pedestal outside his mansion. It was hard to see from this distance and the failing sharpness of his aging eyes, but he remained content to know everything was under control. Mass groups had formed and fell outside his mansion's walls more than once since the public questioned the disappearances of their more educated laborers.

"All in good time," Avital told himself before he disappeared into the pristine haven of his home. A stark contrast to the world that awaited him outside, he slipped into his chair; a cane assisted him as he lowered onto the soft cushion. The Eastern Time Father pulled his hat from his head and removed the breathing device that hid beneath it. He placed it over his face and took a deep inhale, feeling the comforting expanse of oxygen in his lungs through the weaves of tubes and purifiers attached to his hat.

Once satisfied with the oxygen he had consumed, Avital's trembling hands pulled the Chronometer from his pocket. His face reflected in the glass that shimmered atop the metal clock. His ears perked as they heard a large thud and a short rumble. He guessed the people had brought down the statue, though he did not get up to verify it. Their little victories meant nothing in the grand scheme of things. He wound the crown of the Chronometer, ensuring time ran in his realm for another day, as it always did.

"Yes," he said to himself, slipping the Chronometer into his pocket. "All in good time ..."

EDVARD ADDIHEIN'S MENTAL condition deteriorated more with each passing day Nicholai remained unfound. Every letter that arrived in the post stressed his heart. Each second that ticked by until his uneasy fingers pried open the parcel was a second that separated him from the news of his son's assassination. Though every letter he received and opened so far had failed to bear that news, each additional letter that followed soon became that doomed note in his mind.

He stared at the wax-stamped letter in his hands for a long time before he convinced himself to open it. Edvard's eyes hesitated before they focused; the words appeared blurry until the message took shape—just another follow up of other divisions' goings-on. They were all the same—chaos, questions, and uprisings in the more-conflicted divisions.

It seemed Southern and Eastern experienced the brutalist public outcries. They had tried to keep it from the citizens in the beginning, but the growing passage of time made them impatient. Avital and Darjal had paid no need to their peoples' distress and carried on with their efforts to construct the ship and stock it with supplies. Edvard knew it was only a matter of time. Carlo and Vadim would soon follow suit. Patience wore thin regarding Nicholai's capture and the restoration of Southeastern's time.

Vocal disapproval from the public was not the only thing that kept him up at night. The state of Panagea was dreadful and became sorrier with each additional earthquake, sinkhole, wildfire, and volcano eruption. The number of lives lost due to the natural disasters in all Panagea encroached upon a million in the months since Nicholai had abandoned Southeastern.

While most of his people weren't as violent as those in Southern and Eastern, his ability to quell their growing concerns fell short. Edvard had exhausted his resources as far as sending aid to the townships most ravaged by the tragedies. The short supply of medics had forced most towns to organize crash courses in basic first aid, but, even if all the people in Western knew how to clean and bandage a wound, medical supplies still dwindled. There were too many wounded to sustain production, and it only got harder to transport supplies, with Panagea's shows of protest ripping up and destroying the roads. Panagea had suffered the occasional disaster before, and, even though the frequency of those events increased with each passing year, Nicholai's sin in Southeastern had unleashed a new quickness on the crumbling world.

Edvard closed his eyes and placed the letter on the table near a pile of others. The mounting pressure for Edvard to prove his alliance with the Time Fathers grew tiresome. Nightmares plagued him in the evenings, and the nightmares of reality afflicted him in his waking state. He was tired. So tired.

"What have you done, Nicholai?" he asked himself, his voice graveled and fatigued. The man rubbed his eyes and leaned back on a wall for support. How his son had fallen so far was beyond Edvard. It put him in mind of Enita for a moment. Edvard sighed. He wondered what Nicholai was doing. Did Kazuaki treat him well? Had he found the Earth Mother? If he had, did he discover the truth of the past Time Fathers? If so, how did that affect how he saw Edvard and the other Time Fathers?

The Western Time Father felt the weight of every night he didn't sleep. On typical days, he busied himself with the duties required in his division, but thoughts of his son plagued him often. If Edvard thought any less of his son for stopping time in Southeastern, he suspected his son thought the same of him, if he discovered the secrets of the Earth Mother and his title.

The whole ordeal confused Edvard Addihein. A man navigated by his inner sense of what was right, in this case, he found his moral compass struggled with where its true north pointed. It spun round and round in an endless circle as justification and rationalization tried to break the surface of his internal debate. Logic and emotion battled in long stretches, and he was no closer to arriving at what was right than he had been when he had first heard of Nicholai's betrayal.

"Mr. Addihein," a voice called out from the entrance to the Time Father's sanctuary. "A Mr. Olebbows is here to see you, a representative from Western's town of Dygier. He has concerns he'd like to discuss with you. He didn't make an appointment. Should I send him away?"

"That won't be necessary." Edvard adjusted his vest and hat. "I'll make time for him."

The footman nodded and turned to show Edvard where he could find the delegate.

The Western Time Father followed, grateful to have something else to put his focus on. A town representative, regardless of how agitated, was a much kinder alternative than his thoughts as of late.

A FLICKER OF LIGHT from a kerosene lamp cast dancing shadows across Aggi Normandy's face. He sat and assembled the countless documents that covered his tabletop into piles—accounts of how many people had died due to the disasters versus how many had perished during the construction of Darjal's ship, how many towns had suffered catastrophic structural damages, how many people remained homeless. Another pile contained information he had gathered about Southeastern during Nicholai's reign, assessments of the peoples' morale, references made to Nicholai's successes and failures; it was a short pile. Most of the Southeastern Time Father's documents remained stuck in Southeastern. From what Aggi surmised, the people enjoyed Nicholai's rule. He couldn't imagine what had made the man doom all those people to their current fate.

The state of Northeastern reflected that of Western—controlled chaos. The Northeastern division's citizens respected Aggi Normandy and trusted he would not lead them astray, but, with fewer resources available to showcase his support, some people distrusted his ability to maintain their safety. His primary focus remained on his people. It always had been. That reason alone ignited his decision to challenge Nordjan at his border. Having witnessed the negative influence the Northern Time Father had birthed in his division, Aggi wanted nothing more than to shut it down before Nordjan tried to push his questionable tactics on Northeastern. Aggi would not allow his people to suffer the same conditions as those in the Northern division.

They put up a valiant fight. Though they were unsuccessful in changing Nordjan's mind; they kept his influence contained within his borders. Aggi lamented the lives lost and did not consider it a victory for anyone. The Northeastern Time Father suffered a huge blow of confidence by the scenario's outcome; his penchant for ruling was far different from those of the other Time Fathers. All he did, he suspected, was buy himself more time before Nordjan tried to exert his control outside his division again. He suspected that was why he took such a vested interest in Nicholai. Now the Northern Time Father remained the least of his troubles.

Aggi wished he knew what Nicholai's end game was. No other Time Father in history had betrayed their cause to this level. Time had stopped before—but never for this long. Even seasoned men panicked, unaware of the full extent of damage a division frozen in time for this long would create. Though Aggi did not know Nicholai well, the more he learned about his ruling tactics, the more he thought the man aligned with his own ideals. But stopping time ... that was something Aggi never would have done.

The man frowned. His inability to piece the puzzle together increased his frustration. Something was missing from the equation. He could not put his finger on it, but he intended to find the missing piece ... hopefully, *before* they found Nicholai. It was getting harder to keep the peace.

MUCH LIKE THE PANIC in the divisions across Panagea, Nordjan's annoyance grew. He considered himself a fair man. He kept his mind open to new ways of benefitting his division and Panagea since the day he accepted the responsibility of guiding Northern to greatness. But things had progressed outside his realm of control; Nordjan was neither accustomed to it nor appreciative of the challenge.

He never thought Nicholai would have separated himself from Panagea for so long. He surfaced on no shore, no division. His lingering absence caused Nordjan to conclude Kazuaki had sailed to that little island which contained the Earth Mother. Nicholai either had accompanied him by choice or by force, but regardless of the semantics, each action the Time Father committed spat in the face of everything those before him had built. He would not allow things to return to their previous state.

Nordjan was not a stupid man. He predicted this chaos would erupt amongst the people if things drudged on as long as they did. He had tried to avoid it coming to the public's attention for as long as he could, but Avital and Darjal's brazen disinterest in hiding their efforts had spoiled any chance. Much as he wanted to, he couldn't interfere without consequences.

After his attempt to infiltrate Northeastern and enforce his ways of ruling onto them, all the Time Fathers had decided each division would operate to maintain peace amongst the individual rulers. Bitter acceptance tainted Nordjan's memory of the event. He understood keeping the peace amongst the rulers was necessary but had a hard time accepting the other divisions wouldn't utilize his superior ideas and practices. If only they listened, they would see for themselves.

Winter covered the Northern division, but the seasons were irrelevant. A thick blanket of snow always covered his division. Though he stood indoors, Nordjan's breath clouded around his face. The cold of his division penetrated even the strongest wall. The man made a mental note to have someone fetch more coal for the stove. With enough fuel, he could banish the cold for a short while. If only he could banish his thoughts of crippling resentment.

Nordjan had poured a lot of himself into Nicholai when the Time Father had accepted Southeastern. More than Nicholai's father, Nordjan had guided him in hopes he saw the perks of Nordjan's ruling methods. But Nicholai had been slow to adopt Nord-jan's ideals, and Nordjan was not a patient man. It was his impatience that had caused the rift with Northeastern. He hadn't been able to influence Nicholai to conform to his ways of ruling and had thought a more forceful approach would prove effective. But Nordjan couldn't force his ideas on others in another border war; he had lost a lot of men to Aggi Normandy, and, even though it was years ago, gaining recruits proved difficult. Men weren't eager to enlist when Nordjan showcased his desire to solicit war. With Nicholai's actions, having to dispatch men across Southeastern's border, he did not have soldiers to spare. He considered it his biggest blunder as a ruler, only accomplishing unease among his people and a constant stiffness between Northern and Northeastern, but he didn't wish to dwell on the poor results.

The waiting game was the most vexing part. Not one person knew where Nicholai might surface when he returned to Panagea. They all had their speculations, but speculations were all they had, and anything not rooted in logic was a waste of supplies and energy. It was with some luck the next decennial gathering of the Time Fathers approached. They would be one man short, but the remaining divisions needed to choose a new successor when Nicholai's inevitable death occurred.

Nordjan harbored disappointment that his attempt to mold Nicholai had failed. Despite their obvious differences, he had high hopes for the boy. If only he had channeled the energy he put into helping people in the short-term and applied it to long-term solutions, but Nicholai always struggled with pulling the trigger on things that required any amount of discomfort to his people. He had the ability to be a great ruler. Nordjan saw it. But he doomed himself in his failure to make unpopular decisions, regardless of how necessary.

The Northern Time Father frowned. It didn't matter now. Nicholai was not long for the world, and Nordjan did not allow himself to experience any remorse at that fact. Regardless of how much he invested in him, he couldn't mourn a man as traitorous as Nicholai Addihein. He tried not to dwell on it and thought instead about who would be the next successor to the Southeastern division. Each Time Father would nominate a potential candidate at the decennial, and Nordjan wanted to make the best choice; once Nicholai was dead, they'd have a lot of work ahead of them to clean up Panagea, and he needed someone who could do it with the greatest amount of efficiency.

Chapter Fifteen

The island served as a wonderful home during their stay, more accommodating than Panagea had ever been to the outcasts. The food filled their stomachs, clean water replenished their bodies, and the remoteness made the land a haven to careen the ship. They repaired the dry rot, pried off the barnacles and tarred the exterior with the last of the supplies the ship held in its storage. The undertaking stretched across several days, but Kazuaki Hidataka's ship returned to its glory days.

It was unfortunate all good things ended. The time to bid the island farewell had come. At Umbriel's insistence, they prepared to return to Panagea. They needed to make haste. The land ran on borrowed time.

The crew hauled in as many fresh fruits and vegetables as they could, informed by Umbriel to take as many as would fit in the ship; there was no risk of the food rotting with her ability to regenerate the harvest's freshness. Vegetables and fruits weren't the only delicacies they took from her island; to everyone's excitement, fresh meats stocked the galley. Penn delighted at having found a way out of barnacle removal; he kept busy processing animals and prepping them in salts for travel.

Kazuaki stood beside Umbriel as he watched Granite load the last of the supplies onto the cockboat. Everyone else waited on the ship, ready to depart. The captain placed his boot in the small boat, one foot still planted on the watery shores. He offered a hand to

Umbriel to help her into the vessel and noticed she held an uncharacteristic look of sadness. "Umbriel? Everything all right?"

She stared across the land she called home for the last several centuries. Though the Time Fathers of the past had fashioned it to be her incarceration, Umbriel never saw the landmass as a cell. She cared for it in much the same way her companions had cared for Panagea lifetimes ago. It provided for her, kept her safe, and nourished her. She returned the favor. The island had become more than a lump of grass, trees, and rocks. In her isolation, it had become a sentient friend.

The gentle wind blew her hair around her face. "Forgive me, Kazuaki. I'll just ... miss this place."

The captain frowned and let his arm drop. He couldn't relate. The last island he had fallen on had almost killed him until he ate that mermaid, and he did not remember having a ceremonious departure from his hometown. When he had left, he did not know it would be for the last time. Even if he had known, he held no bond with it. Though he always fancied the idea, Kazuaki called no place *home*. "Umbriel, I cannot claim to understand the sadness of leaving a place behind. But I can speak for the thrill of finding a new place to rest your feet in every corner of the world. No matter where you land, you're within the walls of where you belong. The world is full of new places waiting to give you that same feeling."

"Thank you, Kazuaki." She grinned and extended her hand to allow him to help her into the boat. She stole one final glimpse of her island and sighed. "I'm ready."

The captain smiled as she sat on the wobbling wood of the cockboat.

Granite looked to Kazuaki to see if he had any additional commands before departing, but the captain shook his head and motioned forward.

Though she appeared comforted, Kazuaki noticed Umbriel stared at her island the entire time the cockboat rolled toward the ship. As she separated from her element, soon he'd be back in his.

Kazuaki did not burden the crew with any knowledge of his plans while they stayed on Umbriel's island. The benefit of a worry-free environment on land was something they hadn't enjoyed for a long time, and, aside from gathering supplies and careening the ship, he wanted them to be free from any additional concerns. It was the closest they ever got to paradise; it didn't seem fair to deprive them of the opportunity.

The cockboat reached the ship, and the three individuals exited to join the others. Granite hoisted the cockboat into place, and Kazuaki called everyone's attention to the main deck. The time to tell them had come.

"Comrades!" he shouted, his hands behind his back as he paced the deck, making eye contact with every person who fell into line. "We've enjoyed a rejuvenating stay under Umbriel's gracious hosting, but the time to take leave is now. This may come across as unorthodox, but we will not be hunting any myths. We will not be tracking down any legends, and we will not be plundering for any treasures." He gauged the looks of confusion on his crew's faces. He had been trying to think of what to say to them all week. He still wasn't sure he was prepared to say the right thing, but that never stopped Kazuaki before. "I realize there's no way to say this without coming across as dramatic ..." He admitted stopped to stand at the center of the line and straightened his posture, appearing as serious as he ever had before. "We're going to Panagea. We're going to save the world."

A series of hushed whispers came from the crew as they exchanged glances.

Umbriel stood alongside them and remained quiet as they digested what Kazuaki had said.

Nicholai narrowed his eyes, skeptical of the captain's announcement. He had indicated nothing of the sort on the island, though Nicholai had been busy feeling sorry for himself after discovering the unflattering truth of the early Time Fathers. He didn't have much of an opportunity to dive into his book, with the expectations Kazuaki had of him during the ship's careening, but every spare minute he earned went into reading it. The Earth Mothers' slaughter was not mentioned and, to add insult to injury, nothing that would be of any use to help Lilac. But something Kazuaki had said caused him to perk up for the first time in a while. The way the captain spoke filled him with a hint of hope.

After a moment of quieted discussion, Iani stepped forward to separate himself from the rest. "The world, Captain?" He tilted his head, skeptical whether he should make a sarcastic remark or try to understand the gravity of Kazuaki's seriousness. "Seems a bit of an undertaking for just the ten of us."

"Eleven," Umbriel sounded. She smiled as everyone turned to look at her. "I'm certain I can heal Panagea, under the right conditions."

Nicholai's gaze fell as he tried to make mental calculations. He had witnessed Umbriel's ability to grow plants from her own energy. Her place was a paradise, rich with oxygen and food sources, everything Panagea was not. If she could remedy Panagea from what ailed it, if the world was not collapsing, not only would he have more time to save Lilac but they could save the people of Panagea too. "Twelve," he announced, straightening up as he stepped forward. "I'll help in any way I can."

Kazuaki arched a disbelieving brow. He had familiarized himself with Nicholai's energy shift after the revelations he had reached on Umbriel's island. The captain suspected the man would wallow longer in his pity. He did not have much time to dwell on it though, as his comrades fired more questions.

Rennington stepped forward. "With all due respect, why do we suddenly care about Panagea now? She's never cared for any of us. We can't even set foot on her shores without risking our own lives."

"That's not Panagea," Umbriel interjected. "The wrath stems from those who rule. We mustn't punish her for the deeds of those who tread upon her."

"I understand this must come across as confusing," Kazuaki admitted. "You're not wrong. It's dangerous, and the people of Panagea *have* spurned us. But this world is to be my home forever, as I refuse to join Mimir in his afterlife. I will *not* stand by and watch the world die, knowing I cannot go with it. I've resigned myself to my fate, but I will not force it upon any of you. Umbriel and I discussed it. We plan to get her to land and let her regrow Panagea one ecosystem at a time. She is confident once the plants grow large enough, long enough, they can leach out centuries worth of toxins and create a more suitable place to live—less environmental deaths, fewer natural disasters, no more walking around with oxygen injections in your pocket, no more black lung, just ... a better place." Kazuaki trailed off as if lost in his vision. He respected the sea and all it gave him; he'd be damned if anyone told him where he couldn't walk anymore. He cleared his throat to push it from his mind. "We'll meet resistance. The Time Fathers will not appreciate the change, I'm sure, and they'll use their militaries to make that point known." A slow grin spread across his face. "But it sure would be nice to give them one final feck you, wouldn't it?"

Brack matched the captain's grin and stepped forward, clenching his fist. "I'm always happy to stick it to those self-righteous feckers." He faced Nicholai. "I mean, not you."

"It's okay, Brack." Nicholai forced a small smile. He hoped he was nothing like the Time Fathers Brack wished to *stick it to*.

"I want you all to know you keep the option to leave," Kazuaki added. "You've all exceeded my expectations. You've served me well, and you've served me long. Should you wish to take your leave, I will not blame you."

The captain's plans were a far cry from their traditional undertakings. But, behind every bad memory, under each rotten experience, Panagea was their home. Nostalgia crept into their minds, and they pondered what it could be.

Elowyn could challenge the patriarchal society. Bartholomew could initiate a desire for learning again; he could teach the people there was more to life than machines, that knowledge paved the way for a better tomorrow too. Revi could build a better world for the children he had abandoned, even if he was too terrified to return to them. Iani and Rennington could regain their patriotism by fighting for a land they believed in. Granite could invite wilderness back into Panagea and pave the way for a place where animals like the beast could live without fear of death. Penn would follow anywhere. Bad tempered but loyal to a fault, he would never abandon his family. Not when he knew how terrible it felt to be without one. And Brack was just happy to be along for the ride. With the right guidance, it could be the home they all wanted.

Bartholomew placed a hand on the captain's shoulder. "You know I would never leave."

"Nor us." Rennington stole a glimpse of Iani. "It'll be nice to fight for something we believe in for a change, aye, little brother?"

Iani grinned and saluted Kazuaki. "The Platts brothers are here for you, Cap, through and through."

"And me." Elowyn stepped beside her self-appointed brothers with a nod.

"And me," Granite added without flare.

Penn shrugged, feigning half-heartedness, though anyone who understood him well enough knew he'd never abandon his family. "Well, someone's got to feed you."

Revi watched everyone else fall in line and nodded after he found Kazuaki's gaze. He had left too many important people behind. He wouldn't do it again. "Til the bitter end, Captain."

Kazuaki returned the nod and eyed Bermuda, awaiting her reply.

She stared at him with disassociation. "We're not heroes, Captain. Since when are we in the business of saving lives?"

If the captain suffered at all from Bermuda's hesitation, he did not show it. The old Bermuda would have seized the moment and never looked back. But she was not the old Bermuda. Not yet. Though he knew it was pointless, as she had not yet begun her treatments with Umbriel, Kazuaki laid both hands on her shoulders. "We've always been in the business of saving lives, Bermuda. We just always tried to save our own. This ship served as a lifeline to every one of us, cradling us in the waves of the sea, far from the reach of whatever we ran from on land. The lot of us, we've run from prosecution, from the military, from the oppressive thumbs of our division leaders, from ourselves—we've all taken refuge on this ship."

Bermuda stared at the captain, her face blank. She tried to find meaning in his words, but she couldn't. She parted her lips to say something, but nothing came out.

Kazuaki closed his eye for a moment, reveling in the seconds he got to be in proximity to her, even if she didn't understand. He opened his eye again and gave her shoulders a gentle squeeze. "I know. It's out of our realm. You're right, Bermuda, we're not heroes. We're something far better." Kazuaki leaned forward and whispered, "We're *legends*."

Umbriel observed the two as Kazuaki shut out the world around him. He only existed at that moment with Bermuda. She smiled as the other members of the crew grew excited. To be a part of something big, they developed anticipation. She saw it in their eyes.

Bermuda's face lingered a handful of inches from Kazuaki's until she nodded. "All right, Captain. I'm in. You never steered us wrong before."

A brief look of relief washed over the otherwise poised captain's face. Nicholai watched it appear as quickly as it vanished. He stepped backward and let the heat of the moment fall over him. In the last months, he had witnessed these people steal and kill if it suited them without a second thought. But he also had witnessed little moments of redemption—the duty of protection the Platts brothers shared, the love between Granite and his dog, the fierce threads of loyalty which weaved through them all, and now, as he watched this small band of misfits pull together to save Panagea, he thought perhaps he had judged them too soon.

"What division do you plan to start with?" Revi asked.

Kazuaki tore himself from Bermuda and readjusted his focus. "It would be wisest to choose a place where the reigning Time Father is the most ... disliked. If people are hungry for change, it will be easier implementing it."

They all faced Nicholai and awaited his reply. He blinked and shrugged as they had caught him off guard. "Uh, it's a tossup. It would be between Eastern and Southern. Avital York has always put out the lowest collective morale as far back as I can remember, but he also possesses one of the largest militaries. Southern has also boasted low happiness amongst the public, and Darjal's army is impressive but not as heavy as Avital's."

"Eastern or Southern," Kazuaki asked the crew. "Which is it then? It makes no difference."

At once, the Platts brothers shouted, "Southern!"

Kazuaki smirked. "Eager to return to the homeland, boys?"

Rennington scoffed. "The only thing I'm eager to do is turn that place into something worth fighting for."

"And maybe some capital punishment for Darjal Wessex," Iani added with a grin.

Nicholai frowned, about to open his mouth to protest the killings of any reigning leaders, but Umbriel interrupted him. "Then it's decided. I'll plant the seeds that will detoxify Panagea, but she'll need a large-scale reforestation effort in a short amount of time. Nicholai, I'll need you to lend me your abilities if we're to experience success."

"Abilities? I'm sorry, Umbriel, I don't understand what you're talking about."

The Earth Mother tilted her head. "You do not know how to isolate time? For a specific object?"

"Nobody has ever done that, so far as I know." He rubbed the back of his neck. "I've never heard of such a thing. It seems all fantasy."

"Not in the least." She crossed toward Nicholai to bridge the distance between them. "Much like the Earth Mothers, the Time Fathers can give of themselves. We can give our energy to produce and grow the plant, but its growth is limited by the energy we house within ourselves. I could escalate a tree's growth days but never years. Not without time. Not without you."

Nicholai put a hand to his temple and tried to absorb what Umbriel had said. It seemed farfetched for her to know something about Time Fathers that he or any of his predecessors didn't know. "I'm afraid I still wouldn't be of help. Even if what you're saying is true, I don't know how to isolate time. Nobody does. Our Chronometers control our divisions' times, but ... that's it."

Umbriel's expression shifted to one of pity. "It seems in their attempt to make themselves something greater, they lost more than they've gained. No matter, it's simple. You can isolate an object and quicken its time by exchanging years off your life."

"Years off my ..." Nicholai arched a brow. "Sure, sign me up. Let it be known worldwide that I restored plant life in Panagea and perished immediately after."

"Nicholai ..." Umbriel laughed and shook her head. "I would not let you die. Any years you exchange from your life to grow the plants, I will replenish. That's what made Time Fathers and Earth Mothers such great assets to one another."

Nicholai remained skeptical. His boots paced the ship deck. He tried to make sense of things. He did not know how any of the Time Fathers would react to Umbriel's return after she had remained banished for so long. He wasn't even certain if all the existing Time Fathers knew about her. Maybe if *he* didn't know, some others didn't either. Edvard, he hoped at the least, did not know. Then again, whether they knew of her, they knew the earth was crumbling. Nordjan had mentioned it at every meeting with Nicholai; it had been the primary focus of their discussions and their efforts to combat it all had failed. If there was a way Umbriel could reverse the negative effects that ravaged Panagea, wouldn't they give it a shot?

Nicholai inhaled a deep breath before he turned to Umbriel. "How can we be sure this will work? How does planting a few trees fix an entire continent?"

Umbriel smiled. "All good things take time, Nicholai. I do not know the full extent of Panagea's pain, but no matter where I stand, I can feel her. She loves mankind so much she accepted the poisons he pumped into her for centuries, but it's a toxic relationship. It cannot continue forever. We need to restore the balance, lest she withers away, and we're left without land to walk on. With enough plants, we can expel these venoms, repair the ecosystems, and restore her to her former glory. The quest to further technology will be much easier if we have a healthy place to call *home*."

Nicholai tried to get a sense of comfort with her plan of action. When she mentioned furthering technology, he appeared confused. "You still want to continue on their path, even after what they did to you?"

"Of course. I understand the nature of their ambition. If we do not move forward, we remain stagnant—and a stagnant pond is never as useful as a fast-moving stream."

"You harbor no resentments? No bitterness for how they treated you?"

"None." Umbriel craned her neck skyward. "They did what they thought was right. Now I must do what I think is right. I'm not returning to destroy technology. I'm returning to restore the balance. The people of Panagea deserve the best of both worlds."

Nicholai nodded and spied the Chronometer that dangled around his neck. He had wallowed in his bitterness for long enough. His lamenting did nothing positive for Southeastern and it did no good for Lilac. "Right." He straightened his posture. "Well, that's it then. Though I'm sure Darjal will be unforgiving since we destroyed his library and stole his escape boat supplies ..."

"And killed his footmen," Iani interjected.

Kazuaki smirked and looked toward Bartholomew. "I live for the moment I see Darjal's face. Take us to Southern."

The navigator nodded with a confident grin. Newfound resolve filled him to the brim. To go down in history existed as one of Bartholomew's greatest ambitions. Even better that it would be for something honorable. "Right away, Captain. We'll be there in no time."

THE DAY GAVE WAY TO night as the ship rocked closer to Southern's borders. Even with favorable winds pushing the sails along, many days and nights separated them from Panagea's shores.

Bermuda sat on the makeshift bed and scanned all corners of Umbriel's room. Kazuaki gifted it to the Earth Mother for her stay on the ship. It had been Jirin's old room and remained vacant since Bartholomew shot him dead years prior. Paraphernalia still littered the space, but Umbriel whisked through it, gathering the pieces as Bermuda sat.

"How long will this take?" Bermuda asked. She craved the ability to resume her duties.

"Not long." Umbriel placed the bag of trash she had accumulated into a corner of the room. She sat beside Bermuda with a gentle smile. "Sorry to keep you waiting. I find I work better when I'm not surrounded by clutter."

"What exactly will you be doing?" Bermuda eyed Umbriel with apprehension. Kazuaki had been cryptic when he told the quartermaster Umbriel would administer treatments to her. Bermuda didn't question it; though times existed where she second guessed the captain's motives, he never steered her wrong before. He mentioned something about her heart, but her heart felt fine. It pumped blood to all the right places, kept her alive and fulfilled its purpose.

The Earth Mother raised her hands, an aura of calm emanating from her. "It's a detox of sorts. May I touch you?"

Bermuda's brow arched. "It's been a while since anyone ever asked me that. But do what you have to do."

Umbriel smiled again, unbuttoned the top three buttons of Bermuda's clothing and laid her hands on the woman's chest.

The quartermaster stiffened, unprepared for the Earth Mother's touch despite her having gained consent. She tried not to breathe for fear her heaving chest would make Umbriel's palms sink more into her skin. It was a foreign feeling to have another hand on her without clothing in between. The warmth of Umbriel's hand on her caused the quartermaster visible discomfort.

Across from her, Umbriel closed her eyes.

"Are we done yet?" Bermuda murmured.

Umbriel laughed, her eyes still closed. "I'm afraid not. My apologies."

The heat from Umbriel's palms radiated outward. It began like a fire, sweltering and unbearable, but shifted to a comforting temperature that penetrated a shiver in her chest she didn't know existed. The feeling was subtle, but she felt the warmth spread through her torso, into her shoulders and hips, down through her arms and legs. It traveled through her bones and veins until the heat stopped in the tips of her fingers and toes. It was the strangest feeling she ever came to know. The two women sat in silence, Bermuda too tense to move.

Umbriel's shoulders slumped forward, and she sighed. The Earth Mother removed her hands from Bermuda's chest and wiped the hair from her face. Beads of sweat collected around her forehead, and her eyes, which moments ago appeared alive and youthful, now looked drained. "There we are," Umbriel whispered, breathless. She tried to banish her fatigue, but it remained clear. "How do you feel?"

Bermuda frowned and touched the spot on her chest where Umbriel's hands had rested moments before. "The same. Well ... warmer, I guess?"

Umbriel leaned back on the bed, her hands in her lap as she tried to relax. "It's a start."

"I suppose it is," Bermuda replied, though uncertain what it was a start to. She stood and buttoned her shirt. "And we're to do this every day?"

"If it pleases you. I know you're a busy woman, but the more we do it, the faster you'll see results."

Bermuda frowned again but hitched a shoulder in a casual shrug. "If Kazuaki says it'll help ..."

"He cares about you a lot." Umbriel remained on the bed, unable to summon the strength to pull herself off. She had poured much of her energy into Bermuda but still hadn't broken through the pool of toxins Mimir had injected into her heart. It would take time before the quartermaster returned to her true self.

"Yes." Bermuda crossed her arms. "He's a good captain."

Umbriel slid farther up the bed. The look of intrigue outshined the look of struggle as she pulled her tired body forward. "Tell me how you met."

Bermuda hesitated. It had been so long ago, remembering the details proved difficult. "We met at a pub. He rarely set foot on land. It was a chance occurrence. He shrouded himself well. Nobody recognized him, at least not to my knowledge." A smirk tugged at the corner of her mouth—the first time Umbriel witnessed Bermuda attempt a smile since they met. "We got drunk together. Absolutely shitfaced." Her smile grew more recognizable. "We both lamented our situations and eased them with liquor. He balked about having to find new crew members. I deplored that Ty joined the—"

Umbriel tilted her head, concerned. Her distress grew when Bermuda's eyes collected more alarm. "Bermuda?" She summoned fragments of energy to scoot closer to the bed's edge.

Bermuda wildly scanned the room as the emptiness in her brain engulfed her. She remembered the name but not the person it belonged to. Like an apparition that haunted her mind, she tried to place the title to a face but struggled to connect the two. "Joined the ... I ..." She looked to Umbriel, embarrassed and scared. "I don't remember."

"It's okay," Umbriel said in a soothing tone. She redirected to positive things to decrease Bermuda's growing panic. "You two are lucky to have the company of one another. I can tell you and Kazuaki share a deep connection."

Bermuda's heart still thudded. It felt different. It felt alive, as if shocked by lightning. She laid a gentle hand on her chest to steady the beating organ. "Yes ..." She focused on the calm of Umbriel's words to help return her to a controlled state. "Yes, Kazuaki is a dear friend."

Hints of sincerity hid in her once bland, neutral words. Umbriel could tell she had ignited a change. It was slight, but given more time, she was certain she could restore Bermuda to her true self.

A knock at the door caused both women to shift their attention elsewhere. It was for the best, Umbriel surmised. Bermuda teetered on the edge of a meltdown. They needed a distraction. "Come in," Umbriel called out from her place on the bed.

The door crept open several inches, and Nicholai peered into the opening. "Am I interrupting anything?"

"No," Bermuda retorted and cleared her throat. "I'm due back on deck." She gathered her things with haste and pushed passed Nicholai in the doorway. The quartermaster hoped if she exited fast enough, she could run away from the uncomfortable feelings she experienced by replacing them with dutiful tasks.

Nicholai stood back as she left and forced an awkward to Umbriel. "She's never taken a shine to me. I hope I didn't intrude."

"Not at all. We finished her session. And don't be so hard on yourself. I'm sure she'll grow to like you just fine. She's a good person, just struggling to find her way." She patted the bed, a silent offer for him to sit. "Did you have something you wished to ask of me, Nico? Please forgive me. I'm afraid I must take comfort in the bed a little longer."

Nicholai noticed a look of fatigue about the Earth Mother as he sat beside her. "Is everything all right? Do you want me to fetch you something from the galley?"

"No, no." She shook her head with a tired smile. "I'll be all right."

Nicholai nodded. He stared at the door Bermuda had exited. "Are you helping her? To find her way, I mean?"

Umbriel sighed as she followed Nicholai's gaze to the door. "I hope so. Matters of the heart are always the most challenging."

"The heart, you say?" Nicholai chortled. "Forgive me, but she's always come across so ... unemotional. I surmised she was incapable of feeling matters of the heart."

Though she knew Nicholai chose his words in jest, dark humor existed in the truth they contained. "Love is a powerful thing. It can turn even the best of us into monsters. I have experienced its power. That's one of the many reasons I understand Bermuda. She's not a terrible person, just a person who has encountered terrible things."

Nicholai's face softened. He had never considered why Bermuda behaved the way she did. He hadn't thought of why any of these individuals behaved the way they did. Love drove sensible people to the brink of insanity. That much he knew. Rodgie's love for his daughter had made him pull the trigger. Nicholai's love for Lilac had made him freeze Southeastern's time. Though he knew nothing more about Bermuda than he had a moment ago, he felt sheepish for judging her.

"Never mind all that," Umbriel replied when she saw his look of shame. "What can I help you with, Nico?"

The Time Father let his other concerns fall to the back of his mind when she spoke. He resumed his original quest, though he wasn't sure how to approach it. He placed his fingertips on his chin and contemplated the right delivery, but there was no way to discuss it without avoiding embarrassment, so he blurted, "Can you help me learn how to expedite time?"

Umbriel's exhausted eyes lit up. "I can try my best. I learned from a Time Father a long, long time ago. Though I'm unsure if I remember exactly how to go about it, I'm eager to help however I can."

"Did you know him intimately?" Nicholai asked, curious about the relationships she shared with the men who doomed her.

Umbriel blushed and tucked hair behind her ear. "One far more intimately than the others."

"I see." Nervousness tainted Nicholai's faint laughter. "He ... He wasn't one of those who betrayed you, was he?"

"Oh, no," Umbriel replied, wistful as her eyes faded further into the recollections of her past. "He was my knight in shining armor, ruler of the Northern Division." Her blissful smile faded. "He suffered a fate very similar to my companions. When he did not comply with the other divisions' wishes, they ... well ..."

Nicholai lowered his fingers to the mattress. They dug into the soft material, driven by his rising anger to such a degree that his skin whitened. "I'm so sorry, Umbriel." His apology was rough. A rage tainted it that was unfamiliar to the otherwise peaceful man. "You have suffered many atrocities."

"None more than any other." She laid a hand on top of Nicholai's, easing his anger. "We all have demons, Nicholai. Some of us vanquish them with bloodshed and sword, others remain in denial and ignore them altogether. Some even turn into demons themselves, and the rest of us, we coexist with them, acknowledge their presence, learn why they're there, and hope to avoid inviting any more into our circle. Have you decided yet how you will handle yours?"

Nicholai lifted his head. "Excuse me?"

"Your demons. The ones you thought you left behind in Southeastern but still cling to you, like hungry wolves on a wild deer."

The Time Father clenched his jaw, unsure of how to react. His first instinct was to portray his shame for his actions, but the more time separated him from his wrongdoing in Southeastern, the more he came to terms with the consequences of his actions. "I don't know. I'll take them as they come, I suppose."

"I see. Just be sure you're cognizant of which ones you starve and which ones you feed." She laid on the mattress to look at the ceiling. "I do not wish to pressure you, Nico, but you realize you must restart Southeastern at some point. The world operates as a whole design. I'm afraid it cannot function long term if an eighth of it is unmoving. The definition of life is to breathe, to move, to be. You are suffocating an entire portion of the planet."

Umbriel's words were firm, but her delivery was gentle. Nicholai still didn't know what to do with Southeastern. The fate of his division consumed him daily. He collapsed backward on the mattress, staring at the ceiling in silence with Umbriel. After many moments of collected quiet, he said, "You know, they gave you a much better room than they gave me."

The Earth Mother released an exhausted laugh. "You don't say?"

"I mean it. This place is a mansion compared to my little supply closet. I think the captain likes you."

"He's a good man," Umbriel said through tiny giggles. "They all are."

Nicholai's light laughter waned. "Can I ask how you concluded that? These people baffle me. They project humanity for one another but killed so many footmen in Southern. How one can take another's life like that without a shred of remorse, I'm sure I'll never know."

"Death comes easily to those who grew up with it." Umbriel fell deeper into the comfort of the mattress. "If you witness it every day, it feels commonplace. I, too, find it unnecessary. They're just doing what they think is right."

"That's what everyone keeps saying. I can't help but feel *my* way is the right way, though I know different solutions exist to the same problem."

"And there are. They harbor different values on various scales. They have a code of ethics, just as we do. It is not our job to dictate their lives, only to live ours how we see fit. Imposing our values on others does not differ from what the past Time Fathers did to my companions and me. You need to separate yourself from the accountability you feel to change them. A man must wash the blood of his actions from his own hands. You can hand others the soap, but, if they refuse to use it, there's little else you can do."

Her words about death and slaughter were so nonchalant. Nicholai laid there for a moment before he turned on the bed to face the Earth Mother. "I mean no disrespect, Umbriel, but isn't you traversing the seas to restore Panagea an imposition, when you know the Time Fathers do not want such action?"

Umbriel smiled to herself. "My intention isn't to impose. It's restoring Panagea. That is my purpose."

Nicholai propped himself on his elbow. "They'll try to kill you, especially if you're in my company."

"I suppose they will." Her eyes were somewhere far away. "But it's much easier to die if you're doing it for the right reasons."

It took a moment before Nicholai absorbed her words and accepted them. He settled onto the mattress again and stared at the ceiling again. Despite the questionable ethics of his newfound company, he felt relieved they were on his side. They made an incredible team and showed him the fierceness of their camaraderie. It felt good to be a part of something like that. His thoughts drifted to Southeastern, how he had abandoned it and had left those who dwelled within its borders to a cruel fate. He wondered how Kazua-ki would have handled it; despite their differences, he recognized the captain as a capable leader.

Panagea needed the revolution. When he figured out what to do in Southeastern, his people could awaken to a better place, a less hostile world. Not just those in Southeastern, but all of Panagea. It could change everyone's lives, so long as they were open to the transformation. He suspected the people would be; though some divisions boasted higher morale than others, optimism suffered in every division as the world deteriorated further, and the efforts the Time Fathers implemented to improve things were not making it better. In fact, it seemed to worsen.

Nicholai closed his eyes. Umbriel was right, he decided, as he felt the boat sway on a large wave. Some things were worth fighting for. Some things were worth dying for.

Chapter Sixteen

Rennington leaned his crutch against the wall. He remained cautious in his optimism, hoping to abandon the tool there and never look back. With care, the man applied weight to his injured side and smiled with relief when he did not feel much pain. Elowyn had taken great care to ensure it healed well. With a content sigh, he turned to Iani. "She's been a steady companion, but I think I'm ready to break up with her."

"Just as well," Iani replied as he stared at the crutch. "She was too good for you anyway."

Rennington smirked and punched the younger Platts brother's shoulder before he walked past him. His gait was stiff but otherwise normal as they climbed the short steps to the main deck. "What do you think the captain wants to see us about?"

"Not sure, but I hope—" Iani almost ran into Rennington when he halted. "Hey, what's the holdup?"

"I don't know." Rennington stared at the Brack's backside.

The man blocked the entrance to the main deck, oblivious to their presence.

"Hey, Rabbit, the feck you doing?" He poked Brack hard in the side.

Brack startled and faced Iani and Rennington with a look of surprise. His cheeks flushed red, but he recovered well, returning to normalcy. "Thank the gods it's just you two. I was afraid you were Bermuda."

Rennington's brow rose. "I know the quartermaster is rough around the edges since the whole Mimir thing, but we've had years to get used to it. Why are you hiding from her?"

Brack's mouth broke into a slow, devious grin. "Umbriel is sunbathing."

Iani and Rennington tilted their heads and exchanged glances with one another before both brothers struggled to push past the other. They squeezed their bodies through the narrow space of the staircase that connected the main deck to the hull. Limbs flailed as the three men tried to find a good position. Once they settled into a suitable location, they spied on a topless Umbriel as she laid in peace on the deck.

The sun melted upon her flawless skin; her long silver-white hair pooled around her in silk strands. She was free in her state, uninhibited by her brazen nudity.

"She's been like that for a solid ten minutes at least," Brack said without taking his eyes off her.

"Gods-damn," Rennington muttered. He felt perverted for staring, but the sentiment didn't stop himself from gawking. He paused, directing his words to Iani, though he could not break his gaze from Umbriel. "Iani, we should ... uh ... we should ... the captain wanted to see us."

"Shush your face." Iani swatted his brother. "I didn't get a good enough look the last time—"

"A good enough look at what?" Elowyn's voice sounded from behind the three men who turned around in a panic. Their look of guilt was enough for Elowyn Saveign to know she had interrupted something.

"Sorry, gotta go see the captain, EP. No time for chats," Rennington stuttered as he shoved passed Brack and Iani to make a mad dash for the captain's quarters.

"Yeah, yeah, me too." Iani tried to charm his way out of any ill-mannered actions from Elowyn. He stumbled over Brack and ran as fast as his feet could carried him toward his older brother.

Elowyn frowned and placed a hand on her hip. "I don't know what you three were doing"—she climbed passed Brack and rose to the main deck—"but, if you're infected with this much shame, I don't think I want to know." As she reached the top of the stairs, her gaze fell on the naked Umbriel. She blinked, wondering if she was seeing things, before she spun on her heels and glowered at Brack. "Gods, Rabbit, show some chivalry for a damn change!"

"Oi, I'm only human!" He raised his hands. "She's just the way nature intended her to be. Don't go stiflin' her sense of self!"

Elowyn rolled her eyes and crossed the distance to Umbriel. She cast a shadow over the woman as she loomed above her. "Um ... Umbriel?"

The Earth Mother opened one eye and found Elowyn's face as she towered over her. "Oh, hello, Elowyn." She smiled and propped herself up onto her elbows. "Is there something I can help you with?"

"You could put on a shirt, for starters." Elowyn checked the deck for something she could use to cover her.

Umbriel sat upright and pushed her hair from her face. "My apologies, Elowyn. I hope I did not offend you. I'm grateful for the clothing, but I find it's easier to absorb the sun's rays when I'm not hindered by apparel. I'll put something on, if you prefer."

Elowyn pursed her lips and rubbed the back of her neck. She was a medical doctor. A naked body should not have bothered her. But, when she regarded Umbriel in her perceived vulnerable state, Elowyn recalled every instance when a man had made her feel less than she was because she had breasts and a uterus. Elowyn cursed the patriarchal society she lived in. She wanted women to feel empowered, but now she just felt prudish. "Um, no, it's okay. You do what you must do. "It's just, Brack is over there watching you. I figured ... I don't know, I told him to bugger off."

Umbriel laughed and put a hand on her chest. "Thank you for looking out for me, Elowyn. Mr. Joney is a simple man who delights in simple pleasures. I'm certain he's no more ashamed of his actions than I am of mine. His watchful eyes do not bother me. I'm confident in who I am and how I present myself. But it bothers me I've made *you* uncomfortable, and, for that, I apologize."

"No, I, um—" Flustered and more than a little embarrassed, she forced a smile. "You know, I should see if I need to ... medic ... anything. Um, have fun, and ... and make yourself at home." She dashed off, confused how she went from feeling like the savior of Umbriel's purity to the thief of her comfort. But something the Earth Mother had said stuck with her. Though Elowyn perceived her as vulnerable, Umbriel's confidence showcased no weaknesses. The medic found it strangely inspirational. She stored it in the back of her memory, should she ever need it.

Iani and Rennington strode to the captain's quarters after their awkward encounter with Elowyn. Both felt too obstinate to discuss what had happened as they knocked on the door. It felt like their sister had caught them in an unflattering circumstance, and they hoped to never speak of it again.

"Come in," the captain's voice sounded from inside the room.

The two men entered.

"You wanted to see us, Captain?" Rennington closed the door behind him.

Kazuaki narrowed his eye. One of his guests was missing. "Where's Nico?"

Iani shrugged. "We went to get him like you wanted, but he was in the spare parts room. Said he was working on something important and didn't want to put it down."

The captain's face adopted a look of irritation. He turned to the scholar who sat beside him. "Bartholomew, would you fetch Nico and clarify it is a command, not a request?"

Bartholomew nodded as he pulled himself from a pile of parchment on Kazuaki's desk. He laid his glasses on the table and stood. "Yes, Captain."

Kazuaki's gaze flicked to Rennington as Bartholomew exited. He notated his crutch's absence. "Good to see you could say good-bye to that thing." He pointed to where the crutch used to be.

"Ah, yeah." Rennington laughed and flexed his leg for good measure. "Happy to say goodbye too."

"Right." Kazuaki leaned over his desk, weaving his fingers together as he stared at the two men. "We're reviewing the plan of action for when we arrive in Southern. I called you here, because I need your expertise, gentlemen."

"We're here to help however we can, Captain." Rennington and Iani grabbed chairs and slid them over.

Kazuaki stood from his chair, far too consumed with energy to sit. He positioned his hands behind his back as he paced the room. "We already destroyed the catacombs in Avadon. I'd like to finish what we started."

Iani tilted his head. "I'm with you, Captain. I'd love to see all of Darjal's division crumble, but ... Avadon is one of Southern's larger cities. It might be easier to start somewhere ... less aggressive. A smaller town that would put up less resistance, perhaps?"

"It would be easier." Kazuaki stopped pacing to stare out a small window. "But Avadon is right on the coast, and it borders Darjal's hometown. I want that bastard's head on a pike."

Iani shrugged and leaned back in his chair. "Sure, Cap, whatever you decide. We know a few alleys and abandoned industrial plants that don't see the light of day. We could take refuge there while Umbriel does whatever it is she needs to do, at least until we need to take things out into the open."

"Captain ..." Rennington shifted his weight and sat forward, a look of distress on his face. "I'm with you on the whole decapitating Darjal thing, but can you get Nico and Umbriel to go along with that? I mean—"

"Nico couldn't even kill those footmen when Rennington got shot," Iani interrupted. "Renn's right. He's shit with a gun. And Umbriel seems to be a bit of a pacifist herself."

Kazuaki narrowed his eye. "Just leave them to me."

The two brothers exchanged glances and shrugged in unison.

The three sat in silence until Bartholomew returned with Nicholai.

Irritation appeared on the Time Father at the interruption from his project, but he put on a good face as he wiped grease off on his pants. "You wanted to see me, Captain?"

"We're starting our revolution in Avadon. I know you drudged around that town for long enough to find the catacombs that ran beneath the city. I need to know of any other places we might seek refuge long enough for Umbriel to get a head start on her forestation project. She said it would be best to sow a multitude of seeds in secret until we're forced to make our presence known. That will accelerate the detoxification process before we're interrupted by the Southern military."

Nicholai frowned and shook his head. "We should choose somewhere far from Darjal's reach at first. You know, build alliances with disgruntled civilians before we try to infiltrate Avadon again. Starting so close to his hometown is a death sentence."

"Darjal signed his death sentence when he tried to kill Rennington and Iani."

Iani grinned and nudged his brother. "Ah, Captain's gettin' sappy."

"Ha!" Rennington smirked. In a singsong voice, he taunted, "You *love* us."

"Belay that." Kazuaki glared at the two before he turned back to Nicholai. "Do you know another entrance to catacombs that remain? I know you referenced Darjal's paranoia when we first met. I suspect more exist that we didn't destroy."

Nicholai shook his head, his face stern. "Even if I did, I really think Avadon is too dangerous. If anything I've ever heard about Darjal is true, as soon as he knows we're back in Southern, he will unleash his army. That man would summon hellfire to rain from above if he could, and he wouldn't give a damn who got in the way."

Kazuaki huffed. "I'll bring an umbrella."

The Time Father approached the captain. He emphasized his certainty in the tone of his voice. "Kazuaki ... you don't get it. Darjal is a prideful man. He considers himself a god. He will stop at *nothing* until I and, by extension, all of you are dead. I am certain innocent people will perish if they're close enough to his rage."

"This is an uprising, Nico. A revolution. People will die. The sooner you accept that, the easier this will be."

Nicholai inhaled a slow, measured breath. He exhaled and recalled what Umbriel had told him in her quarters. It wasn't his place to impose his beliefs on the captain, but he would not bend his ethics to suit the situation. "I'm not a murderer, Kazuaki. I will not take a life."

"That may win you a popularity contest, Nico, but it won't win you a war."

Nicholai closed his eyes and summoned what little calm he had left, waiting until he knew he could speak without rage tainting his words. "I won't stop you from doing what you think is right. I hope you afford me the same courtesy. Just remember, you're the one who must sleep with those demons at night, not me."

Against everything, the captain chortled. "I appreciate the moral lesson, Nico. But, when you've seen as many nightmares as I have, it's the demons who are the ones too fearful to sleep."

There was no reasoning with him. He was a man cemented in his design. Nicholai sighed and tried to find contentment that, while he could not convince Kazuaki to refrain from killing, he, himself, could stand by his principles. "Additional catacombs run through the city all the way to Darjal's hometown."

"Great. We have options. That'll be all, Nico." Kazuaki motioned toward the door.

The Time Father loitered, perplexed by the short meeting, before starting for the door.

"Nico—"

Nicholai spun on his heels toward the captain.

"What would you do? If you're staring down a barrel and there's a finger on the trigger, what would go through your mind?"

With a pause, Nicholai contemplated. "I would hope he had a terrible aim." With that, he left.

Kazuaki watched him depart then remained focused on the closed door. He faced Rennington and Iani then cracked his knuckles. "Make sure everyone keeps an extra eye on him when we dock, boys, otherwise, that idiot will get himself killed."

THE VISITS WITH UMBRIEL got less awkward with time, but Bermuda still dreaded them. A dull ache seemed present in her chest whenever she entered the Earth Mother's quarters. It had nothing to do with Umbriel. After an initial dislike, Bermuda found her calming presence nice to be around. But, every time she approached the door, a hesitation lingered inside her, weighing her feet to the floorboards. The quartermaster pushed herself forward at her captain's reassurance. If he said it was for her greater good, then it must be. She trusted him with her life.

Bermuda knocked three times and pushed open the door with a forced smile when Umbriel called her inside. "Hello again."

"Come in, Bermuda," Umbriel welcomed her with warmth, as she always did, and sat up straighter with the quartermaster beside her. "How have you been feeling since your last treatment?"

"Um ..." The woman could not make eye contact. She did not wish for her confession to offend the Earth Mother.

"It's okay. You can tell me, even if it's unflattering."

Bermuda cleared her throat and tucked a strand of hair behind her ears. "Well ..." Her face twisted into soft confusion. "I feel ... heavier. Not in a physical sense. When the day ends and I'm about to drift off to sleep, there's just ... this overwhelming weight." She pressed her hand into her sternum. "Right here. Not sharp, like a dagger, just ... an ache. I don't know how to explain it."

Umbriel nodded. "I thought there might be. You've spent years with an emptiness there. I suspect it's normal to feel an uncomfortable pressure as we dispel the toxins."

"Is that what you're doing?" Before, she was content to blindly follow the captain's orders. A base part of her always did and still wished to. But now, as the cobwebs of Mimir's influence dissipated, she grew more curious about what Umbriel was doing to her.

"It is. Is there anything else you'd like to know before I continue?"

"No." Bermuda unbuttoned the top part of her shirt to allow Umbriel access to her chest. She felt guilty for questioning Kazuaki's intentions and wanted to proceed without delay. But, as the Earth Mother laid her hands on her skin, the quartermaster's expression showed a lingering question.

Umbriel inhaled as the familiar warmth spread from her fingertips to Bermuda's skin. "Please don't hold back, Bermuda. I'm here to help. The process will work much better if we clear your mind and your heart."

"My heart." Bermuda frowned, allowing the familiar feeling to flood her body. "I know the captain has my best interest but I must admit, I wished I knew why he insisted on these treatments."

Umbriel ran the energy through her, plucking away the internal sludge of Mimir's doing. She wanted to choose her words with care; matters of the heart were fraught with fragility. "He has your best interest." She tried to concentrate on her words as her body depleted itself. "Kazuaki loves you very much. I loved a man myself once. He always said I breathed life into his soul ..." She smiled at the pleasant memory.

A nervous laugh escaped Bermuda as she tried to hold her body still. "It's nothing like that." The quartermaster didn't know why the topic made her stomach rise, but she pushed through it. "The captain puts on a front, but he's dutiful to every one of us. I'm sure his actions would be the same whether it was me sitting here or Revi or Elowyn ..."

Umbriel's lips shifted into a sly smirk. Kazuaki's feelings were transparent to the Earth Mother, but it seemed Bermuda wore a convenient pair of blinders. Whether her denial existed before or after Mimir's curse, she did not know. "That's a shame. It's wonderful to love and be loved in return. Have you ever felt that way about anyone?"

Bermuda quirked a brow and became more aware of her beating heart. It felt stronger now somehow, more present. With it came memories of a face, a man. She narrowed her eyes and tried to pull more details forward. "I ..." Her quickened pulse distracted her. "I think I did. Once."

Umbriel felt the panic rise in Bermuda. It reflected what happened before. Her anxiety correlated to her inability to fit the pieces of her mental puzzle together. To comfort her and provide reprieve in the form of a distraction, Umbriel shared one of her memories. "My A'ronn, he would whisper sweet nothings as we laid our heads in the grasses, staring at the night sky." She grew weaker the more she poured into Bermuda, but she carried on, determined to make more progress. "He was a dear man, my love. A vision, he called me. He had a way of weaving words. Poetry comes easy to those in love."

Bermuda nodded as her eyebrows knitted together. "A vision. Gods, that sounds so familiar." She allowed the thought to pass. In a moment of clarity that struck her like lightning, she faced the Earth Mother. "Ty. His name ... it was Ty Aldon."

"Your lover?" Umbriel pretended Bermuda hadn't mentioned him once before as she tried to maintain an air of tranquility. Bermuda had made great progress, but the endeavor had taken its toll on the Earth Mother. She tried to steady her trembling hands as Bermuda called forth more memories.

"Ty." She repeated it as if the name itself helped bring her lucidity. "He worked for the Northern military. He wanted me to join him, but they only allowed men to enlist as soldiers. I ... I could only join as a medic. But I couldn't. They wouldn't allow me to undergo the training process, because I had a history of petty crimes."

Umbriel's hands quivered more. The weakness moved up her forearms and shoulders, but she steeled herself in position and remained calm. "I'm so sorry to hear that. What happened?"

Bermuda's face fell, too deep in her flooding memories to register Umbriel's tremors. "He enlisted anyway. He said he wanted to help people. That man was always trying to help people. I was so mad at him for joining without me. That's why I was at the pub that night when Captain Hidataka arrived ..."

Umbriel winced, and her arms collapsed into her lap. She hunched over, trying her best not to show evidence of distress, though it remained obvious with her labored breathing. "I'm so sorry, Bermuda," she said again as she tried to catch her breath. "You were doing so well ..."

Bermuda's eyes widened as she reached with her hand and stump to help Umbriel sit upright. "Gods, are you okay?"

"Yes, yes." Umbriel waved her hand to lower the dramatic overtone. "What happened?" she asked again, clammy under Bermuda's hand as she forced herself to sit taller. "To you and Ty? It must have been painful."

The quartermaster turned away, lost in thought again. She surveyed the handless limb she used to prop up Umbriel and jumped to her feet. The last revelation hit her. She opened her mouth to speak, but no words left. Ty. The military. Her anger had steered her to the pub after Ty had enlisted to stand with Northern. She had felt abandoned by him. She had been furious, hurt. Her pain and several rounds of shots had driven her to tell Ty she would be joining Kazuaki Hidataka on his ship, hunting myths and legends with other outcasts Pangea had shunned. He had been heartbroken but had said he would wait for her. After months at sea with her temper cooled and her heart aching for the man she loved, she had returned to Northern to find him. "He died," she uttered, her eyes shining with tears that went unshed for years, though none spilled down her cheeks. "They told me he died in the battle of Northern and Northeastern."

Umbriel's expression underneath strands of hair that stuck to her sweat-soaked face fell to one of sadness and compassion. Bermuda could not forgive herself, Umbriel surmised. Too often, the crushing weight of heartache was heavier if the individual felt responsible for it. "I'm so sorry, Bermuda. I know it's hard. But, my dear, Mimir cannot take away that pain for you. He can only numb you to it."

The hair on Bermuda's arms stood on end as she laid a hand over her chest, over her heart. Her agony had lingered with her for months. Years. There was no forgiveness, not for what she'd done. Her gaze fell to where her hand used to be. She remembered now why it was missing. She had traded it away to be free from the crippling pain that consumed her again.

The quartermaster shot a look of daggers at Umbriel as everything fell into place. "I was content with that bargain." Her fist clenched so tight her knuckles whitened. The heartache had returned in full force. It reminded her with every beat why she had given her hand to be rid of it. With everything illuminated in her once-clouded mind, she felt a sense of betrayal. She was back to where she had started, doomed to live the rest of her existence with this horrid feeling. "Why would Kazuaki ask you to rid me of Mimir's medicine?"

"That was not medicine, Bermuda. That was an illusion. Life hands all of us pieces of darkness. You need to carry them with you to grow stronger. Carry them until you realize the darkness was a gift, giving you more strength than a life of ease ever could."

"I *have* carried it! For years, I've carried it!"

"No. You set it down. You sat with it and grew weak with it. But you're one of the strongest women I've ever encountered, Bermuda. If anyone can come back from this, it's you."

"*Puh-leese!*" Bermuda scoffed and turned away. Though her anger dissipated in Umbriel's supernatural presence, she still seethed. "You barely know me."

Umbriel scooted across the bed and propped her back and head against the wall. She sighed, exhausted, but still a smile found its way to her tired face as she closed her eyes. "I know enough. I'm certain Ty was a great person, and it's a crime you lost him. But you're with great people now, and they felt it was a crime to lose you too. That's why Kazuaki asked me to help."

Bermuda let the Earth Mother's words envelope her. They tempered her fire, but feelings of hurt still lingered. She saw Umbriel suffered from fatigue and cleared her throat. She did not wish to engage the weak woman further. "I ... I'll leave you be."

"Bermuda," Umbriel called from the bed as Bermuda approached the door.

The quartermaster cast a glance over her shoulder.

Umbriel's eyes searched the woman across from her. "What happened with Ty was an unfortunate accident. You did nothing wrong."

She nodded once, though Umbriel suspected she didn't believe it. Then she slipped out the door.

Chapter Seventeen

S he knew where to find him. After all the time they had spent together, Bermuda predicted the captain's movements with a level of accuracy unmatched by anybody else on the ship. It didn't take a scholar to know where he'd be. Ever since they left Umbriel's island, Kazuaki lived in his quarters, obsessing over battle strategies. Bermuda allowed none of what the Earth Mother had said to slow her brisk pace to his room. Without knocking, she flung open the door, a gust of wind blew her hair as she stood tall in the entryway.

Unaccustomed to such a barbaric intrusion, instinct propelled Kazuaki to reach for his weapon. When he realized who had barged in, his hand dropped, and a look of confusion swept over him.

"Bermuda?" Bartholomew's chair screeched as it slid on the floorboards beneath. "Are you all right?"

"Leave us be." Her words dripped venom, her stare fire.

The navigator cleared his throat and stole a quick glimpse of the captain. Kazuaki looked perplexed. Bartholomew granted him an apologetic look as he collected a few papers from the desk and stood. "As you wish, Quartermaster." He saluted a silent good-luck gesture to Kazuaki and eased past the woman on his way out the door.

Kazuaki, still paralyzed by his incomprehension, watched Bartholomew leave before he shifted his attention to Bermuda and rose. "What's the matter?"

"Why?" Fresh betrayal shook her voice.

Kazuaki blinked. At first, more confusion fell over him. It didn't last long until a strange excitement replaced it. Malice infected her words, but it possessed emotion—something he had not heard from her since before Mimir. "Why, what?"

"Why did you tell her to undo what Mimir did? I gave my *hand* to destroy that pain, and here you are, instructing her to put it right back in my chest. Why would you do that?"

Kazuaki Hidataka was a stoic man, but his body still felt the chilling thrill of paralysis when her words poured from her. His heart skipped. With pure ecstatic excitement, he whispered, "Then it worked?"

Bermuda scowled. "Your damn right it did. I can't believe you, Kazuaki. I thought we were ..." She shook her head. She never knew what she and the captain were. A connection existed between the two, she couldn't deny that, but whatever they were, she didn't expect this from him.

"Bermuda." He stepped toward. "I did it for your own good."

"No!" Her cheeks flushed red with anger, she clenched her jaw and her frustration mounted. "You were selfish." Her fist, clasped at her sides, shook as she flooded with emotions unfelt for years. It was hard to contain them all.

Kazuaki took another cautious step before he lowered his voice. "Bermuda ..."

"I *never* wanted you to relinquish your immortality, knowing every bullet from then on that pierced your flesh could be the last. But I cared about you too much to deprive you of something you wanted. Why would you take away what *I* wanted most?"

The captain stopped. He opened his mouth to speak but couldn't find the right words. He panned the room as he searched for the correct thing to say, but he could think of nothing poetic, nothing that would paint him as anything other than what she labeled him—selfish. He was. He knew it and couldn't deny it. After a moment of collection, Kazuaki forced himself to look at her again. The man took a deep, steady breath, feeling the emptiness in his lungs as he exhaled. "Because I missed you."

Bermuda stood before him, unmoving. His confession was simple but powerful. Never did her captain appear as exposed as he did now, a raw nerve standing before her in brutal honesty. "I didn't go anywhere."

Kazuaki tilted his head a fraction of an inch. "Yes, you did. You went far, far from here, somewhere I couldn't reach you. Bermuda, I know my actions troubled you. I know you're distraught and understandably livid. But I am *so* glad you're back."

Bermuda searched his eye, an eye that often held nothing but a rigid duty inside. She saw his sincerity, his alleviation. It softened her. "There's nowhere else I belong."

Kazuaki grinned and wrapped his arms around her, his tall frame engulfing the petite woman. Years of guilt melted away. If Mimir took him now, he could die happy, vindicated. She had returned to her true self, to her home. He closed his eye, and her hair's scent filled him, salty from the ocean winds. Had unadulterated jubilance not overwhelmed him, he would have found temptation in her proximity, but Kazuaki remained far too lost in the luxury of the moment to pay the tension any mind.

Bermuda allowed him to scoop her up. She stood on the tips of her toes to rest her chin on his shoulder. The warmth of his arms consumed her, and the quartermaster felt her tensed muscles relax. "I'm still mad at you," she said, her voice muffled as he squeezed her.

Kazuaki did not let go. He eased his ambitious grip but still craved her closeness too much to release her. "Stay as mad as you like." He could handle her wrath. So long as she experienced emotion, he would take her however he could get her.

The two remained embraced in the captain's quarters. The sun shined through the small glass windows. It illuminated particles of dust floating in the surrounding air. Kazuaki surrendered himself to the moment for as long as time allowed him. But, with each second that ticked by, his brain beckoned him closer to crossing the boundaries of his unthinkable feelings. Her proximity was too alluring. A nervous grin swept across his face. "You know, I don't think we've ever—"

"We haven't." Bermuda chuckled nervously as she pulled herself from the embrace. The pair had known one another for many years, but never did they find their bodies pressed for so long against each other. They would take a bullet for one another, but neither the captain nor Bermuda ever considered themselves the embracing type. "Chalk it up to the moment."

Kazuaki's hands lingered on her shoulders after she pulled herself from his arms. "I hope you forgive me. I know you wanted to vanquish that pain. But he didn't just take your heart. He took all of you. It was selfish of me, yes. But know I would have done anything to get you back."

"It's okay." Feelings of sheepishness crept into her bones. She wanted to be numb to the demons that haunted her, but she couldn't blame her comrade. "In all honesty, I'm sure I would have done the same for you."

"Well ..." Kazuaki sighed, a content smile still plastered on his face. "It's good to have you back." He blinked, more aware of the time in which his hands lingered on her person. With the heat of the moment passed, he forced himself to withdraw his touch. His palms felt cold without her skin against them. The captain tore his gaze from her as he edged toward his desk. "Bartholomew and I were just ... reviewing some things. Tactics and strategies."

"Yes, that's right." She followed him to the table and scanned the papers. "I almost forgot we're in the business of saving the world now. It's odd, Captain, to want to help Panagea. I don't think she or those who rule over her would grant us the same favor."

Kazuaki smirked. "So dramatic. It feels less odd if you shift your thoughts. We're not saving the world so much as we're toppling an empire and rebuilding it from scratch." He shuffled the papers and stacked them in a corner. "I like to focus on the empire-toppling part."

Despite herself, Bermuda laughed. But her jovial nature was short-lived, and her face grew serious. "I know you're doing what you think is best, Kazuaki, or you would not be doing it. But this whole thing ... it's more dangerous than any other challenge we've taken. The entire crew is risking their lives for this. What are we gaining from it?"

He stared at the notes he and Bartholomew took, the strategies they laid out. He knew it was an incredible undertaking. It was bold to think a handful of people could undo centuries of damage and alter thought processes and social and cultural constructs that had existed for too long.

Kazuaki feared outliving a dying world. But he would never admit it. Selfishness was not his only motivator though. "They condemned us to the sea for a long time, Bermuda. I love the ocean, but even the boundless waters have started feeling small after so many years. We know if we set foot in Panagea, our past crimes will carry us to the grave or a prison cell. I'm done with it. I want all of you to walk wherever your feet will carry you. Panagea wants the ocean to be our prison, but I want my freedom back. And yours. Elowyn's. Rennington's and Iani's. Brack's, Bartholomew's, Penn's, Revi's Granite's. Even his damned dog. I'd risk it all and more for every one of you."

Bermuda eyed the faux-leather cover around Kazuaki's socket. Through Umbriel's abilities, she was free from Mimir, but she knew his fate remained bound to the creature. "I wish you wouldn't. Risk it all, I mean. I let what happened with Ty wound me greatly, Captain, but ..." She looked away, embarrassed. "Kazuaki, if you died, it would kill me."

Her admission lifted him. He felt every word she breathed course through his veins. But her pain made him frown. "Bermuda, look at me."

She raised her head but refused to make eye contact, too put off by the weakness she showed. It burned her. Bermuda, a woman who slaughtered many men in their onshore excursions, stood tough as diamonds in every way. But, with matters of the heart, she was powerless.

Kazuaki leaned forward until he found her gaze. Though her expression harbored disappointment, he smiled. "I'm not going anywhere."

One corner of her lips pulled into half of a smile. "Promise?"

"Cross my heart and hope to die."

SINCE THE DEPARTURE from Umbriel's island, the moments spent in the dining hall shifted into something greater than they were before. At first, Penn was inexperienced with the fresh ingredients; the only access to fresh food he had before was the occasional non-mutated fish plucked from the ocean. But the cook was a fast learner. Bartholomew had dredged up old books from his collection that lent themselves to Penn's learning experience. Though the literature didn't have a strong focus on cooking, they detailed the structural integrity of plants, vegetables, and meats, giving him a vague idea of how much heat they could handle before they broke down.

Umbriel had also been an incredible resource, though her knowledge remained limited to raw foods and how long to cook various meats over an open flame. She did not understand luxuries, like pans and utensils, but the two learned together. They had a lot of time to kill as the ship soldiered toward the Southern division.

Revi, Granite, Brack, Elowyn, Bartholomew, and the Platts brothers all found spots at the wooden table while Penn put the finishing touches on the meal in the galley. They each held servings of various spirits in their hands, taking relief in their drinks as they relaxed from another long day. The room filled with soft chatter until Brack approached the topic on everyone's thoughts.

"So, how about this revolution, eh?" He tried to gauge his companions' reactions.

Daily ship maintenance kept them all busy, with little time to discuss their futures. The concept remained foreign for them all. The only similarity the inevitable uprising shared with their traditional activities was that it would piss off the Time Fathers and the affluent citizens of Panagea. Though they hadn't made enemies with everyone, some detested Kazuaki Hidataka and his band of outcasts.

Bartholomew sipped from his drink, having sought solace in the dining hall after Bermuda had booted him from the captain's quarters. He looked contemplative. After a while, he lifted his head and recited, "A world may suffer because of the evil that dwells within it, but it suffers far greater when its people do nothing to change it."

Rennington bobbed his head as Bartholomew's sage advice fell over the crowd. He stared at his drink as he swirled it in his hands. "Makes no difference." He watched the brown liquid settle. "Even after we left Southern, we never stopped being soldiers. We signed on a long time ago to fight the good fight. At least this time, we'll actually be doing it." He turned to Iani. "Am I right?"

Iani grinned and clinked his glass with Rennington's. "Through and through, big brother." His smile faded as he lost himself in thought. "Have to be honest though. I always wished to fight *for*

Southern and not against it. I know I shit talk the place a lot, but we were born there. It was home. I loved it." He paused; his brows knitted together as he took a big swig of his beverage. He exhaled when the burn of the alcohol seared his tongue. "I mean, I loved what it used to be."

"It could be that again." Elowyn rested her cheek in her palm. "All the divisions could, as Bartholomew said." She noticed her reflection staring back at her in her glass of liquor. When she had been a young medic freshly indoctrinated into the Northern military, she had possessed a passion for helping people. Mankind's general abrasiveness and the battle against Northeastern had beaten the passion from her. But, somewhere deep inside, that dormant feeling remained alive. "It's kind of exciting to think about it, to help rebuild a world into something better."

Granite nodded and watched his mongrel tire itself with merciless running about the main deck. The beast curled into a tight ball and slumbered at its master's feet. It would be nice, he thought, to encourage a place where animals roamed free again.

Revi shrugged. "It'll be nice to do something you can be proud of, for a change ..." Though he directed his words at them, they knew he spoke of himself. A chaotic, last-ditch attempt at doing the right thing was what Revi Houton needed. After a series of bad decisions and abandoning his wife and kids, he yearned for something to clear his conscience, something that brought him one step closer to personal redemption. Perhaps, if he succeeded, wherever the Houton children were, he could make a better world for them. He'd like for them to see good days. Gods knew they didn't have many when he and Arabella had lived together, and he couldn't imagine they got much better after he had left. They deserved a shot at something greater than they'd known.

"Oi, I was always proud of what we did," Brack said at Revi. "We found a shit-ton of legends under Captain Hidataka's guidance, eh?" His face beamed with pride at the memories, and he laughed. "You all recall that time we found Pandora's jar, and Captain told us not to open it?"

Iani joined the laughter, so amused he almost spit out his drink. "And then you feckin' dropped it, and it shattered to pieces. Yes, I remember!"

Even Elowyn chuckled. "That's right. He didn't want us to open it, because it"—she curled her fingers into air quotes—"'contained evils untold of.'"

A small smirk crossed Revi's lips. "I thought he was going to kill you, Rabbit. You all remember what he said after you dropped it?"

Rennington stood from his chair and mimicked Kazuaki with a baritone voice. "Ah well, the world's already full of evil. I suppose a little more won't hurt it."

"Almost shit myself." Brack wiped a tear from his eye as he busted a gut. "I don't know what put him in a good humor, but I dodged a bullet that night, I did."

Even Granite harbored a small smirk.

The laughter diminished as the seven members sat at the table. Many more memories existed similar to Pandora's jar—good ones, unpleasant ones, and everything in between. They had been with each other through more blood, sweat, and tears than they remembered. Though injuries slowed them or death separated them or disappointments arose when certain myths and legends didn't prove to be truthful, they always counted on one another to be there. And, at the forefront of each exploit was Captain Kazuaki Hidataka, leading them every step of the way.

"I'd take a bullet for that guy," Iani said, breaking the silence as he leaned back in his chair.

Rennington scoffed and smirked. "Then he'd call you an idiot, seeing as how he can't feckin' die." Though his words were sarcastic, he gave a short nod afterward. "But I know what you mean."

"He *could* die," Elowyn corrected Rennington, "if he uses that eye of his."

The crew fell quiet again. Imagining a world without the captain was strange. They all had grown accustomed to his immortality, but Elowyn was right—he could die. It was why he erred on the side of caution and had put the plate over his socket. They knew the captain lamented having his chance for a noble death taken away, but they also knew he lamented spending his afterlife in Mimir's well more.

"Captain's been good to us," Granite said, surprising everyone at the table, as he always coursed through an entire day without saying more than three words. The behemoth raised his glass for a formal salute. "To Kazuaki."

Everyone nodded and raised their glasses. "To Kazuaki," they repeated in unison before each threw their respective drinks into the backs of their throats. The empty glasses were all turned upside down and placed on the table as Umbriel sauntered into the room.

"Good evening all." She smiled, sitting beside Granite. "How has the day treated you?"

A quick collection of pleasantries filtered through the group. Though rare, everyone took an immediate liking to Umbriel.

Kazuaki and Bermuda entered the room after the Earth Mother arrived.

Umbriel found Bermuda's eyes across the room, curious if the quartermaster remained angry with her for ridding her heart of Mimir's influence.

Bermuda caught her looking and flashed a small, forgiving smile. It was enough for Umbriel to relax her shoulders as she melted into her chair and inhaled the scents wafting from the galley into the dining hall. "I'm looking forward to what Penn has cooking in there."

The group shot their heads toward her, a look of absolute puzzlement on their faces. Emotion dotted her voice, and pleasantness hung in her words—something none of them had heard for years—but, in their skepticism, they said nothing.

Bermuda noticed as it was obvious. She rubbed the back of her neck, an awkward feeling creeping through her. "Gods, have I been all that bad that it's weird to compliment the chef?"

"Umbriel's kindness and skill have rid our quartermaster of Mimir's poison." Kazuaki pulled two dusty and rare bottles from the deep interior pockets of his long jacket he had smuggled from his personal stash. "I dare say it's worthy of a celebration."

The crew sounded, delirious in their merriment as they stood from their chairs to pat Bermuda's back.

She felt vulnerable being the center of attention but handled it well with pleasant nods and gratitude. "Thank you, everyone. You have my apologies, if I treated any of you poorly in my state."

"Just glad to have you back." Elowyn held out her glass as Kazuaki popped the cork from one of his bottles. "It's been too long."

The captain poured a glass for everyone and set one aside for Penn. As he performed his rounds about the table, he paused. Someone was missing. A small look of dissatisfaction appeared on his face. "Where's Nico?"

"Probably still working on whatever the feck he was doing in the storage room," Rennington said as he returned to his seat to sample the beverage.

Penn pushed open the swinging door with his backside and turned to unveil the first of many platters he had prepared. The stewed meat's scent made everyone's mouths water as he placed the tray on the table. He looked proud as he wiped the sweat from his brow with the back of his wrist. "Take a bowl." He motioned to the empty vessels on the serving platter. "I got sautéed veg coming out too and some vanilla bean-soaked apples with nuts for after."

As everyone lusted over the food, Nicholai crept into the room. He went unnoticed as the boisterous group celebrated Bermuda's freedom and Penn's meal. It wasn't until after everyone helped themselves to a heaping bowl of Penn's stew did he clear his throat to get their attention.

Kazuaki narrowed his eye. He noticed the Time Father cradled something in his hands. "What do you have there, Nico?"

"Right, well." Nicholai lifted it to allow everyone a better view. "I, uh ... found some parts in the storage room. I built a few working machines in my day in Southeastern, and ... I noticed you had a lot of useful components down there ... Anyway"—he crossed the distance to Bermuda and presented it to her—"you won't offend me if you don't want it, but ..."

The quartermaster inspected the object, confused. It was clearly a hand with five discernable digits, though they were all made of various metal pieces and gears. She turned it over to see each of the intricate pieces worked together in a way that allowed for a full range of motion. The fingers bent at the natural joints with ease, lubricated and smooth. Various tones of brass, bronze, and steel adorned the invention, with a fastening device near the artificial hand's wrist to allow her to strap it to her stump and fasten it as tight as she needed. "I don't know what to say," she admitted, unsure of whether to find offense or gratefulness.

"I was limited to what was available." Nicholai pointed out different parts on the mechanical hand. "Improving technology was something many people in Panagea pursued, myself included. Particularly concerning new machinery. I limited myself mostly to clockwork, but I experimented with brain control interfaces at a few of my conventions. It's not just decorative. It has the potential to restore movement, to respond to your cues."

Bermuda's eyes lit up as she tore her stare from the hand and searched Nicholai's face. "Restore movement?" Hope lingered in her voice.

Nicholai nodded. "Biotechnology and neural engineering are still far from being mastered, but the science reminds me of a machine's brain. Unfortunately, I can put the components together to fashion a functioning unit, but"—he frowned, disappointed with his limited knowledge—"I don't know a lot about the human body. It's capable of being a fully functioning hand, but I haven't figured out how to link it to the nervous system."

Umbriel sat upright in her chair with excitement. "I could help with that."

Bermuda flushed, the attention overwhelming her again. "Umbriel, you ... you've already done—"

"Not nearly enough." Umbriel stood from her chair and approached Bermuda. She took the hand from Bermuda's grasp and fastened it to her wrist. "You plucked me from that island after hundreds of years. You're ushering me to Panagea so I might save her and honor my departed companions. I'm grateful you're helping me fulfill my purpose. This is the least I could do."

The device strapped to Bermuda's wrist felt heavy, but she said nothing as Umbriel laid her hands on her wrist. "It may take a moment. I'm still drained from our last session."

The group watched in awe as Umbriel closed her eyes. With one hand on Bermuda's head and the other on her spine, the Earth Mother manipulated the cells in the axons and fibers that comprised the quartermaster's nervous system. It differed from a plant, but Umbriel had mastered her abilities, which only grew in success with the centuries she possessed them. The room fell silent for a full minute. When the tip of Bermuda's index finger on her artificial hand twitched, everyone jumped back.

"Hot damn!" Brack leaned forward to get a closer inspection. "Did you do that?"

"I—I think so," the quartermaster said. She stared at her new hand with incredible disbelief. She dared to move another finger. It twitched again.

When Umbriel dropped her hands, she appeared exhausted and slid into the open seat nearest Bermuda and rubbed her eyes. "It'll take getting used to. But I know you'll come around to it in no time."

Bermuda tried a third time to move the tip of her index finger. The metal digit flexed at her command, and she gasped, unable to contain her disbelief. "Thank you, both. I can't believe it. I can't believe *this*. Thank you."

Kazuaki watched the scene unfold with his own series of heavy disbelief. He turned to Nicholai, who accepted Bermuda's gratitude. The captain eyed the glass of wine in his hands then silently offered the priceless merlot to the Time Father.

Nicholai turned with a start and accepted the wine with hesitation. "Thank you, Captain, but I don't—" He paused. The Time Father did not drink, but he also did not want to offend Kazuaki. It was the grandest gesture the man had made to him in all the time he knew him, and he didn't wish to sully it. "I don't deserve it. I was just ... I thought it would help."

Kazuaki poured another glass for himself from the bottle. Without saying a thing, he tapped his glass against Nicholai's in a quiet salute, took a long drink and returned to his seat.

The Time Father got lost in the ripples of the crimson liquid in his hands as he recalled the many hours it had taken him to build the hand. He did not skip a single detail. It had cost him precious time studying his book and searching for answers for Lilac, but he tempered his guilt with the validation that Lilac would be proud. Though she remained frozen in Southeastern, he carried her spirit with him everywhere. To give a missing piece back to Bermuda, it was something she, herself, would have done had she possessed the ability. Moments like this were one of the few ways he kept her alive.

Gods, he missed her.

Kazuaki inclined his chin and stood tall before his crew. He raised a glass high into the air. "I've traveled the lands and seas of this world for much longer than I care to count. While the time I've served with all of you has been short compared to the life I've lived so far, they have, without a doubt, been the best years of my life. It has been an honor and a privilege. I want you all to know that."

The crew of Kazuaki's ship nodded and raised their glasses in the final of many salutes throughout the evening.

"We'll drink to that," Bartholomew said, speaking for the collective.

"That's it then. Drink up, ladies and gentlemen." Kazuaki sipped a long, thoughtful drink from his precious wine. He lowered the glass to the table and grinned, a maniacal look about him. "Tomorrow, we go to war."

Chapter Eighteen

Leaving the ship was like leaving a lover or a child. Kazuaki slid his hands across the rough railing as he traipsed along the main deck. He didn't flinch when the splinters in the aging material stabbed at his fingers' calloused skin. He knew he had to leave her but distanced himself from the reality until they entered Southern's reach. It was far too dangerous to drop anchor within sight of land. He positioned her in the same spot he did previously when he neared Southern's coast. But this time, he knew he would not be staying with her.

Kazuaki sighed and stopped to rest his palms on the old surfaces of the ship. His hand lingered on a tall mast that reached into the sunrise's bleeding colors. It was a rare occasion he left her. Even in the infrequent instances when he craved the touch of land, he left the ship for only a day, too accustomed to the familiarity of the sea to venture far from it. But the captain knew in his heart this adventure would keep him from her for much longer than usual. It was for the best. He needed to adapt.

Penn stood beside the captain, waiting patiently. He knew the reason Kazuaki had called him forward, and he didn't want to rush him. Penn recognized it was a difficult departure, even for the stone heart of Captain Hidataka.

The ship adopted a sentient nature to Kazuaki. She became a fixture of his identity. She remained as much a legend as he had become throughout the years. The care he had put into her showed despite her age. He'd never let only a single pair of eyes keep watch over her unless it was himself, but today that would have to be the reality. He needed every hand he could take for their vast undertaking. His blood ran cold at the thought. But even the greatest of relationships needed to experience a goodbye now and again. Kazuaki told himself he'd see her later, though he recognized it may not be for a while.

"You'll have more than enough supplies to keep yourself stable," he said to Penn as he stopped to undo a knot that did not fit his standards. After retying it to his satisfaction, he turned to the cook. "Are you sure you'll be fine here by yourself?"

Penn flashed the captain a grin. He was not a jovial man by nature, and so the expression appeared odd on his face, but he knew this moment came with difficulty for Kazuaki, and he wanted to put him at ease. "Story of my life, Captain. I'll do all right." In all truth, Penn found relief he had escaped the inevitable hand-to-hand combat the rest of the crew would endure. Though he sent his heart with each one, he wasn't skilled with weaponry. His efforts would be much more useful tending the ship than engaging in a revolution.

"Good man." Kazuaki patted his shoulder. He knew Penn could handle it. He trusted him. The ship sat far enough away from prying eyes that the cook would be safe, but logic did not banish all the captain's apprehension. Apprehension, however, never stopped Kazuaki Hidataka from doing what was required.

The captain ripped himself from the mast and traversed the distance to the ship's ledge. After checking that everyone was situated in the cockboat, he looked once more at Penn. "Godspeed," he said before he gave the solitary man a quick nod. Kazuaki grabbed a loose rope and lowered himself halfway before he jumped the rest of the way.

The boat rocked as the captain landed in it, but it did not faze the inhabitants. Nicholai tried not to appear vexed as Granite's dog wagged its tail in his face.

As the cockboat rolled toward the shores with the manpower of those who rowed, Brack voiced his concern. "Are you sure we should bring the beast?"

The dog's tongue lolled out the side of its muzzle, unfazed by Brack's words.

"It's unavoidable," Revi said. "Granite goes nowhere without him."

Granite nodded as he rowed, his powerful strokes bringing them closer to the shore with each concentrated effort. Revi was right. No matter the danger, the beast was there for his master, and the master was there for his beast.

A thick mist blanketed the land, obscuring everyone's vision as the cockboat approached the coast. They quieted as it neared land. They exited silently as the hull scraped against the rocks of the shore. Granite hauled the small craft farther onto the sands and stone, positioning it in the same spot the getaway boat they had ransacked many weeks prior had hidden.

"It's so hard to see," Umbriel admitted as she trudged up the misty shores to approach Avadon's edge.

The remnants of the crumbling catacombs remained as they had left them. It seemed no efforts had ensued to clean the mess. She walked ahead of the rest and stopped once she had gained enough height. White ash floated in the air, settling on and around her as she stared into the expansive scenery. Panagea differed greatly from how she had left it. Many buildings had established themselves since she last walked this earth, but they had suffered as much as the land had in her absence.

Seeing through the thick fog was difficult, but what was discernable was heartbreaking. Smoldering wreckage, likely still coming off a fresh disaster, lingered in the distance. The toxic smell of smoke wafted from burning fires, comingling with the mist coming off the waters. It created a distressing curtain of dystopia that covered the city.

Somewhere in the distance, hidden by the translucent haze, she heard people shouting as they tried to extinguish the blazes. The Earth Mother raised an arm to shield her eyes from the suffocating smog. It was much worse than she had imagined. Though she felt the pains Panagea experienced even from her far-off island, she never prepared herself for the decrepit world that awaited her. It was a far cry from the one she had left hundreds of years ago.

"Oh, Panagea." She stared at the remnants of the failing city. "What have they done to you?" Umbriel could not stop her eyes from glossing over with tears. Only a select few escaped and stained her cheeks, but she quickly wiped them away. The Earth Mother returned. She could fix this, she thought. She had to.

The crew joined her side to behold the chaos.

Nicholai looked horrified. The earth had deteriorated so much in the short time he was gone. It made his blood run weak. The Time Father could not deny the hand he played in this. It was undeniable Panagea had been failing for some time, but Southeastern's halt expedited this horrid aftermath. It was the first time the true gravity of his crime weighed on him. All the guilt and regret he held prior paled compared to seeing it with his own eyes. He thought he had more time to figure things out for Lilac, for Southeastern, but seeing Panagea now, like this ... He had been dead wrong.

"This is what we're fighting for?" Brack shook his head and reached into his pocket to be sure he had his oxygen syringe. The way the environment presented itself, he assumed he'd need one handy.

"Sure is," Kazuaki replied, his voice flat. Even the captain was surprised by the wretched state, but he refused to show it. "It'll be too obvious if we enter in a large group. Iani will take Elowyn, Brack, and Bartholomew. Rennington will take Granite and Revi. Nicholai will take Umbriel, Bermuda, and myself."

Rennington nodded and faced his brother. "You remember how to get to the abandoned industrial plant we saw last time we were here?"

Iani bobbed his head. He recalled the building rested near an alleyway they had taken refuge in before they had plundered Avadon, before they had run into Nicholai. "Near the market, Nico," he said as he turned to the Time Father. "Down by the church. You know of it?"

Nicholai struggled to recall that far back, but, after prying the old memories from his brain, he nodded. "Yes, I think I know of it."

"Alright then." Rennington motioned his group forward. The fog's thickness did not deter him. No matter how long he stayed away, this place became one town he knew like the back of his hand. "Off we go."

THE THREE TEAMS ARRIVED at the crumbling industrial plant with little fuss. The streets of Avadon were in such a sorry state the public had much more to worry about than the new faces who traveled into their borders. A surprisingly small number of footmen were patrolling, much less than anyone expected. The streets themselves appeared ghostly, with nothing more than the haunting vocals of the morning church choir fading from the cathedral walls. It was an unsettling sound, emphasized only by the defeated looks on the faces of the few townsfolk they encountered.

The steel door creaked in protest as Kazuaki pushed it open. He led the last of the three groups to enter the failed industrial plant.

Nicholai crept inside when the space allowed for it and surveyed the familiar interior. It had been a water purification plant, much like those he had established all over Southeastern. Why Darjal had left it to rot confused him. The rusted tanks inside showed visible damage. Natural disasters, he guessed. He did not know why Darjal wouldn't put the time and effort into fixing the space with how vital they were.

Nicholai frowned. It was likely if a disaster occurred in this area, any extra funding went into the church's restoration. Darjal loved his pristine cathedrals, almost as much as he loved himself.

Though broken glass and rusted metal chunks littered the floors, it appeared much of the factory's components were stripped. Steel beams and other various metal pieces that should have been there were missing. It was almost as if the larger pieces of metal were harvested for something else. For what, he did not know.

"This will work." Umbriel knelt to an exposed piece of earth. Large chunks of the metal flooring were missing, leaving the rocky terrain below exposed. She reached into the pockets of the pants Elowyn had gifted her and sprinkled seeds she had reaped from her island into small holes she had dug in the ground. It required much less of her energy to grow existing seeds than to make her own.

The crew watched in silence as Umbriel's hands hovered over the earth. None of them knew much about plants. Doubt lingered in their minds that anything could grow in such rocky, depleted soil. But, despite their lack of faith, a multitude of tiny green sprouts soon poked from the terrain.

"The first plant Panagea has seen in many years," Bartholomew said in awe as the little seedlings crawled upward. "It's incredible."

Nicholai knew Bartholomew's statement wasn't true. Malcolm Finn had produced several plants in his greenhouse, but he did not care to correct the scholar. Instead, he thought about how much Lilac would have loved to see this.

"Nicholai," Umbriel said with a smile from her place on the ground. "It's time for your first lesson."

The Time Father blinked and eyed the rest of the crew as they surrounded him. "Really?" He felt burdened with all the gazes on him. Though he hesitated, he convinced himself to kneel beside Umbriel. "I ... have no idea where to even start."

"You'll get there." She took his hands and positioned them over the seedlings. "A'ronn told me he channeled his focus, almost like he was walking down a narrow hallway. Pretend nothing exists to your left or your right. The only thing that exists at this moment are these plants." She gazed at the frail seedlings with pride. "I'll hold your hand. Don't worry, I won't let go. Any years you give to these plants, I'll give right back to you."

Nicholai frowned, unconvinced. "Alright. Here goes nothing." He gave his best effort to direct his focus to the plants.

A large silence followed with no results.

Brack scrunched his face and fidgeted in his boredom. "Is it supposed to take this long?"

"He won't get it right away," Elowyn said as she loomed over Nicholai with a curious, watchful stare.

"He's probably not concentrating enough," Bartholomew offered.

Brack grinned. "He should pretend it's a woman. That always helps me concentrate."

"He should—"

"*He's* standing *right* here," Nicholai muttered.

Kazuaki motioned for the crew to follow him to a decaying vat. "Leave him be for now. I have plans for two of you." Kazuaki scanned the group, trying to make the best choice. He pointed to Revi. "You'll go to the market posed as a traveler. Your back story can be as in-depth as you deem necessary." He reached into his pocket and tossed a small satchel of coins at the man. "Gather whatever information you can about what's happened since we were last here. A lot has changed. The lack of footmen is disconcerting. I want to know where those bastards are."

Revi nodded as he slipped the satchel of coins into his pocket. "Yes, Captain."

"You." He pointed at Elowyn. "You'll pose as his wife, lover, what have you. People look harder at strange, single men appearing out of nowhere than they would at an unassuming man and wife. Should things get rough, you'll have an extra set of hands to wield an extra set of weapons."

Elowyn scoffed. She was always the wife. She tried not to take it to heart. Kazuaki sent her because she not only possessed the physique to play the unassuming wife, she also possessed the skill to slay any obstacles who made the mistake of getting in her way. Elowyn's raw medical knowledge made her a fierce opponent. One expert pop with a knife to the carotid artery made short work of anyone, and she knew just where to find it, along with many other Achille's heels in the human body. "Yes, Captain."

While Revi did not enjoy the roleplay—having mixed emotional baggage regarding wives—he forced himself to fall in line. "Come along, *dear*," he muttered as he hauled open the loud, steel door and slipped outside.

Rennington watched them go with visible frustration. "Why didn't you send one of us, Captain? We know this place like the backs of our hands."

"Which is the problem," he replied, removing one of his many guns to inspect it. "The risk is too great that someone will recognize one of you. Revi and Elowyn are more than capable and twice as easy to overlook."

Rennington accepted it for the logic it held, though he wished it had been him to go. Watching Nicholai loom over those tiny plants with no success in growing them made him aware that time would tick by slower in here than it did in Southeastern.

A MORNING COLD CLUNG to the air. The chilling atmosphere of ash, coal dust, and smog infecting the sky sent a chill up Elowyn's spine. She shivered as she walked alongside Revi but brushed off the inconvenient feeling as best as she could. These pedestrians walked like the living dead, trudging forward with somber, expressionless faces. Each one tried to get through their day with no additional stresses. It was one of the most depressing things the medic had ever seen.

"Looks like the market's up ahead." Revi readjusted the cloak he wore over his shoulders.

The pair ambled into the business center. It was a disturbing sight. What Rennington and Iani once described as a bustling center of activity was barren. A series of unkempt infrastructures lined the street ahead, but, for each that appeared operational, four to five sat dormant, unattended, and abandoned.

"This place gives me the creeps," Elowyn murmured as they entered the market.

The pair searched for a business they could make a purchase from that might also lead to useful information.

"There ..." Revi motioned to a garment peddler with a nod of his head. He extended his arm without emotion, so Elowyn could weave her arm into his. They presented themselves as a couple as they approached the stand. "Excuse me, fine sir," Revi said, trying to sound dignified, "as you can see, my wife is in dire need of some clothing. She's been reduced to these sorry rags."

Elowyn clenched her jaw, resisting the urge to punch Revi as he motioned to the clothing she always wore. "Yes," she said with a forced smile. She slid her other hand up Revi's arm and discreetly pinched the delicate skin of his inner bicep. "Anything you have would be wonderful."

Revi remained steadfast as her strong fingers clamped on his tender skin. It took all his willpower; the burning pain that emanated from it was sharp. He kept his composure through the pinch and reminded himself not to offend Elowyn, for she fought dirty.

The peddler straightened up, surprised to see someone near his store, let alone interested in buying something. "Right, yes, sure." He scrambled to find something suitable for Elowyn to wear. As he rummaged through some garments, he tried to keep the only two customers he'd seen in days close by, engaging in conversation. "Sorry to hear your garments suffered so much." He glanced at the various holes and torn threads in the piece Elowyn wore.

The woman feigned another smile through pursed, irritated lips. "You are sweet to say so."

Revi tried to stifle his amused grin while the peddler returned with a surcoat. He laid it over his arm to show off the details. "This piece is handcrafted with durable materials. It'll survive the conditions we've experienced as of late. You could try it on, if you assure me you won't run off with it." He chuckled.

Elowyn grabbed the surcoat and inspected it with care.

"We'd never be so bold as to steal anything," Revi replied with a charm and a smooth grin Elowyn didn't know he was capable of. "I'm sure we wouldn't get very far before Avadon's footmen apprehended us."

The peddler scoffed, keeping a sharp eye on the surcoat as Elowyn handled it. "That's a laugh." He crossed his arms. "Footmen are sparse around here. Have been for weeks. You two aren't from around here, are you?"

Without hesitation, Revi nodded. "You've got a keen eye, my good man. We came in from Southwestern, seeking refuge."

The peddler laughed, but the sound was not one of joy. It was sad and filled with pity. "Then I'm afraid you've come to the wrong place, stranger. I find it hard to believe things in Southwestern are as terrible as they are here."

Elowyn pretended to fawn over the surcoat.

"Pray tell, if things have gotten so poorly around here, why would they disband your footmen? One would think they'd want to keep the peace. We all know the military does that better than anyone." The words were like poison on Revi's tongue, but they spilled out of him with dutiful necessity.

The peddler shrugged. "Feck if I know the truth. Darjal Wessex made no formal announcements about it. Word on the wind is they were all sent to Southeastern's borders. I heard about a small band of men and women who ventured that way a week ago. Rumor has it they couldn't even travel close to Southeastern before military descended on them and forced them to turn back."

"You don't say? Well, Carlo Angevin isn't much better. He's tight-lipped about the goings-on, that one." Revi turned to Elowyn to break up the conversation to avoid coming across as suspicious. "What do you think, darling? Should we get the surcoat?"

Figuring the peddler would open up more if they bought some of his wares, she nodded. "I would love it very much."

"How much for the surcoat, friend?"

The man appeared nervous. Revi knew he was desperate to name a high price, as he needed the money, but feared naming a price so high it would scare away his potential customers. "Th-three hundred."

Revi removed the satchel Kazuaki had given him. He knew there was more than enough there. The captain hoarded currency as he hoarded just about everything, but he put on a show, pretending to count each coins' individual denominations. "I don't know, love." He stared at the money in his hands. Purposeful hesitation ensued as he shuffled the metal disks around with his finger.

"Two hundred eighty," the peddler interjected. "It's a steal at that."

Revi allowed a slow smile to cross his face. This man needed the money. Revi surmised he had a family to feed. If anyone understood the mountain of pressure that accompanied fatherhood, it was Revi Houton. Perhaps the sale would cause this man one less sleepless night and feed his children's bellies. "We'll take it." He handed him the money.

The peddler exhaled a huge breath he hadn't realized he'd been holding. "Thank you, sir. It's a great piece. Your wife will love it."

Elowyn smiled and folded the surcoat over her arm. "Thank you. It's beautiful."

"No, no, thank *you*. This'll keep us out of the slums for another week at least."

Revi arched an inquisitive brow. "The slums, you say?"

"Aye." The man nodded; a look of pity crossed his face. "The slums—where all the poverty-stricken dwell now. Families forced there by homelessness brought on by the disasters or just the inability to pay their dues. I'd give my right arm to avoid bringing my children there. Crime rates are high enough as it is in town with nearly all the footmen gone. I shudder to think of how chaotic the slums are."

Revi narrowed his eyes, absorbing the information to relay it to the captain later. "Does Darjal Wessex not send aid to those who suffer? From what I understood, he had more than enough in his church coffers, let alone the taxes he collects—"

"You really *are* out of your division. No money left for aid. Darjal poured all the division's finances into constructing that ridiculous ship."

Both Revi and Elowyn couldn't contain their surprise. They stared at the business owner with alarm.

"Ship?" Revi asked, trying to erase any shock he portrayed by injecting calm into his voice.

"Yeah, a big metal waste of money. They said it was for colonizing other islands, but, with all the damn cannons on that thing, I can't say I'd want to set foot in any world that ironclad had a hand in building. Darjal had engineers from all divisions enter Southern's borders to help in the construction." The man tilted his head. A new air of caution surrounded him. "I'm surprised you didn't know. From what I heard, Carlo Angevin was a big supporter of its construction."

Revi flashed another suave grin to dissuade additional skepticism from growing. "You must forgive our naivety in the matter. We were so busy fleeing Southwestern we barely paid mind to its politics as of late."

The peddler accepted the answer with a nod. "Well, I'm afraid you won't find happy-ever-after here, stranger. Southern has really fallen from grace in the last month."

A low rumble sounded beneath their feet. Revi and Elowyn both extended their arms at their sides to steady themselves.

The peddler appeared unaffected as he returned the garments he had pulled out earlier to their places.

The thunderous rolling felt strange on the bottoms of their boots. Vibration from below rattled through their ankles and into their legs. It only lasted ten seconds, but it was enough to startle the man and woman.

The peddler gazed upon them, confused. "You two still haven't gotten used to it yet, aye?"

Not wanting to appear out of the loop, Revi collected himself and flashed a contrived smile. "Not yet."

"At least that was a little one." The peddler placed his palms on the top of his stand and leaned forward. "Can I do anything else for you two?"

"As a matter of fact, you can." Revi slicked his hands through his hair. "I'd like to protect my dear, frail wife from the dangerous of your slums." He winced as Elowyn pinched him again. "Could you please let us know which areas we're to avoid?"

"Of course." The peddler pointed behind him. "It pains me to admit it's not far from the market. It starts about a mile or two outside the market's edge and declines from there. You'll know you're close when you smell it. Lots of hungry, angry people out there. Watch your wallets, and watch your lives, 'cause they'll take both in seconds."

Revi nodded and slipped another coin from his satchel before he pushed it toward the peddler. "Thanks for the tip." He turned his attention to Elowyn. "Shall we?"

The peddler accepted the coin graciously and stuffed it into his pockets.

The woman agreed and walked alongside Revi as they headed to the abandoned industrial plant.

The peddler waved in the air with a smile after them. "Thank you both! Be careful out there!"

"YOU'RE DOING GREAT, Nico."

Umbriel's encouragement was the only thing getting the Time Father through the difficult task. It was one thing to say he would channel focus but another to figure out what that meant. He sighed, disappointed he had achieved nothing resembling success in the hours he had sat with Umbriel in the dingy factory. "That's kind of you to say." Nicholai dropped his arms. "But I can't help but feel I'm not making much progress."

"You've barely given yourself any time. Masters aren't made in a day."

"I'd settle for a novice." Though his words were depressing, they weren't incorrect. The seedlings looked no different now than they had when Umbriel birthed them hours ago.

Kazuaki watched from a corner of the wide-open room. Several crewmembers passed the time playing simple dice games.

Iani, however, had caved under the pressures of boredom and plopped next to Bartholomew, who was nose deep in a book. "I thought the revolution would have been a bit more exciting."

"I could lend you some reading material."

"I'd rather die of boredom."

"That would certainly make things quieter."

"It's only been a few hours." Kazuaki cast disdainful stares at those who voiced their complaints. "You've spent much longer stretches at sea doing nothing than you've spent in here."

"It's the walls." Iani eyed the tall metal container they dwelled within. Though they crumbled and several large, open gaps let daylight filter through the holes in the ceiling, it was much more of a claustrophobic prison than the ship had ever been.

The screeching doors of the building's entrance gave way to Elowyn and Revi. The group sat upright, excited to hear whatever news they came to share. It would be a pleasant distraction from the overwhelming silence they'd lived in.

Kazuaki crossed the distance, leaving Umbriel and Nicholai to their studies. "What's the good word?"

"The *good* word," Elowyn started, "is Darjal has dispatched most of the footmen to patrol Southeastern's borders. That's the word on the street, at least. Darjal has made no formal announcements, but it makes sense they'd send their armies there to wait for Nico in case he returned."

Kazuaki nodded, though the way she'd said it left him to believe there was a bad word to follow the good word. "I like the sound of that."

"Right." Revi's expression showed what the captain suspected; there was bad news. "They also constructed a ship, Captain. I fear our days of being the only souls commanding the seas has ended. I suspect that's also were a lot of Southern's footmen have gone."

Kazuaki frowned. "A desperate attempt from a desperate man." He felt limited apprehension for the state of Penn and his ship, but he remained calm. "They don't know we're here," he said, trying to reassure himself as much as the crew. "The ocean is a big place. They won't find Penn unless they're tipped off."

Bermuda grimaced. The news unsettled her. "Why now would they craft a sea vessel? We've angered them in the past, but none of the Time Fathers tried to hunt us by sea before. It was never worth it."

Kazuaki lowered his voice. "I'm guessing it is not us they are hunting." He motioned discreetly in Nicholai's direction. "They saw him with us when we destroyed the catacombs. I'm sure they surmised he was in our company. I'm certain they'd shed no tears at our deaths or capture, but I believe Nico is the true object of their efforts."

"It's strange to think about, that they would hunt him so aggressively," Rennington said as he stared in the Time Father's direction. "The man wouldn't hurt a fly."

"Don't be so sure," Bartholomew interjected. "He left an entire division frozen in time. He may not have killed them, but he's certainly denying those millions of people their right to live."

"Did anyone ever figure out why he did it?" Elowyn asked.

They all turned to look at Nicholai, who still struggled to isolate the seedlings' time and expedite their growth. In the time they had come to know him, damning an entire division of people to a cruel fate seemed like the last thing he'd do. But everyone on the ship made questionable decisions in their day, and it stopped none of them from accepting one another along with their faults.

"Gods damn it all!" Nicholai shouted in frustration, pressing a clenched fist into the rocky earth.

Umbriel laid a gentle hand on Nicholai's shoulder. Her voice was soft as she leaned in closer. "Don't put so much pressure on yourself, Nico."

The Time Father tightened his jaw. "It's hard not to when so many lives depend on my success."

"Use that. My A'ronn told me you had to give of yourself to make it work. It came so naturally to him, to give to other people. That's what made it easier to give his years to the object of his focus. You're cut from the same giving cloth as A'ronn. You're just overthinking it. You've already mastered the hardest part—benevolence. Now you need to channel it."

Nicholai inhaled and sighed. "I'll try again." He held his hands over the plants and closed his eyes. He thought of Lilac, of Southeastern. His face shifted to one of disappointment, but he felt a soft squeeze from Umbriel that redirected his focus. Though it pained him to stop thinking about Lilac, he cleared her from his thoughts and refilled his brain with the people of Panagea. He thought of all the men and women he had ever stopped to help, all those who had ever helped him. He thought of his mother Enita, the one who birthed his bleeding heart. He smiled at the memory. She rarely entered his thoughts since she passed away when he was a boy, but he couldn't help but think of how good she would have been at this. He whispered a silent prayer to any god who listened

"Nico," Umbriel whispered. "Open your eyes."

The Time Father opened his closed lids and stared at the seedlings. They had doubled in size. He looked dumbfounded and faced the Earth Mother with cautious optimism. "Was that ... was that me?"

She smiled and nodded excitedly. "You did it."

"I did it," he repeated, his face etched into a look of awe.

The group did not have much time to revel in their enthusiasm. The familiar creak of the steel doors filled the hollow room.

Kazuaki drew his dual pistols in both hands.

The crew followed his example; the slick sound of unsheathed blades and cocking guns filled the air as they struck offensive stances, positioning themselves between the door and the Time Father and Earth Mother.

Kazuaki growled. He stared at the five silhouettes that lingered in the doorway.

Granite's dog barked, the fur on its back standing on end.

Even with the loud echoing sound, the captain's harsh voice penetrated it all. "Who goes there?"

Chapter Nineteen

No fear presented itself in the five figures who entered the building. The group of men fanned out, outnumbered but unintimidated. Some held knives, others machetes, while one possessed a firearm. The individual with the gun stepped forward to defend his four companions. He fixed his aim on Kazuaki, the clear leader of the group.

The leader cocked his pistol. "Surrender your money and your possessions, and nobody has to die."

Kazuaki's face blossomed into a slow grin. He cracked his neck twice and squared his shoulders. "Now where's the fun in that?"

A sudden bout of nerves crept into the attacker. Kazuaki's response was not one he received often. "Have it your way. Get 'em, boys."

Though they were far from the impending fight, Nicholai placed himself in front of Umbriel, a human shield should the situation arise. Though he did not condone the violence, it was mesmerizing watching Kazuaki and his crew engage. He had witnessed Rennington and Iani's skill in Avadon and Kazuaki's abilities in the catacombs, but this was something different. Like a choreographed dance with bloodshed, they fought.

Bermuda leaped forward with unmatched grace. She slid low to the ground, avoiding a knife swing. The blade of her dirk slipped into her opponent's calf.

He fell to his knees with a scream.

25

With matched speed and poise, Elowyn's blade found another in a clash. She snarled at the man. Her arms possessed as much strength as his as the power behind their blades battled.

The leader seemed surprised. One of his men fell to his knees in the blink of an eye. Panic pulled the trigger, aimed at Kazuaki.

The captain's quick reaction mocked the bullet; it only grazed his arm. He advanced. He craved information more than a quick kill and dropped to the floor to sweep his opponent's leg. As the man staggered to catch his balance, Kazuaki stood. He caught him by the throat with one hand. The fear in his eyes fed the captain's ego. He tried to lift his gun again, but the captain wrapped his free hand around the muzzle and shoved it aside.

It became clear the fighters possessed no training. Kazuaki and his crew were experts in hand-to-hand combat, but securing victory was too easy.

"Retreat!" the stranger choked out under Kazuaki's grip.

The remaining men obeyed. But, before they reached the door, Granite positioned himself before them and slammed the heavy steel shut. His dog barked, running circles around the group with no sense of direction.

"Tell me"—Kazuaki pulled the man closer—"how terrible are your lives that you would throw them away today?"

The man's face turned purple from the lack of oxygen.

Kazuaki did not take joy in killing untrained assailants. Easy tasks failed to provide a rewarding feeling, so he waited.

The stranger tried to speak but could not with Kazuaki's fingers digging into his fleshy throat.

The others dropped their weapons and raised their hands in a universal signal of surrender. One tried to apply pressure to the calf wound belonging to the screaming man.

"We'll leave," the uninjured man declared and motioned to his leader. "Please. Spare him."

Nicholai approached the man Kazuaki held captive in his grip. He neared unconsciousness with each passing second.

"Kazuaki, he's done. Let him go."

The captain frowned. He was not keen on taking orders from the Time Father but dropped the man to the floor. He planned on letting him live. His death denied the captain the information he wanted.

Nicholai knelt beside the man after he crumpled to the floor.

His eyes grew panicked as he tried to suck in air around him, but the thinning oxygen coupled with the trauma Kazuaki had caused to his neck made it difficult. When the fear became clear, Nicholai removed his oxygen syringe and held it up, a silent request to see if the suffering man wanted it.

After a few hurried nods from the stranger, Nicholai jammed the needle into his flesh. With the medicine flowing through his veins, his breathing steadied, though damage to the skin remained around his throat. The captain's grip possessed a crushing weight, and this instance was no exception.

"Are you all right?" Nicholai asked.

"He asks them if they're all right," Kazuaki muttered, disgusted. He stepped away and shook his head. Nicholai was the only man in the world who looked an attacker in the eye and offered him a lifeline.

The man nodded again, waiting before he trusted himself to speak. His throat felt as though a steam car had run over it.

One other piped up, talking for him instead. "We'll leave. Just please spare our lives. We only wanted the money to feed our families."

"The sob story of a lifetime," Kazuaki replied. Bitterness exuded from him as he crossed his arms. The captain was unmoved, but he recognized the man's words held a truthfulness. These weren't soldiers or assassins. They were simple civilians who had found pointy objects and a gun and tried to be heroes. "How did you find us?" He loomed over the collective to establish his dominance.

"We followed the husband and wife," one confessed, motioning to Revi and Elowyn. "They bought that pricey surcoat in the market. We figured them good for some money."

Revi narrowed his eyes, disappointed he hadn't realized they had followed him. The smog was so thick, it was hard to see three feet in front of him, let alone see anyone who may have had a wandering eye.

Elowyn eyed the machete on the floor that the man who had engaged her in battle had dropped. It wasn't the standard falchion issued to Southern footmen, but she had to ask. "Do you report to Darjal or the military?"

"Feck's sake, no." He stiffened as she loomed near him, her weapon still steady in her hand. He wasn't sure if she associated herself with the Southern Time Father, but he could not hide his disdain. He would rather die than pretend to honor that man. "Darjal is the one who doomed us to the gods-damned slums. I'd gladly roll over and die hungry if it meant he'd die too."

"Well then." Kazuaki bent to retrieve the guns he had dropped earlier and put them where they belonged. "It seems we're bound by a common thread." Though his words were comforting to the assailants, his tone still held an authoritative horror to it.

Bermuda regarded the man whose leg she'd ripped open. She was not sorry for what she'd done. He had invited it. But she couldn't help but cringe at the sounds of agony he made. "Elowyn can probably help with that." She looked at the medic. "I mean, if you want to."

"Here's the thing, gentlemen." Kazuaki knelt to look the leader in the eyes. "How am I to know I can let you walk out that door without giving away our position?"

The stranger met Kazuaki's stare and wrinkled his nose. "What's so critical about your position? You're in an abandoned factory. This isn't exactly a feckin'—" His gaze went passed the captain's shoulders to rest on Umbriel. A mixed look of confusion and surprise spread across his face as he noticed the plants. "What are those?"

Umbriel stood and placed her hands on her thighs. "Those are seedlings. I'm sure you don't remember a time when she was in her most beautiful state, but, with enough of these plants, we can drain this toxicity that has befallen Panagea and restore her to her former grandeur."

The man stood, still out of breath. "You all must be out of our damn minds."

"I'd watch that mouth of yours," Kazuaki stated. "Or your throat won't be the only thing burning."

The leader pursed his lips and nodded. "Look. I can't promise to understand what you're doing here, but, if what you say is true and you are enemies of Darjal, we're gathering a resistance in the slums. It's nothing great, just more civilians like us." He placed a hand over his chest as he tried to catch his breath. "My name is Emont. You lot seem like skilled fighters. Though you ripped Jodathyn's leg half open, we'd love to let bygones be bygones, if you wish to join the movement."

Bermuda scrunched her face. Seething sounds of pain from Jodathyn accosted her ears as he clutched his bleeding leg. "You may not want to speak for him. He still seems pretty pissed."

"It's not the worst thing that's happened to him. It's not the worst thing that's happened to any of us."

Kazuaki pondered the request. An army of people who already despised Darjal seemed like a tempting offer, but what was the value in an army of civilians? They might make one lucky shot in a dozen attempts, but all they would become were corpses in an unpleasant war. Then again, it was better than nothing. "We'll let Umbriel finish what needs to be done in this factory. Then we'll allow you to take us to your slums."

Emont frowned and eyed his companions. All appeared to accept their fate. Kazuaki and his crew had made short work of them. They dared not disagree with his plan.

"Can someone at least assist Jodathyn while we wait? He's got a wife and kids waiting for him."

Elowyn waited for the captain's response. Though his face remained stern, he issued her an approving nod. The medic wasted no time and rushed to her pack to gather supplies.

"Forgive me," Emont said as Elowyn returned to Jodathyn's side and cleansed the wound, "but how are a few plants going to help Southern? How could something so small could make much of a difference?"

Umbriel motioned Nicholai to her, and he approached. She spread more seeds and grew them several inches in height within seconds. Her gaze fell on the Southeastern Time Father as he tried once again to advance their growth, succeeding far sooner in raising the plants an additional several inches higher now than before.

His surprise remained clear, and he smiled in astonishment despite the small growth.

Umbriel smiled too, congratulating Nicholai with a light pat on the shoulder. She looked over her shoulder at Emont. "I'll show you when we get to your slums."

THE TIME SPENT IN THE factory stretched into the fourth day. While the five assailants remained captive during that time, as Kazuaki had no intention of letting loose ends run amok, they weren't treated like prisoners. Everyone received their three-square meals.

Brack, Bermuda, and Bartholomew switched shifts on who gathered the market supplies. There was no new information. They returned with enough food to feed the people who dwelled within the safety of the crumbling factory. But, while the crew gained no new insights during their stay, they exposed Emont, Lakow, Jodathyn, and the others to an environment far beyond what they were used to.

Umbriel and Nicholai worked around the clock to fill plant life throughout the building. Various mosses covered the rusting shreds of metal, turning the dull browns and oranges into multiple shades of fresh green. The floor, once half-covered with remnants of old metal, flourished with an assortment of perennials that stretched through the factory's entirety.

Vines crawled up the edges of the building, finding any little spot in the decaying metal where they could grip and climb. Dwarf trees sprouted and reached to the height of an adult. Vegetables and flowers sprouted and bloomed, bringing pops of color to the cacophony of earth tones.

The Time Father and Earth Mother worked in amazing synchronicity. Whatever years Nicholai gave of himself to the plants, Umbriel replenished with her skillset, manipulating his tired body and breathing new life into it. When both felt the heavy effects of their efforts, they stopped and rested then jumped back in as soon as they felt they could. What once existed as a dark, sullen place shifted into a veritable forest trapped inside the walls of an abandoned building. It was, for all intents and purposes, like living in a giant greenhouse.

When they found no more room to grow additional plants, Nicholai admired their work. It represented Umbriel's island, a place he never thought he'd see the likes of again until this moment. To know he'd had an active part in creating it eased the burden he placed on himself for his past sins. With more effort like this, perhaps he *could* save the world he had helped destroy.

Lilac would love this place, he thought. It was a larger version of the vision her father held, with hundreds of species living inside the walls as opposed to a handful. When he figured out a way to free her from her fate, he would take her here and show her where it all had begun.

Umbriel approached the group, her hands behind her back. "I think we've done all we can here. Just think, in ten years, most of Panagea could look like this."

Emont was impressed at the evolution the building underwent in the days he sat trapped inside it. He couldn't deny how impressive it was, but, even with days' worth of conversation from the others detailing how it helped Panagea, he failed to see its future effectiveness. "It's ... certainly something else."

"This is for you." Umbriel handed him a plump, ripe tomato.

Emont arched a brow, confused as he accepted the smooth vegetable. "Thanks?"

"It's food. Try it. A bunch of them are back in that corner."

Emont did not seem eager to try it. But, with the heat of Kazuaki bearing down on him, he forced himself to take a bite. After some thoughtful chewing, his disinterest faded, replaced with surprise as he wiped liquid and seeds off his chin with his sleeve. "This is delicious."

"Almost everything here is edible. I can educate you on their nutritional content. But know, if anyone in your slums is starving and they're unable to afford the food at the market, they can always come here. I can teach a few of you what to look for when certain harvests are ripe, how to sow your own seeds, how to keep this place thriving. With enough gentle hands and more expansion of our efforts, you'll never put your children to bed hungry again."

Emont looked overwhelmed. He inspected the tomato in his hands, a look of awe on his face. At that moment, he saw. He witnessed the raw power of Umbriel's creation. Perhaps this strange band of people *could* initiate a change for the good. The realist in him held on to a shred of skepticism, but he opened to the possibility. "Thank you. Anything we can do to help, just let me know."

Umbriel smiled and tucked a strand of hair behind her ear. "You could take us to your slums. I would like to plant there too."

"Yes." Emont nodded as he looked toward his companions. He wished to return to those he had left behind. They likely assumed him captured or dead after the days he had spent here. His return would bring relief, especially since hopeful news accompanied him. "I'll take you there right away."

Both groups gathered their belongings and readied for departure. Two men flanked either side of Jodathyn to help him walk; his calf imposed on him.

While Kazuaki remained apprehensive about departing in a large group, the lack of footmen eased his concerns.

Nicholai stared at Umbriel's and his efforts for a moment longer. It was incredible to think this much life could hide inside a building that appeared unassuming from the outside. The more decrepit structures they filled like this before the footmen discovered their efforts, the more hope he harbored for their overall success.

Following Emont to the slums replaced much of Nicholai's hope with nausea. The several mile walk displayed nothing but chronic deterioration. The marketplace and Avadon's center, while depressing looking, resembled pieces of pristine beauty when compared to the land that led to the heart of the slums.

Instead of somewhat functional buildings, most of the architecture existed as rubble. Clear evidence of the natural disasters that had ravaged the town was visible upon entering Emont's home. Makeshift tents, propped up with fallen steel beams and chunks of metal, served as shelters for the hundreds of people who struggled across the decrepit place.

The smell matched the visual in its revulsion. Kazuaki recognized the scent—rotting corpses. It was so thick he tasted it on his tongue. While it appeared the people who lived here tried to bury their dead, not enough tools were available to dig a hole. Even if they possessed the tools, the sheer amount of deceased was overwhelming; no way the hundreds of people who made their homes here could keep up with the intense demands of burying the many bodies, especially since much of the still-living inhabitants were hungry, feeble children.

Emont read the crewmember's expressions as they carried themselves farther into the tangible torture pit. "I know it's not an easy place to look at. But we're doing the best with what we have."

"Daddy!" Jodathyn's children ran to him—two girls and a boy, none of which had seen over eight years of age.

The man's eyes widened with extreme intensity as the children wrapped their arms around his legs, applying pressure to his throbbing calf injury.

"What happened? Where were you?" They fired questions at him without mercy, ecstatic to see their father returned from whatever had kept him away.

Revi couldn't help but watch. That could have been him if he had the guts to go back. But several days was a far different time span than ten years. Some of his children were almost adults now. With any luck, they faired at life far better than he had. The current state of the world dimmed his hopes. The large number of people who had perished in the disasters made a small part of him wonder if his children were still alive. His stomach twisted at the thought as he surveyed the bodies they had passed. Any of those faceless corpses could have been one of the Houton children. It filled him with a resolve to continue the mission.

"Never mind all that," Jodathyn said to his children as he placed his hands on two of their heads. "Where's your mother?"

"Over here!" the eldest daughter yelled, pulling Jodathyn from the arms of the two who provided him with standing support.

His eyes widened as the heat of a thousand suns burned through the back of his leg, but he forced himself onward with limited signs he was in pain, as not to cause additional alarm to his children.

Emont watched him go with mild concern but left the man to his own decisions. "This way," he told the collective group, bringing them to a large tarp that stretched twenty feet in the sky supported by ropes and stakes. It was a mangled-looking thing, offering limited protection from the elements, but it still housed many people.

Most huddled around three large drums filled with burning rubbish. Though it was not cold, their skin's paleness and sunken eye sockets left little doubt they were ill, feeling even the minor absence of heat through their bones.

"What exactly is your plan?" Kazuaki muttered, unimpressed by the haggard individuals who surrounded him. "You cannot stand there and tell me you would expect these people to successfully mount any sort of resistance. They're half dead as it is."

"Kazuaki." Umbriel sent him a stare that encouraged him to show empathy.

Emont sighed. "It's okay, Umbriel. Your captain speaks the truth. Though the footmen's presence is low and we have numbers on our side, unfortunately, the state of our numbers is sad. It hasn't grown beyond an idea. A hopeful one at best." He crossed his arms. "But we can't very well sit here and continue to rot."

"You need your people in good health, if their voices are to be heard," Umbriel said. "How often do you see foot soldiers in the slums?"

Emont laughed. "This is a lawless place. They don't care what happens to us here. The closest they'll come is the edges of the marketplace in the heart of town. Rumors have spread about the dangers that await in the slums. They don't want to be here anymore than we do."

"Good," Umbriel said, a smile coming to her face. "Then, with your permission, Emont, we would like to help."

It did not take long to see a change. Those who were strong enough cleared the rubble from the earth and placed it in piles. 'Round the clock, the forgotten civilians of Avadon and other surrounding cities who sought refuge in the slums abided by Umbriel's instruction.

Once the grounds opened to expose the dirt beneath, Umbriel planted her seeds, and Nicholai, growing more successful in his efforts with each passing day, brought new life to the decaying place. They were careful not to grow anything that may come within eyesight of those in the town center—no towering plants, only low-growing vegetables and fruit-bearing shrubs.

As the project continued day after day, Bartholomew offered instructional classes on how to nurture the plants, information he had learned from Umbriel and a few of his books.

Elowyn provided medical care for as many individuals as she could, though the number of injured people was great. Her supplies dwindled by the second day. Despite the setback, she made do with the medicinal plants Umbriel and Nicholai grew upon realizing the need for them. Natural pain relievers and plants with antibacterial capabilities were amongst the most necessary, but, for each one they cut down to use, the Earth Mother and Time Father grew ten more in its place.

Kazuaki instructed Emont on battle tactics, unleashing hundreds of years' worth of strategies on the man who rose to be the voice of the slums.

Granite showed those who listened how to fashion weaponry from everyday garbage. Anything that filed to a point was enough to pierce a person—the duller, the better. He made many close-combat pieces with other civilians while his dog roamed and played fetch with the children of the slums. The animal was the biggest provider of joy amongst the young ones, a fine babysitter while the adults labored long into the day.

At night, they gathered by the various fires and showed the people how to prepare foods plucked from the gardens. The forgotten people congregated in droves for the stews and soups, regaining their strength as they recovered from starvation and found remedies for infected wounds. Physical differences weren't the only notable changes. Mentally, emotionally, the people grew in spirit and resolve.

Once their efforts outgrew the slums, Emont snuck Umbriel and Nicholai into the city limits, with Kazuaki, Bermuda, Revi, and Brack as their eyes and ears while they worked. In the many trips he had made to the marketplace to scout out patrons to mug, he had familiarized himself with which buildings remained abandoned. Fortunately, or unfortunately, there were many.

It was strange for him, a man who grew up in Avadon his entire life. When he was a child and into his young adult years, an unutilized structure wasn't probable. It was required that not a single piece of land went without serving a purpose. But, as the disasters grew in frequency and Darjal poured more of Southern's finances into the ship's construction and the integrity of the churches, more factories and plants fell into disrepair.

It was exhausting work. Umbriel and Nicholai toiled in yet another uninhibited factory, putting the finishing touches on any usable space available for more greenery. The Earth Mother looked fatigued, matched only by Nicholai as he wiped sweat from his brow.

"How are you doing, Nicholai?" Umbriel asked, panting as she leaned against a wall.

Nicholai spun a complete circle to behold the surrounding sight. Though he had grown accustomed to seeing vast assortments of life clinging to eroded metal and rocky terrain, he still smiled at the magnificence. "I'm doing all right. No matter how many times we do this, it reminds me of a place I hold near and dear to my heart." He yawned then turned to her with calmed contentment. "It makes it easier to keep going. Even when exhaustion sets in."

"Indeed, it does." She took a cue from Nicholai and yawned herself. "Our efforts put me in mind of the redwood tree. I would love to grow one when the time is right."

Nicholai stretched his arms over his head and tried to banish the tiredness from his limbs. "What's stopping you?"

"Oh, they're far too grand a tree to grow in secrecy." She closed her eyes to revel in the quiet, for she knew it wouldn't last long. "They can grow one hundred feet tall in only fifty years, an impressive feat on its own, but, when you think of their true potential, they can reach heights of over three hundred and fifty feet and live for thousands of years." Her eyes opened and her gaze fell on the Time Father. "Just like our little revolution. Such impressive growth in so short a time, but, when I think of the potential, it sends a positive shiver up my spine."

Nicholai's lips tugged into a silent smile. He extended his hand as he gave his years to a patch of immature ivy. The plant sprawled along the length of the wall, falling into the imperfect cracks in the building's questionable structure. It grew six feet before he dropped his hand to his side.

"You're getting very good at that." She touched his shoulder, re-generating the life he had gifted the vines.

Nicholai smirked. "I had a good teacher."

"Looks like we're about to wrap it up here," Kazuaki said, careful as he walked over some colorful flowers on the factory's ground. "You both have enough left in you to do one more today?"

Umbriel and Nicholai nodded in unison as they looked to Emont.

"Where to next?" the Time Father asked.

Before Emont answered, a low rumble sounded below their feet. Familiar with the reverberations by now, though he remained calm at first, he grew more concerned as the vibrations continued. When they grew in length and intensity, his expression became one of full-on panic. "Run! This quake's a big one!"

Everyone bolted for the door. It was chaotic running on the ground as the earth thundered beneath their feet.

Kazuaki threw open the door, ushered everyone out and slammed it behind him after they all had exited.

Screams rose from the townsfolk who walked Avadon's streets. The violent shrieks escalated in hysteria as a tall housing complex shattered from the base. The screech of yielding metal pierced the brains of all within earshot as floor by floor the building collapsed, the foundation weakened from months of on-going plates shifting below Panagea's surface.

Dust and ash climbed into the sky. The crew stood, staring onward at the horrifying loss. It was the first of many buildings to suffer. There seemed to be no safe place to take shelter. A structure that appeared stable dissolved seconds later.

"Stay together!" Kazuaki shouted over the roar of destruction and the stampede of terrified citizens. It seemed the best place to be was also the most vulnerable—open ground.

The handful of footmen who patrolled the area tried in vain to contain the residents' panic. "To the church!" they shouted, motioning the scattering people to the gothic cathedral. Of all the buildings in Avadon's heart, they knew it would be the safest. Darjal had reinforced it a hundred times over to ensure it remained standing.

The people who possessed the wherewithal dashed to the safety of the church doors.

Nicholai's face twisted into one of horror. Wall after wall of the factories they had forested fell, exposing the secret greenhouses within.

Despite the dust and chaos, two footmen noticed the stark contrast of the greenery against the grays of their metal world. "What the feck is that?" one asked his comrade, gesturing to the building Kazuaki and his crew had exited.

"Forget it," the second foot soldier said as he ran toward the crew. "Hey, you! You can seek shelter in the church!" He stopped when he got close. A well-timed wind gust blew the debris from his clouded vision, unveiling the faces that stood before him. He recognized one, the one issued to every foot soldier in every division since Southeastern fell victim to its current state. "Shit," he said in a heavy breath, stumbling as he backpedaled. "It's Nicholai Addihein!"

"Bloody shit." Kazuaki removed a dagger with one hand and a pistol with the other. "Jig is up, ladies and gentlemen." He lunged forward to stab the footman in the neck, but a bullet pierced his wrist, and he dropped his weapon.

The first foot soldier clung to his smoking gun, a look of unadulterated alarm on his face. He watched the captain curse as he grabbed his bleeding wound. "Go!" he shouted at his friend, motioning him to run. "Alert Darjal!"

With a fleeting glimpse of appreciation to his companion who had saved his life, he ran. The foot soldier disappeared into the mists of the disintegrating city.

Bermuda scowled and started after him, firing several rounds. It was difficult to see. She was on unfamiliar ground. The woman gave chase until a house collapsed twenty feet in front of her, causing her to lose visual. She halted, clenching her weapon. "Damn it all."

Kazuaki's eye pierced through the thick clouds of smog at the foot soldier who had shot him. He said nothing, but his expression spoke volumes.

The footman stared, trapped in the captain's glare. He turned on his heels and rushed to alert the others while he still had the benefit of a head start.

"Are you all right, Kazuaki?" Umbriel shouted over the noise.

"Peachy," he growled, hand soaked with blood.

Emont ushered them forward. "Let's get out of here!"

"We can't go back to the slums," Nicholai said. "They'll follow. You'll be exposed."

Emont scowled as cinders swirled around him. He was tired of running. He was tired of hiding. He was tired of his family and friends existing in the squalor Avadon's elites had condemned them to. They did not have much time to grow in strength, but they couldn't wait anymore. "Let them come."

Revi shook his head. "No." He gripped Emont's shoulders. "You lead them to your camp, you lead them to your children. Go back and get the others. Rennington, Iani, Elowyn, Granite, Bartholomew, and whoever else will follow. We'll bring the fight to them."

Emont paused but nodded with newfound determination. "I'll be back." He rushed into the black and gray powder that littered the air.

Umbriel looked to Kazuaki and Nicholai. The burden of the moment was heavy in her eyes. "What do we do now?"

Revi and Brack withdrew their weapons.

Bermuda emerged from the ashes and joined their sides again, her gun still clutched in her hand. Her look of disappointment told everyone the soldier had escaped.

Kazuaki frowned as he released his bullet wound and retrieved the weapons he had dropped. "We fight."

The quakes continued without a break. The incredible vibrations below them ripped through the city, leaving behind nothing but destruction and death.

With the chaos of the disaster in full force, Kazuaki knew it would be difficult terrain to fight off their attackers. It didn't matter. The footmen would descend upon them soon. The soldiers were an organized bunch. Though small in numbers, they were still formidable opponents. Kazuaki did not move. He waited. They hold their fire long enough, giving the plant life a head start. It was time for their voices to rise and for blood to spill. Umbriel and Nicholai had thrived in their element. Now it was his turn.

Silhouettes appeared in the dust. Five, ten, fifteen men came into view, ready with their standard-issue falchions. Though most of their guns had been melted to make metal for the ironclad, a few held fast to their long-range weaponry.

The captain smirked. He pushed through the pain to grip his gun in one hand, his dagger in the other. The perfect combination of close and long-distance combat.

Bermuda, Brack, and Revi followed suit, surrounding the Earth Mother and Time Father. They all knew the duo's crippling ethics prevented them from taking a life, so they made it their priority to keep them safe.

"Brack," the captain ordered, "get these two somewhere safe."

"Right-o, Cappy." Brack motioned Nicholai and Umbriel to follow.

With hesitation, they fell back into the dust and followed the man.

As the soldiers marched forward, each eager to be the one who claimed the title of being Nicholai's killer, the crew readied themselves. A slew of unsettled ash distorted any accuracy for the few who remained capable of issuing gunfire, but, as soon as a semi-accurate aim showed, the sound of bullets unleashed.

Bermuda, Kazuaki, and Revi lunged forward, each taking their own course as they hurled themselves into the crowd.

He was a marksman. Kazuaki squeezed a bullet into an oncoming soldier's forehead. He targeted those with long-range weapons, preferring to rid himself of the dangers that stemmed from unexpected attacks.

Bermuda and Revi were familiar with the captain's battle tactics. They, too, made it a priority to drain the lives of any gun-wielding footmen.

Bermuda snarled as she fired her gun. Dodging the swing of an oncoming falchion disrupted her aim. But even well-trained men were no match for the agile huntress. She gutted her attacker.

The contents of his stomach spilled onto his fingertips. He suffered the unfortunate delay of death from a wound that wasn't immediately fatal.

Revi's attacks held less finesse. The frenzied man, who hated himself far too much to fear death, was a madman in battle. Without mercy, every blade thrust found flesh. A whirlwind of bloodshed followed. He suffered blows of his own, but adrenaline fueled him with infinite energy. He would feel it later. But, at the moment, Revi Houton felt no pain.

"This way, guys!" Brack looked back to be sure the Earth Mother and Time Father kept pace. As he climbed over the clutter of fallen rubble, he glanced forward, finding himself face to face with three other footmen.

Nicholai put his hand in front of Umbriel.

The footmen withdrew their weapons.

Brack spat and reached back to grab his cutlass and pistol and dug his heels into the earth. "Go on then."

Two advanced on Brack while the third went for Nicholai and Umbriel.

Weaponless, the Time Father edged back, keeping Umbriel behind him.

Brack tried in vain to free himself from the fighters who flanked him, but all his effort channeled into staying alive against two men. "Run! Or fight, dammit! But at least run!"

Nicholai grabbed Umbriel's hand and pulled her from the fight. He believed Brack could defend himself. If Nicholai drew the third footman far enough away, he could spare his comrade from dealing with more attackers than he could handle.

Umbriel ran ahead, though she still held his hand. The woman was far more accustomed to reacting within her natural surroundings than Nicholai, and her pace illustrated as much. With an unmatched swiftness, she leaped fallen rubble with grace, dragging the Time Father along with her.

"Umbriel!" Nicholai shouted, having lost their pursuer to the Earth Mother's quick feet. "We should take refuge in the church. We can blend in amongst the civilians. I know Darjal's soldiers are hungry for our capture, but he stresses the sanctity of the church. With any luck, they won't dare spill blood on holy ground."

Umbriel nodded, though she didn't appear convinced. "It's worth a try." She pulled Nicholai with her back toward the cathedral.

Cutting through the narrow alleys, the two returned to where they had started. Nicholai glimpsed Kazuaki as he decapitated a man with a single swing. The captain dripped in blood—his enemies' and his own. He was almost unrecognizable under the sea of scarlet liquid. Nicholai forced himself to look away, following Umbriel up the unguarded church steps and into the cathedral's open doors.

Bodies crammed inside.

Umbriel squeezed through with ease, her nimble body seeking any opening with a quickness.

Nicholai's palms sweated from the adrenaline that coursed through him, but he kept his grip on her hand as she weaved through the crowd. They came to a standstill near a tall marble statue that featured Darjal crafted to look like a god among men.

"I hope they'll be all right." Umbriel stared in the direction they had left their companions.

Nicholai tried to catch his breath and slow his beating heart. "They're very capable," he reassured her, though he, too, hoped they had fared well in the slaughter.

Children cried within the cathedral walls. Their scared protests echoed in the tall ceilings. Mothers tried in desperation to provide comfort, but the panic was suffocating.

Umbriel clutched Nicholai's arm and gasped. She pointed to the mouth of the church. "Nicholai ..."

He followed her alarmed gaze to the entryway to see several footmen enter. His face fell. They had been followed. "Too many people are here," he whispered. "They'll never find us."

"Come forth, Time Father!" one soldier shouted into the crowd. "We know you're here!"

The panicked people inside looked to the footmen, confused. Half exchanged hushed conversations while the other half feared for their lives.

"Citizens of Avadon, in the belly of our own church is a traitor to Panagea! Southeastern's very own Time Father, Nicholai Addihein! We must find him, and we can bring these disasters to an end!"

Those who hadn't paid attention before listened now. The crowd eyed one another with skepticism. It didn't take long for the public to separate Nicholai and Umbriel as strangers to their city. A small opening formed as people backed away from the pair; whether by fear or confusion, it was hard to tell.

Nicholai found the footman's gaze. Despite the wild beating of his own heart, he stood tall. "You would not shed blood in the church of Avadon," he announced with vindication, hoping he was more correct about that than he had been about being undetectable within the cathedral's walls.

The footman scowled. They advanced through the crowd, but the volume of people made it difficult. They freed their falchions from their scabbards. "That's where you're wrong. Darjal put a high enough price on your head. I'll simply buy his forgiveness for sullying his church."

The impending fight caused a riot. Finding the church to no longer be the haven they thought, the people spilled back into the streets, screaming.

In full fight mode, Revi lunged at the closest body he saw, stopping his dagger inches from the face of a terrified mother. He withdrew just in time and narrowed his eyes as he wondered what caused them all to abandon the safety of the church's sanctuary.

Nicholai edged backward as the footmen advanced. It was much easier now that most of the people had cleared the area. A few lingered inside and watched with horrified curiosity. "You don't have to do this." The Time Father held out his hands to ease the tension.

"Get 'em!" the soldier ordered, but, before they moved forward, another deep boom roared from beneath the earth louder than any they had experienced.

The floor shook with an intensity that rattled the stained-glass windows until they shattered into countless pieces. Shards of red, green, and blue collapsed to the floor. Decorative stone figures carved into the ceiling's molding weakened, and the heavy statues plummeted.

The footmen stepped backward as the compromised flooring gave under the weight of the collapsing figures, punching large holes in the floor as they fell into the church basement.

Nicholai edged away, creating as much distance as he could between himself and the decaying floor. But to no avail. His stomach leaped as the floor buckled and sent him flying toward a hole. Umbriel fell victim too, but, with quick acting on both their parts, they seized one another's hands. Nicholai gripped the edge of the flooring as he struggled to keep Umbriel from falling into the basement.

One footman fell through the floor. Others backpedaled to avoid the same fate. Though the unfolding scenario terrified them, catching sight of the Earth Mother and Time Father in a vulnerable position eased their displeasure.

"Umbriel," Nicholai grunted, straining to hold both with one hand, "do you remember what you said at the greenhouse? That tree you wished to plant—do you think I have fifty years in me?"

The Earth Mother gasped as she comprehended his hints. She summoned a redwood seed from inside her, opening her palm to unveil the delicate thing. "We'll do it together."

"Right. Brace yourself for impact then." He let the edge of the flooring go.

With a thud, the two landed into the darkness below the church. Nicholai hurriedly searched for any breaks in the foundation, hoping to find exposed earth to place the seed. It took longer than he hoped with the limited light. The skin on his hands split open on the jagged rubble as he ripped loose pieces from the floor.

The two footmen above ran down the church steps to the basement, holding the fragile railings as they approached their comrade who had fallen earlier. They helped him to his feet, and the three stared at Umbriel at Nicholai.

"Umbriel ..." Nicholai's bleeding fingers pried the last piece of rubble from the floor to reveal the natural ground hiding below.

The Earth Mother's eyes adjusted to the darkness and located the spot in the earth.

Nicholai stood and stepped forward, using himself as a barrier while she knelt and dropped the seed into its new home.

The foot soldiers progressed, weapons drawn.

Nicholai held his ground.

"It's ready," Umbriel said from behind.

He had little time to react before a blade descended toward him.

Umbriel tripped Nicholai, causing him to avoid the attack by inches as he fell to the floor. The Earth Mother stood, her eyes shining and fixated on the footmen. "Don't worry. I will not take your lives."

The men laughed at her confidence, but she cut their amusement short when she lunged forward with incredible agility and accuracy. Her fingers thrust into one larynx. His falchion clattered to the floor as he threw up his hands around his throat, gasping for air as he fell to his knees.

The other men scowled. They turned their agitation into attacks. Her mercurial athleticism made it difficult for them to land a hit.

Nicholai struggled to concentrate, finding this the first time he needed to perform with distractions. His hands shook as he closed his eyes. "Come on, come on," he goaded himself on until he heard Umbriel fall beside him, gripping an injury on her arm. The men had landed a lucky hit.

"It's over, Nicholai," one footman said, Umbriel's blood still clinging to his blade.

"Not yet," the man said in a deep exhale, covered in sweat and ash. "I still have time on my side." With Umbriel gripping his shoulder, he steadied himself and gave it one final effort.

The soldiers stepped backward, alarmed.

In seconds, the delicate twisting of the seed took on bark growing outward in width and upward. Branches turned into limbs as the tree spiraled, crashing through the flooring above and raining shards of rubble upon them.

Nicholai clenched his jaw as it grew, finding every cell and atom inside him depleting as the redwood scrambled to the church's ceiling. It compressed under its weight for only a moment until the sheer power of nature broke through the top. Branches spewed from the holes in the cathedral where beautiful stained glass once stood. In seconds, the church became nothing more than a small box surrounding the magnificent symbol of power.

"Dark magic," the footman whispered in awe. He stepped backward from the impressive base of the tree that had aged fifty years before his eyes.

"It ... It doesn't matter." The other tried to collect his disbelief and replace it with duty. "Your parlor tricks will not save you, Nicholai Addihein." His voice quivered with a mixture of shock and terror, but his training pushed him onward.

The Time Father couldn't lift his neck. His head lolled on his spine as he struggled to keep his focus on the soldiers. It was a massive undertaking. Even with Umbriel throwing all her energy into him, he felt drained. He couldn't even part his lips to speak.

Umbriel remained standing, but Nicholai felt her using him for support. She, too, felt depleted beyond measure.

"Get the Chronometer," the soldier ordered. He swung his falchion back, ready to decapitate the Southeastern Time Father. His arm was unsuccessful. Something pulled him to the floor, hard.

Granite's dog snarled as it flailed its head from side to side, teeth deep in the arm of Nicholai and Umbriel's would-be attacker. His scream echoed off the broken walls as the animal mangled his flesh.

The last footman standing did not have much time to react before Granite ran him through. The point of his blade pierced his lung. He withdrew it as the man's failing body slumped to the floor. Still suffering from his laryngeal fracture, the third gasped for oxygen as he regarded Granite with pleading eyes.

"Please." Umbriel unlatched Nicholai's shoulder and took two shaky steps toward Granite. "Leave him be. He is no threat."

Granite paused. After a moment of consideration, he grabbed Umbriel and threw her over his shoulder. He hoisted Nicholai after, hauling both parties from the crumbling cathedral walls and into the open streets of Avadon.

The rumbling below the land ended, but the scene it left behind was an absolute horror. Confused people littered the blood-soaked streets, calling out for loved ones lost in the chaos.

Nicholai summoned the energy to look up long enough to see Kazuaki and the crew coated in crimson red and black ash.

The captain found Granite and tried to approach without alarm, but he harbored anxiety at seeing the two individuals in their haggard condition.

One by one, the crew regrouped. Bermuda, Elowyn, Brack, Bartholomew, Rennington, Iani, and Revi joined the others. Emont followed suit soon after.

"Brack," Nicholai said in a cough through his relieved smile. "You're okay."

The man looked worse for wear, sporting a new series of blood-caked wounds, but he smiled. "Wish I could say the same for you, mate. You look like something that crawled out of the Underworld."

Nicholai grimaced as Granite set him down. "At least I'm not *in* the Underworld."

"Don't speak too soon," Rennington gazed around the decrepit remnants that surrounded them. Only a handful of buildings within eyesight survived the onslaught.

"Impressive," Kazuaki said, motioning to the redwood tree that towered from the church. "We knew exactly where to find you after you pulled that little stunt."

Iani nodded, surveying the decay that surrounded them. Dead footmen cluttered the ground. Those who survived had fled. The church looked desecrated, replaced by a grand symbol of everything they had fought for. The factory walls around the greenhouses had crumbled, exposing their secrets. Though the streets remained peppered with frenzy, the young Platts brother felt something he hadn't in a long time—hope. "Does that mean we won?"

The others looked to the captain.

He knew they had not slaughtered all the footmen. Some likely had fled to bordering cities. "Celebrate our small victory while we can," Kazuaki murmured as he cleaned the blade of his weapon. "We're in the thick of it now. Darjal will be upon us at any moment."

Chapter Twenty

A terrifying silence claimed the air. Darjal sat at his ornate desk, his eyes glazed over. His mind wandered far from the walls that contained his physical body. His palms laid flat on his desk, fingers splayed, pressing with unnatural pressure as his shoulders and arms stiffened. The man lived in such stillness he looked as if he wasn't breathing. The Time Father's reaction showcased so strong a strangeness it made the soldier in front of him cringe.

"My Lord?" he uttered, unable to handle the eerie stillness any longer. "Did you hear what I said?"

Life shot back into Darjal's eyes, and he flicked his gaze to the footman. The had soldier arrived fresh from the events in Avadon. He had trekked to Darjal's hometown as fast as his feet and the nearest steam train could carry him. He had described it all: the Nicholai sighting, Kazuaki's slaughter of the soldiers, the strange woman's presence, his church's desecration, the plants that dominated the abandoned factories' interiors. The messenger left no precious detail unmentioned.

"Yes," the Southern Time Father murmured; his fingers curled inward as he balled his hands into tight fists. "I heard you loud and clear."

"What do you wish to do, Lord Wessex?"

The man eased back in his chair and tried to lower his mounting blood pressure. He rubbed the sides of his temples, hoping it banished the migraine that assaulted his brain. "Send word to the other divisions, the other Time Fathers. Then send word to the elected official of Guress in the Northeastern division. If Jernal remains on schedule, that will be his next stop. Detail in the letter he is to journey to Southern as fast as the waters will take him."

"Yes, sir. Anything else?"

"Yes." The Southern Time Father sat upright in his chair. "Ready whatever footmen we can. I'm taking them to Avadon to deal with Nicholai Addihein myself."

The soldier frowned. "Forgive me if I speak out of turn, Your Grace, but wouldn't you be much safer here? Avadon is in dire straits. I feel the rebellion on the wind. I can get a competent commander to lead the militia into battle—"

"No." Darjal's blood boiled in his veins. "Nicholai destroyed one of my beautiful churches, a place where I exist for the people of Southern outside my hometown. If he is turning the people of Avadon against us, then like the mighty smite the non-believers, I will see to it the entire town watches as I rip out his sinful heart. I will make an example out of him and drive the people back on the righteous path."

A heavy pause followed as the footman forced himself to nod. He did not agree with the Time Father placing himself in a vulnerable position. Not after he had witnessed Kazuaki Hidataka's merciless battle tactics. But Darjal Wessex's ego was grand; it had to be, to believe he was a god. The soldier knew no chance existed in changing his mind. "Yes, sir. I'm uncertain how many men we will gather. Many still patrol Southeastern's borders. We placed a large number on the ironclad, and we suffered a heavy blow in Avadon. But I'll let you know as soon as we have a suitable army assembled."

"Off with you then." Darjal flicked his wrist.

The soldier departed, relieved to create distance between himself and the Southern Time Father.

Darjal's heart thudded from deep within his chest. Victory was within their grasp. Nicholai had made his location known. It was only a matter of time now. To be the one who brought down the traitor would not only showcase his godliness, but he would go down in history as the savior of Panagea. The people would witness his ability to cleanse the world of the sinful.

He laced his fingers together and leaned forward, his expression one of sadistic excitement. "I'm coming for you, Nicholai Addihein. May you beg me to have mercy on your soul."

THE DISCORD AMONGST the people was palpable. Those from the slums poured into the heart of Avadon, causing even greater pandemonium amongst the citizens. They thought of the poverty-stricken as filth who brought nothing but theft and assault along with them. The men and women of the lawless land saw the footmen's bodies as a victory and reflected it in their excited state. But the corpses seemed like a bad omen to the townsfolk, now having no protection from the horrid conditions in which they lived. Confusion and panic clung to the air. It fueled the already fragile environment.

"The people are scared," Bartholomew announced as he looked to Kazuaki. "We need to calm them, or word will spread that our presence brings chaos instead of composure."

Emont showed his agreement. "They've been left in the dark for so long. Darjal has fed us one lie after another. First about the state of Southeastern, then with the ship. They need to know what's going on."

Bartholomew peered at Nicholai from behind his glasses. "You need to expose the goings-on, Nicholai. Tell them everything. It's our best shot at reaching them."

The Time Father didn't have much time to recover from his endeavor in the church. He looked nothing like a diplomatic convoy who could usher the people into an understanding state. "I wouldn't know what to say." He forced himself to sit upright.

"The truth." Bartholomew motioned to a tall pile of rubble that lingered in the city center. "Get up there. They need to hear it. The sooner they know we're a positive influence, the sooner this revolution can get the people behind it."

The Time Father stared at the crumbling debris the scholar intended to serve as his soapbox. Bartholomew was right. The people had lived in the shadows long enough. He dragged his tired body forward, forcing one foot after the other until he climbed the garbage heap and raised his hands to gather attention.

"People—" He doubled over in a coughing fit. His heart thudded as he tried to steady his breathing. The man's body remained ravaged from the growth of the redwood tree.

Kazuaki reached into his pocket and took several long strides to Nicholai then injected him with an oxygen syringe.

The Time Father's coughing slowed, and he straightened himself upright. His breathing returned to normal, and he patted the captain's shoulder in a silent gesture of thanks.

Nicholai turned to the scared citizens and invited a deep breath into his lungs.

"People of Avadon—"

The residents' panic proved too great. Only a few stopped to look at him.

Kazuaki frowned, irritated. "Steady yourselves!" His loud voice cut through the air with the power of cannon fire.

More stopped and turned.

"Listen to what this man has to say," he growled and stepped aside.

The Time Father cleared his throat as a small crowd gathered. Everyone lived in desperation, hungry for direction. Though the confusion in their faces plagued him, he carried on. "I know you

all must be scared. I'm here to shed light on the anarchy you've endured. No lies." He stared across the growing audience. "Just truth."

"How can we trust you?" a random voice shot forth from the
crowd.

Nicholai nodded. "You raise a valid point. I know about what
I speak, about the state of Panagea. About everything." He pulled
his Chronometer from his shirt and held it near his neck. "I know
because I am Nicholai Addihein, Time Father of the Southeastern
division."

The energy shift was tangible. A series of whispers grew, weaving in and out of the mouths of many as the gathering gained more
citizens. Questions fired at Nicholai from the terrified men and
women, but only a few were discernable amongst the many.

"Is Southeastern frozen?"

"What was the ship really for?"

"What is causing all these disasters?"

"Where did that thing in the church come from?"

Nicholai raised his hands to silence the onslaught of questions.
"Please, people, please—" He had lost them. He regarded Kazuaki
for answers.

The captain met his gaze and nodded to the crowd, a silent order for him to regain control.

Nicholai frowned and gazed across the pandemonium before
he stood taller. "Silence!" he shouted with an authority he didn't
know he possessed.

It gathered a reaction. The voice's quieted. He had their attention again.

"I regret to inform you all that Southeastern is, indeed, frozen
in time. It has been for months." He tried to remain authoritative,
though evidence of shame lived in his tone. "Panagea has been in
dire straits for years, but this has certainly expedited the frequency
of the natural disasters deteriorating the continent."

"What are you waiting for then?" an angry voice yelled from the crowd. "Go unfreeze Southeastern and save us from this nightmare!"

Nicholai winced but remained strong. "Southeastern's state is only another blow given to an already dying earth. Unfreezing the division would only delay the inevitable. We need to correct this from the inside out. That's why a tree is growing through the church."

His delivery failed to make sense to the people. They continued to balk, but some seemed relieved to get answers.

"For too long we have abused Panagea, sucking all she had within her in exchange for the conveniences of metal and machines. We cannot deny how important technological advancements are, but, in our eagerness, we became blind to the fruits of nature." He gestured to the exposed plants grown in secrecy, now flourishing in the light despite being surrounded by dust. "Here you will find food, medicine, natural materials for clothing. The possibilities are limitless. But, most important of all, you will find Panagea's salvation. She cannot exist without these complex ecosystems to nourish her. By destroying the creations that extend from her, we are slowly killing her."

"He speaks the truth." Umbriel joined Nicholai on his mountain of rubble. "We have asked so much of her and given little in return. For thousands of years, Panagea has been the food in our stomachs, the water in our veins, the oxygen in our lungs, the home where we plant our feet. Is that not enough?"

Stillness fell over the crowd. It was hard for them to absorb the gravity of Nicholai's and Umbriel's words.

"I understand that it is difficult to grasp," the Time Father started, "having never seen the full force of nature. But those Avadon has rejected—the weak, the poor—they have seen it with their own eyes. They've eaten the food grown from the earth, and they've found relief in nature's medicines. Please, speak with them, let them show you. Do not take my word for it. See for yourselves."

Rising whispers floated about, comingling with the dust in the air.

Cautious whispers of hope, of careful optimism, Nicholai thought. With one final effort, he addressed the people. "We will stay as long as we need to, to show the positivity of our efforts. I only ask that if your feet carry you outside Avadon's borders, you speak of our accomplishments here. Spread the word. Darjal has labeled all of you as faceless, nameless denizens of Southern. He has insulted you by keeping the truth from you. But, when I look out at you, I see possibilities. I see not only Southern's deliverance but Panagea's as well."

It was quiet. The wind howled as it twisted through the broken rubbish of fallen buildings. Bartholomew gazed at the crowd then at Nicholai. He clapped, guessing on a psychological level people would follow. His hands remained the lone producer of the sound until Iani and Rennington joined, followed by the rest of Kazuaki's crew. It didn't take long before the slum's inhabitants voiced their applause, thankful for the wonders Nicholai and Umbriel brought unto them. Several of Avadon's citizens joined, having experienced the brutality of living in a city that received only religious platitudes from Darjal with no follow through. They, too, grew excited by the prospect of something better.

Though some held fast to their skepticism, Nicholai took it as the best outcome. He exercised care as he climbed down from the rubble and offered his hand to Umbriel.

"Well done." Kazuaki gazed at the two exhausted individuals. "Now, let's find you both a bed and get you some rest. You'll need all the energy you can muster soon enough."

TIME TREATED THEM BETTER than it had at the beginning. True to their word, Nicholai, Umbriel, and Kazuaki's crew brought the same knowledge to Avadon that they had brought to the slums. Help came in physical labor, educational offerings, medical services, and emotional support. When Nicholai wasn't busying himself with the plant life's expansion, he answered the peoples' questions. Some stayed, too attached to Avadon to abandon their home despite its poor condition. Others ventured forth in search of new beginnings, carrying the tale of the rogue Time Father and his ethereal companions with them.

Every day was a wait for Darjal. They knew he wished to unleash a storm upon them. But it was not just the Southern Time Father they awaited. As word of their efforts spread, the risk of dwelling in Avadon grew. Other Time Fathers would seek out Nicholai. He knew he could not linger in Avadon much longer, but he stuck to his promise. The man brought as much of himself as he could to the citizens before they discussed their impending departure. It put him in mind of Southeastern. It felt good to return to a version of himself he used to be. If only for a moment.

Nicholai knelt beside a squash plant. He held out his hands, and the green vines crawled outward with speed, climbing the lattice the people fashioned from recycled rubbish. Plump, weighted vegetables sprouted and hung from the plant as a shadow fell over Nicholai.

"Nicholai, what you're doing here ..." Kazuaki said, towering over him. His words still held a permanent jaggedness, but he cleared his throat to soften his tone. "You're doing well."

The Time Father arched a brow as he stood and dusted the dirt from his knees. No hidden insult. No verbal attack. "Captain Hidataka, that's quite possibly the most encouraging thing you've ever said to me."

Kazuaki scoffed and rolled his eye.

Nicholai knew by the captain's gesture he had ruined the moment. He grinned despite himself. "We're all doing well. Better than I ever thought possible. Thank you, Kazuaki."

"Right." The captain forced a small smile. "Just keep it up."

Nicholai returned his smile. He thought they could have saved a thousand worlds before he'd ever receive praise from Kazuaki Hidataka. "So ... you must be excited Umbriel restored Bermuda's heart, huh?"

Kazuaki's expression flattened. "What?"

"You know ... I mean, she told me a little about what was happening. About Mimir. Siphoning the poison. That's why she was so ... heartless?" He paused. The heat from Kazuaki's stare made him feel uncomfortable. "I thought, I figured you'd be the happiest of all, you know."

Kazuaki narrowed his eye. But before he opened his mouth to speak, Bermuda ran to the two men, out of breath. "Captain! I saw an army on the horizon carrying a sedan chair. It bears the Southern insignia. I'm certain it's Darjal."

"About damn time," Kazuaki muttered. "Tell Emont to ready those who wish to fight."

"And give those who wish to flee the opportunity," Nicholai interjected. "We can't force everyone to take part."

Kazuaki scoffed for the second time. Nicholai's ethics surfaced at the most inopportune moments. The captain motioned the two to follow as he broke into a run. "Stay out of the way if you don't plan to put yourself to use," he said to Nicholai. "I will be too preoccupied with the soldiers to save your ass."

They readied those who were willing. The impending battle lived at the forefront of everyone's minds since Nicholai had mentioned it to the townsfolk after Avadon's destruction. Boxes of handmade grenades filtered through civilian hands. Those who did not fear close-handed combat gripped their sharpened shrapnel.

Makeshift armor, fashioned from metal scraps, fell over countless bodies.

They looked the part, but Nicholai still harbored concerns about whether the people were battle ready. They were citizens, a far cry from the trained footmen who would descend upon them in minutes. He reminded himself they wanted this. They wanted to contribute to Panagea's shift, to be the ones who stood against their oppressors and said, *We want a change.* He could not deny them that.

Rennington and Iani seemed the most excited. They swung their machetes around in their hands with an anxious energy that bubbled inside them.

"Good luck, gentlemen," Nicholai said to the Platts brothers. "I know you've waited for this day for a long time."

Rennington grinned, his arm around Iani as he beamed. "You don't know the half of it, Nico."

Nicholai patted both of their shoulders. Though their integrities on how to handle certain situations did not align with his own, he cast their differences aside. They lived in comfort with the path they chose. He had plans to try his own way. Though it went against Kazuaki's wishes to stay out of harm's way, Nicholai needed to try. He exchanged words of encouragement with the rest of the crew he came to know and respect, despite everything. He turned to Kazuaki. "Good luck, Captain."

Kazuaki shoved one last dagger into his boot. "Go on then." He motioned Nicholai off.

The Time Father nodded and vanished from the battlefront.

Kazuaki's crew stood at the forefront with the collective group of outraged citizens who awaited Darjal's arrival. It did not take long.

The Southern army stood in eyesight. Kazuaki could not analyze their expressions from the distance, but he hoped they portrayed shock at the organized group of residents ready to challenge them. He turned to his makeshift warriors. "Remember, this is *your* home ground! Use that advantage, use the terrain, and show them what happens when they spit in the faces of Avadon!"

The people roared and ran forward, weapons held high above their heads.

Darjal's army followed suit. The sedan chair, still flanked by four soldiers who carried the poles, headed toward the church. The lines of opposing forces met. Bodies collided with great ferocity. The clangs of metal and heated cries of the people rose high.

The battle had begun.

Nicholai knew Darjal would not take part. He came for the religious and political appearances he assumed he'd need to make after his victory. The Time Father kept a close eye on the sedan chair as it weaved out of danger's way and into the crumbling streets of Avadon. He wished he could see the look on the Southern Time Father's face as he exposed himself to his dying city, but the cloth that hung in the windows shrouded the man inside. If Nicholai could see a small shred of guilt, regret, *something* that gave him hope he could reach Darjal, it would have given him more confidence for success.

The four footmen carried the sedan cart to the church. They lowered to their knees as Nicholai pressed his back against the walls of the alley, the same one he took refuge in months earlier. He watched from the shadows as Darjal lifted himself from the carrier and brushed at his suit. Fury infected his face as he beheld the once magnificent cathedral.

His precious church, once a symbol of glory to his godliness, was destroyed. The tree towered out the top in defiance, disappearing from eyesight in the low-hanging clouds. Darjal spat and turned to his men. "You four guard the door. Wait out front for the others. Bring him as soon as you have him. I'll show these heathens what happens when they follow demons into the darkness."

The footmen nodded and assumed their posts in front of the church doors, weapons visible, as Darjal slipped inside to assess the structural damage. If anything was worth saving that hadn't fallen, he wanted to know about it.

Nicholai eased into the shadows of the alley and searched the base of the church for the entry to the catacombs, but, when he found the hidden handle and tugged, he frowned. The church's foundation had shifted in the quakes. The damage had compromised the opening. It wouldn't budge.

With a sigh, he eyed the tree limbs that had crashed through the stained-glass windows. He'd have to find another way in.

BERMUDA GRUNTED AS she stabbed a man in the chest. The dagger ate with hunger before it moved to the next meal. She did not linger to see if her victims died. Even if they escaped death, a weakened soldier made an easier target for the inexperienced citizens to finish. A tornado in the masses, the quartermaster brought chaos wherever she went.

Elowyn focused on immediate deaths. She did not fear taking another man's life, but her compassion wouldn't allow them to suffer. A soldier raised his weapon to attack. She severed the exposed brachial artery in the armpit. Main arteries, jugular veins, the temples of the skull, the eyes—those were her targets. Anywhere that brought a sweet, merciful death.

The medic's focus held a disadvantage. She paid little attention to her surroundings while she perfected her aim, but she never feared. That's what the Platts brothers were for.

Bartholomew was no expert in close-handed combat. But, even with his imperfect eyesight, he knew his way around a gun. His calculating mind was his biggest asset. He was intimate with the human mind's inner workings. Predicting a man's move was easy. The scholar waited for the best shot to appear. Then he took it.

Kazuaki fought beside Granite. The captain's blade ran a soldier through. Granite made short work of those who neared him. His size made him slow, but the beast picked up the slack. Wild jaws brought down any assailants who dared to hurt his loving master.

Granite was a steady fighter, slow and methodical. Above the chaos, his dog's shrill yelp sliced through his eardrums. The man's head whipped toward the cry. The beast laid on the rocky ground, howling as a soldier loomed over him. His foot fell in waves as he stomped the fallen creature.

If a more dangerous weapon existed, Kazuaki had not seen it. Granite's dog never suffered before—none had ever gotten close enough. The captain, who witnessed horrors beyond man's imagination, watched in revulsion.

Granite bellowed a sound of raw supremacy. He grabbed the dog's attacker's skull with his giant hand and ripped him from the beast. The soldier's head twisted under Granite's force. He separated the cervical spine from the skull. The head dangled on the body, held on only by skin. Granite grabbed the corpse and hurled it at another foot soldier who dared to approach his dog.

"Gods alive ..." Kazuaki couldn't stare long. He returned his attention to the battle. If he had cleansed his soul at all before this moment, Granite's grotesque display had soiled it again. He didn't let it slow him. The slaughter ensued.

Gentle hands scooped up Granite's dog. The giant man cradled the beast in his arms. The whimpering creature laid over his shoulder while he continued the fight one handed. This handicap did not slow him. The true fury that was Granite unleashed itself. The footmen suffered much for their egregious error.

Kazuaki scowled as his blade met another. A quick pop from his gun brought the clash to an end. He spied Iani and made his way beside him, cursing as a footman's bullet found his side. He felt the familiar burn. It radiated through him as he flung his dagger toward his assailant. The blade sank into its target with success.

The soldiers were stronger than he thought. Bodies of Avadon's citizens cluttered the red earth. "Iani!" he shouted through the noise of the fight. "Did you see where Nico and Umbriel sought safety?"

The younger Platts brother dodged a swing. Raw iron from his pistol split open a soldier's skull before one of Avadon's citizens dug their steel pipe into the footman's side. He screamed and fell to his knees. "No idea, Captain!"

Kazuaki scowled. They didn't hold them back as much as he expected. Southern's soldiers crawled farther into the city. He hoped Nicholai wasn't doing anything stupid.

NICHOLAI'S FINGERS burned as he pulled himself up the moss and vines that grew on the church's exterior walls. The soles of his feet scraped against the foundation. He dragged himself closer to a broken window. With exertion, he gripped the window too hastily, cursing as his fingers sank into the jagged edges of broken glass.

Exercising more care the second time, he found a place to rest his fingers where the glass was obliterated and hauled his body upward. A thick tree branch lingered nearby, and he tested the integrity with his foot before he walked onto it. He spied Darjal below, running his fingers over the broken statues and relics. After his initial mourning, he disappeared into the decaying steps that led toward the basement. A glance at the door showed the footmen remained posted outside.

With cautious steps, Nicholai crept across the tree's limbs and positioned himself above the church's entrance. He drew a deep breath and jumped to the bottom, absorbing much of the impact in his joints. Quick feet carried him to the church doors, and he slammed them shut before shoving a decorative wrought iron sword that had detached from a statue into the handles. He heard the footmen on the other side of the door as they approached.

They tried to rattle open the door but to no avail.

The commotion summoned Darjal from the basement, and he ascended the steps, appearing once again in the church interior. The two men met one another's gazes, standing before each other in the distance. Darjal appeared horrified at first but took note Nicholai possessed no visible weapons. Confident strides carried him forward. "And just like that, as if from a piece of folklore, the demon stands before the god."

"They will kill you, Darjal. I came to talk sense into you before that happened."

The Southern Time Father sneered. "Gods do not bow down to the demands of the demons."

Nicholai rolled his eyes. "Will you cut the religious ranting? You're no more a god than I am a demon. Darjal, I'm *trying* to help you."

"Help?" Darjal laughed. The eerie sound echoed in the large room. "You abandoned your division, betrayed everything the Time Fathers stood for, and sent our continent into turmoil. Nicholai Addihein, if you wish to help, you will do the noble thing and remove your Chronometer, strip yourself of the Time Father title before the people of Avadon and have the good decency to die a public spectacle, so others might never make the same mistake you did."

"I don't disagree I played a part in this chaos. But Panagea was failing far before my sin in Southeastern. She was in trouble the second the past Time Fathers killed the Earth Mothers. It's just taken hundreds of years to see the long-term consequences." His face shifted to one of morose. Though part of him already knew the answer, he needed to hear it for himself. "Did you know, Darjal? Of Umbriel, locked away on that island?"

The Southern Time Father frowned. "We all knew. The fact Edvard Addihein did not shed light on this information only speaks to how little he thinks of you."

Nicholai narrowed his eyes. He suspected as much. "You would banish a woman to a cruel fate for *hundreds* of years? For what, Darjal? Why?"

He scoffed. "Your empathy has blinded you, Nicholai. We left her there for the same reason our forefathers left her there."

"This is madness! You boast of advancement, of the importance of change, of pushing mankind forward, and yet you continue to embrace an archaic, outdated belief system. You're accepting the pieties of men long dead. They're not even here to see the consequences of their actions, Darjal. What we're doing, what we've done, it isn't working. But there is still time to fix this!"

"Our forefathers built a life for us. They turned unrefined beasts who prayed to old-world gods for favor into men who could answer their own prayers with technology. I will not invite those omnipotent heathens back into this world. I am all the god Panagea needs."

The man was sick. Delusional. But Nicholai had to appeal to him if he wanted a chance at nonviolent change. "We can coexist. The Time Fathers and Earth Mothers were meant to maintain the balance."

"You always were an idealist, Nicholai." The vigorous pounding on the door outside the church almost drowned out Darjal's voice. "A few Time Fathers shared your ideals throughout the years, but history has shown us that ideals never thrive outside the minds who create them." He walked forward and pulled a gun from his breast pocket. "If you're not with us, you are against us. And we are too powerful to fall."

Nicholai eyed the weapon before he flicked his gaze back to Darjal. His face showed no fear, only disappointment. "Should you meet your end tonight, remember I tried to save you, Darjal."

Darjal raised the gun. "Confident words. They'll be the last ones you speak."

Nicholai tried to stay ahead of Darjal's gunfire as he unleashed his bullets. To his relief, the redwood's thick trunk provided cover.

"You ran for a long time, Nicholai." Darjal rounded the base of the tree. "But you cannot run forever. Not from me. I am Panagea's god. I will smite the immoral before you sully my world further."

Nicholai doubled around the back.

The Southern Time Father followed. He spotted Nicholai and squeezed off another shot.

Nicholai ducked back in time to avoid being hit. The metal connected with the edge of his shoulder before it came out the other side.

Darjal snarled, frustrated. He lifted his weapon again but collapsed under the weight of Umbriel as she descended from her hiding spot in the redwood tree.

The woman's feet dug into his shoulders and brought him to the floor before she flipped off. With grace, she landed on her knee while one hand steadied her.

Nicholai looked to Umbriel, surprised.

"You weren't the only one who thought they could change his mind," she said as she came to a stand.

Darjal's age felt the pain as he laid on the floor, but sheer determination pushed him to his feet. He seized his weapon from the floor and raised it with shaking hands. "The Earth Mother," he said in a loud exhale as his cruel eyes fell on the silver-haired maiden. "Perfect. Two for one."

"Darjal!" Nicholai held up his hand as the man aimed the Earth Mother. "Stop! I beg you."

"You'll be begging soon enough," he said with a grunt as he squeezed the trigger.

The Earth Mother avoided it, but both individuals knew they could not outrun his gunfire forever.

As the Southern Time Father lifted his gun to the Earth Mother again, Nicholai stepped in front of him. "Darjal, *please—*"

There was no reaching him. His ego allowed him to live in delusional invincibility. In Darjal's mind, he was a god sent to cleanse Avadon of the demon Nicholai. The Southeastern Time Father watched as his finger caressed the trigger. He did not wish to put Umbriel in any additional danger. They couldn't risk it.

Nicholai threw his hands forward to stop any more damage from occurring. The metal of Darjal's gun eroded. The decay happened fast. Despite pulling on the trigger, the weapon deteriorated too much to function.

Darjal's eyes widened at the sight. "The dark magic," he whispered. "So it's true." The Southern Time Father watched in horror as the age crept up his fingers, wrinkling the skin on his hands and wrist.

Nicholai panicked as the effects traveled up Darjal's arm, withering any visible flesh. He only intended to erode the weapon, but Darjal's touch was inseparable from the gun's handle. Nicholai dropped his hands and stepped backward, horrified as the Southern Time Father aged countless years in minutes.

His skin creased and dried, his already graying hair turned ashen white and fell from his scalp in patches as his body slumped to the floor. Eye sockets sunk deeper into his skull. Teeth fell from his jaw as his hands crippled and curled inward.

Nicholai's heart pounded. He couldn't rip his gaze from his unintended act.

Darjal laid before him in the fetus position, the withered remnants of the man he once was. He moaned a grotesque sound of agony that would haunt Nicholai forever. His bulbous eyes quivered as they looked at the Southeastern Time Father. Terror reflected inside them until they lost the light that showed life.

Nicholai stared at the frail corpse, his face one of pure shock. "I ... only meant to ... the gun." A burning acid that boiled from his crime ravaged his stomach.

Umbriel joined beside him. She banished her shock at the sight and laid a gentle hand on Nicholai's shoulder. "It was an accident. You tried to reason with him."

He didn't hear her nor the forceful pounding on the church doors. He fell victim to his appalled mind. He had killed a man. Accident or not, he had drained Darjal's life from him in the most traumatizing way. Everything he ever stood for crumbled, like the city of Avadon. Nicholai was so lost inside himself he didn't even flinch when the homemade grenade blew open the church doors.

Umbriel shielded her eyes with her hand and squinted as dust and debris floated in the surrounding air. Too far from the door to suffer any hits from shrapnel, she stood tall until she recognized the bodies coming forth through the dust.

"Iani! Rennington!" She rushed to hug the men.

The Platts brothers returned her embrace but quickly pulled away to assess the situation. It seemed no threat existed.

Rennington stepped forward when he realized Nicholai's back was to him. "Nico?" He edged close enough to see Darjal's wilted corpse on the floor. "Bloody shit!" He jumped backward. Rennington had witnessed many traumatizing things on the battlefield, but the dried-up face of Darjal Wessex was a nightmare unmatched by any corpse he'd seen prior. "What happened here?"

Nicholai stared at the body, unmoving. "I killed him."

"I'll say you did." Rennington gave the corpse a little kick. His face scrunched when he felt the femur fall off the pelvis from inside the pants. "Didn't think you had it in you. Let's go tell the captain the good news."

Iani walked over to see the body and stuck out his tongue at the sight. "Ugh, damn, Renn, why didn't you warn me? That's sick."

Rennington grabbed Darjal's decayed arm. It separated from the body with ease, and he waved it in Iani's face. "Need a hand telling the captain he's dead?" He laughed at his dark humor and found more amusement as Iani shied away from the limb.

"You're feckin' off in the head, Renn." Iani swatted the hand, refusing to watch as it struck the floor with a thud.

The Platts brothers started out the door, walking over the bodies of the four footmen who had once guarded the entrance.

"Darjal's army is retreating. They had the upper hand for a while, but ..." Rennington shook his head and shuddered. "Let's just say, never mess with Granite's dog. With Darjal done and dead, the battle's as good as won. You both coming?" Rennington asked, oblivious to Nicholai's mental anguish.

Umbriel forced a gentle smile. "We'll catch up."

"Right-o. We'll be in the town center." Rennington stole one last glimpse of Darjal's withered corpse—the symbol of Southern fell, the man who had ordered the Platts brothers to send those children to their deaths. It felt good, he thought as he followed Iani out the door. Justice was finally served.

Umbriel acknowledged Nicholai's tangible anguish. She grabbed his hand to let him know she was there. "Will you be okay?"

Nicholai startled. He drew a sharp gulp of oxygen. He hadn't even realized he had stopped breathing. Numbness engulfed his entire body as he knelt and scooped up the Chronometer once possessed by Darjal Wessex. "I'll be okay."

She wasn't convinced. But, with little else to do, she whispered a silent prayer for Darjal that the old-world gods swept his soul to a better afterlife. She hoped he found peace. With that, she followed Nicholai out the church doors, leaving Darjal Wessex to his tomb inside his precious church.

THE GATHERING IN THE town center was a mixture of triumph and mourning. Many had perished, still sprawled on the broken grounds of the battlefield. The tragedy came at a cost, but the people saw it as a pivotal moment for Avadon. Their city's voice stretched far across the land and shouted its disapproval for their division's condition. It was a drop in the ocean, but they reveled. It was the start of something, a part of a movement so grand it filled their tired hearts and provided a sense of purpose and relief to the injuries they had suffered in battle.

Caked in blood, Kazuaki found Bermuda in the crowd. A look of relief climbed onto his face when he realized she had survived. One by one, others joined the group. They reveled in the safety of their comrades. The only one who did not celebrate was Granite, far too consumed by his injured dog to give much care to anything else.

Elowyn separated herself from the group and slipped to Granite's side. "May I?" When he nodded his approval, she felt the creature's bones. Her expertise relied in human medicine, but she couldn't abandon Granite to his concern. There were obvious breaks in the dog's legs. She regarded Granite with as much reassurance as she could muster. "I'll do everything in my power to help him, Granite. I promise."

Kazuaki noticed Nicholai approach with Umbriel. He could tell the man was beside himself. His face was pale, emotionless. He recognized the look. The captain saw it in many others throughout his lifetime. Rennington had briefed him on what had happened in the church. Nicholai's mental trauma was fresh; Kazuaki thought it best not to mention it. "Our work in Avadon is finished. Our efforts here were successful today, but, if the other divisions send their armies at the same time, we'd be unable to beat them back. We need to move on to Southwestern and stay ahead of them." Kazuaki scanned riotous crowd. "They have the tools to rebuild this place. They'll be safer if we're not here."

Emont stepped forward. "I'm coming with you."

The captain frowned. "We can't leave Avadon without structure. It's clear whoever held office of this city isn't present. They'll need guidance during reconstruction and help to bury their dead. You're needed here, Emont."

"I will resign my position to Jodathyn. He's a stand-up man. He knows how to take charge. You must amass more followers as you move. I'm familiar with the surrounding towns that stretch beyond Avadon. I'll spread the word of what we did. I'll gain more soldiers, not just for the cause, but I'll send additional hands to Avadon to assist. Morale is low elsewhere. I know they'll stand up and fight when news of our success reaches them. You need us, Kazuaki. You can't do this alone."

The captain clenched his jaw. Emont was right. Were it not for Avadon's people, they would not have succeeded in their efforts. "Very well, Emont. Gather whoever you can. Meet us outside of Denicee. We'll enter Carlo Angevin's hometown together. If we beat you there, we'll wait."

Emont nodded. "You paved the way to rebirth Avadon anew. I won't let you down."

Nicholai shared a grim glance with the two men as he clutched Darjal's Chronometer in his palm. "There's just one loose end. We need to appoint a new Southern Time Father. With Darjal dead, no one has the power to wind the Chronometer. Southern will freeze in less than twenty-four hours and all of you with it."

Kazuaki frowned. Nicholai spoke the truth. But they couldn't choose anybody. It was an enormous undertaking, ruling a division, let alone a fragile one. They needed someone intelligent, someone capable, someone as abrasive as they were understanding to the peoples' needs. Most important of all, they needed someone they trusted. "That doesn't give us much time to find someone we can rely on."

The crew fell quiet. Time was not on their side. They couldn't throw anyone into that position. Even if they could, few would jump at the opportunity.

Without the approval of the rest, the new Time Father would have just as big a target on his back as Nicholai. Especially if it was known he was the rogue Time Father's ally.

The weight of the moment crushed upon them until Bartholomew stepped forward and looked Nicholai in the eyes. "I'll do it. I'll be Southern's Time Father."

Chapter Twenty-One

The victory in Avadon fueled the people with new hope. Most embraced Bartholomew's offer to rule; they craved leadership in their desperate hour. They'd felt an absence of it since Avadon's mayor had abandoned his position. Bartholomew assured them he would lead with fairness, but they weren't selective. A leader gave them optimism that someone would change their ravaged land. And, if he failed, they at least had someone to blame. Bartholomew welcomed the challenge.

Kazuaki and the crew stood before the scholar as did Nicholai and Umbriel. Darjal's Chronometer swung back and forth in the Southeastern Time Father's hand as he held the chain.

"Are you sure, Bartholomew?" Nicholai asked for the last time. "You'll be bound here inside Southern's borders, unable to leave for more than a day. It's a far cry from the life you knew at sea."

Bartholomew nodded. He understood their uncertainty but felt none of his own. "I am sure."

The Southeastern Time Father returned his nod and popped open the clock's face, exposing the gears that clicked and whirred within. He knelt and scraped open a healing wound on his hand by slicing it over a piece of sharp rubble. Nicholai hovered his injury above the clock until a drop of blood fell inside, the first step in preparing the Chronometer for a new member. Prepped with the blood of the old, he looked to Bartholomew. "Your turn." He extended his hand.

Bartholomew did not hesitate. He rested his hand in Nicholai's. With a quick swipe, the Southeastern Time Father split open his skin, allowing Bartholomew's blood to commingle with the Chronometer's gears. Bartholomew's DNA spilled into the corners of the watch's interior. He belonged to Southern now.

Nicholai closed the Chronometer's face and handed it to the man before him. "Congratulations." He forced a smile, relieved to have found someone capable yet saddened to leave him behind. "Southern couldn't be in better hands."

Bartholomew accepted the Chronometer with gentle hands. He wiped his thumb over its smooth face before he affixed it to his clothing by the chain. "I won't let you down."

"It never crossed my mind." Nicholai patted Bartholomew's shoulder before he stood aside to allow the others to issue their goodbyes.

Kazuaki approached and stared at Bartholomew with a sigh. "Good luck, old friend." He surveyed the barren environment that surrounded them. It looked dreadful. "If anyone can turn this place around, it's you."

Bartholomew smiled. "I know the sea has always been your place, Kazuaki. But know as long as I'm here, you will always have a home on Southern ground."

It was a struggle to bid farewell to such a good man. Kazuaki extended his hand for a shake, but Bartholomew pulled the gruff man into an embrace. He remained stiff under the show of affection, but, after a moment, Kazuaki softened and patted Bartholomew's back.

When he pulled away, he eyed the crew. They all stared at Bartholomew, their faces encouraged, save for Bermuda. She portrayed a look of uncertainty.

"See you, Bart," Brack said as he shook the man's hand.

Iani and Rennington approached together, smiling at Bartholomew as they stood before him. Intelligent, accomplished, and well-spoken, he was the picture of perfection. None better could fill the role. "Finally," Iani said, "a Southern ruler I would gladly die for."

"Let's not be dramatic," Bartholomew replied as he shook the brothers' hands with a quiet laugh. He stepped backward and beheld those he had come to know well. "Go on then," he said, enveloped in pride at having had the pleasure of knowing them. "Go liberate the world."

The departure did not come without pain, but duty carried them forward. They commandeered two steam cars with the respective owners' permission. Avadon faded into the distance as they trudged forward. The cars rattled over the uneven terrain. Avadon was only a small part that comprised the Southern division, but they remained confident word would spread. Everything here lived in the capable hands of Bartholomew now. They needed to keep going. The vehicles headed southwest into Carlo Angevin's division.

WEEKS PASSED. THEY stopped at several places along the way to make camp. Nicholai and Umbriel took advantage of the breaks, crafting small ecosystems in secrecy as they went. The group often sought shelter in decrepit buildings along the way, trying their best to stay low and progress. It was disheartening how many existed. Panagea's desecration spread beyond Avadon. Every village or city they drove through suffered. Some were more obvious than others.

In the daylight, Umbriel summoned and sprinkled various seeds as she hung out the side of the steam car. Her tactic did not give Nicholai any opportunities to isolate and speed up their time, but it required little effort of her, and she let nature take its course.

If the seeds were strong, they would survive, and the survivors would reseed themselves with stronger, more durable offspring.

It felt no different when they crossed Southwestern's border, save for the gaping absence of Bartholomew's wisdom. Though emotions ran high, the crew remained in great spirits coming off the victory in Southern. Nicholai did not share their enthusiasm. He suffered through his disgust with himself but hid it well.

Night approached after another day of many logged hours driving. Their vehicles crawled into a small town, the terrain crackling under the tires as they pulled the cars behind a tall building to shield them. Fruits Umbriel had packed fed their hungry stomachs, and they readied themselves for rest.

The moon hung high in the distance, beaming a soft illumination onto the dark town. Evening was well upon them. The streets lived in stillness with not a person in sight. Small towns did not share a bustling nightlife; the residents were all inside their homes, finding sleep in their beds.

"We can stop in a few more places to allow Umbriel time to grow her plants," Kazuaki said, breaking the silence as everyone readied themselves to find rest. "That'll give Emont more time to gather recruits. As soon as he meets us in Denicee, we'll isolate Carlo Angevin. A handful of the footmen are just blindly following orders. If we assassinate Carlo first, with any luck, most will surrender."

Nicholai looked up from his untouched fruit. "That's not what we're trying to do." His conviction on the matter was strong, a side effect of the despair he felt at killing Darjal. "We're helping the people. Helping Panagea. This isn't a Time Father murder party."

Kazuaki scoffed. "One and the same. One accomplishes the other."

"For everyone you kill, we'll struggle to find a suitable replacement. We got extremely lucky with Bartholomew. He made the ultimate sacrifice. Do you intend to condemn others to the same fate?"

The captain arched a brow. "Condemn them? Is that what you feel your title is, Nico? A punishment?"

The man flinched. He had started to. "Just ... think about it."

Kazuaki looked unimpressed. "I'll know what to do in the moment."

Nicholai was too tired to argue. He closed his eyes and felt the sting of many sleepless nights attack his lids. The man collapsed back. Against his body's wishes, he pried open his tired eyes and looked skyward. No stars shone through the surrounding town's smog and lights. He wasn't surprised. He only saw them when they were far off Panagea's shores, rolling on the waves of Kazuaki's ship.

Umbriel laid down beside him, her eyes on the heavens. "How are you holding up?"

"Fine."

He answered too fast to sound reassuring, but she sensed he did not wish to discuss it. She wasn't sure if leaving him alone with his thoughts was a good idea, but Umbriel knew she couldn't force him to talk. The Earth Mother turned over, closing her eyes to summon sleep.

Granite ripped little pieces of dried meat from his hands, feeding the beast the small morsels as he sat in the steam car. Despite both Elowyn's and Umbriel's best efforts, one of the dog's legs had suffered far too much damage and required amputation. Umbriel's abilities had facilitated in healing the dog's soft tissues, but reconstructing the shattered bone was beyond hers or Elowyn's medical expertise. The beast did not seem to mind. He wagged his tail and licked Granite's face as he fed him.

Bermuda sat beside the captain who propped himself up on the steam car to take the first watch. She rested her arms on her bent knees, sighing after a full day of travel. Everyone around them laid down, trying to find rest. The orange glow from the fire brought light to her face. She recalled the countless bodies they had abandoned in Avadon. She thought of Bartholomew. "Do you really think we can do it, Kazuaki?" Her voice quieted in the stillness. "Do you still believe it's all worth it?"

The captain watched as the others slept. Revi would rise in four hours to take over the watch so he, too, could get a small amount of shut eye. "It went well in Southern." He faced Bermuda when he was certain everyone else found sleep. "I'm optimistic."

"For what?" A hint of frustration tainted her query. "We had a home at sea. We don't need another one. Penn is stuck with the ship. We lost Bartholomew forever to Southern. It seems like everything is falling apart, and I'm still not sure why we're doing it. Why doesn't Nico just restart Southeastern and spare us all this headache? That seems to be all the Time Fathers want."

Kazuaki squared his shoulders and shrugged. "I'm sure he has his reasons. We'll deal with that when the timing is right. But for now, we fight. We fight for what Panagea used to be, for what she could become."

"Which is?"

The captain smirked. "A new beginning. Seems we could all use one of those." He knew his crew well. They all harbored reasons for taking part.

Bermuda pursed her lips and slanted her neck back to look skyward too. Her look of disapproval shifted to one of slow acceptance. She trusted him. The quartermaster always followed the captain into the dark. With a smirk, she used her shoulder to nudge him. "Careful, Captain. The crew will think you're going soft."

He chuckled, resting his head on the back of the steam car. "Gods damn it all. I hope not."

Bermuda grinned. "Don't worry. Your secret's safe with me."

Kazuaki gazed upon her, drinking her in. When the familiar feeling of desire crept into his veins, he tried to banish it. "Get some sleep, Bermuda."

"Nah." She felt the cool touch of the steam car's metal on her back. Perhaps the cold would temper the rising heat inside her. The quartermaster leaned farther into it and listened to the surrounding sounds of the night. She knew she should sleep. But she couldn't. "I'll keep you company for a while."

The captain accepted her reply, though it meant another night of torture sitting beside the woman he could not have. The ecstasy of her proximity often outweighed the agony. He steeled his nerves and tore his gaze from her, staring into the darkness. "I'd like that very much."

MORNING ALWAYS CAME quicker than anyone prepared for. The crew pulled their tired bodies from the earth and carried on. Raw adrenaline and mental determination drove them forward. The days blurred together—a slew of planting, growing, moving on. They spent so much time growing new miniature forests in various decrepit buildings Kazuaki suspected Emont had beat them to their destination. But, when they pulled into the small town outside Denicee, it appeared as though he hadn't arrived at all.

The steam cars rattled across the broken roads. Their eyes stayed as alert as possible, on the lookout for any sign of Emont or his recruits. A veritable wasteland surrounded them. The crumbling infrastructures put the crew in mind of Avadon, but it seemed the people who used to live here had abandoned it entirely.

"Perhaps he moved on to Denicee without us," Bermuda guessed. "This place is barren."

Kazuaki frowned as the steam car came to a slow crawl. A vacant town would have been an ideal place to organize before they entered Denicee, but Emont was impatient for change. Perhaps his unrest drew him into the city's walls. Entering Denicee without their army was a gamble, but it seemed they had little choice.

As they were about to continue to the next town, Elowyn spotted a shadow. "There." She pointed. "I'm sure I saw someone."

Kazuaki grew inquisitive and steered the vehicle toward the sighting.

A figure stood in the road, unmoving.

The captain stopped before the skeptical looking individual with a pack over his shoulder.

Umbriel hung her head out the vehicle. Despite his abnormal presence, she still flashed an approachable smile. "Excuse me. Has a man named Emont been through these parts?"

The man narrowed his eyes. "Who's askin'?"

Umbriel tilted her head as she regarded the crew. Her attention returned to the strange man, and she smiled again. It would either be a death sentence, a warm welcome, or a complete lack of acknowledgment, but she took the chance. "Kazuaki Hidataka and his crew."

The man examined the vehicles and scrutinized the occupants and their appearances. He appeared satisfied with what he saw. "Emont told me he expected you much sooner. He's already taken everyone into Denicee."

Kazuaki frowned. He suspected they had spent too long planting, but he saw no sense dwelling on it now. It, too, remained a critical step in the revolution. "Very well. Are you a part of the rebellion? Do you need a ride into Denicee?"

The man nodded and jumped onto the back of the steam car. "I'll be fine back here." He thrust his arm ahead. "Better get a move on. Emont's followers are anxious. I don't know how long he can contain their aggression."

Iani grinned and nudged Rennington. "I like the sound of that. They got some fight in them, aye?"

The nameless man nodded. "The people are hungry for change. Many jumped at the opportunity. Better to die fighting than roll over like a dog."

Granite shot the man a hateful stare, but Elowyn patted his leg. "At ease. No harm meant."

He scratched behind his dog's ear as the vehicles rolled toward Denicee.

Stillness dominated the trip. The gravity of the situation sank in. Relief existed that Emont had success gathering soldiers for the cause, but the ease in which he collected them spoke to how terrible their living situations were. They craved a revolution so much they would relinquish their lives to achieve it.

Nicholai grew more disheartened knowing their soldiers were the common folk of Panagea, people like his residents, people he cared for. Lilac plagued his thoughts every mile. He saw her life in every flower they grew. Months passed, and he was no closer to a solution than when he had left. He fooled himself into thinking the resistance would buy him more time; if he could heal the world, it would slow the disintegration process. But it continued to fall.

Every dilapidated town they passed through was one more glaring symbol of how many people suffered because of his actions. Though they would have suffered from this regardless, freezing time in Southeastern had made it much worse. Nicholai stared ahead, finding the battle within his mind far more difficult than any he experienced with the footmen. With all the natural disasters, it felt as though Darjal Wessex's blood wasn't the only stain on his hands.

He couldn't stall much longer. He had to address Southeastern. But, every time the Time Father thought about heading back, his boots refused to move. The thought of ending Lilac's life ... he couldn't do it.

The thoughts plagued him all the way to Denicee. Nicholai hardly realized they had arrived until the vehicles halted.

The stranger from earlier released himself from the back of the steam car when he saw Emont loitering in the town's entrance. After crossing the short distance, the two men shook hands.

"Glad to see you all made it," Emont said, grinning at the crew. "I've been waiting out here every morning for the past several days. I worried something had happened."

"Where is everyone?" Kazuaki surveyed the unassuming citizens of Denicee walking with complete ignorance that their town would be the center of bloodshed within the day.

"They're hiding in some decommissioned factories beyond this road. I know they'll find relief to hear you have arrived. Not as many abandoned buildings here as there are in Avadon. They're packed in there pretty tight. It's getting a bit claustrophobic."

"Ready them immediately." Kazuaki looked to the horizon as he spied the tall tower that housed the Southwestern Time Father. It was an iconic structure, rising higher than any other building. The captain didn't need to harbor too much information about Carlo to know his ego claimed the grandest building as his home. "We've waited long enough."

"You don't want to rest? Collect yourselves a little?"

"Not today." Kazuaki spoke for everyone as he walked away from the steam car and toward the tower.

Emont shrugged and clapped his hands together. He looked to the crew, an eager grin on his face. "Alright then. Let's do this."

It took a while for the townsfolk to realize what was happening. Confusion appeared on their faces as hordes of people poured from otherwise unutilized industrial plants. It was a surreal sight that garnered initial disbelief. But, when the denizens identified the defensive clothing, armor fashioned from scrap metal and witnessed the weapons pulled from their hiding spots, the collective's intentions became obvious.

They marched with impressive form toward Carlo's tower. A handful of Denicee's citizens scampered to the safety of their homes. Others gawked when patrolling footmen tried to stop the mob from advancing on Carlo's home. They never stood a chance. Even with the benefit of training, the few scattered footmen could not combat the hundred angered citizens pulled from the impoverished grounds of Panagea's ravaged cities.

The element of surprise resided in their favor. Carlo did not have the foresight to rally an organized defense against their infiltration. The footmen were tired, exhausted from long days of hauling protesting citizens who cried out for help into Denicee's jails. They had been dealing with resistance from the townsfolk around the clock. While they were ill-prepared for a full-scale uprising, they were intelligent. The remaining men fell back and sank into the jail's walls, gathering numbers to match the mob before they returned to the confrontation.

The footmen's fallback granted them the ability to get close to Carlo's tower. Emont's soldiers roared, beating on the walls of Carlo's home with their sharpened points and makeshift shields. It was almost too easy.

Nicholai thought it would be a replay of Avadon until the now organized soldiers poured out the prison gates. Though they only gathered half the numbers held by the mob, their weapons were superior. One footman stood tall before the fifty men behind him, holding a flame thrower.

Nicholai's eyes widened as several brave rebels charged forward, weapons drawn, only to fall victim to the cruel flames.

Burning flesh tainted the air. A shift occurred in the fight. Half the mob panicked while fury swept through the veins of the others. Chaos followed.

Nicholai stepped back from the anarchy. Though his stomach turned, he forced his attention to the building. He had to reach Carlo. He couldn't allow a second Time Father to die. Nicholai's hands wrapped around the door's iron handle, but it refused to budge. Locked. His boots carried him backward several paces, and he looked up.

Carlo stood on the balcony. He watched with disdain at the display of treason below.

The sounds of the dead and the dying clashed with the bullets fired. Blades clanged as they met. Feet from footmen and revolutionaries scuffled. Several of Denicee's citizens ended up in the firefight, shrieking in the disorder. Everything happened so suddenly.

Nicholai needed to act. It was hard to raise his voice above all the noise, but he tried. Saving Carlo from death would ease the guilt he harbored about Darjal. "Carlo Angevin!" He cupped his hands around his mouth to carry his voice. "We are the voice of Panagea! Please, listen to what we have to say. This slaughter is unnecessary!"

He could not see his facial expression, but Nicholai felt Carlo's scowl. "Nicholai Addihein," he hissed, feeling no fear from the safety of his balcony. "So you've resurfaced. Darjal will be pleased to hear it." The Southwestern Time Father was familiar with Darjal's hatred for Nicholai. His desire for revenge had begged Carlo to send many men to Southern to construct Darjal's ironclad.

Nicholai remained unmoving. Smoke from the burning corpses slithered upward. "Darjal is dead." His words were remorseful but steadfast. "I'm here to save you from the same fate. All we ask for is an opportunity for change. These people are suffering. Panagea is suffering!"

Carlo scowled. His rage grew at the knowledge of Darjal's passing. "You speak of the fate *you* have doomed them to. I do not negotiate with traitors of the continent, Nicholai." He gazed at the clamoring bodies, the flying metal, the fire. He sneered. "When you see Darjal, tell him Carlo sends his regards."

The Southeastern Time Father clenched his jaw. "Carlo, please—"

The Southwestern Time Father withdrew into his room.

Nicholai cursed and faced the crowd. His brain scattered to devise another way into Carlo's tower, but it was too late. The fire spread. A window shattered. Napalm spilled into the opening.

Nicholai had not observed much of the fight in Avadon. What he witnessed here appalled him—children separated from their parents, compassion left and welcomed turmoil, bodies fell in waves. A moat of blood surrounded him. And the screams ...

Others saw the fire enter Carlo's tower. Matching the flames' destruction, they joined in an inferno. Nicholai backed away, horrified to watch the citizens decay into wild monsters as they tried to smoke Carlo out, hurling more burning rubbish into the open window. Smoke obscured his vision, but Nicholai found Umbriel in the chaos. She caught his eyes; they shared his concern. The peoples' anger was so thick it was tangible, matched by the ferocity of the footmen who massacred them. The revolutionaries' inexperience was clear. Great losses occurred on both sides.

Elowyn, Iani, and Rennington stuck close together. They worked in sync to annihilate any threats.

Kazuaki and Bermuda neared the prison, subduing the footmen who poured from the walls.

Nicholai lost the others in the blanket of bodies.

The flames climbed higher. The screams grew louder. Panic escalated. Denicee burned as the war raged on. Citizens scattered, finding nowhere safe from the fight. A full-on blaze ate Carlo Angevin's tower.

Nicholai threw his body into the door, hoping the flames may have weakened its integrity. He couldn't leave Carlo to die in there. The exchange of blades, bullets, and smoke billowing off the tower brought nothing but confusion to the people. Nicholai felt the searing heat from the flames that surrounded him as he slammed himself into the door once more. It was so insufferable he feared the worst; Carlo's ego would be the death of him.

Just as he wrote off Carlo's life to death by smoke inhalation, the doors of the tower burst open. Nicholai stumbled backward, falling into the madness of the mob.

Smoke wafted off Carlo's body, and his mad eyes dashed about. Knowing he was the target of the uprising, he needed a shield. His smoldering arms seized the small arm of a nearby child who wailed in terror at being separated from his parents in the insanity. Carlo's pupils were small pinpricks as they darted around, stressing his delirium. A gun surfaced from his pocket. He pressed the cold metal against the child's temple. He shuffled away from the blaze, searching for an exit.

"Shit!" Nicholai tried to rush forward but couldn't force himself through the frightened bodies.

Iani beat him to the punch. The young Platts brother stood before Carlo, blocking his exit. "Carlo ..." Ian outstretched his blood-soaked hands. "What the feck are you doing, mate?"

"You will get me out of here!" His hand trembled as he felt the heat of the fire behind him. "Or I will cover you in this boy's brain tissue!"

"Easy ..." Iani's voice was so soft it was almost lost to the shrieking crowd. He looked into the little boy's eyes. Terror lived there, horrified fearfulness that had no business being in a child's eyes. It was not the first time he had seen that fear. It had reflected in every child's face in Southern the day Darjal had ordered them to kill the offspring of the small revolution. "Let him go. I'll take his place. I'm Kazuaki's right-hand man, a much better bargaining chip than some kid."

Carlo panted, panicking under the pressure as his heart pounded deep inside his chest. "Drop the weapon." He appeared maniacal, lost to the psychosis from his flight-or-fight response. His fingers dug deeper into the child's soft arm. "No sudden movements."

Iani nodded. He took slow, deliberate steps. "You got it, mate. No sudden movements." He tossed his weapon aside. "Here." He extended his hand, though he tried to maintain a safe distance from Carlo. "Hand me the kid, and I'm all yours."

Carlo's corneas were bloodshot from the pressure mounting in his body. His hands trembled. If this man was Kazuaki's right-hand man, his death served as a great distraction. With a shockwave that pierced his brain, he lifted the gun from the child's head and fired three rounds into Iani's chest. He hurled the child at the Platts brother's body and ran.

Nicholai paled as he witnessed the attack.

Iani caught the kid, but the child did not linger long. His terrified feet carried him into the crowd as he screamed for his parents. Iani took three or four quick, panicked breaths as a slow spread of red crept through his shirt.

"Iani!" If anything rose above the unmatched volume of the battle, it was Rennington's voice as he fought through the horde of people. Whether footmen or civilian, he fell anyone who stood in his way until he reached his younger brother. He caught him in his arms.

Umbriel ran toward the brothers, but a footman's blade swept her side. She shrieked and fell as her fingers grasped the gash. The woman rolled to avoid another stab. Her fingers clawed into the dirt as she tried to pull herself to Iani, but the footman pursued her, relentless.

"Iani, feckin' shit," Rennington stuttered, frenzied as he tried to keep his brother from moving.

"Renn ..." Blood spilled from Iani's mouth and trailed down his cheek. He blinked at his brother with a grin, feeling a wave of redemption knowing the child had escaped from Carlo. He gripped his brother's wrist, his words muffled as he gargled through them. "F-For Southern."

"Hey, hey, hey. Shut it. You'll be okay." Rennington's voice broke. "You'll be okay," he repeated as he gripped Iani's hand.

Umbriel's patience wore thin. The pacifist huffed and spun, seizing the blade with her hands. The blade ate into her fingers and palm, but she held her grip, forcing it from her attacker's shocked grasp. She drove the blunt handle into his throat, and he fell to his knees, gasping for air. It wouldn't kill him, but it guaranteed her freedom. Her rushed feet flew to Iani, and she skidded into the ground beside him.

She laid bleeding palms on his chest. She closed her eyes. A swift concentration consumed her. What felt like hours had only been seconds. The Earth Mother scrambled to manipulate the living tissue, to close the wounds.

She was too late. He was gone. Iani Platts, a soldier to Southern reborn, had died in the line of duty.

Umbriel didn't need to speak. Rennington knew by her morose expression. His fists, soiled by his little brother's blood, clenched as he stood. He stared into the crowd where Carlo had disappeared.

The Time Father hadn't gotten far, caught in the same typhoon of people that consumed Nicholai. He was easy to identify; his regal ensemble clashed with the townsfolk's common clothing and the soldier's uniforms. Carlo tried in desperation to force through the horde, but a life of luxury had softened his muscles. He fired at anyone who stood in his way, but, for every person he fell, five more got in his way.

Rennington unleashed a war cry. A man possessed, he fought through the people. The sheer volume and horror of the noise that emanated from him banished both footmen and civilians from his route. They stumbled to clear themselves from his wrath, from that psychotic sound. Adrenaline, rage, and raw power drove him forward with great speed. In one leap, Rennington tackled Carlo Angevin to the ground.

Carlo didn't stand a chance. The frail leader suffered under the force of Rennington's unbridled strength. He forced the flailing man onto his back, unleashing an unforgiving onslaught of fists onto the face of his brother's killer with a disgusting display. The dynamism in which Rennington dropped his fists was inhuman. His attack was as brutal as it was relentless.

Several of Carlo's teeth flew from his jaw at the impact. His arms, which he lifted to defend himself, dropped to his sides, motionless. The man's face became nothing more than the shattered remnants of what was once a skull.

Rennington's knuckles swelled, bones in his hands fractured. He continued, though Carlo was visibly dead. Rennington's onslaught did not cease, but the rest of the battle did.

The captain and his crew had annihilated much of the footmen. Those who remained alive surrendered at the sight of their dwindling numbers. What citizens remained ran to their homes. The revolutionaries fell from a hundred to a handful, less than twenty having survived the butchery. Carcasses blanketed the streets. People shied away from the scene of the overkill.

Granite and Revi pushed from the crowd; the beast limped behind them. When they saw Rennington, they rushed forward and grabbed his arms.

"Renn," Revi tried to pull the man back as he delivered punches on what was only bone fragments and tissue attached to a body. "He's dead, mate. He's dead."

Rennington didn't hear him. Even when Granite's colossal strength joined to help Revi, he continued the assault. It wasn't until Nicholai also joined the other two men that the three pulled him off what remained of Carlo Angevin's body.

"Rennington ..." Nicholai didn't know what to say.

The man remained under their grasp for only a moment, panting before he pulled himself away and stormed off.

Nicholai followed, but Revi stopped him with a well-timed hand on his shoulder.

"Let him go, mate. There's nothing you can say right now."

Nicholai's eyes fell. He felt for the elder Platts brother. It was clear to him long ago when he saw the two for the first time in Avadon their bond ran deep. Iani's death was not the only thing that gnawed at him. He forced himself to observe Carlo's body. He had let another Time Father fall. Though the sight disgusted him, he scooped up the Chronometer, still wet with Carlo's blood.

As more people witnessed Carlo's corpse, word filtered through those who remained standing that the battle was a success. The small crowd cheered and voiced their overwhelming joy at the sight. Nicholai wondered if these people knew what success was. As he stared at the bodies that climbed into the triple digits, all he saw was failure. Carlo's death changed nothing unless they found a suitable replacement they trusted. It was Avadon all over again.

IANI'S FUNERAL WAS short. What it lacked in time, it made up for in sentiment. The crew wrapped him in a thick sheet and laid him in a steam car's back seat. Rennington was adamant his grave would not rest in Southwestern. After all their goodbyes, a revolutionary drove him toward his home, toward Southern. Kazuaki assured Rennington he'd send word to Bartholomew. He would give him a proper burial.

The flames reduced Carlo's tower to garbage. Though a shell of the building still stood, the black soot inside along with the questionable strength of the infrastructure made it uninhabitable. The footmen relented to Kazuaki and the others. Citizens jailed for igniting small revolutions of their own were freed from the prisons into the welcoming arms of their family. Husbands, wives, brothers, sisters of those who found freedom sought the crew, thanking them for their efforts to save those who wished to start a change.

The crew found refuge in a large armored building outside the prison walls. With Carlo's tower in ruins, it was the best place to devise their next move. Emont, Kazuaki, Bermuda, Revi, Brack, and Granite stood beside Nicholai in the main area while Elowyn and Umbriel comforted a silent Rennington in the next room.

"I know it's not the time," Nicholai said, his voice hesitant, "but it's been ten hours since Carlo's death. We're running short of time to initiate a new Time Father."

Bermuda narrowed her eyes, irritated at Nicholai's statement. Contained rage poisoned her stare. "How can you even think about that right now? Iani is *dead*, Nico."

Nicholai squared his shoulders. "It's not as if I want to, but, if we don't, Southwestern's time will stop."

Unwavering aggression poured from her as she hissed, "That doesn't seem to bother you about Southeastern."

The room grew quiet. Nicholai took a deep breath. "Bermuda, I mourn for Iani too—"

"As you should." She glared, crossing her arms. "I would feel terrible too if someone in your family died fighting a war *I* had created."

"Bermuda." Kazuaki took her arm and ushered her from the room and out of earshot of the others before things escalated. His expression reflected stern remorse. "We're all grieving. I know it's not easy. Burying good men never is."

She glowered at him and shook her head. "This is getting ridiculous, Kazuaki. This feckin' revolution is tearing apart our crew. First Bartholomew, now Iani. How many more do we have to lose before you realize this isn't worth it? These *people* aren't worth it!"

"We all have our reasons, Bermuda." He stole a quick glance at the crew. "I'm sorry you haven't found yours yet." It gutted him to say it. But he needed her to know. "I stand by what I said before. You can take your leave whenever you want. I won't force you to do this."

The quartermaster scoffed. "I see Nicholai's been wiping his damnable ethics off on you. He needs to restart Southeastern. If he does, it'll take the heat off. He's the one they're hunting, not us."

Her words cut him, but, like every other injury he had suffered, he showed no sign of weakness. "Nico is part of the crew now," Kazuaki said, having gained a surprising amount of respect for the man in the months they had spent together. "And we've never forced our members to face their pasts before. I know you're fuming now, Bermuda, as am I. But let us keep our anger directed to the right target. Nico is not the one who killed Iani. The Time Fathers did. Their tactics did. The world they built is what killed Iani."

Bermuda narrowed her eyes. "Seems you forgot he's one of them, not one of us." The woman turned, her anger carried her far and away from Kazuaki Hidataka and Nicholai Addihein.

The captain closed his eye. His jaw tightened, and he threw an aggressive punch into the wall. Kazuaki understood her frustration; he knew from where it stemmed. Bermuda was a maiden of strength and grit. But her Achilles heel remained. She never handled the death of a loved one with grace.

Kazuaki dragged himself back into the others' presence. He found Nicholai's eyes across the room. "So? What did we decide?"

Nicholai sat up straighter, surprised Kazuaki returned. "Emont has graciously accepted the risks of assuming the title."

Kazuaki flicked his gaze to Emont. He didn't know him long, but he gave an approving nod. The captain trusted him. He was a man who did not shy away from a challenge, and best yet, Kazuaki did not have to part with another member of his dwindling crew. "Good man. Now everyone get some rest. We'll figure out our next move on the morrow."

NICHOLAI'S ARM SHOT up out of bed. He reached for the bullet that hurled toward Lilac. It struck his palm, and, for a moment, he felt the sting of the metal as it pierced his flesh. But, when cognizance returned to his otherwise cloudy brain, he realized it had all been a terrible dream.

Funny how the pain felt real.

He rubbed his palm to banish the strange, lingering ache as he pulled himself to his feet and threw on his shirt. The man's face twisted into an uncomfortable frown. Something was off. Though distracted by the phantom pain in his hand, Nicholai soon realized a weightlessness around his neck. His fingers reached down. Dread consumed his eyes as he searched his empty chest.

His Chronometer was gone.

Kazuaki burst into his room. Though he disguised it well with his experience, Nicholai isolated a fraction of the same panic he felt. "Bermuda is missing," the captain announced, staring at the Southeastern Time Father.

The light from fresh dawn outside filtered through the building's small windows. The others in the room stirred due to the commotion.

"So is my Chronometer."

The captain's face shifted into one of intense frustration as he balled his hands into fists. He feared she had taken him up on his offer. With no initiative to fight, Kazuaki assumed Bermuda had abandoned the cause. But no. She had started her own. He drew a deep breath through his nose and exhaled. "Of course, it is. Nicholai, I have reason to believe she's on her way to Southeastern. She's going to try to restart your division's time."

"That's ridiculous," Nicholai replied as he paced, sweeping his hands through his hair. "She can't. The Chronometer won't respond to her. Only a Time Father can restart his division's time. She won't even be able to enter the border—" His expression became one of increasing concern as he recalled all the soldiers dispatched to Southeastern. "Kazuaki, as soon as she sets foot there, they'll kill her."

The captain squared his shoulders. "Get dressed," he ordered, looking to the rest of the crew as they pulled themselves into a waking state. "We'll intercept her before she gets too far."

In the heat of the moment, Kazuaki did not hear Emont as he approached from behind. "Excuse me, Captain, but I need to speak to Nicholai."

"I can't now, Emont. I'm sorry." Nicholai hurriedly gathered his belongings, trying to assemble himself with efficiency.

"With all due respect, Nicholai, I really think you'd wish to address this—"

"I don't have time. We're in a bit of an emergency state."

"But, Nicholai—"

Another body appeared in the doorway.

Kazuaki arched a brow and stepped aside as not to stand so close to the figure.

The man held a commanding presence despite the fatigue that emanated off his body. "Hello, Nicholai."

The captain's eye shifted to a skeptical slit as he shot a glance at Nicholai, irritated a stranger was delaying their efforts to find Bermuda. "Who's this?"

Nicholai spun around to see the man who stood in the door. His face dropped, but he recovered well. It was the last man in the world he expected to see. After clearing his throat, he declared to Kazuaki, "This is Edvard Addihein. My father."

Chapter Twenty-Two

Nicholai could not shake the shock. He had not laid eyes on Edvard Addihein since the last decennial gathering of the Time Fathers at Panagea's center. It was almost ten years ago when he took command of Southeastern's time. Nicholai possessed mixed feelings about Edvard's arrival. It couldn't have come at a worse moment.

"I'm sorry, Edvard," he said, unable to address him by his familial title since he had entered adulthood. "I'm not sure why you came, but the timing is ..." He trailed off, not wanting to come across as rude to a man who had made a long and tedious journey, but there was no way around his immediate departure's necessity.

"It's okay, Nicholai." Edvard lifted his hand to dismiss his son's concern. "I cannot stay long. With most of the roads and train tracks in disrepair from the disasters, it took much longer to get here than I expected. I have little time before I need to head back if I'm to return in time to keep Western in check." He patted the Chronometer chained to his breast pocket.

Nicholai slipped his arms inside a long-sleeved coat, keeping his eyes on Edvard the entire time. "You traveled a long way," he said with skepticism. "Why?"

Edvard frowned. A sigh escaped his lips. "I came, because I received word of what happened in Southern. I know Darjal is dead. The other Time Fathers are hunting you tenfold now, Nicholai. I need to know why—why you froze Southeastern, why you're doing ... *this*." He waved his arms around.

Kazuaki noticed his hands lingered in his direction.

The captain glowered at Edvard as the others acquainted themselves with a more wakeful state.

Granite's dog wagged his tail as he ran to the tired bodies and licked them.

Rennington did not sleep much. His eyes held an absence, while the others held confusion.

They looked to the captain for answers, but he was far too focused on Edvard to pay them much mind.

Nicholai closed his eyes as he tried to find the right words. "We need a change, Da— Edvard." He tried in vain to address him by his title as his father, but it felt too strange. They shared a bloodline but little else. To Nicholai, the man was, for all intents and purposes, a stranger. "Panagea was dying long before I froze Southeastern. Nordjan knew it. He'd tell me as much in every monthly meeting. We can't correct it continuing as we have. Panagea needs the Earth Mother." His tone fell as he paused. "Now you answer a question for me. Why didn't you tell me about her?"

The Western Time Father cringed but remained honorable in his stand. "Sometimes people do things they think are right at the moment, like what you did in Southeastern. A thirst for change isn't the motivation for your treason, Nicholai. I know you learned of the Earth Mother *after* you doomed Southeastern to its fate. Tell me why."

He should've known Edvard would see through his explanation. The Western Time Father had been a perceptive man during his childhood. It only made sense the skill had deepened as he aged. Nicholai glanced at the crew behind him then eyed Kazuaki. With hesitation, he refocused on Edvard. It was time to own up to his crime. He had been running from it for far too long. "I did it for Lilac. Certain death lingers an inch or two from her face in the form of a bullet. If I did not stop Southeastern's time ..." He summoned the conviction to continue. "She would have died."

The crew exchanged glances. This was the first they had heard of Lilac.

Edvard stared with more regret than understanding reflecting in his eyes. "My son, I know it may not seem like it, but, if you leave her in her state, she's already as good as dead. Along with the hundreds of thousands of people who live in Southeastern with her."

"I'll find a way to save her," he retorted with unintended aggression. "I have to. She means everything to me."

Edvard's expression revealed his disappointment. "Take it from me, boy. The fates of others are beyond our control. We may control the time that surrounds them, but we're powerless to the inevitable."

Kazuaki watched the Addiheins. He bristled at Nicholai's confession. He took Nicholai for a smart man. As his respect for the Southeastern Time Father grew, he speculated the man's reasoning for freezing his division stemmed from grand importance. Nicholai had showcased his intelligence the entire time he had been in the captain's company, and, while Kazuaki had given him a brutal beginning, he had grown to trust the Time Father's instincts and ethics. As Bermuda had observed, some had even rubbed off on him. But this whole time, hundreds of thousands of lives hung in the balance for one woman.

Before he could vocalize his anger, Emont pulled him aside. "Captain, Edvard's arrival is not the only thing that needs addressing." He removed a wax-sealed parchment from his breast pocket. "This came by currier from Southern with great haste. It seems the news of Darjal's death has spread like wildfire. Aggi Normandy delivered this overnight to Southern in hopes we were still there, but, when Bartholomew received it, he sent it to us straight away."

The captain ripped it open then scanned the letter's contents. It seemed Aggi Normandy celebrated their exploits with cautious optimism. "The Northeastern division wishes to give us aid." He looked to Emont for insight. Kazuaki was far too removed from Panagea to know much about the individual Time Fathers. He could only speculate so much. "What do you think, Emont? Can we trust him?"

"Aggi and Edvard have always been the most well-received, Captain." Emont looked over his shoulder as Nicholai and Edvard continued to talk. He returned his attention to Kazuaki. "But Aggi Normandy is the only one with a history of standing up to the other Time Fathers. I'm certain he means what he says."

Umbriel entered the room, surprised to see their alarmed faces. She had risen with the sun to help the citizens of Denicee bury their dead. After blessing the fallen, her feet had carried her to the building where her comrades rested, but their concern distressed her. "What's going on?" Her gaze fell on Edvard as he and Nicholai shared a quiet discussion in the room's corner.

Kazuaki ground his teeth. "Bermuda's gone. She took Nicholai's Chronometer. She's headed to Southeastern to restart his division. Aggi Normandy of Northeastern has promised us his aid. This letter dictates he's given his word to support our efforts. And *that* is Nicholai's father. Edvard Addihein of Western."

Umbriel's grace showed in her face. Without hesitation, she placed a hand on his arm. "I know you must go to Bermuda. But please know I cannot stop now. Take the crew to ensure your safety. I'll continue planting seeds in Southwestern. The threat of capture is nonexistent with Emont in charge. If what Aggi Normandy says is true, I will make my way to Northeastern. It'll be easier to travel in secrecy if it's just me. Once you secure Bermuda, we can rendezvous in the safety of Aggi Normandy's hometown."

"Absolutely not," Kazuaki replied, unable to quell the harshness of his words. "I can get Bermuda by myself."

"Don't be foolish, Kazuaki." Her words were strict, but a gentleness existed in her tone. "Southeastern's borders are crawling with men. You'll need every hand available if she's gotten herself into a dire situation. The crew cannot do much for me while I plant anyway, and they will only draw attention to my efforts."

The captain's jaw tightened with irritation at the sense behind her words. She was right, and he did not have time to argue. "I will not leave you defenseless." He looked to Granite. "You and the beast will travel with her. Keep her safe."

Granite nodded as he stroked the top of his dog's head. It would be strange traveling without the crew, but, if any one of them could keep Umbriel safe single handedly, it was Granite.

"Meet us in Northeastern, in Aggi Normandy's hometown," he reiterated to both, his stare's intensity showing his rigor. "Emont, issue a letter to Bartholomew. Instruct him to send a man to Southern's coast. Get word to Penn to meet us near the coastal town of Brechita. We'll shave time off our journey to Northeastern if we travel by sea."

"Right away. And, Captain, track your friend at the station in Norridon. All the routes to Southeastern closed after the imports and exports ceased. They only left one route open to move the soldiers there. If Bermuda is going to Southeastern by steam train, that's her only way to get close to the border."

Kazuaki nodded. "Thank you, Emont."

"Of course. Good luck." He slipped passed Nicholai and Edvard as he went out the door.

Nicholai watched Emont depart, unsure of why he had made such a hasty exit. He faced Edvard, but it seemed his attention lived elsewhere. "Edvard?" He narrowed his eyes. "Are you listening?"

The Western Time Father blinked to clear his cloudy eyes. "Yes, Nicholai, I apologize. The state of the world has the people scared. Their complaints ... they keep me up at night."

Nicholai's expression fell flat. He felt Kazuaki's impatience grow as he spoke. "I'm sorry, Edvard, but I have to cut this short. I really need to be going."

"It's just as well. I should be off too. One never knows how difficult it might be to get home if another disaster strikes. Nicholai, promise me you'll be careful. And please, *please* consider unfreezing Southeastern. I hoped I could talk sense into you, but love ... it has ways of driving a man insane, I know."

Nicholai rubbed the back of his neck and forced a nod. "Right. I'll think about it."

Edvard sighed and started for the door but paused. "Nicholai, if you ever need a place to stay ..."

The Southeastern Time Father flashed a small smile. In the wake of all the chaos, it felt good to know his father had his back, even to a trivial degree. "Thanks, Dad."

The word struck him. Edvard lingered. A strange look crossed his face. Nicholai thought for a moment he might say something, but he forced himself to exit instead.

Kazuaki huffed. "Now that that's over with, let's get the feck out of here."

THE STEAM TRAIN'S INTERIOR felt cramped compared to the outside world. The black locomotive split through the jagged cities with precision, clamoring closer to its next station with each passing second. Rennington stared out the rattling window. Darkness clung to him since they left many hours ago. It rattled around in his soul with a heaviness that matched the weight of the steam train.

Elowyn stole occasional glimpses of him, assessing his mental condition. Everything was still so fresh. Iani's death cut her to the core, triggering a series of flashbacks of her blood brothers when they perished in battle. Losing Iani was like losing them all over again. But Elowyn Saveign's empathy exceeded her emotional distress.

She rose from her seat and slid into the open space beside Rennington. "He was a great man. Iani died a hero, Renn."

Rennington acknowledged her words with a microscopic nod but continued his long, unending gaze into the bleakness of the towns that passed outside his window.

Elowyn sighed and leaned back in the comfort of the cushion that supported her. "He was a great brother. I'm going to miss him so much."

Revi perked up. He listened from his place one seat behind Rennington. Though he wasn't the most sentimental man, he could not deny the pain Rennington experienced. He felt Iani's loss himself. Revi leaned forward, trying to lend emotional support, though it was beyond his expertise. "Iani was a soldier. He died doing what he signed up to do. Except, this time, he died fighting for someone he respected. He loved Southern, and he knew Bartholomew could turn it around. Iani played a huge role in your home division's eventual success."

"He did," Elowyn added as she fidgeted with the hem of her shirt. "I'm sure he knew the power of his sacrifice. Iani Platts had a great heart. I don't think he would've done it any other way."

If Rennington listened, he did not respond. He stared out the glass, lost to his mind's replaying clip of his brother getting shot. Three rounds. Boom, boom, boom. He must have relived his death a thousand times.

Elowyn and Revi sat back, concluding their kind efforts wouldn't gather any positive results.

"I'll tell you what Iani Platts would've done," Brack's said from the seat in front of Rennington and Elowyn. He turned around, resting his arm on the seat back as he faced the sullen Platts brother. "He'd tell you to quit your damned pouting. Then call you a whiny piece of shit."

Elowyn's eyes widened with horror.

Even Revi appeared appalled by Brack's callous statement.

But, before they chastised him for his vulgar speech, Rennington cracked the smallest of smiles. He continued gazing out the window but looked a little less plagued by his thoughts. "You're gods-damned right he would."

Kazuaki watched Nicholai as he sat in silence several seats ahead of him. He'd been quiet since their departure, neck-deep in his battle. Darjal's death could not have been easy for the pacifist to accept, let alone the worry that followed the theft of his Chronometer. And then there was Edvard's appearance ...

Still, the captain harbored little pity for the man. It was a useless emotion, and he was far too consumed with rage that Nicholai had escalated the failure of an already dying land to delay the inevitable death of one woman. Kazuaki knew he had told Bermuda no judgment lived on his ship. All good men made mistakes. But the quartermaster's absence ate at him. If she got hurt, or worse ...

Unable to dwell in his imagination any longer, he stood from his seat and walked over, forcing Nicholai aside as he sat beside him. His words were cold. "Do you know what makes a man a capable leader, Nico?"

The Southeastern Time Father pulled himself from his reverie. "Excuse me?"

"How long did you govern Southeastern for?"

Nicholai blinked, confused where the conversation was going. "It's been ... almost ten years since I was initiated."

"It's no wonder you're terrible at it. I've been captain to various crews for hundreds of years, and I've never once doomed them to a future of lifelessness."

Nicholai's expression fell flat. He felt a great irritation rise inside of him. The need for survival and his general kindness had carried him this far with Captain Kazuaki Hidataka. But everything he had endured in the last several months finally crushed his patience. The Time Father sat up straighter as sarcasm spilled from him. "Yes, because governing over a handful of people is the same as governing over hundreds of thousands. I'm sure it must have been very trying for you. How many did you command at most? Ten? Fifteen?"

Kazuaki scowled. "Belay that!" He dug into the seat cushions in front. "I took you for an intelligent man, Nico. I suspect you never mentioned why you froze Southeastern because, on some level, you also knew how asinine your actions were."

"Do not preach to me about asinine actions, Captain, lest the sword also calls the dagger sharp."

"You cast your peoples' wellbeing aside for one life, Nico. Where do your priorities lie?"

Nicholai kept his gaze, his facial features firm. "I should ask you the same question, Captain. Or did you forget we abandoned the revolution to chase after *one* life?"

Kazuaki flinched. He did not have an immediate reply. After a moment, he said, "This is completely different."

"How so, Captain?" Nicholai feigned ignorance as he leaned forward. "Because you love her? Because she is every bit a part of you as your own hand? Or your lungs? Or your heart?"

Silence followed. Though Kazuaki said nothing, his stillness spoke volumes.

Nicholai knew he had struck a nerve. He had observed Kazuaki's interactions with Bermuda, how she could knock the powerful man from his composed pedestal with a single word. "I know that's why we're pursuing her, Captain, and I went along with it. I went along with it, not just because I need my Chronometer back but because I am *intimately* familiar with the sentiments that plague you. Will she be okay? Will I get to her in time? If I don't, how can I live with myself after?" His words grew more heated as he continued. "I know because I *am* you, Captain. I may not slaughter an army of footmen without guilt or command a ship at sea or become a feckin' immortal legend, but, in this circumstance, whether you like it or not, you and I are one and the same."

Kazuaki stared without emotion at the Southeastern Time Father. His words settled over him like dust. He drew a slow, deep breath and allowed a moment to pass to collect himself. He looked to the front of the steam train.

The locomotive slowed. A member of the train crew appeared at the front of the cart. "This is as far she goes to Southeastern. If you want to enter the borders, you'll have to go the rest of the way on foot."

Kazuaki and the rest of the crew stood to their feet. "That's fine."

The attendant noticed Nicholai, tilting his head and breaking into a grin. "Wait a second. You're Nicholai Addihein. And you," he said with excitement, turning to the captain, "you're Kazuaki Hidataka. You're the ones who started the revolution!"

Brack gathered his belongings and chuckled to himself. "News travels fast, aye?"

"It does when you're doing justice for the people. On behalf of all Panagea, thank you. It's about time someone did something about the state of this place." His eyes fell on Elowyn, and he gasped. "You must be the Earth Mother!"

Elowyn forced a smirk but did not bother correcting him. "We appreciate your enthusiasm"—she threw a pack over her shoulder—"but we really need to be on our way. Time restraints, you know."

"Of course, of course." He moved out of everyone's way as they departed the train. He waved, a huge grin plastered to his face. "I can't wait to tell everyone I met the people who will save Panagea."

"Let's keep that bit hush-hush," Kazuaki muttered as he turned to the man from the station platform. "We're trying to keep from getting murdered and all that."

"Oh! Right!" The man nodded as the steam train hissed. "Good luck and thank you!"

The crew turned away, creating distance between themselves and the train.

Kazuaki removed a small compass from his pocket.

Revi leaned over as the captain flipped it open.

Kazuaki looked up when the needle pointed toward Southeastern. "That's it then?"

The land stretching outward before them appeared ominous. Fog shrouded whatever hid beyond their eyesight, but even the limited expanse of what they saw reflected a land that bordered a forgotten place.

Kazuaki looked down, trying to find a sign of where Bermuda may have gone. When he had carried himself far enough away from the train station's platform, he found a set of footprints carved into the soft ash that settled over the decrepit ground. "We're on the right track."

The crew followed behind, wordless as they trudged forward.

Kazuaki moved with purpose, his desire to find Bermuda before she got hurt compelling him onward. Nicholai's words filtered through his brain, causing a frown to appear on his face. Though he denied it with every breath, he knew Nicholai was right. A victim of his hypocrisy, Kazuaki's long strides carried him deeper into the dismal direction of Southeastern's borders.

Despite his best efforts, it seemed he shared more in common with Nicholai Addihein than he had first thought.

THE WESTERN DIVISION was cold. The winds brought a chill with them. While Edvard Addihein was typically a stoic man, it sent a shiver through his bones. His thoughts were as unforgiving as the wind. His arms wrapped around himself a little tighter as he waited, his feelings tormenting him as he stood on the cliff's edge.

Perhaps it wasn't the winds that made him shiver.

He heard the ornithopter before he saw it. The clunky machine appeared in the clouds, swirling the mist with its blades and wings as it edged closer. Edvard stepped backward to give the flying contraption a clear space to land.

Nordjan pulled himself from the ornithopter's seat, an eagerness about him that Edvard had never witnessed before. "Well?"

Edvard felt his entire body tense under his own touch. He looked Nordjan in the eyes. "They're meeting in the coastal town of Brechita before moving to Aggi Normandy's hometown. If they survive Southeastern's borders, you can intercept them there. They travel by steam train now, but I overheard the captain instructing the new Southwestern Time Father to send word for his ship to carry them to Northeastern."

Nordjan tightened his fists. His excitement grew. "Excellent. Thank you, Edvard. You've served Panagea well this day. It's a huge step toward regaining favor."

The Western Time Father remained emotionless. With fatigue infecting his words, he replied, "I would do anything for Panagea and its people."

"I will send word to Jernal. He was on route back to Southern before Darjal's death." His brain fired as he tried to calculate the soldier's next stop. "If he cannot reach Southern's coast before the captain's ship is on the move, perhaps he can follow their route to Brechita and intercept them there."

Edvard nodded dutifully. "Kazuaki's crew has experience over Jernal. I'm sure they'll move fast in the waters, but, if he can head them off, he'll have a much better chance at catching them."

"Right." Nordjan rubbed his hands together. "We mustn't waste any time. I'll send the necessary letters immediately." He returned to his ornithopter and turned with a look of pride. "Edvard, I know that must have been difficult for you. Well done."

Edvard Addihein said nothing. He watched in silence as Nordjan fired up his ornithopter. Even after he had vanished outside the Western Time Father's field of vision, he remained standing on the ledge. Though he had done right by Panagea, by Nordjan, Edvard Addihein could not shake the poisonous feelings of guilt that churned in his stomach.

As the cold winds brushed against him, he turned to head to his home. With any luck, a series of messengers would be there, bearing various complaints about the state of Western. They, at least, would keep his mind off the burning ache in his chest.

Chapter Twenty-Three

The ash fell like snow the closer Bermuda edged to the border. Delicate gray and black flakes settled on the ground, cast off from the volcanic eruptions Panagea had experienced in the last few months. The quartermaster lifted an arm to shield her nose and mouth as she walked. She tasted the ash through her nostrils and on her tongue. It held the flavor of death.

Nicholai's Chronometer waved back and forth in her mechanical hand as she walked, the chain clanking against her steel digits. Fortitude pushed her to her destination. The military had vacated the smaller towns she walked through since leaving the train station. Posted signs on various structures left little doubt. Another symbol of Darjal's selfish efforts to keep the people of Southern from discovering the predicament that befell Southeastern.

Even if the military hadn't ordered them to leave, Bermuda doubted anyone in their right mind would stay. The towns closest to the unmoving division had received the brunt of Panagea's tantrums. Jagged chunks of rubble jutted from the ground, but it was otherwise a barren wasteland, devoid of life and forgotten under a blanket of powder and debris.

Her solitary trek gave her many hours to think. Anger gripped her. Her heart bled for Iani. Once again, Bermuda had blindly followed Kazuaki into an adventure. The captain always possessed an aptitude and foresight she respected, but this endeavor was an egregious error on his part. Worse yet, the crew shared his vision. The revolution called to them. It had cost them Bartholomew and Iani.

And for what? For Elowyn to prove something to herself by challenging patriarchal views? For Rennington to ease his guilty conscience and fulfill that sense of patriotism he had lost? So Granite could give the beast a more conducive living environment? For Revi to pacify his remorse at abandoning his family by giving them a less chaotic world to live in? So Brack could have bragging rights? So Kazuaki's ego could walk where others told him he couldn't?

A misstep interrupted her anger. She tripped over something hidden beneath the dust. Bermuda stumbled but caught her balance and turned to cast an irritated glare on whatever had caused her to stagger. At first glance, it looked like nothing more than an unnatural lump. But her boot scraped away a layer of ash covering the object. Clothing.

The quartermaster's gaze traveled down the form's length. A torso. An arm. A head. Flesh still clung to the bones. The skin appeared withered, but she could still discern the expression. A permanent look of horror and sadness lived on the nameless citizen's face. Bermuda had seen countless bodies in the life she made with Kazuaki. But this corpse's sunken, lifeless eyes invaded her mind. She suspected it would live there a long time as she turned her back and continued onward.

It was hard to walk through land that had once bustled with people. Ghosts of their lives lingered here. So many suffered. Uprooted from their homes—either by natural disaster or by order of their division leader—conditions had forced them from everything they knew into unforgiving places. All those people in Southwestern, jailed for speaking their minds, for voicing their dissatisfaction—it gutted her. Bermuda reacquainted herself with why she despised Panagea. It was a cruel, merciless place.

The quartermaster eyed the pocket watch curled around her mechanical fingers—such a small object and yet such a devastating impact. Sometimes it was the smallest things which had the biggest influence, she thought. Her attention shifted to the artificial hand Nicholai had crafted. Also small. Also a vast impact.

Despite herself, her heart softened. He wasn't a bad guy. Bermuda did not get to experience Nicholai for as long as the others. Her affliction prevented any emotional development. But what little she knew of him, after Umbriel had cleared the clouds from her heart, she did not hate. The Time Father was eager to please. He worked hard. He let the kindness of his soul guide his actions, and though it blew up in his face, he held fast to his beliefs, no matter how naive. Bermuda ventured to think if they had met under different circumstances, she might even like him.

But he wasn't her family. She would do anything for her family. And his presence, whether it was his fault, tore them apart.

Abandoning Penn on the ship, Bartholomew's takeover of Southern, and Iani's death should have infuriated Kazuaki as much as they infuriated her. The captain's selfishness commanded Umbriel to erase the bargain Bermuda had made with Mimir. Now his selfishness overshadowed the integrities she knew him to hold fast to. All this because he was too egocentric to continue living a life at sea.

He should have done better by them. He always did before.

The quartermaster saw her goal up ahead. She took cover behind a tall mound of rubble, remnants of a once-proud apartment complex that lived in the Southern town bordering Southeastern. She stared ahead. Dozens of footmen patrolled the area. They did not appear attentive. Bermuda knew as soon as she made her presence known they would descend upon her without question, bound by duty and desperation for action. She needed to devise a plan if she were to get anywhere near the border, let alone inside it to restart time.

It was a strange, empty feeling, looking into the land of Southeastern. It was almost as if an invisible wall stood between the two divisions. A soft wind blew more ash with it, creating movement in Southern. The footmen played simple dice games, gambled and exchanged conversation with one another, but their actions all lacked spirit. Autopilot dictated their activities. She remembered it well, functioning without thought or heart. It had been the only way she endured another day when Ty's death was fresh. It must have been how they, too, powered through their existence. They severed their emotions from experiencing their grim reality.

Despite how dead Southern looked at first glimpse, comparing it to Southeastern made it seem alive. Southeastern was devoid of wind. Bermuda witnessed civilians along the edge, unmoving and statuesque in appearance. Everything sat suspended in time. It was inherently wrong. She feared she'd become ill if she looked at it long enough.

The quartermaster turned away and pressed her back against the decrepit wall. Her eyes closed. The expressions on the footmen's faces were barren, lonely. She saw why, being surrounded by this place. Isolation lived here. They had only been patrolling Southeastern for several short months, and all looked as though they wished themselves dead rather than gaze at the inertness that surrounded them for another second. She almost felt bad for them. No soul should live in a place like this. It was too ... inhuman.

Her eyes slowly peeled open. It hit her then. Blind rage gave way to a deeper understanding. The quartermaster noticed countless lumps in the dust surrounding her. The same lumps she had tripped over minutes ago. What her wrath labeled as garbage were bodies. Hundreds. It wasn't the ash that made her taste death. It was the whole environment. This was the world the footmen lived in.

This was the world that awaited Kazuaki if he did not save Panagea.

She knew then. His actions weren't bred in selfishness. His actions were bred in fear—fear this would be his afterlife. Bermuda never saw fear in the captain. Not once. Perhaps that was why she overlooked it. Her stomach squeezed from a sudden feeling of regret. Bermuda could not condemn Kazuaki to this life. She couldn't.

She loved him too much.

The quartermaster surveyed the Chronometer once again and sighed. She peered around the corner of the rubble to spy the footmen one last time. Her metal fingers lowered the device into her pocket for safekeeping. *I'm so sorry, Kazuaki.* With any luck, they were still in Southwestern. She had to go back.

Her thoughts were interrupted as hands wrapped around her mouth and waist. They pulled her backward behind the crumbled wall. Bermuda's eyes widened in surprise, but she summoned the mental wherewithal to fight back. Driving an elbow into the stomach of her assailant gathered a response; he released her and doubled over. She spun from his grasp and faced him. Her metal hand found his throat and squeezed as the many shadows of her attacker's companions came forth in her peripheral vision. They outnumbered her.

"Belay that," a familiar voice Bermuda recognized immediately sounded from the darkness.

"Kazuaki?" She squinted to get a better view.

"You're killing Brack." Kazuaki gestured to the man she still held in her grasp.

Bermuda whipped her head to her captive.

Brack's face had turned a horrid shade of purple.

She released him without delay. "Shit! Rabbit, I'm so sorry." She dusted him off, as if that would help his lungs from being deprived of oxygen.

Brack coughed and reached into his pocket to find his injection. The warm feeling of relief as air filled his lungs and blood again soothed him. He rubbed the tender skin on his neck. "No worries, love," he uttered through a hoarse voice. "Nothing a great handful of women before you haven't already done."

The others stepped forward from the shadows. Nicholai was last to showcase himself, his arms crossed. "I believe you have something that belongs to me."

Bermuda hesitated. She lacked the skill to admit she was wrong, but her hand pulled the Chronometer from her pocket. "Yes. I do."

Nicholai frowned. "What were you thinking? You wouldn't even be able to cross the border, Bermuda. Southeastern will let nothing in I don't bring with me. A Chronometer is a tool, only bowing to the instruction of the Time Father whose blood runs through its gears."

She scowled. The woman understood his anger, but she was not accustomed to being berated. "Take it." Bermuda tossed it toward him.

Nicholai caught it, confused. The intervention went much easier than he thought it would. He had been so consumed with finding Bermuda. When the threat of her betrayal subsided, the proximity to Southeastern assaulted him. It was the first time he was this close since he left months ago.

A large part of him still wasn't ready to face what he'd done. It was easier to keep running, but he could not witness the horrors Panagea and her people endured and continue to delude himself into thinking it was avoidable. The Time Father beheld his division's stillness from behind the safety of the wreckage. All those people. He knew he had to restart it. But a paralysis gripped him, and he was helpless to its power.

Kazuaki, looking both relieved and defeated, approached Bermuda with a low voice. "I thought you left. I thought you had taken me up on my offer to part when you realized this wasn't your war."

"I was wrong, Kazuaki. I'm sorry. If this is a future I can save you from"—she gestured to the wasteland that surrounded them—"then it *is* my war."

An invisible hand squeezed his heart. Her words invaded him and ruptured him. He said nothing. He didn't need to.

Bermuda rested her head on Kazuaki's chest as she stared at the ground. "I'm sorry I keep doing this. I didn't want to lose anyone else." It disgusted her, how little control she held over her emotions. Weakness had never infected her, not before Ty. Since his death, she dug her nails into those precious few in her life and vowed with every ounce of her being to protect them from harm. But, in her efforts to be everyone's savior, Bermuda highlighted her fatal flaw: her crippling inability to let fate happen, the same fate Nicholai tried to control.

Near his chest, Bermuda felt the captain's heart quicken. Believing her close presence caused him discomfort, she withdrew. The quartermaster approached Nicholai and found his distant stare. She recognized the look—raw conflict. Bermuda summoned everything inside her that pushed her through the shame of stealing his Chronometer. "You must restart it at some point, Nico. Panagea can't take much more of this. Some things are just ... beyond our control. But I understand the desire to live in the illusion. I know you'll do the right thing when you're ready."

Nicholai pursed his lips as he closed his fingers around his Chronometer. "I will. I promise."

"For what it's worth, I'm sorry. I just wanted my family safe."

Nicholai positioned the Chronometer over his head, letting the piece fall to its familiar place at his chest. He returned his gaze toward his hometown, toward Lilac. "I know exactly what you mean."

Being here, back in this place, only highlighted how much things had fallen. Southeastern looked just as it had when he left. While it was never perfect, seeing the stark contrast between his division and the Southern land that bordered it was moving. All the buildings in Southeastern within eyesight remained pristine, unburdened by the harsh hand the disasters had brought. Meanwhile, in Southern, partial clumps of infrastructure surrounded, covered in sheets of colorless powder. The people inside Southeastern looked happy. Their frozen faces reflected contentment, a purpose, a sense of naivety to the state of the world around them. And yet the soldiers who loitered around the border showcased depression. Misery. They wore the knowledge of the dying earth on their faces.

Panagea suffered so much. If ever a more obvious visual confronted him, he could not think of it. Nicholai clutched the Chronometer that dangled around his neck. He had the power to ease part of Panagea's burden in his hands right now. All he had to do was make it across the border and push a single button. But every time he felt a moral push to move forward, something weighed down his legs. Lilac.

He couldn't do it.

"Come on, mate." Revi's hand fell onto Nicholai's shoulder. "Brechita's not far from here. Let's go."

"Revi, you told me once that time rarely ever solves your problems, no matter how much of it you have." Nicholai stood, unable to tear his gaze from his home division. "Do you still believe that?"

Revi shrugged. "I do." He followed Nicholai's gaze to Southeastern. "But, as time goes on, it becomes less about waiting for the problem to solve itself and more about waiting for your head and your heart to accept the knowledge it won't. Only then does it become clear what you have to do."

"How did you know when it was time?"

Revi Houton inclined his chin. "Still don't. Head's accepted it, but the heart ..." He hitched a shoulder. "Some things just need more time than others."

Nicholai nodded in slow acknowledgment. It was clear the Time Father could not bring himself to restart Southeastern this day.

Kazuaki cleared his throat to get everyone's attention. "Let's move out before the footmen become keen to our presence. With any luck, Penn is waiting for us in Brechita."

THEY SAW THE MAST FIRST. The low clinging mist on the ocean waters shrouded much from their initial vision. Kazuaki's ship crept through the translucent clouds like a ghost, but what would be an ominous sight to most was a relief to the captain's crew. Kazuaki delighted in seeing it most. It was like reuniting with a long-lost lover. The ship was much a part of him. He missed it.

Penn dropped the anchors as close to the coast as he could. When he arrived in the cockboat, he looked the part of a man who had not slept in days. His eyelids bobbed up and down like the waves as the cockboat slid into Brechita's shores.

The captain placed his boot on the small vessel's edge as he leaned over and grinned. "Penn Elmbroke, it's feckin' great to see you."

The corner of the cook's mouth tugged into a tired smile and nodded. "Captain." He eyed the others. "Can't speak for my counting skills, as one man manning an entire ship has wiped every bit of logic from my brain, but it seems we're missing some bodies."

Kazuaki said nothing.

Elowyn, Rennington, Revi, Nicholai, Bermuda, and Brack climbed into the cockboat and settled into the wooden benches.

"At ease, Penn." The captain took the oars from the ragged man's arms. "You look like the dead. Get some rest. We'll brief you as we head to Northeastern."

Penn abided without argument. He collapsed into the bottom of the cockboat, sliding down into a sitting position to rest the back of his head on the vessel's side. Sleep found him as Kazuaki rowed the little boat to his ship. It was an incredible feat, being captain, quartermaster, navigator, cook, and every other title assigned to their crew. Penn had outdone himself getting the ship to Brechita alone.

Elowyn woke him when they reached the ship but only long enough to move him to his quarters, where he soon found rest again. Though they were short-handed, they found inspiration in Penn and readied the ship for departure. They secured the cockboat, prepared the canvas and raised the anchor.

Nicholai helped as much as he could, but, as the ship carved through the waves toward Northeastern, he placed his hands on the thick wooden ledge and stared. They would pass through the entire coast of Southeastern on their way to Aggi Normandy's division. He could not see much with the fog on the waters, but he imagined it was for the best. Not only would it spare him from having to confront his biggest mistake, but it would make things harder for the Southeastern soldiers to see them pass through.

Nicholai pictured the ocean waves lapping against the shores of his division. The water's liveliness would prove a blunt contrast to the land's stillness. His jurisdiction did not stretch to the sea. No Time Fathers' did. Only the land of Southeastern bent to his command. The ocean did not bow to the rules of time. He suspected that's why Kazuaki loved it so much.

The next few hours crept by. Everyone returned to their roles aboard the ship as if they'd never left. Nicholai was not as comfortable as the others aboard the vessel. This was their home, not his. He walked below deck to what used to be his room and sat on the side of the bed. He noticed the book he had taken from Darjal's library. The Time Father grabbed it and flipped to a random page.

The object he once thought to be Lilac's salvation had only been pages and pages of information that dictated what he didn't want to hear. There was no way to undo it. He could not manipulate the bullet. He could not manipulate Lilac. He could stop time but couldn't go back in time. Nicholai approached every potential angle and arrived at the same conclusion each time: Lilac was helpless to her fate. Though it seemed no other options existed, it was not something he wished to accept.

His thoughts drifted to Umbriel. He hoped she, Granite, and the mutt had success in their planting. She had accomplished amazing things so far. There was still a lot to do, but they gained the power of Southern and Southwestern. Aggi Normandy of Northeastern voiced his desire to help. And Edvard ...

Nicholai recounted his father's appearance. It was strange how he had appeared out of nowhere. Edvard Addihein never left Western. The most he ever ventured was on diplomatic convoys through Western's various cities and to Panagea's center for the decennial gathering of the Time Fathers. So much time had passed since he last saw him. He had been haggard in his appearance, but the mass of his peoples' concerns must have gutted him. Nicholai always remembered Edvard as being dedicated to his people.

The Time Father set down the book and drew a deep breath. Perhaps he should prepare the meal for tonight, he thought. Penn needed the rest. He couldn't claim the title of a chef, but he had listened to Umbriel teach the citizens of Panagea how to cook. He *should* be able to pull something together.

THE DAY DISAPPEARED as it did countless times before. Somewhere in the dark sky, the moon lingered, but it was hard to tell where. The suffocating fog from earlier still clung to the waters, and the clouds above matched in thickness, obscuring the white orb. Only a soft glow that lit the surrounding mists showed any sign of where the moon hid. It was a surreal environment, as if the ship floated in nothingness.

Kazuaki laid in his bed, a hammock of his own design—simple and efficient, the way he liked it. His hands laid across his stomach as he stared at the ceiling. Iani was dead. He had lost members of his crew before, to death, old age, retirement. He'd even killed a few himself if they were insolent enough. None left a crater in him like Iani Platts.

In the beginning, the deaths of those around him had burdened him. Exposure to loss in volume had numbed him as the years passed. Death became a commonplace thing, like eating, drinking, and breathing. Iani's death was the first one that had come back to haunt him in a long, long time.

Perhaps Bermuda was right. Maybe he was going soft. Kazuaki frowned at the thought. If that was the case, it was all that damnable Nicholai Addihein's fault. He had been as cutthroat as ever before the newbie had arrived on his ship's deck. Despite his best efforts, a small smirk crept onto the captain's face. Never in his life did Kazuaki think he'd take to a Time Father, but Nicholai and his unwavering morals bore into him without warning. Though the two men were cut from different cloths, Kazuaki respected Nicholai's resistance to be anything other than who he was—a man who made mistakes but only wished to help those who couldn't help themselves.

The Southeastern Time Father was an idealist stressed by a boundless heart. Kazuaki suspected Darjal's death and being confronted with the frozen people of Southeastern had damaged the man's psyche more than he let on. He suppressed his demons and kept them locked inside as not to burden anyone else. That, too, earned Kazuaki's respect.

Rennington had the first watch on the main deck. This knowledge allowed the captain's eye to close. The luxury of potential sleep did not last long. A loud boom sounded, bellowing in its power. His eye shot open. Kazuaki had become accustomed to a similar sound on Panagea's soil. The natural disasters resonated with comparable intensity. But this was no quake. Kazuaki was familiar with this sound, though he hadn't heard it in several hundred years.

Cannon fire.

He didn't need to crawl from his bed to know Darjal's ship was upon them. He did not blame Rennington for failing to sound an alarm; it was likely the mist obscured their arrival. As he stared at the ceiling, his small smirk from before spread until it consumed his face. Those fools. Domesticated dogs came to the woods to battle the wolf, but he had the home team advantage. They had abandoned the sea long ago. It belonged to Kazuaki Hidataka now.

The captain sat upright from his hammock. His boots landed on the wooden floor with a thump. He grabbed a bottle of manufactured booze and lifted it to his lips. A long, slow drink followed before he returned it to the table and exhaled. The burn in his throat fueled him. Broad arms grabbed his long jacket and threw it over his body. A quick check insured his weapons were ready. Both guns and steel lived on his hip.

The sounds of a scuffle outside his door pierced his ears. They were boarded.

With one swift kick, he blew open his door and engaged. His knife found flesh straightaway. Bermuda was not far. Bullets and blades shredded the air from both captain and quartermaster. The two fought with synchronicity, with precision.

Rennington, Brack, and Elowyn were also on deck. The fire-fight commanded them.

Revi prepared a cannon for fire. The instrument roared like thunder but did minimal damage as it connected with the enemy ship. A large metal monster in the ocean, Darjal's ironclad was a magnificent homage to the madman's wrath.

Revi cursed and ducked before a falchion found his head. His dagger found the soft skin of his attacker's jaw. He kicked the body into the unforgiving sea where waves swallowed it whole.

Nicholai burst to the main deck. His eyes absorbed the battle. All footmen, bearing Southern's insignia—it was like they had traveled back in time to Avadon. His nerves charged as he avoided an oncoming attack.

Rennington appeared beside Nicholai. A man possessed, he grabbed the opponent's arm on another long swing. Weapons made most men weak. They relied too much on the instrument to rely on skill. With his other hand, he raised his machete to sever the footman's hand at the wrist. The falchion clattered to the floor. As fast as Rennington had appeared, he vanished, off to paint the deck red.

Nicholai scooped up the weapon, more for a shield than anything else. Adrenaline attacked his bones. Surrounded by the ocean, there was nowhere to run. He watched as Revi fired another cannonball. It struck an unlucky footman but did minimal damage to the vessel. It was too powerful. Nicholai found the captain in the chaos. "Kazuaki! You must take out the ship from the inside!"

Kazuaki was engaged in the slaughter. Those bold enough to set foot on his ship stood no chance. Kazuaki was the lightning, Bermuda the thunder. Together their storm ravaged any soul who got in their way. The footmen were easy. The ironclad was not.

Cannon fire from the enemy ship met his vessel's exterior. Splinters of wood and shrapnel littered the sky. The captain cursed.

Their experience at sea would not matter if the footmen landed enough lucky hits. Darjal's ship was a war machine.

But a war machine was still a machine. Nicholai knew his way around their inner workings.

Kazuaki hurled a handmade grenade. The explosion sent footmen on the metal ship's deck through the air. The captain growled. "Nico, you're coming with me!" Before the Time Father protested, the captain fired the last rounds in his gun and tossed the empty weapon aside. He seized grappling hooks from beneath a tarp and shoved one into Nicholai's hands. "Cover me!" Favorable winds and skill helped Kazuaki's hook soar through the air. It caught the metal ship's ledge in a single effort. Kazuaki jumped.

The crew flooded to the edge, providing Kazuaki with cover fire. Any footmen who tried to cut the captain's rope received an unforgiving bullet.

Penn popped his head to the main deck from below, a look of obliviousness on his face. "I leave you all alone with the ship for a few hours! Feckin' shit!"

Nicholai stared at the grappling hook in his hands. "The feck am I supposed to do with this?"

Bermuda scowled at the *click, click, click* of her empty gun. Enraged, she tossed it aside and gripped another hidden on her person. "Get over there and disable the ship! Kazuaki will cover you!"

Revi forced the grappling from Nicholai's hands, hurled it with the same accuracy as the captain and shoved the rope into the Time Father's grasp. "Hold on tight." Without warning, he pushed Nicholai over the edge.

Instinct kicked in, and Nicholai gripped the rope as he fell. Strong winds whipped at his face as he thudded into the side of the enemy ship. Despite trying to absorb most of the impact with his legs, his unskilled landing left his bones vibrating. With relief, the panicked chemicals spilling from his brain dulled the pain.

Kazuaki had left a pile of bodies by the time Nicholai clawed his way to the ironclad's main deck. The captain suffered many wounds but the rips and tears in his clothing and body did not stop him from ravaging his opponents.

An oncoming soldier approached Nicholai. He borrowed a falchion from a fallen soldier. His oncoming attacker met his blade. He didn't need to defend himself long. Kazuaki ran the footman through. The Time Father stared at the body with regret but returned his eyes to the captain. "We have to get to the boiler room. If we disable the engine, they'll be dead in the water."

Kazuaki scowled as a soldier's bullet found his stomach. He peered through the gun smoke to identify his target. A well-thrown dagger sank into the soldier's eye socket. "Hurry and find it, Nico. The ship can't take much more of this!"

"I don't know the layout!" Nicholai ducked, using his falchion to ward off further attacks. "It could be anywhere!"

The captain seized an injured footman who tried to crawl away. He threw him to the floorboards, the only part of the ship that wasn't wrapped in iron. He pressed his boot onto his chest, his blade to his cheek. "Tell us where the engine room is."

The soldier tried to spit at Kazuaki, but all that came out was blood. The captain carved what would later become a deep scar into his face for the show of disrespect. "I'll ask again. Where is the engine room?" Kazuaki felt the man's hysterical breathing under his boot. He was a multi-tasker. He fired at those who approached, and bodies fell around him.

It wasn't until the footman saw the dead eyes of his comrade collapse next to his face that he relented. "It's through the hull ... at the ship's bow."

Kazuaki withdrew his weapon and motioned to Nicholai. "Move on then."

The Time Father followed Kazuaki and, at the footman's instruction, disappeared below deck toward the engine room. Their hurried footsteps echoed off the metal walls. "You didn't kill him."

Kazuaki shot another man, an easy target in the narrow hallway. He pushed his way toward the engine room. "Not yet."

Back on the wooden deck, Brack slipped in the pool of blood. Landing on his back, he took advantage of his position, driving a blade through a boot and into the tendon of a looming soldier.

Revi slid by, using the blood as a lubricant to glide until he stopped before Brack and helped him to his feet. The ship deteriorated. "I don't know how much longer we can keep this up."

"Keep firing!" Bermuda's machete ate through another man as if it were starving. Their experience in battle carried them far. But, as an explosion rocked the stern and a fire erupted, she knew they ran on borrowed time. *Come on, Kazuaki,* she thought as she locked steel with a soldier. *Hurry your ass up.*

"There it is." The engine room door. Nicholai climbed over the bodies Kazuaki left in his wake. His fingers never reached the handle. A bullet pierced the back of the Time Father's leg, and he collapsed. Nicholai's panicked fingers wrapped around the injury to apply pressure.

The captain spun around to confront the familiar face of the man who had dropped his comrade. "Well, well," Kazuaki growled and raised his gun at Jernal. "Look who bribed the reaper." He had escaped death in the catacombs, but he would not be lucky today. The captain squeezed the trigger. *Click.*

Jernal glanced at the captain's empty gun and aimed his own. "For Southern." He fired.

The captain lunged forward to put himself between the bullets and his mortal companion. He tossed flint, steel, and a grenade Nicholai's way.

The Time Father caught it in his bloody hands.

Kazuaki winced as the bullets found his flesh, and he advanced toward Jernal. The pain was getting to him. He took countless bullets. But he powered through. "I hate to kill a man who fights in the name of Bartholomew Gray." He hurled a dagger at Jernal, comfortable using it as a long-range weapon when consequences were dire.

Jernal raised his arm, and that was where the dagger struck. He grimaced as he ripped it out. Jernal was a stoic man, but his alarm was ruining him. He riddled the captain's body with many bullets. It seemed the rumors were true. Death did not come to Captain Kazuaki Hidataka. Still, he found his courage. "I stand for Darjal Wessex."

"Then you stand for a dead man." Kazuaki leaped at Jernal and pinned him against the wall. "Send him my regards."

Nicholai dragged himself to the engine room and opened the door. He struggled; his blood-soaked hands made it hard to grip the flint.

Jernal looked his reaper in the eye. He had received Nordjan's letter from the mainland. It had dictated the need for a hasty return but nothing of Darjal's fall. "Spew your lies, demon, I will not listen."

Kazuaki smirked.

Nicholai lit the grenade. He tossed it into the room and forced himself to stand.

The captain leaned forward, his face inches from Jernal's. "You'll see for yourself soon enough."

"Leave him. We have to go." Nicholai limped to the captain, forcing weight onto his injured leg.

Kazuaki's gaze flitted to the engine room. Nicholai was right. Though it went against every instinct the captain possessed, he released Jernal. Kazuaki threw Nicholai's arm over his shoulder to expedite his mobility while Jernal watched in confusion.

The soldier glanced into the engine room and spotted the grenade. "Shit." The engine room contained most of the explosion. The shell of iron that surrounded it absorbed the blast.

Kazuaki spotted his ship as he emerged from the hull, finding the back quarter in flames. "Gods-damn it all!" He hurled Nicholai and himself into the first auxiliary boat he found that his crew's cannon fire hadn't damaged. The captain's blade cut the ropes to free the ship from the side of the ironclad, and the two men plunged into the sea.

Nicholai grunted at the harsh landing. He gripped his leg injury again to still the blood loss.

Kazuaki abandoned the small vessel and dove into the violent ocean. He surfaced at his ship's edge and climbed the sides with dual daggers as his assistants. Plunging the blades into the wood, he scaled the vertical obstacle and landed on the deck. Smoke swirled around him as he found Revi in the chaos. "Get to the engine room! Full power!"

Revi abandoned his efforts to subdue the flames and vanished into the ship's hull. Rennington, Brack, Bermuda, Elowyn, and Penn tried their best to quell the damage but did little with the constant threat of footmen at their forefront.

Kazuaki ran to the bow and gripped the wheel. With the enemy's engine destroyed, the ship created a distance between its opponent. The smoldering ironclad floated in the sea, powerless to catch up to the burning wreckage that was Kazuaki's ship.

Fewer and fewer footmen littered the deck as the influx from the warship ceased. Though riddled with injuries, the crew showed no mercy. Soldiers who did not wish to die jumped into the sea by their own doing. The threat of death by falchion was eliminated. The crew shifted their efforts toward the fire.

Kazuaki looked over his shoulder. The flames grew, feeding on the wooden masts and canvas. Despite its condition, the ship parted from the ironclad with efficiency, but the captain knew it wouldn't last. She would soon fall, the biggest casualty of his entire crew. It took a moment for him to make the call. Denial tried to infiltrate his thoughts; he loved his ship. She was a piece of the Kazuaki Hidataka legend. But it was the ship, or the ship *and* the crew.

His gaze flitted to Nicholai in the waters below. The man struggled to row the lifeboat in the power of the waves alone. Coupled with his injury, Kazuaki showed surprise he kept a close pace. Survival instinct played a strong role in keeping a man alive. The captain tightened his lips together, his hand gripped around the wheel's handle. It hurt to let go. But he did.

Kazuaki marched forward, looking passed the bodies that besieged his deck. He found his crew in the back, fighting the flames. Though it ripped his heart in half and gutted his heavy soul, he raised his hands to his mouth to help carry his voice. "She belongs to the sea, mates! Abandon ship!"

Chapter Twenty-Four

The beloved ship drifted in the unforgiving waters. It was far off, but they still saw it. Though the haze remained over the swelling waves, the dying vessel's orange glow vessel burned like a lighthouse in the distance. They fled to Nicholai's lifeboat, their own cockboat far too damaged in the battle to be of use anymore. It was one last affront to the captain. Not only did he have to part with his precious ship, but he couldn't even claim the small boat she carried with her.

Kazuaki rowed with persistence. The sting of the bullets in his body mocked him with every stroke. He remembered the day he bought the vessel. He had purchased her for almost nothing several hundred years ago when it became clear the art of seafaring was dying. Men and women no longer found their fortunes in the briny waters; the advancements made on land afforded them all the luxuries they needed. The wanderlust died. Maritime adventures died with it.

Once again, the ocean belonged to no one.

Elowyn stitched a knife wound in her abdomen, biting hard on a bullet between her teeth with each thread the needle made into her skin. She reached into the emergency pack of medical supplies she had grabbed before their hasty abandonment. When her hands found the antiseptic, she used care to pour it into her gash. The medic needed to conserve as much as she could. There were many wounds to go around.

Brack dug into his arm with a pair of Elowyn's forceps, trying to fish out a bullet. Blood oozed from the hole as he sunk the metal pliers in farther, rummaging them around until they found the foreign object hiding inside. He tried to stifle his howl when he ripped it out. He was only somewhat successful.

Anguish lived in the small boat. With the adrenaline from the fight long gone from their bodies, all that remained was the crippling fatigue.

Bermuda sanitized the forceps as best as she could when Brack finished with them and sat beside the captain. "Want me to get those?" She motioned to the dozens of tiny holes.

"Tend the rest," Kazuaki murmured, knowing full well Rennington, Revi, and Nicholai still held shrapnel under their skin. "I'll live."

Bermuda nodded and went to assist the others.

Penn, who had endured several cuts from falchions but avoided any flying bullets, grabbed a set of oars after he had stitched and cleansed his injuries. He rowed in silence with the captain, figuring the man knew which direction they needed to go.

Revi groaned as he removed another bullet. He huffed and hurled the metal chunk into the sea. After a few deep breaths, he slid the only cask of water they had loaded into the lifeboat toward him and took a much-needed drink. The cool liquid eased the fire inside him. He wiped beads of trailing liquid from his jaw. "How far do you think we'll get before we run out of supplies?"

Kazuaki rowed on. "Not far enough. We'll have to land on Eastern's shore. No way we'll make it to Aggi's division with what we have."

Everyone nodded. The surrounding atmosphere grew solemn. They suspected as much.

With everyone's battle scars attended, each member grabbed an oar. They needed every shred of strength they possessed if they would make it to Eastern's shores in a lifeboat. The crew rowed until their arms screamed in protest. It felt as though the tearing muscles may never recover. And then they rowed more.

"I just don't understand it," Elowyn said between panting as she forced her arms to move. "How, in an entire ocean, did that ship happen upon us?"

"Only the luck of the gods could have sent them upon us." Rennington scoffed as he pulled his oars through the resistant waters. "Maybe Darjal's delusion had some truth to it, and he was a god, after all. Fecker is haunting us or some shit."

"I don't think it was anything supernatural," Nicholai murmured. He had sat quietly the entire time. His leg throbbed where Elowyn had extracted the bullet. He felt every heartbeat within it.

Elowyn eyed Nicholai. "If not by omnipotent force, then how?"

The Southeastern Time Father squeezed the wooden oars. A strange feeling had boiled inside him since Kazuaki hurled him into the lifeboat, and he shared the same question as Elowyn. He took a lot of time to ponder it. Worse yet, something inherent within him told him it was true. "The only other man who overheard we were going to Brechita," he replied with a bitter taste in his mouth. "Edvard Addihein."

IT TOOK TWO DAYS OF rowing for the boat to find Eastern's shores. It was just in time. Though everyone tried to find resilience, the lifeboat grew claustrophobic.

Kazuaki splashed into the waters and hauled the boat to the shore with Rennington's and Nicholai's help.

The Time Father still felt the seething burn in the back of his leg as the saltwater seeped into his healing wound.

Smog billowed from the tall smokestacks of Eastern, constant and concentrated. No glimpses of blue remained in the sky. Everything within eyesight adopted a dull, gray hue—the buildings, the roads, the atmosphere. Eastern was a colorless division, devoid of anything resembling natural life.

"We'll have to find a market," Kazuaki muttered as he rifled through his pockets. He possessed no currency for the Eastern division; it had sunk with the ship. With any luck, they'd accept Southern money. He still possessed a few coins in his pocket. "Someone will have to stay with the ship—boat," he corrected himself.

His words were flat. Bermuda felt his defeat. She wished something existed for her to ease the burden in his head, but everyone suffered. The collective was in no condition to survive in Eastern if they met any resistance. It was the most populated division, packed with prying citizens who crowded every inch of the city. "I have doubts we'll be able to cross Northeastern's border on foot, Captain. Eastern has eyes everywhere, and we don't know who's on our side."

"Right." He slicked his hands through his hair. They weren't unassuming. Riddled with knife and bullet wounds and caked in dried blood, the crew would stick out like sore thumbs amongst the common folk of the Eastern division. "We'll get what we can and float the rest of the way. We'll stay far enough off the coast to avoid unwanted sightings but close enough that we can land, should a storm occur." He spied the lifeboat; a disapproving sneer crossed his face. Not even the great Captain Kazuaki Hidataka could keep that dingy afloat if an ocean storm was violent enough.

The churning of factories in full production and hissing steam cars in the distance almost covered the sound of the cocking shotgun. Tired eyes followed the source to a woman. She stood on a hill overlooking the coastal embankment. The twin barrels pointed down at the haggard group, threatening to fire at any moment.

"Who goes there?" the gun's owner asked, her words thick with fearlessness.

Kazuaki glanced beyond the woman to a small, shabby building. He could only see the topmost part, but the decrepit structure was likely her home. He did not think they'd find residential properties so close to the coast, but, with Eastern maximizing the entirety of its land, it should have come as no surprise. "Madam, I am in no mood."

Nicholai took gimping steps ahead of the captain and raised his arms. Kazuaki was not in the best frame of mind. None of them were. He needed to intervene before the hostility escalated and their cover blew even further. "We mean no harm to you or your family, I assure you."

The woman chortled. "Even if you did, doesn't look like y'all could do much damage."

Nicholai mustered a charming grin despite everything that ravaged him up to this point. "Well, you're certainly right about that."

Her pressure around the gun's trigger eased, but she did not risk lowering her protection. "If you ain't here to cause trouble, what *are* you doing crawling from the bay like sea scum?"

"We've just come in search of food and water for our travels. We'll be gone in the blink of an eye," the Time Father replied, a gentleness in his tone.

The woman studied each person, but her gaze lingered on Nicholai the longest, scrutinizing him. "If you leave your weapons in the boat, I'll give you a warm meal and a floor on which to sleep. Won't be much, but you don't look like you're in a position to complain."

Nicholai smiled. "Right you are again, m'lady. We'd be most grateful." He turned to Kazuaki with a quizzical shrug.

The captain mulled over the offer for a moment before he nodded to his crew to leave their weapons in the boat. Should any real confrontation arise, Kazuaki remained confident they could use their fists as a temporary solution. The woman's primitive home was as far from the city center as they would get, though it still lingered too close for his liking. "Someone will still have to stay with the boat."

"I will," Rennington volunteered, placing a boot on the lifeboat's floor. "Could use time to myself anyway."

"Nonsense," Elowyn argued, unwilling to leave him alone in his state. "I'll keep you company."

"You can bring 'em some food, so long as I get the bowls back." The woman at the top of the embankment rested her shotgun against her shoulder.

"Right." Brack grinned, rubbing his hands together as he beheld the gun-toting maiden. "Well then, love, what's for eats?"

The food was warm, the house even warmer. Their assailant introduced herself as Mairyn Catteral but assured them they could call her *Catty* for short. She never asked for their names in return. Her home was simple but well kept, with three children also dwelling inside the one-bedroom establishment. The quarters were tight with the rest of the crew inside, but no one complained. It was far better than being crammed in the lifeboat, where it was hard for one to stretch their legs.

Revi played cards with the kids—two boys and a girl. He showed them various magic tricks and illusions in-between structured games. It was the first time since Nicholai laid eyes on him that he wore a genuine smile. The man seemed every bit the father, sitting with those kids.

Catty returned from her bathroom with a handful of things—gauze, medicines, astringents. She set them on the tabletop after Penn and Brack cleared all evidence of the meal they had eaten. "There's not much here," she said, offering half-empty bottles, "but you're welcome to take whatever you need."

Nicholai surveyed the belongings before returning his attention to Catty. "You're too kind, Miss Catteral. I know we look every bit the sorry bunch, but you don't have to give us your things if you require them yourself."

The mother leaned back in her chair, watching as Revi engaged her children in play. "You take what you need, Nicholai. You'll need it more than we will."

The Time Father blinked when she addressed him by name. He knew he never gave it to her, and, if she had asked, he would have given her a false alias. It was too dangerous to introduce themselves to potential enemies. "Excuse me?"

"Don't be too shocked. In a world as grim as this, good news spreads quick. People crave any shred of hope they can get." The gaze from her green eyes landed on the visible Chronometer chain peeking from his clothing's collar. "Caught a glimpse of it in the light outside. Very identifiable piece of jewelry you have there, my friend."

Instinct issued him to rest a hand on the metal that hid beneath his shirt, and he flashed Catty an apologetic smile. "I suppose it is. I hope our presence hasn't put you in any danger."

"Not yet. Truth be told, I wish you arrived sooner. Maybe then Mr. Catteral would still be with us ..."

Nicholai observed the woman with visible pity. He did not wish to pry for further details and extended his compassion. "I'm sorry for your loss."

Catty leaned forward, resting her chin on her open palm. "Thank you, Nicholai, but waste no pity on me. Everyone has losses. It's just nice to know a band of people are out there trying to make less of them for people like me." She looked at her children. "Like us. It's every bit worth the risk."

Bermuda eavesdropped from a chair she had found in the main room. She locked Catty's words into a far corner of her brain, should she need to revisit them later if doubts about their mission resurfaced. It felt good at the moment, knowing they honored the desires of a woman like Catty, knowing they paved the way for a better future for her children. She'd use that to keep her moving.

"I'll send some food off with you." Catty motioned to the small cupboards of her kitchen. "Water's a bit harder to come by. Rations have gotten low. They use a lot to extinguish the fires. I have some in the rain barrel out back, but the smog in the sky gives it a foul taste."

"Whatever you can spare," Nicholai said with a small smile. It felt wrong to take food from this woman's home, but no matter how they looked at it, they needed it to complete their journey to Northeastern.

Catty leaned forward, reaching across the tabletop to grab Nicholai's hand. She squeezed it in hers. Though Mairyn Catteral presented herself as a strong, fierce mother, he felt a vulnerability in her hold. "Thank you, Nicholai. The people have heard of the Earth Mother's efforts as she climbs through the divisions. Know the change is small, but we see it. We feel it. You are doing right by us, and by Panagea."

Nicholai stared at the woman's hand and pressed his lips together, absorbing the gratitude that she emanated. "We'll keep trying, Catty. We'll fix this."

She gave his hand a final squeeze before she released it. The woman leaned back in her chair, a peace about her he didn't notice hiding in her rigidness before. She nodded. "I know you will."

Morning came fast for the exhausted group. Catty's quarters were small but comfortable. Kazuaki traded posts with Rennington and Elowyn halfway through the evening, offering them the shelter of the indoors while he took up the watch of the lifeboat. As well-rested as they could be in the short time they had, the crew felt a small sense of rejuvenation as they readied themselves to continue their journey to Aggi Normandy.

Revi had the hardest time leaving. The kids wrapped themselves around his limbs and pleaded for him to stay. "You don't need me here," Revi replied to the young ones with a smirk. "Your mum's got all the qualities you need to learn in this world. She needs no man to do right by you three."

Catty smiled, handing Revi the last of the food she set aside for them. "Good luck, Mr. Houton."

Revi accepted it with gratitude. "Best of luck to you too, Miss Catty." He looked down at the kids. "Be good." With that, he traipsed toward the lifeboat, loaded it up and helped Kazuaki push it into the waters once again.

Catty watched for some time on the shores of her Eastern home. Her children retired to the home's interior. Though the lifeboat was long gone from her sight, she lingered, letting the feelings of hope creep through her veins. Having met the Time Father now and those in his company, she felt a new life breathe into her bones. It felt good.

She was about to return to her home, but something caught her eyes. On the ground rested the two cleaned bowls Rennington and Elowyn had left on the shoreline. Catty started for them and bent to scoop them into her arms.

A noise from the right trapped her attention, and she turned with haste. A small vessel, identical to the lifeboat the crew had departed in, pulled onto the shoreline. Her eyes narrowed. She didn't have time to fetch her shotgun. The mother watched as a dozen men crawled from the craft and collapsed onto the shores of Eastern. All donned Southern military regalia and looked as haggard as Nicholai and his crew.

Jernal heaved the boat onto the dry rocks with the last of his efforts, breathing hard. When he caught movement from the corner of his eye, he startled.

Catty stood several feet from him, fearless.

"Pardon me, miss," Jernal said, exhausted. "It seems we found ourselves on your property."

"Yes," she replied, her tone sharp. "It seems you have."

"Forgive the intrusion." He tried and failed to look presentable. He scanned the shoreline and turned a quizzical eye to Mairyn Catteral. "Pray tell, I know it may sound odd of me to ask, but have any other men washed up on your shores?"

Catty gauged Jernal from head to toe. She examined every tear in his outfit, every healing injury, every symbol of the torment he'd endured. After a long pause, she returned her gaze to his, unwavering. "Not a one."

IT WAS MUCH EASIER getting into the lifeboat the second time around. Refreshed from Catty's generosity to the point of being able to function, the crew ferried down the coast of Eastern into Northeastern territory. In their chests, the men and women remained warm despite their exhaustion. Mairyn Catteral had filled them with enough life to push their tired bodies onward without risking mental collapse.

The currents were favorable. The wind accommodated them. Flowing on the calm ocean waves almost made it difficult to remember what a sorry state the land was in, though they caught glimpses from their position in the water. A minimal exchange of words occurred. Everyone tried to conserve their energy to allow their slow-healing wounds an opportunity to rest. But, as soon as the tip of their lifeboat pressed into the Northeastern shore, adrenaline returned. Touching welcoming land was a huge, unadulterated relief.

"What should we do with the boat?" Penn asked as he removed the last of the supplies from inside the small vessel.

Kazuaki placed his boot on the vessel's edge and gave it a hearty shove. It floated back into the sea. With nothing to hold it down, the waves carried it farther and farther away.

That was not enough for Kazuaki Hidataka. With unreleased frustration, he withdrew his gun and fired multiple rounds of unnecessary bullets into the vessel until his pistol's chamber emptied.

"Guess that answers that," Penn muttered. The boat was slow to take on water, but he knew the rest of its life existed at the bottom of the ocean. He shrugged and trudged up Northeastern's shore.

The city that greeted them bustled with activity. It, too, experienced negative effects from the disasters that frequented Panagea, but people were active in their repairs. The damage was greater than they could keep up with. Many decrepit buildings remained, but it was the most encouraging effort the crew had witnessed in their travels. They walked farther into the city, not fearing any retaliation in the hometown of Aggi Normandy. The Northeastern Time Father had made it clear in his letters he wished them nothing but wellness, and, with Emont to back up his words, they exercised no caution.

The peak of Aggi's tower loomed in the distance. It would take at least a mile of walking and weaving through the city's streets to reach it. Nicholai's leg still bothered him, and the crew's injuries plagued them too. It would be an effort to reach the tower but nothing worse than they had already endured. As he was about to cross a busy street, he spotted a familiar face.

The soft, silver hair blowing in the wind was unmistakable. The flawless skin, the delighted smile—he'd recognize it anywhere. "Umbriel!" Nicholai grinned as he ran toward her, his excitement quelling the sting in his leg. Relief showered over him knowing she had safely arrived at Northeastern's borders. He scooped the woman in a tight embrace, lifting her feet from the ground before he set her down. "How did you know where to find us?"

The woman smiled, tucking strands of hair behind her ears. "I felt it in the earth." The Earth Mother waved with joy as she spotted the rest of the crew across the street. She wrapped her arms around each of them as they met her.

Kazuaki regarded Granite and smirked. "Thanks for keeping an eye on everything."

Granite, who was silent as he stood beside Umbriel, nodded an acknowledgment. His faithful canine stood beside him and jumped onto everyone's legs, wagging its tail in the commotion.

Rennington stooped down to pet it, happy to see the amputation did not slow the beast's classic exuberance in the least.

"You all must be dead tired." Umbriel noticed the various wounds that inflicted them all. "Let's get you back to Aggi's home."

THE BEDS WERE LIKE rectangular slices of utopia, the most comfortable things any of the crew had slept on in months. Aggi Normandy's introduction had been short. At first glimpse of their weary bodies, he had immediately issued them all a place to rest, as they looked in dire need. Feeling a sense of safety surrounding them, the members slept an entire day away. Twenty-four hours of rest for their aching bones somehow did not seem like enough, but everyone was grateful for the opportunity.

Nicholai sat upright in the bed Aggi had gifted him. A comfort existed in the room, but he did not pay much attention to his surroundings. Too many thoughts of Lilac and her predicament ravaged his brain. And Southeastern's predicament. And Panagea's predicament. He ran out of ideas ... ideas he did not have to begin with. It was not the only thing he ran out of. Revi's words weighed on the Time Father. His optimism was fading, paving the way for reality to surface. It was as painful as it was uninvited. Nicholai lost himself to it, a victim of his thoughts, until a soft knock at the door tore him from his reverie.

"Nicholai?" Umbriel pushed open the door and peered inside. "Would you accommodate me for a visit?"

The Time Father rubbed his face to pull himself back to the present world. "Of course." He slid his legs off the side of the bed and motioned her in.

Umbriel strode across the floor and sat on the bed beside him. Her gaze drifted to the exposed injury on Nicholai's leg, his parting gift from Jernal on Darjal's ironclad. "I wonder why you haven't bothered to heal that yet."

Nicholai arched a brow. "A full day's rest did me a lot of good, but I'm still not as capable in the medical arts as you or Elowyn."

The Earth Mother smiled, the picture of wisdom. "Time heals all wounds, Nicholai. Particularly physical ones. Why not quicken the process?"

The Time Father withdrew. A hesitation splayed on his face. It wasn't as if he hadn't thought about it. If the principle of speeding up time applied to human skin as well as it applied to plants, it made sense he could isolate his injury and heal it. But he couldn't pull the trigger. "You saw what I did to Darjal in Avadon. I tried to isolate the time to the gun, but ... it spread. I didn't know how to stop it."

Umbriel tilted her head. His concern stemmed from understandable apprehension. "It was a pity, what happened in that church, but it was an accident. I can see why you'd hesitate, Nicholai. I just don't want to watch fear cripple your opportunities to enhance your gift."

He nodded. "I appreciate your kind words, Umbriel," Nicholai thanked her with a small, sarcastic smirk. "But I think I'd prefer to practice on something other than myself." He joked to ease the discomfort, but that image remained burned in his mind and probably would for the rest of his natural-born life.

"Understandable. I could take care of it for you if you'd like."

The pain was uninvited. The throbbing bullet hole in his leg only reminded him of the lives lost on the ocean that night. Though he was relieved to disable the engine as opposed to sinking the ship, he couldn't help but wonder if the soldiers who survived the crew's gunfire could survive being adrift at sea. "I would like that very much," he finally said, hoping to rid himself of one more terrible reminder of a bad memory. He had enough of those floating around.

As Umbriel laid her hands on his leg and manipulated the damaged tissues, Nicholai's thoughts drifted to the crew. They all needed a few days to mend, if Kazuaki would allow it. They were in good hands in Northeastern; Aggi Normandy boasted the highest ratings for advances in medical science. His brows knit together at the thought. "Umbriel, do you know if Aggi is available for a chat? I'd like to discuss something with him, aside from the obvious."

"I think he's getting ready to call a meeting soon." She removed her hands from his leg after she completed her objective. "Now that everyone is awake and well-rested, he's eager to discuss the next plan of action."

"Great." Nicholai slid off the bed and onto his feet. He surveyed his leg, flexing it as he stood. It was incredible what Umbriel accomplished on a cellular level with minimal time. "You're a miracle worker."

"I do what I can." She came to a stand beside him. "Come on then, let's find Aggi."

"On a first-name basis with him, I see." Nicholai nudged her playfully as they exited his room.

"He's nice." Umbriel laughed as they walked to the Northeastern Time Father's office. "He's been very accommodating since Granite and I arrived several days ago."

"I bet he has." The Time Father chuckled, finding refreshment in sharing spirited banter with another individual again. He had missed it. But all jokes aside, he guessed Umbriel's presence came as a relief for Aggi Normandy. She had a calming presence about her, and the Northeastern Time Father probably saw little of that in the days since the disasters grew in frequency. "I'm sure he was delighted to have a beautiful woman in the room to offset the chaos he's been dealing with as of late."

Though no attentive eyes were present to bear witness, the Earth Mother's cheeks reddened. A long time had passed since anyone had called her a beautiful woman. Though she knew in her heart he had said it in innocence, absent of any lingering undertones, Umbriel could not deny how much she enjoyed hearing it come from Nicholai Addihein. "Here we are," she announced, trying to quell her unusual wild nerves as they stood outside Aggi's door.

Before Nicholai raised his hand to knock, the door opened. Aggi appeared to be in a hurry, almost running into them. He jumped with a start, but his anxiousness dissipated when he realized it was Umbriel and Nicholai, and he grinned. "You're awake."

"Yes, thank you for your hospitality." Nicholai bowed his head in a show of gratitude. "We could sleep another week if you let us, I'm sure."

Aggi chuckled. "It was my pleasure. Anything to help those mounting the revolution." His expression grew dim. "Really, Nicholai. Thank you for what you're doing. Your methods are a little unorthodox—freezing Southeastern and all—but we've needed a change for years. It's certainly one way to get everyone's attention."

Nicholai forced a smile. Aggi believed he had frozen Southeastern out of strategy. Though he thought it might be best to correct him, he let it slide. "Speaking of Southeastern, Aggi"—Nicholai cleared his throat—"a lot of our people are stricken with black lung. I heard Northeastern's researchers made a breakthrough in an experimental treatment."

Aggi tilted his head. "You heard right. It performed well in early trials, but we abandoned the release date to the public. Everyone needed to put their efforts into ... *this*." He motioned all around him.

"I understand." Nicholai tried to summon charm from his still-tired body. "Aggi, you have gifted us with insurmountable kindness since our arrival, but I hope it would not be too bold of me to ask for one more favor."

Aggi Normandy blinked, shrugging a single shoulder. "Of course, Nicholai. Anything."

The Southeastern Time Father stood taller. "Might I claim a vial of your black lung treatment?"

Evidence of confusion dotted Aggi's eyes, but he saw no harm in relinquishing. "It's all yours. I have business to attend in town. The vials are in a storage facility until these disasters sort themselves out, but I'll find someone who can get one for you. When I return, I'd very much like to discuss our next move, if everyone is well-rested."

"Of course. We'll ensure they're all ready. Thank you, Aggi."

"My pleasure." He turned to the Earth Mother. "Umbriel," he acknowledged her presence with a gentle smile and a tip of his hat before he slipped off to tend to his duties.

Nicholai pointed at Aggi's back, looking at Umbriel with a broad grin. "See that? He's got it bad," he teased. His expression shifted to a more mischievous nature when he saw her face. "Umbriel—are you blushing?"

The stoic woman's eyes widened at the accusation. "Let's wake the others." She dismissed his interrogation with a quick smile before starting toward the other rooms.

Nicholai watched her depart, stifling a chuckle. The Earth Mother was always the picture of composure. Seeing her flustered entertained him in a way he couldn't explain. It was nice to know she, too, despite being a six-hundred-year-old maiden able to summon seeds and heal with a touch was also human.

Aggi wasted no time in town. Whatever his duties were, he had performed them with great efficiency. It was hard for the crew to get themselves together, but they pulled their aching muscles from their beds and helped themselves to the hygiene products made available in the Northeastern Time Father's residence. Aggi summoned the group into a large room for the meeting, ensuring everyone had a chair around the multi-leafed wooden table in the center. He could not contain his eagerness to begin, but he investigated their comfort before they continued.

"Is there anything else I can get anyone?"

Brack grinned. "A bottle of whiskey and your finest Northeastern broad."

Elowyn swatted him. For a petite thing, she packed power behind her hit. She looked to Aggi as Brack whined and rubbed at his arm where she had struck him. "Ignore him, Mr. Normandy."

"Please, Aggi is fine. You've all made some incredible advances toward rerouting Panagea. Plants growing again in Southern, Southwestern, and even those you seeded in Northeastern before you made your way to my home—it's amazing. I never thought I'd see anything like it in my lifetime. I'd only ever heard the stories."

Everyone watched as his once-excited expression fell into one of regret. Aggi crossed the room to Umbriel and got onto one knee, taking her hand into his. "I knew of your plight in those stories. I knew the past Time Fathers left you to rot on that island, and I did nothing. I didn't think one man could ignite such a huge change, especially after our loss in the battle with Northern." He squeezed her hand and searched her eyes. "Umbriel, please accept my deepest, most sincere apology. I am a division leader. As such, I am a man of the people. I *should* have done the right thing, and I did not. Can you ever forgive me?"

The Earth Mother seemed surprised by his grand gesture. His words were genuine; she felt it in his voice. Umbriel issued him a smile and patted his hand. "Of course, I can, Aggi. None should punish the sons for the sins of their fathers. I harbor no grudge, not for you or them."

Aggi released a breath he didn't realize he held. He made no efforts to disguise his relief at her forgiveness. "Thank you." He slid back to his feet and released her hand. "I will make it right. You all have whatever is at my disposal. I will help however I can. If we can get Avital, Nordjan, and Vadim to see the light, this will be much easier."

"And Edvard," Nicholai interjected.

Aggi quirked a brow as he tilted his head. "Edvard too? I assumed, as your father, he may be swayed, if he was not already."

"No." Nicholai laced his fingers together on the table to squeeze his frustrations into his own hands. "I can say with a great deal of confidence he revealed our position to Darjal's ironclad. That ship couldn't have found us any other way in a limitless ocean."

The Northeastern Time Father's expression fell flat. "I'm sorry to hear this, Nicholai."

Kazuaki leaned forward on the table. "We must decide who to persuade next." Whether through means of discussion or violence, it mattered not to the captain. "Speaking of Edvard, my vote is on him." The heathen was responsible for losing his ship. Kazuaki hoped Edvard's mind wouldn't change with words alone, as he wanted to drive a dagger into the man's heart. If he wasn't Nicholai's father, he wouldn't have hesitated to do so.

Aggi nodded, closing the door so listening ears would not be privy to any information discussed in the room. "We could visit the division leaders one by one, ladies and gentlemen, or"—he traipsed to a desk and unlocked a drawer with a key he had withdrawn from his pocket, removed a few letters and returned to the desk—"we could reach them all at the same place at the same time."

Everyone's eyes widened. "How?" Revi asked. "I thought those feckers were bound to their divisions?"

"They are. But the gathering is upon us."

"The decennial," Nicholai said in a heavy exhale. How could he have forgotten? The ten-year gathering of the Time Fathers at Panagea's center. It would be the perfect opportunity to present their case. Darjal had been one of the major obstacles; he was as stubborn as he was delusional. But the personalities of the others still left him with some concerns. They were all stern; it made them good leaders but would also make it that much harder to convince them to alter how they've done things the entire time they'd been in power.

Vadim might relent if they presented the change in a way that highlighted monetary gain. He was a money-driven man, boasting the largest treasury of all the divisions. He hoarded every coin he earned. While there was no guarantee altering his leadership tactics would bring him an additional fortune, it would at least spare him from Kazuaki's blade if he cooperated.

Convincing Avital would take effort. As the eldest of all the ruling Time Fathers, he remained the most attached to the old-world ideals. He modeled his division off the original Time Fathers' foundation—no wasted space, ultimate efficiency, never stop progressing.

Nicholai wanted to believe Nordjan could see the potential of change. Despite his rough exterior, the Southeastern Time Father grew to respect Nordjan's powerful ability to rule with necessity in their meetings together. He was a stubborn man, but, at the core of it all, Nicholai believed he was fair. If he convinced Nordjan it was for the good of his people, his mind could change.

And Edvard ... Edvard was the wild card. Everything Nicholai thought he knew about the man, which wasn't much to begin with, had sank to the bottom of the ocean with Kazuaki's ship.

"It'll be a good opportunity," Aggi started, "but it won't come easy. This won't be like any other decennial I've attended." He eyed the stacks of letters. When Nicholai had first betrayed Southeastern, Aggi had received countless letters detailing every aspect of what the other divisions had endured to secure Nicholai's capture. The invitation to the decennial had also arrived in the post. But, as time went on and it became clearer Aggi Normandy did not supply as many resources into finding Nicholai as the other division leaders, the letters slowed. Even still, the Northeastern Time Father had a critical inside look into the goings-on of the others. It was that knowledge that concerned him.

"What can we expect?" Nicholai asked. He had only attended one decennial, the one where they had inducted him. It was a tedious, hours-long endeavor detailing the state of Panagea, the people, whether they needed to start looking for potential Time Fathers if others wished to retire—a whole slew of political chitchat that rambled for an eternity.

"They're scared, Nicholai." Aggi's face grew serious, and he lowered his tone. "Darjal's and Carlo's deaths have them reeling. They know you're in Kazuaki Hidataka's presence, and his immortality has proven dangerous in your battles. I fear they may act in desperation. They're already taking their armies with them, leaving their divisions defenseless."

Nicholai frowned. It was a common show of respect that the Time Fathers arrived at Panagea's center alone. The fact they were bringing their armies raised a red flag. Aggi was right; it was a desperate move. "We'll have a hard time getting to them if we have to go through four division's worth of armies."

"Indeed," Aggi agreed with a sigh. "Avital's army alone is insurmountable. The sheer volume of people in Eastern grants him an incredible advantage. Even if we take Northeastern's armies, and Bartholomew of Southern and Emont of Southwestern send whatever men they can spare, we're still outnumbered."

Brack sat upright, shrugging a shoulder. "Ain't some way we can bypass the militiamen? A flying machine perhaps? If we could get the drop on the Time Fathers themselves, that'd save us a damn bit of bloodshed."

Everyone turned to look at Rabbit. Each face matched the others in the amount of confusion they displayed.

"What?" Brack stared. "I got ideas rattling up there too. Sometimes."

"A flying machine *could* work," Rennington said, glancing at Aggi. "Do you have access to any that would house us all? I don't think we could all fit in a standard ornithopter."

Aggi stroked his chin. "A majority of the larger flying machines are housed in Northern. They're mostly used here for recreational purposes, all single-manned machines. But I could scare one up. We confiscated one of Northern's larger vessels when we battled years ago. It's in sorry shape, and it's been locked in a facility for years, but it's repairable."

"Sounds like that's our best bet," Bermuda offered, trying to gauge everyone's reactions. The crew never minded a little bloodshed. Or a lot. But trying to engage the armies put many lives at risk. Losing Iani was tragic enough; if they could avoid any additional losses, they would take it.

"The flying machines will get us close, there's no doubt about that." Aggi paced the room. "But make no mistake, Nicholai. They want you dead. I have every reason to believe bringing their armies to Panagea's center is only the start of their desperation."

Nicholai's brows furrowed. "What do you mean?"

"I wouldn't put it passed them to freeze their divisions too, Nicholai. They know Kazuaki Hidataka is their biggest threat, and they'll render him immobile. If they feel like they're backed into a corner, they'll do just about anything."

The Southeastern Time Father lowered his head, thinking. Only Time Fathers could traverse the realms when time stilled. If they did paralyze their divisions, it would be Nicholai and Aggi versus Vadim, Nordjan, Avital, and Edvard. Their odds of success increased if Bartholomew and Emont attended, but he suspected they did not receive an invitation. Still, he would not throw Bartholomew and Emont into that situation. He couldn't risk sending good men to their potential deaths. Not many were left who were willing to step up and rule a division. Emont and Bartholomew needed to sit this one out.

Kazuaki and the others would be useless. Nicholai was not an unintelligent man; though it ate at his conscience, he knew the success of their efforts rode on the captain and his comrades' ability to kill men in the blink of an eye. If the other Time Fathers did not listen to reason, there was a high probability they would try to kill him. With the others paralyzed, it would be on him to fight back. But Darjal's death still haunted him. Taking a life went against everything he believed.

The crew stared at Nicholai. The stillness of the situation emphasized their concerns. They knew he wouldn't kill a man. And, if he wouldn't, that left things to Aggi. And if Aggi couldn't ...

"Why would they freeze their divisions?" Nicholai asked in anguish. "They would participate in the very thing they're hunting me for."

Aggi cast Nicholai an empathetic look. "They're terrified. What you've accomplished—what you've *all* accomplished—you've taken this further than any of them thought possible. Desperate men act recklessly. It's their ace in the hole, their last resort."

A lingering quiet commanded the group. Everything relied on Nicholai's and Aggi's ability to take a life. While the Northeastern Time Father did not seem to shy away from the challenge, Nicholai struggled. Aggi was a strong, capable leader, but his combat skills remained limited. He was a politician not a soldier. To expect he could slay four opponents was naïve.

Everyone knew better than to convince Nicholai to abandon his ethics. While he had made his protests earlier, the Southeastern Time Father accepted Kazuaki and his crew held different solutions to different problems. After a period of adjustment, he had let them execute their slayings without protest, keeping his concerns to himself. They respected him enough to offer him the same courtesy, but it left a shadow of uncertainty hanging in the room. Nobody had any advice to offer. If the Time Fathers froze their divisions, they could do nothing.

Kazuaki leaned forward to study the members of his team. His gaze lingered on Bermuda the longest; he wanted to memorize the look of her, as she was now, before he brought the weight of his decision onto her—perfection, down to the last strand of salt-scented auburn hair, with her dark eyes to match; her skin, ravaged by a series of battle scars, each inch more flawless than the last; the way her collar bone swept to the curve of her shoulders. He committed it all to memory.

She caught his stare and tried to assess his expression, her brows drawing together.

The captain closed his eye. He didn't want to see the look on her face when it changed. "Aggi, if you can get us to the Time Fathers in your flying machine, I will immobilize them. Then we won't have to worry about them stopping their divisions."

Bermuda narrowed her eyes.

Aggi cocked his head. "With all due respect, Captain, we really should spare as many as we can. It'll be a feat finding suitable replacements. And even still, as soon as you kill one, I'm certain they will trigger their Chronometers. You wouldn't have the time to deal with all four."

"I didn't say I'd kill them. I said I would immobilize them. That would give you all time to confiscate their Chronometers without retaliation."

He felt the heat from Bermuda's eyes upon him, but he dared not look at her.

Aggi stepped toward the man, curiosity consuming him. "What do you mean, Captain?"

Kazuaki felt a churning in his guts, something he hadn't felt in a long time—the anxiousness of a man with an expiration date. But he was certain. He lifted his hand and tapped the metal plate hiding beneath the patch that covered his eye. "Just get me in front of them. I have my own last resort."

Chapter Twenty-Five

To everyone's relief, they had almost a week to prepare for the decennial gathering of the Time Fathers. It took time to get everything organized. Aggi sent for immediate repairs to the flying machine pilfered from the battle between Northern and Northeastern. They addressed letters to Bartholomew of Southern and Emont of Southwestern. The contents detailed the goings-on, urging them to keep as many soldiers they felt they needed to maintain their division, but they were grateful for whatever soldiers they spared. The men would be a boundless asset at Panagea's center. With the promise of blood flowing like rivers, they needed all the help they could get.

Everyone scrambled. Even in the chaos, the nights the crew spent under Aggi Normandy's hospitality were some of the most peaceful they'd had in a long time. With no threat of immediate death on the horizon, there was no need to stay on edge. But, as the days ticked down and the decennial drew closer, everyone grew restless. Each sunrise meant one day closer to Kazuaki Hidataka's looming death.

The captain laid flat on the bed in Elowyn's room. She layered sheets of plastic on the blankets. The medic did not want to soil Aggi's sheets with Kazuaki's blood. Her hesitant hands reached for the instrument sitting beside her, the one that would free the screws holding the plate to her captain's skull. Elowyn delayed her movements. She was not eager to take part in the chore, but, at Kazuaki's insistence, she could do little else.

"Are you sure, Captain?" she asked again for the tenth time that morning.

Kazuaki laid on the bed, staring at the ceiling. "I'm sure."

"Right." She sighed. Of course, he was. Kazuaki Hidataka did not announce his plans if he did not intend to follow through with them. "Hold still ..."

The captain closed his eye and took a deep breath. He felt the pressure as Elowyn freed the first two screws holding his plate in place. It was an uncomfortable feeling, the twisting of regrown flesh, the sound of grinding bone as it released from his skull. Even in his agony, he made no noise. He did not wish to make it any harder for Elowyn than it already was.

After unscrewing the third and fourth bolt, she set them in a metal pan by her side.

Kazuaki counted as the metal pieces fell in one by one. "Be sure to shield your vision before you remove the plate," he reminded her without opening his eye.

Elowyn nodded, though she knew he couldn't see her. She prepared to stick the flat end of her instrument under the plate to pry it up, but, as the tip touched the metal, she stopped. "Are you afraid, Captain?"

"Can't hurt more removing it than it did when you put it there."

The medic sighed again. "Of death, I mean. Of spending the rest of your afterlife with Mimir in that well."

Kazuaki frowned. He knew what she meant but thought he could buy himself time from answering it. "Not afraid. Not of Mimir, anyway." The only thing that birthed fear in him was facing Bermuda one last time. She actively avoided him since he made his announcement in Aggi Normandy's chambers.

"It's just unfair," Elowyn lamented, resting her arm and the instrument she held at her side. "You spent hundreds of years hunting the ability to die. After everything you've endured, all the nightmares on this earth you've seen, I just think you deserve something more fitting than an afterlife trapped with Mimir."

"It's my own doing, Elowyn." Kazuaki opened his eye. It did not seem that Elowyn possessed the mental wherewithal to remove his plate yet. He'd have to ease her into it. "It's not ideal. But a man is only as good as how he approaches his demise. Mimir may have stolen my fantasy of a peaceful afterlife, but I'll be damned if he tarnishes my last act in life. Best to enter the fray in a blaze of glory."

Elowyn forced a smile. "That must've been where Iani got it from. You've done a lot for us, Captain. You took a slew of tainted individuals the people of Panagea had chewed up and spit out and turned us into something better. We have a lot to thank you for."

It was then Kazuaki knew what caused Elowyn's delay. She was saying goodbye. He filled his lungs to the brim before he exhaled in one quick breath. He did not know how to sound comforting. It was not in his skillset. But he knew she hoped for a poignant moment. It was understandable. She never got the chance to say goodbye to anyone else she had lost—her brothers, Iani. Kazuaki flashed her a small grin. "I did nothing any of you wouldn't have done for me."

Her eyes welled up. The gloss of unshed tears strained the captain. Elowyn tried hard to keep her grief contained, cleansing the instrument she was about to use to pry off his plate, though she had already sterilized it several times before. When it became clear she could stall no longer, she sat up a little straighter, forcing a smile through her shining eyes. "This may sting a little."

Kazuaki closed his eye and leaned back on the plastic-covered pillow. "That's all right. No matter how much it stings at first, eventually, it always feels better."

With the captain's eye closed, she allowed her tears to fall. She stuck her instrument under the plate and pried it from the skin it had embedded into for the last few years. As it yielded, Elowyn closed her eyes, not wanting to subject herself to the nightmare-inducing iris Mimir cursed Kazuaki with.

Though she felt the wetness from beneath her lashes, and the moment gutted her from the inside, she experienced a small sense of peace from Kazuaki's words. He was right. Time healed all wounds. Though the pain of losing her brothers and Iani was still intense, the scar did not hurt as much as when the wound was fresh.

She felt the plate loosen, and she gave it a final pull. No matter what happened from here on out, she held fast to the last words Kazuaki Hidataka had shared with her.

NICHOLAI SAT ON THE steps leading to Aggi's residence. They showed their age. Though magnificent in their craftsmanship, the disasters reached far and wide. Aggi's hometown reflected a good condition compared to the others they had witnessed, but the aftermath remained. Several buildings gave way under the fragile ground. The sky shed ashes blown in from a far-off volcanic eruption. The passersby showed evidence of the stress on their faces. Nicholai's face matched theirs.

He had lost himself since Kazuaki's offer to paralyze the Time Fathers with his eye. While he did not know the gravity of his offer at first, he was quick to surmise what it meant. The behavior of the crew and helpful hints on the captain's backstory from Brack filled in all the gaps.

Who would have thought the legendary Captain Kazuaki Hidataka possessed a weakness? Nicholai knew now why he trapped his eye underneath that metal plate. The Time Father long assumed Kazuaki had lost it in battle. That it was an enchanted eye a lesser god had placed there to cleanse his soul by unleashing his darkness onto others who looked at it was certainly the last reason in the world why he thought the plate was there.

Umbriel watched him in silence. She leaned against one of the grand pillars that sprawled from the ground in front of Aggi's home. Darkness exuded off his body the Earth Mother couldn't ignore, yet she found herself hesitant to approach. The feelings that had surfaced inside her a week ago only grew in their intensity. The warmth was inviting, though she had not intended to expose her heart to the complex nature of intimacy again.

Even after hundreds of years, A'ronn's memory remained a powerful part of her. But, as the Earth Mother learned, the laws of attraction did not bend to a set standard of rules. But this revelation was not what weighed down her feet. Umbriel embraced the potential. It was the unknown result of Nicholai's reaction that glued her to the concrete. Never did Umbriel hesitate in her sentiments; she was a confident woman free of restraint. But the way Nicholai's eyes often drifted to the sky, a part of her suspected someone had already laid claim to his heart.

She sighed. Despite it all, she couldn't leave him to battle his internal demons alone. After drawing an encouraging breath, Umbriel crossed the distance, smooth in her motions as she sat beside him on the stairs. "How are you doing, Nicholai?"

Though it was clear he had not expected her, Nicholai did not startle at her sudden presence. He turned to her with a calm look, coercing a smile to appear. "All things considered, I think I'm doing quite well."

His confidence, though translucent, was inspiring. She returned his smile and leaned back on her palms. "Are you worried about Kazuaki?" It seemed to be the central theme amongst the crew. Umbriel suspected the topic plagued Nicholai too.

"Your perceptiveness knows no bounds," he replied with a small, defeated laugh. "I can't believe the man has a weakness." A weakness besides Bermuda.

"Everyone has a weakness." Umbriel craned her neck back to look at the gray, lifeless sky. "Even legendary men like Kazuaki. It's the human condition. Some weaknesses are just more obvious than others."

"I should say so." Nicholai frowned, feeling very aware of his own weaknesses. "I could save him, Umbriel. He wouldn't be forced into his last resort if I could just ... fire a feckin' gun."

Umbriel tilted her head, redirecting her attention to the Southeastern Time Father. "I think it's a little more complicated than all that."

"No. I've been going over it again and again all week. Kazuaki is only using his eye to immobilize them, to keep them from freezing their divisions. He's doing it because he *knows* if they do—and they won't listen to reason—that's it. It's Aggi and me against four men, and I haven't exactly proven to be a useful soldier. It would be Aggi's death sentence and mine." Nicholai rested his forearms on his bent knees. "If we descended on them in the flying machine, he, Bermuda, Brack, Rennington, the whole crew—I know they could all choose different targets. Two or three quick squeezes from the trigger would bring down all four Time Fathers before their fingers even came close to their Chronometers. I know they could do it, because I've seen it." He turned away, his voice collected as he talked it through. "But they won't. Kazuaki's a natural disaster in his own right, sweeping through a battlefield without mercy, leaving countless bodies in his wake. Umbriel, in my heart of hearts, I feel we can solve conflict with words instead of bloodshed, that death is the lazy man's option—a temporary solution. They need to learn where they went wrong, or history is doomed to repeat itself. I've *always* thought that. I believed in it with my entire being. Since the revolution began, Kazuaki has massacred everything that stood in his way, but now he's throwing this one to me, letting me approach with a plea rather than a sword. And it'll cost him his life."

Though he spoke unemotionally, she sensed he still writhed in conflict. "Nicholai, I haven't had the pleasure of knowing Kazuaki for as long as you have. But, in the short time I have spent with him, I can say with great confidence he wouldn't partake in anything he didn't believe in. I know your worry stems from respect, but even if you *could* fire a gun, even if you could take a life, the Time Fathers' deaths would create more problems than it would solve. We'd never find four suitable replacements before their divisions froze. Kazuaki knows that."

Nicholai was silent. She always had sage advice, a pearl of wisdom to her words that surpassed her appearance. It was easy to forget Umbriel was over six hundred years old, until she spoke. Nicholai was a victim to his ego as he mulled over Kazuaki's fate. He assumed the captain bent to his ways as a mercy gesture. But perhaps a part of the captain believed in the superiority of Nicholai's approach. Enough of him to give his life for it anyway.

The Time Father still writhed about Kazuaki's impending death, but Umbriel's words brought him a small breath of relief. She had that effect on everyone. She brought the best of herself to everything she touched. His thoughts drifted to how she had filtered the poison from Bermuda's heart. Within a few days, the condition had disappeared, and Bermuda had returned to normalcy. "Umbriel, I'm sure it must have already crossed your mind but could *you* do anything for him?"

Umbriel pressed her lips together as she sat upright. "From the first day he asked me to help Bermuda, I have tried to think of a way to help him too." Her expression fell as she leaned forward, wrapping her arms around her bent knees. "Bermuda's fix was not without its difficulties but much easier compared to what plagues

Kazuaki. Lesser gods are tricky creatures. They used to be everywhere, you know. They loved mankind. But now, they're nowhere. Driven out by those they loved. Anger and revenge fuels Mimir. I know that's why he cheated her. They're powerful beings, but Bermuda's problem rested in her heart, and a heart is a tangible object composed of cells—elements I can manipulate. But Kazuaki, his issue rests with his soul. It's an ethereal thing, made up of abstract concepts that make a person who they are. No cells ae present for me to cleanse, no palpable object for me to heal. Only an equally powerful force has any chance of helping him escape Mimir's trickery now."

Nicholai was crestfallen at her confession, though he hid it well. He knew she would have helped him already if she could. "Yes. I suspected as much."

"Do not harbor so much frustration for yourself, Nicholai." Umbriel tilted her head toward him as she rested it on her arms. "A hard decision for a regular man comes with ease to Kazuaki."

"Yes, Kazuaki was always good at making hard decisions. It makes him an excellent leader." Nicholai recalled his short adventure with the captain. Despite the situation that loomed over them, he smirked. It was easier to smile than to lose himself to the darkness. "If Kazuaki had been the ruler of Southeastern, perhaps we could've avoided this mess entirely. I never could make those hard decisions. Not without hesitation anyway."

"You're too hard on yourself. It takes a strong man to rule a collective." She thought back to how A'ronn had operated his division. "Strength in all aspects. Intelligence, fairness, strategy, empathy. I know you possess at least some of those in great supply."

Nicholai chuckled, the sound dim. "I do love my people, Umbriel. But I think the moment I froze Southeastern, I loved myself just a little bit more. It was selfishness that pulled the crown on my

Chronometer that day, and it continues to be selfishness that refuses to undo it."

"That seems unlike you. Can I ask why you did it? Why you froze Southeastern?"

The Time Father stared ahead, a blank look plastered to him. Kazuaki and the crew had already familiarized themselves with his reasoning. It was only fair Umbriel knew too. "If I unfreeze Southeastern, Lilac will die."

He didn't need to explain who the name belonged to. Umbriel was a perceptive woman. The way he spoke her name, though it was brief, left little doubt in her mind. Lilac was the keeper of Nicholai's heart. She was the little light his eyes caught every time he lost himself in thought. She was the blood in his body that powered him forward through his pitfalls. She was his reason, his strength, and his weakness all rolled into one. Despite the invisible dagger that plunged into her chest, Umbriel smiled; for love, no matter how jagged, was always a beautiful thing to behold.

"You must think that's pretty gutless of me, aye? Damning countless people to spare one life? A life I'm not even sure I can save?" Nicholai did not turn to gauge her reaction.

Umbriel shifted to follow his gaze across the city. "Love makes fools of us all. But I'd rather be a fool than a lone wolf."

The corner of Nicholai's lip tugged into a small grin. "Yeah. Me too."

The Earth Mother nestled her chin into her forearm, finding peace in her proximity with the Time Father. "Then I'll sit with you, so you're not alone."

KAZUAKI'S EYE FELT weird under the bandage. That metal plate became a part of him, in a literal and figurative sense. He felt naked without it. The fear of exposing his eye to someone he cared about was something he was unfamiliar with. Kazuaki did not enjoy feeling fear. It was a filthy, useless emotion.

Blood soaked through the material, despite Elowyn's best efforts. It was hard for her to tend to the injuries left in his skull without vision. Everything she did, she did with her eyes closed, lest she risked falling victim to the nightmares Kazuaki's eye infected onlookers with. It was not just a risk for her but for Kazuaki and the plan. If he cleansed his soul too soon, their entire strategy would be useless.

He didn't get too far down the hallway from Elowyn's room before Rennington, Revi, Brack, Penn, and Granite rounded a corner, stopping him in his tracks. Granite's dog was not far behind, wagging its tail as it sniffed one of Aggi's vases. It lifted its leg to relieve itself on the artifact. Granite rolled his eyes and pulled a rag from his pocket before lowering himself to his knees.

Rennington watched Granite clean the beast's mess before he redirected his attention to Kazuaki. "Captain," he started, holding two shot glasses, "we've got a bone to pick with you."

Kazuaki stared at Granite before raising a confused eyebrow to Rennington. "Better make it quick, gentlemen. I told Aggi I'd help his engineers make the final repairs on that flying machine."

Rennington grinned. He shoved one of the full shot glasses into Kazuaki's hands. "Well, *I* told Mr. Normandy you wouldn't be attending, because you're about to get so damn shitfaced you wouldn't be of much use around heavy machinery."

The captain grasped the offering, feeling some of it spill over the top and onto his hand. He assessed each of his men's faces. Duty called him to the mission, but, after spending time with Elowyn, he knew what they wanted, what they needed. If closure came at the bottom of a bottle, so be it. It was his final moments with them. Best to leave them with a positive memory. He raised his hand with a smirk. "Cheers, mates."

The men clanked their glasses together and made short work of the alcohol they had pilfered from Aggi Normandy's kitchen.

Rennington pulled several small bottles from his boots and topped off everyone's glass. He poured two for Granite, since cleaning his dog's urine had preoccupied him during the first round. "Join us in the library, Captain? Perfect place to continue our soiree. The place is feckin' huge. Books everywhere. Bartholomew would've had a raging boner if he laid eyes on it, that's for sure."

Kazuaki tried to contain his amusement. He threw back the second shot, exhaled and nodded. "Lead the way, Rennington."

The men adjourned to Aggi's library, each finding seats in the Western Time Father's fancy, upholstered chairs. Liquor flowed like rivers as they reminisced. Laughter echoed off the walls. A few candelabras found the floor after some of Brack's more boisterous storytelling. Not once did they talk about Kazuaki's impending doom. It was the perfect send off.

The hours that crept by turned the liquor to slow poison in their veins. The relief it brought was as welcoming as it was intoxicating. Brack laid on the floor, trying in vain to reattach a broken piece of a candelabra to its base. "This feckin' thing's not sticking," he whined, trying to will the delicate metal to fuse together on its own.

"Just put it in that vase. Aggi will ... Aggi can buy another one," Rennington muttered, waving a drunk hand toward a container in the corner of the room.

"Why's this guy have so many vases?" Penn reclined into a resting position in his chair. "What's he got to hide anyway? That's what you do with vases, you, you hide things in them."

Revi arched a brow from his spot on the floor. "C'mon now. Aggi's been really accommodating." He rolled over, not at all agile in his movements, and grabbed the nearby vase to peer inside it.

"Besides, he must not have much to hide, 'cause this one's got nothing in it."

Brack paused. His face grew alarmed. He abandoned his effort to repair the broken candelabra. "Give me the vase, give me the vase—"

Far too inebriated to hand the vase to Brack, Revi tipped it on its side and rolled it over.

Brack seized it with expedience and filled it with the contents of his stomach.

"Shit." Revi wrinkled his nose in disgust. "It's got something in it now."

Granite's dog prodded over and stuck its head in the vase after Brack had finished vomiting. It tried and failed to eat the discharge, unable to get its ears past the mouth of the ornamental pot. Granite, still sober despite having drunk as much as everyone else, appeared relieved. Though the beast had eaten some unpleasant things in its lifetime, Granite did not want to picture Brack's vomit on its tongue when he allowed the dog to lick his face.

"Look, look, look ..." Penn waved a finger at Brack, trying and failing to point at the man. He laughed. "Here we are, trying not to spill our guts in front of the captain, and Brack's, well, he's, he's quite well failed with that one, aye?" He laughed more, as if his joke was the most hilarious thing he ever heard.

The crew joined in his chuckles, but only because it was odd seeing Penn engage in laughter. He was a stoic guy. Alcohol drowned his usual social reservations and left a witty, albeit graceless man in its place. The others loved it when drunk Penn appeared.

Kazuaki grinned. Though he was not as far gone as the others, he wasn't sober. The captain floated somewhere in the middle of complete oblivion and having *some* wits about him. It was a luxury he hadn't enjoyed in a long time. "That's what this is then?" he asked, though he knew from the beginning. "Alcohol and ... a pre-funeral, of sorts?"

Rennington sat upright and belched. He ran his hands through his hair and left them at the back of his head as he found Kazuaki. "Aye, we made a drinking game out of it too. Every time you think to say something mushy to the captain"—he clumsily poured and lifted another shot—"you take a drink."

Kazuaki watched as Rennington slammed his poison and tried to set it onto a table that wasn't there. The glass fell to the floor, and Rennington peered over his chair's arm, staring at it as if contemplating how it got there.

A chortle escaped the captain as he surveyed all the drunkards who filled the room. "Gods alive, you five sure are the sentimental sort."

"Especially Granite." Brack waved an open bottle of booze in the giant man's direction. He shook his head. "Look at him. Pathetic. Can't even hide his pain."

Granite looked the same as he always did, save for the slow arrival of an irritated expression he directed toward Rabbit.

Rennington, still staring at the glass he had dropped on the floor, finally tore his gaze from it and regarded Kazuaki. "You—you just sit there and enjoy it." He slumped to allow his chair to eat him. "You ... I didn't get to do this for Iani. Iani. Iani would have loved this. I don't get to say his name much anymore. Iani."

The room grew silent. Brack crawled across the floor to Rennington with a bottle in his hand and climbed his chair. He stuck the open whiskey's neck into the Platts brother's mouth, and, though he spilled most on Aggi's floor on the way over, he lifted it. "Shh, shh, shh ... there, there."

Rennington swatted it away when the sting of the alcohol burned his tongue. That, tempered with the rotting smell coming from Brack's mouth, caused him to cough most onto his pants and

Aggi's upholstery. His gaze dwelled on the soiled areas, his face dripping in shock. "Gentlemen ... we ... we have not been great right now. To Aggi."

"I don't know. He seemed pretty understanding when ... when we told him we were kidnapping the captain for the night," Revi slurred, pressing his back against the wall for support.

"Yeah." Penn looked to Rennington. "Didn't he say to help ourselves to whatever we wanted?"

It took all Rennington's mental willpower to remember the moment which took place earlier that day. "Yeah, yes. I mean, he offered us a bottle ... That's ... that's the same as offering the whole kitchen though, right? Penn, you're a cook, you know kitchen things. Was he offering us the kitchen?"

Penn nodded. "Yeah, I mean, there's no other way to misconstrue that."

"Aggi's a good guy." Revi slid from his place on the wall to the floor. He laid there, unbothered. "I think I'll visit him after the revolution is over. He's a good guy."

"Here I thought you'd go and give that Miss Catty a visit first." Penn grinned and threw a cork at Revi.

The cork hit him in the chest and rolled onto the floor. "Belay that," Revi muttered lethargically as he stared at the ornate ceiling.

"You visit Aggi all you want," Brack said, looking to Kazuaki. "I'm gonna visit me the Captain. I'll march right up to Mimir's well and say, 'Oi! Let—let Cappy come out, you weird, demony feck!'"

Kazuaki arched a brow. "So much for a peaceful afterlife."

"Hey!" Rennington leaned forward with such haste he almost fell from his chair. "Hey ..." He lowered his voice. "We'll find a way to get you out of there, Captain. Also, Brack said the *M* word, and, as our previous drinking rules dictate, he must now drink an entire bottle by himself."

Kazuaki glanced at Brack and a look of concern crossed his face. "I don't think he needs any more. His liver's not as strong as his breath."

Brack rubbed his stomach as he glanced to the vase. "Don't worry 'bout me, Cap, I made more room."

"Captain." Rennington pointed an index finger at him. "I meant what I said. We'll get you out of that shit of a lesser god's afterlife. That's a Platts promise, mate."

Kazuaki smirked and took another swig. "I appreciate the sentiment, gentlemen. But I made my bed. And I doubt I'll have the ability to crawl in and out of the realm of the dead as Mimir does. He's a lesser god, after all."

"Yeah," Rennington replied, "but you're feckin' Captain Kazuaki Hidataka."

The captain nodded as he sank into his chair. He eyed each of them with a smirk. "Your gods-damned right about that."

The crew raised their glasses though a few were empty. Most of the alcohol found a place in their bloodstreams, but they did not want to pass up the opportunity to celebrate the captain. As they engaged in riotous cheers, Kazuaki sank his fingers deep into his chair's fabric. It was the perfect send off before his afterlife with Mimir.

He couldn't help but think about what Umbriel had said about the lesser god. Though the monster had lived a thousand more lifetimes than Kazuaki ever had to, both were intimately familiar with the trials immortality brought to a soul. Mimir was mankind's creation, forgotten by those who had birthed him, forever living with that wavering hatred for people. The captain knew the wavering hatred well too. Time afforded him the horrors of witnessing mankind's darkness again and again, paving the way for an unending dislike for humanity to flourish.

Mimir remained trapped at the bottom of his well. The ship trapped Kazuaki at sea, where Panagea forgot him, except in the form of terrifying children's nursery rhymes. No wonder the creature was crazy. It was a miracle *he* wasn't crazy. The captain frowned. He was two sunsets away from having to endure the demon for the rest of his afterlife. Perhaps it wouldn't be so bad ...

They seemed to have more in common than he first thought.

SUCCUMBING TO THE ALCOHOL'S effects, Revi, Brack, Penn, and Rennington had passed out long ago. Granite and Kazuaki, inebriated but still possessing basic motor skills, hauled the four men to their rooms. Elowyn took the time to ensure they were all on their stomachs. She admitted to the captain she'd make the occasional check to ensure they didn't choke in their sleep.

Granite and his mongrel retired to their room. An entire distillery couldn't incapacitate the man, but he enjoyed enough to relax his muscles and lull him into a deep sleep.

Kazuaki had no interest in rest. He paced the hallways of Aggi Normandy's home, his hands behind his back as he walked without hurry, investigating room after room. He wasn't sure what he searched for, but he felt compelled to go on one last treasure hunt.

His legs carried him to a formal dining hall, likely where Aggi hosted large gatherings for his political agendas. The ceilings were high, chandeliers hanging from the tops with grandeur. Aggi's residence was stunning. Though it could not compete with the excessive architecture of Darjal's church in Avadon, it boasted a magnificence he did not see in a lot of other places.

Kazuaki slid his calloused hands along the smooth walls as he walked. He noted every minuscule feeling—the coolness of the wall on his fingertips, the way his boots echoed in the large, open room, the thick smell of whiskey every time he exhaled. He closed his eye. A strange smile found its way to his face. These were the thoughts of a man on death row. He'd never delighted in small details before. He loved it.

After opening his eye again, he saw an exquisite phonograph waiting for him across the room. Ornate and elegant, with its shimmering horn sprawled outward in grace, it called to him. Kazuaki obeyed the siren and traipsed toward it. He spotted the circular disc that sat on top. The device was a testament to Aggi's status. If one had enough money for a phonograph, their choice was limited to the model that played wax cylinders. Kazuaki had never seen a model like this before—the cutting edge of music technology. It didn't matter what was on the disc. He needed to hear it. Music hadn't graced his ears in a long time, only what Rennington, Elowyn, and Bermuda played on the ship. What he would give to hear her play her clavichord again. The phonograph would have to satisfy that longing.

After winding the crank and adjusting the needle, Kazuaki stood back. Prerecorded music flowed from the device. Every scratch and crackle from the imperfect machine ignited him from the inside. The sound of the instruments, the voice of a female soprano, it was glorious, all amplified by the freedom afforded to him in the booze that coursed through his veins. Kazuaki lost himself so much in the music he didn't even hear the footsteps behind him. It took a tap on his shoulder to get his attention.

Kazuaki spun, finding himself face to face with the last person in the world he thought he'd see. "Bermuda," he said with a heavy exhale. His liquored-up heart betrayed him as it picked up its pace.

"Captain ..." Bermuda started but wrinkled her nose as the strong scent of alcohol wafted from his body. "I see you've been drinking."

"The crew, they ..." If only he had all his wits about him, he could have presented himself better. "They wanted to celebrate, before ..."

"Your death," she finished, sliding her arms around herself as if the words made her cold.

Kazuaki said nothing. He shrugged a single shoulder in a modest agreement.

Bermuda's gaze fell to the floor, but she forced them back to Kazuaki's face. "You promised me you weren't going anywhere. 'Cross your heart and hope to die.' That's what you said."

"Yes." Kazuaki released a breath he didn't realize he held. "I did say that, didn't I?"

Bermuda stared at him, unforgiving. The music spilled from the phonograph in the background. "How could you do this, Kazuaki? How could you do this to me?"

"Bermuda ..." Kazuaki started, the alcohol in his body making a puppet out of him as he reached for her cheek. He stopped just short of touching her and fought to regain control of himself. "I'm not trying to do anything to you. I'm trying to do it *for* you. Live your life. In a better place."

"Oh, yes," she replied with sarcasm. "Kazuaki, I know I don't have the best track record of gracefully accepting death. I'm trying my best here. That's why I couldn't even stand the sight of your face this week." She felt the heat radiate from the hand he suspended so close to her skin. "You preach of doing this for me, but you, of all people, should know this is the last thing in the world I want."

"Yes, well." Kazuaki convinced himself to return his hand to his side. "Sentiments never were one of my specialties."

"Do not joke, Captain," Bermuda uttered, her voice choking. "Please."

Kazuaki's gaze crept from the boots on her feet and upward to her long legs, her hips, her chest, her neck, her lips, eyes, hair. He wanted to memorize every inch of her down to the look of disappointment on her face, as he saw perfection in that too. "What do you want me to say?" he whispered. "It's our most efficient shot at victory. I can fight for the rest of time, Bermuda, but not you. Not the crew. Not Panagea. The world can't take much more of this."

The quartermaster tried to don a brave face, but he saw through her. Kazuaki had become a critical piece of Bermuda; he was the strength she had lost when Ty Aldon fell. She saw who she used to be when she looked at him—a powerful, unyielding person. At first, she thought if she spent enough time around Kazuaki, she could become that person again. But he had shifted into more than just a tool for her to rediscover herself. "What is a world without you in it?"

Her words pulled him in. His sober brain would have kept him at bay, but the whiskey gave him a push. For years, Kazuaki had kept himself in control around her. Not only was she in a perpetual state of despair from Ty's death, but his feelings for her were impractical in every way. Ty's death had destroyed her. He had vowed never to put her in that situation if he could help it. A separation would kill her ... and separation was inevitable. She lived in pain now, but, if he surrendered to his temptation and pursued a romantic relationship with her ...

No. Immortals and mortals just did not mix.

"Where are my manners?" he asked, listening to the music as it wafted from the phonograph. "Would you care to dance?"

Bermuda looked behind him at the phonograph. "You don't dance," she accused, more than a little relieved to abandon her vulnerability for the moment.

Kazuaki took one of her hands. He summoned all the memories from a few hundred years ago when he had learned formal dances from one of his more jubilant crewmembers. "One dance won't kill me," he joked, though the dark humor only irritated his companion.

He led her across the floor, but her movements were clumsy and awkward. Even when victim to his inebriation, Kazuaki's steps were fluid, but Bermuda had trouble keeping up. "What I meant to say was, *I* don't dance," she admitted, confused how she could slaughter an army with skillful choreography but could not perfect a simple box step.

Kazuaki waltzed into dangerous ground. He thought he could balance on the line without crossing it, but liquor and natural human selfishness prodded him. Her touch did things to him. Despite his best efforts to resist, his fingers pranced on the small of her back spread, trying to take in as much of her as he could before the opportunity vanished. She did not appear burdened by his actions. Perhaps it was his imagination, or wishful thinking, but she even seemed to melt into his touch a little.

Their box step started with them at an arm's distance. But, with each additional step, their bodies crept closer. The gap between them became nothing more than a sliver. Bermuda felt his heart. It was wild with an intensity she only thought it mustered in the heat of battle. Though she tried to quiet it, the beating organ in her chest matched his. It supplied weightlessness in her stomach. "Is there no other way?"

Kazuaki failed himself when he lowered his head. He rested the side of his rough jaw against the softness of her cheek. He was derailing. But damn, it felt good. "It's the only way. With them paralyzed by the nightmares, they can't use their Chronometers as a weapon."

Bermuda knew all of this. His skin against hers sent an invisible shock of lightning through her bones. She, too, was falling. For years after his death, her heart still belonged to Ty. But it was a lie to say a romance with the captain had never filtered into her thoughts. Long nights on the sea could be lonely. She delighted in her strength never to pursue it though. Her resistance was the only thing that tempered her hatred for her otherwise weak heart.

The quartermaster had made a promise to herself to never let her heart stray into another situation where it could crumble as Panagea was. But promises all around broke today. They shattered like glass around her feet. And, in the heat of the moment, feeling the warmth of Kazuaki's chest pressed against hers, she would have thrown her boots from her feet and walked on the shards of those broken promises if it meant one more minute with him.

Still ... the timing was atrocious. "This is the stupidest thing you've ever done," she said, one last-ditch effort to put a wall between herself and a dangerous situation.

Kazuaki smirked. His eye closed as he pulled her closer still. His last shred of volition abandoned him. She consumed him. His ego reassured him it was okay; he deserved this, just one taste of her unadulterated closeness. "I will miss you the most."

Bermuda lifted her chin.

He lowered his gaze.

Her gaze darted around his face. It felt like she was suffocating but in the most thrilling way.

His lips lingered perilously close to hers, teetering on the last microscopic shred of self-control he possessed. The whiskey on his breath surrounded them, but it brought her no discomfort.

The only discomfort she felt was knowing the moment might end. She couldn't let him go. "I'm sorry, Kazuaki ..."

He stopped himself from closing the centimeter that separated her lips from his, but he did not pull back. He couldn't. But her apology was a clear sign they should stop what they were doing, what they were about to do. Though her words pained him, he found some relief in her sense. "You're right." He summoned all his willpower to pull himself back an inch.

He had misunderstood her. Bermuda felt her heart pound harder than it had before. "No— Kazuaki ..." The quartermaster inhaled, trying to breathe in the last seconds of the moment. "Forgive me."

Before he realized what had happened, Bermuda reached up with great speed. Her aim was direct and her force purposeful. She sank her fingertips into the socket that hid behind the bloody cloth tied across his head. In one swift pull, the gelatinous sphere and the cloth popped into her palm as she pried it from his skull. She squeezed the cursed eye in her hand until it burst from the pressure.

Kazuaki cursed and stepped backward. He brought a hand to his bleeding socket as he took to a knee.

Bermuda let her guilt devour her. Along with the potential to lose themselves to each other, the eye was gone. She crushed Mimir's shortcut to cleanse his soul in her hand. Kazuaki would be angry. No, he would be *livid*.

But he would be safe.

Chapter Twenty-Six

The flying machine, restored and functional, waited for its pilot outside Aggi Normandy's residence. Kazuaki stared at it from his place at the window. A weak ray of morning light punctured through the gray smog that clung to the sky. It pierced the glass, highlighting the dust particles floating around the ragged captain's form. Though the light was soft, it was far too bright for him. He pulled back from the window, away from the dull shine that split his dehydrated brain in two. He wished to spare his suffering head. It hurt enough from the alcohol consumption and the familiar sting of having its eye ripped from the socket.

A chair across the room provided him with relief. Kazuaki slid onto the cushion and rested his face in his scarred hands. His mental health's current state matched his horrid physical appearance. He felt like a complete ass for what had transpired with Bermuda. His anger had filled the spacious room last night. He still heard it echo off the walls of his mind as he had berated her for what she'd done. Kazuaki wasn't even mad at her for ripping out his eye; he was mad at himself, mad he had let down his guard, mad he had abandoned rationality and succumbed to his primal desires, that he had illuminated his lingering feelings of lust for her, and that she now had to deal with that on top of everything else.

She had refused to leave while he chastised her. Bermuda had stayed and endured the storm that was Kazuaki's fury. It wasn't until he had admitted her efforts were in vain, that he had tried ripping out his eye many times only to have it grow back, that her broken heart had carried her out of the room. The look on her face, complete dejection, haunted him.

Kazuaki lifted his face from his hands and stared across the room. He wanted to go to her chambers before the light on the horizon rose. But he couldn't. Embarrassment and apprehension paralyzed the otherwise fearless man. He wished to tell her he was wrong. His fingertips touched the cloth that remained wrapped over his head. He was wrong about a lot of things.

Nicholai, Aggi, Elowyn, and Umbriel entered the room first. Donned in defensive armor, they swept across the room and found seats beside Kazuaki.

The Southeastern Time Father couldn't contain his unease. "An emergency meeting on the morning of departure?" He leaned forward to get a better look at the captain. "I have to admit, Kazuaki, your request leaves me a little concerned."

Aggi, Elowyn, and Umbriel shared Nicholai's apprehension in their expressions.

Kazuaki stared at the door. The anticipation to see Bermuda grew despite his best efforts. "We'll wait until everyone is here."

Granite and his mongrel entered next, unfazed by the high volume of liquor consumed the evening prior.

Bermuda was close behind. She eyed the captain for a split second.

He locked gazes with her for as long as he could, but their exchange was over as soon as it began.

She turned away and sat.

The other men dragged themselves in moments later, wearing their hangovers so well a blind man could see it. A series of groans escaped them as they sauntered to their chairs and slumped down.

"I feel like death warmed over," Rennington muttered, rubbing at his face to wake himself.

"So does my upholstery," Aggi murmured. The stench that came off his chairs in the library would take weeks to get out. And the vases ... he didn't even want to think about what he found in there.

"Yeah, yeah." Brack waved his hand, his eyes closed. "Put it on my tab, Mr. Normandy."

Aggi grunted. "Those vases were antiques. I fear it'd take the rest of your life to pay me back, Mr. Joney."

Brack leaned forward on the table and laid his head on his arms. "Then may death take me swiftly in battle today, so I might escape my debt."

The Northeastern Time Father smirked. He returned his attention to Kazuaki. "I received word from Bartholomew. He collected any soldiers Southern could spare. Emont of Southwestern has done the same. I've dispatched a capable army of men as well. They departed from Northeastern in the twilight hours. If the winds are favorable toward the flying machine, we should meet them at Panagea's center roughly at the same time. Everything is in order."

Kazuaki nodded. "Everything but one." He removed the cloth from his head.

The crew shielded their vision, conditioned never to see Kazuaki's cursed eye. The others were slow to react, but it did not matter. There were no nightmares from Kazuaki's eye. It was gone.

Bermuda shifted with an anxiousness.

With excitement, Kazuaki felt her heart skip from across the room.

When Revi realized nothing bad had happened, he faced the captain, cautious. He remained unhurried to trust what he saw. "What the feck happened?"

"The details of the event are irrelevant." Kazuaki tried to steal another glimpse of Bermuda to gauge her reaction while conveying a silent, sincere apology from the distance that separated them.

She stared back, breathless and holding fast to her emotions.

The captain cleared his throat and tore himself away from her. "I don't know why it hasn't grown back, but our ace in the hole is gone."

The atmosphere shifted. Without an ability to stop the Time Fathers from reaching for their Chronometers, they were vulnerable to a uselessness, save for Aggi and Nicholai. One pull of the crown and their best weapons, Kazuaki and the crew, fell powerless.

Rennington shrugged and sat upright from his slump. "Who cares? This is *good* news. The captain doesn't have to spend a shit afterlife with Mimir, and now we can just kill the feckers as we should have from the get-go. Give us three seconds, pop-pop-pop. They'll all be dead, and we can get on with our lives."

"No." Nicholai's tone stood firm. "We can't keep murdering everyone who disagrees with us. We're here to ignite a change, not carry out the same tactic used by the Time Fathers of the past. If we kill them, we're no better than those who executed the Earth Mothers. It would solve nothing. And, even if it did, we couldn't assign suitable replacements in twenty-four hours. If you kill them, you're damning Panagea."

"He's right," Umbriel interjected. "We're making progress with the little we've done, but right now it's but a drop in the ocean. If five of the eight divisions are frozen in time, Panagea will panic. The remaining three divisions will be rubble before the next day's end."

The news disheartened the crew. Until now, a well-timed bullet solved everything for them.

"So, we need a new plan?" Penn asked as he looked to the collective for insight.

"No." Nicholai stood from his seat. "We don't need a plan. I've never needed one before."

"With all due respect, mate," Rennington sounded from the corner, "that hasn't exactly done well for you so far."

The Southeastern Time Father shook his head. "We've survived this long. We can't stop now. We've come too far, and we're running out of time. Southern, Southwestern, and Northeastern armies are already on the march. It's now or never."

Aggi's gaze swept out the window. He stared at the state of his hometown, once a glistening example of near perfection reduced to crumbling buildings ravaged by disaster. Morale was at an all-time low. Joblessness and homelessness infected his land. He was ready for change. His people needed it. The world needed it. "The flying machine is outside and loaded up. We'll follow the Northeastern border to the center and meet the armies there. Let's go." Aggi stood from his chair and led the way, determined to follow through.

Others walked after him, too resolute to abandon the cause.

Kazuaki lingered back. He hoped to steal a moment alone with Bermuda, but she slipped out with the rest of the crew.

Nicholai approached the captain and put a hand on his shoulder. "For what it's worth, I'm glad your eye is gone."

Kazuaki arched a brow. "Then you're a fool. I ensured a shield and a gun were in the flying machine for you. If they freeze their divisions, you will need them."

Nicholai shook his head and spoke in a low voice. "No guns, Kazuaki. Darjal still haunts me." His eyes glazed over as he lost himself to his internal demons. "I will never take another life again."

"They'll kill you, Nico."

"You offered your life to see this plan through. I'm not afraid to offer mine. Truth be told, I prefer it that way." His thoughts drifted passed Darjal to the countless people who suffered from the disasters' wrath. With Southeastern's state escalating Panagea's deterioration, he felt responsible for many of those deaths. "I already have enough blood on my hands."

Kazuaki watched as Nicholai walked off to join the others. He frowned and turned to Umbriel. "He's going to get *all* of us killed. If he's dead and time is frozen, my crew is as good as done for. All they'll have to do is put themselves in a favorable position, restart time and put a bullet in our brains before we even realize what's happening."

Umbriel crossed her arms. "Nicholai is an intelligent man, Kazuaki. I'm sure that knowledge is weighing heavily on him too. But that's not what's bothering you the most today, is it?"

"Umbriel ..." Kazuaki rubbed his temples. "I've had a trying morning and an even harder evening. Two hours of terrible sleep separates me from complete insanity. If you have something you want to say, please skip the cryptic beating around the bush and just tell me what's on your mind."

Despite his verbal tirade, the Earth Mother smiled. "You certainly did have a rough night, didn't you?" She gestured to his missing eye.

Her damnable comforting aura eased his tense shoulders. "I don't understand it. I've tried to rid myself of Mimir's influence for years. I've ripped the feckin' thing out myself a handful of times. I don't know why it hasn't come back this time."

Umbriel tilted her head. "It wasn't you who tore it out then?"

"No. Bermuda did."

A slow smile appeared on Umbriel's face. She did not appear surprised by his admission. "I know they've fallen from mankind's memory now, but I remember a time when the gods ran rampant through Panagea. Their capacity was incredible. We stood in awe of their omnipotence. But even gods have no patent on miracles. The world is full of them. We're blind to them, because we can't see them with our eyes, but it's often the invisible forces that possess the most power."

Kazuaki narrowed his eye. He was hungover. He was tired. Though he considered himself a philosopher, he didn't pick up on the hints Umbriel dropped. "What's all that supposed to mean?"

The Earth Mother maintained her steadfast smile. "I should think it'd be fairly obvious." She slipped off to head outside toward the others.

Kazuaki stood there in his confusion. He dissected her words over and over until he unearthed her subtlety. A powerful, invisible force. He laid a hand on his chest to feel the heart beneath quicken. Could she ...?

Much as he wanted to entertain the idea, Kazuaki pushed it aside. Last night was a mistake. No happy endings existed for men who could not die, not when the rest of the world obeyed mortality's law. Bermuda was a fantasy he could never touch without shattering another of Pandora's jars ... even if a chance existed that she felt the same way about him.

The captain walked outside to join the rest of the crew.

They surrounded the flying machine, donning looks of puzzlement.

"What's the problem now?" Kazuaki asked, irritated.

Aggi rubbed the back of his neck. "We ... We don't know how to fly it. None of us have ever operated one before."

"Just get in," Kazuaki grumbled, ushering Aggi and the rest inside the flying machine. The captain climbed in last and stood before the controls as everyone seated themselves. "It can't be much different from operating a ship."

It was very different from operating a ship. The flight through Northeastern territory was terrifying but efficient. Kazuaki was not a man of the air; the flying machine dipped and jerked whenever an unexpected gust of wind surged through. Everyone gripped their seats' edges in the jolts and prayed to whatever gods they believed in to get them to the battlefield without dying first. But, for every obstacle Kazuaki encountered, a well-timed collection of curses and lever pulling corrected it. After enough time, he found his flow.

The flying machine climbed over the shredded cities below. It was much easier to see the reach of the disasters from their aerial view. Far in the distance, smoke billowed from a series of wildfires. Shrapnel that once comprised entire cities cluttered the streets, ghosts of what they once were. The visual became so disheartening the group found relief when the hours passed, and the sun dipped lower. It seemed cruel to spill more darkness onto the land, but it shielded their vision from Panagea's chaotic state.

The sun lingered on the horizon line. Though nightfall approached, enough light remained to illuminate the movement in the mountains. It was difficult to see from their height, but the crew knew they were the footmen of Southern from the direction they marched. The bodies leaked over the shattered remnants of the mountain village, carrying their division's flag. Together they looked like an ocean wave striking the high rock walls of the coast.

It didn't take long until Southwestern's military also came into view. Their division uniforms' colors brought pigment to the gray landscape. From high above, they pinpointed the last army. Northeastern's men crawled through the broken cities below. Each militia marched closer to Panagea's center with every footfall.

"Gods alive," Elowyn said with a heavy breath as she stared out the flying machine's side. The sheer volume of Avital's army met her eyes.

Battle chants from the sea of men below rose into the sky as they stomped the bottoms of their halberds on the rocky earth in unison. It was harder to discern the other armies. The incredible amount of men Avital boasted consumed most of the land. But hiding amongst the bodies were the cutthroat men of Northern, the humble soldiers of Western, and the warmongers of Northwestern. They encircled the Time Fathers at Panagea's center. Each Time Father held one foot in his division where the cardinal directions split. The soldiers did not remain there long. As soon as they caught the approaching armies' movements, they advanced.

The crew felt helpless watching from above. The men ran toward each other. Metal on metal accosted their ears. They knew the sound well. It became a familiar noise. Soon, the swirling circle of protection around the Time Fathers dissipated. Men melted into one another, becoming one with their weapons—more blood to feed the rocks, more bodies to return to the earth.

The flying machine started its descent. Rennington itched to join those men, the soldier in him screaming as Southern brothers fell. The cries of the dead and the dying and the thunderous pounding of thousands of feet clawing over the jagged earth and broken buildings was unmistakable; the war had begun.

They saw the four men. The Time Fathers appeared confident they remained safe as they stood in the center. Armies sprawled from them on all sides, a wall of protection from the monsters they feared. But their confidence was short lived.

Nordjan was the first to notice the flying machine approach. His eyes did not wish to believe it at first, but the sound was unmistakable. Flapping wings pushed through the darkness and farther into his vision.

As soon as it crept within a safe distance, Bermuda jumped from the craft. She landed before the Time Fathers, a scowl on her face.

The others followed suit.

As the machine touched the ground, Nicholai exited. He pushed to the front of the crew. After adjusting his armor, he surveyed the surprised faces of the men who hunted him. "Gentlemen …" He stood tall and raised his hands, the shield Kazuaki had gifted him strapped to his back. "I am unarmed. I understand you've been looking for me."

The four men stiffened. Diplomatic instincts gripped them, but they showcased caution as they eyed the crew. Nicholai's approach and the obvious absence of weapons kept them from making any sudden movements, but they wore their disapproval on their faces.

Nordjan scowled at Aggi. "Using Northern's own flying machine against me. Very clever, Mr. Normandy."

Aggi smirked but said nothing.

Nicholai cast a glance at Edvard. The man appeared dumbstruck yet relieved to see him. Nicholai narrowed his eyes and took another bold step forward. "We need to discuss the future of Panagea. I ask you to hear me out."

Vadim hissed and withdrew. "You have *destroyed* Panagea. Look around at what you created, Nicholai. You preach of aiding this land, but you have brought nothing to it but chaos."

"I know." Nicholai's admission gathered attention from the other Time Fathers. He drew an unsteady breath. Though it pained him to say it, he decided. "I don't deny my part in this. I will restore Southeastern to its original state as soon as we settle on a better future here and now. You have my word."

"You gave your word you would uphold the Time Fathers' code," Vadim retorted. "But you sullied that as well. Your word means nothing, young Addihein."

Nicholai frowned. He felt Kazuaki grow restless beside him. "I made a lot of mistakes, Vadim. But this, returning the Earth Mother to Panagea, restoring what was lost—this is not one of them."

Nordjan scowled. "You do not know of what you speak, Nicholai. We're trying to prevent you from making an even bigger mistake. Your naivety knows no bounds."

"I have detailed letters from Bartholomew Gray of Southern, from Emont of Southwestern," Nicholai continued, undeterred.

"Their cities continue to fall. The disasters are only increasing in frequency. *Except* for the cities where Umbriel and I reintroduced nature into the environment. They're not even close to full restoration, but they have experienced fewer disasters than the cities that remain untouched. Panagea is responding. Even the smallest efforts we made have already shown an impact. It's minimal now, but, in a few years—"

"Time is a luxury we're running out of, Nicholai. We can't allow you to do this." Avital stole a cautious glimpse of Kazuaki as he slowly reached to his side.

"I implore you to listen." Umbriel pushed passed the crew to stand beside Nicholai. "My island, the island your forefathers chained me to, flourishes with life. Oxygen grows limitless with the trees. It has seen nothing as tragic as this. The ecosystems are Panagea's immune system. Without them, she will fall. We can't continue like this."

"I quite agree," Avital muttered. If Umbriel's island continued to supply Panagea with oxygen without her present, they had no further need for her. It was time to finish what their ancestors had started before she invited chaos back into their lives. Avital brandished a pistol from a side pocket. He aimed at Umbriel, believing his actions would be quicker than his old bones allowed. But the aging Time Father's reaction speed was no match for a real killer.

Kazuaki pulled his pistol, and though Nicholai outstretched his arms in protest, the captain fired before he uttered a word.

The bullet pierced Avital's skull—a mercy kill, right between the eyes.

"Kazuaki, no!" Nicholai watched as Avital's body slumped to the ground.

The other Time Fathers stood, stunned.

"Damnit!" Nicholai spun to glare at Kazuaki. "What did you do?"

"I know the look he had in his eyes, Nico." Kazuaki clutched the smoking gun. He knew it well, because he had patented it—the look of a man who craved victory. He would have shot Umbriel dead without fail. "It was her or him."

That was all it took. Alarm ensued. The atmosphere shifted. It became everything Nicholai feared it would. Another Time Father dead.

Nordjan and Edvard went to pieces, their minds raced.

Vadim reached for his Chronometer.

Kazuaki raised his arm to aim.

Nicholai shoved the captain aside to cause a misfire. He wouldn't allow this to deteriorate into more unnecessary deaths.

The bullet whizzed past Vadim's head as his fumbling fingers pulled the top of his device's crown. All of Northwestern stilled.

Nicholai recognized the aftermath. It matched the eerie stillness he had unleashed on his own division.

Kazuaki cursed as Rennington, Revi, Brack, and Elowyn froze with the rest of Northwestern, their feet across the borders of Vadim's territory.

Nicholai's fingers dug into Kazuaki's sleeve. He pulled the legendary man to face him. "I know you're out for blood, Kazuaki, but we can't kill them! Unless you want to spend the rest of your life chained to a division as its leader, save your bullets!"

Kazuaki scowled.

Nicholai's eyes shined with an unrecognizable rage.

Aggi lunged toward Vadim after he brandished a katana from his side. "You've become the very man you hunted." Aggi advanced toward his opponent. "There's still a chance, Vadim. Change is never easy, but everything Panagea needs is on the other side of your fear. Let it go."

Vadim Canmore dug his heels into the barren ground and glowered. He withdrew his sword, more a symbolic decoration to him than an actual piece of warfare equipment. But he knew better than to come unprepared. "Another betrayal. You should know the dangers he invites into Panagea with his ideals, Aggi."

"Anything has to be better than this, Vadim."

"That's not a gamble I'm willing to take."

The two men charged one another.

Kazuaki growled and looked to Bermuda, Granite, and Penn. Nicholai was right. They could not jeopardize killing all four without putting Panagea at an incredible risk or risking becoming prisoners to the divisions themselves. All they could do was fight and try to get the Chronometers before they stilled their divisions. "Subdue them."

Bermuda, Penn, and Granite approached Nordjan while Kazuaki flanked Edvard.

Kazuaki withdrew his dagger, the only weapon he possessed with which he could restrain his bloodthirsty habits. A small blade would not kill the man if positioned well, but it would slow him long enough to make a play for his Chronometer. "You sank my ship." The captain eyed Nicholai's father. His words were ice. They sent a chill up the Western Time Father's spine.

Edvard clenched his jaw. His hands flexed near his sides. A pistol sat at his hip, and his Chronometer resided in his breast pocket, but he made no grab for either. Not yet. Unlike Vadim, he held fast to his honor, his vow to maintain his time. To Edvard Addihein, it was a last resort not a parlor trick. "You corrupted my son." He backed away, trying to buy himself time from the captain's blade. "I should think that makes us even."

"On the contrary." Kazuaki gripped the handle tighter. "He corrupted me. Were it not for him, you'd be dead right now."

Edvard squared his shoulders.

Kazuaki advanced.

Defensive movements tried to avoid the captain's swings. Kazuaki's confession left him to believe he would not hit to kill. This kept Edvard from drawing his weapon. Though with every fierce swing Kazuaki took, he contemplated withdrawing it more. Not that it would have mattered, not against Kazuaki Hidataka.

It was a challenge for the captain to alter his fighting style. The wolf of war exchanged his kill shots for mercy. He tried to subdue Edvard, but the act proved far more difficult than he thought. With frustration mounting, Kazuaki tackled him to the ground and pinned him, but Edvard put up a valiant struggle.

Nordjan scowled at Bermuda, Granite, and Penn. They looked menacing with their swords and guns, but he, too, knew they weren't out for blood. He withdrew his gun and aimed. He did not want to use it. The man was a politician not a soldier. But he couldn't stand there and let them return disorder to Panagea.

The brandished weapon kept them at a distance. It was enough time for his gaze to slip from his three aggressors, long enough to see Kazuaki corner Edvard across the Northern border. His eyes widened at the opportunity. Though it went against everything he believed, they needed to eliminate their biggest threat. He reached for his Chronometer.

Bermuda followed his gaze to Kazuaki. "Captain!" She ran to him, hoping her swiftness could pull him from Northern's border in time, but to no avail. The quartermaster seized Kazuaki's shoulders as Nordjan plucked his crown, suspending them in the now timeless realm.

Edvard crawled from underneath Kazuaki's grasp and eyed Nordjan, his face coated in concern. Another division rendered immobile. It terrified him.

Granite noticed his frozen superiors. A slow glare consumed him as he faced Nordjan. He grew tired of fighting defensively.

Granite turned his neck to pop it and pointed his machete in Nordjan's direction. "Restart your division."

The Northern Time Father raised his weapon. "Surrender."

At an impasse, the men were about to engage, but a thunderous roll from below their feet stopped them. The incredible noise of the earth splitting beneath them drowned the screams from the armies who weren't frozen in time. As if pried apart by giant hands, a large gash slithered through the divisions that weren't stilled. It crawled over from Western and sliced into Northeastern as far as the eye could see. Rocks and rubble plummeted into the chasm below, bouncing off the jagged edges and disappearing into the darkness of the bottomless pit.

Aggi threw himself from one of Vadim's forceful attacks. He gasped as the canyon called his attention. Horror gripped him as his division divided, everything within eyesight torn limb from limb. Far off buildings fell into the hole in their entirety. He lost himself in that moment; his heart reached out to his people—how many lives were lost? How far did the chasm reach?

His concern was his undoing. Vadim capitalized on Aggi's distraction. His blade tore through the Northeastern Time Father's armor and sank into the skin on his chest.

Aggi howled. His weapon fell to the unstable ground as he took to a knee. His hand clutched his injury as the redness spread through the fibers of his clothes.

"You did this to yourself, Aggi." Vadim stepped backward, panic and alarm on his face. He had never gutted a man before. Not unlike the other Time Fathers, he was no soldier. Having another man's blood on his hands was a strange sensation. It sent his body into shock.

Umbriel spotted Aggi as he hunched over his wound. She ran to him, sliding down and slipping her hands onto his chest.

THE TREE THAT GREW THROUGH IRON   471

Penn rushed to lend her an assist, placing himself between her and Vadim.

The Earth Mother tried to stop the bleeding.

Vadim advanced, adrenaline and an embedded feeling of necessity that they had to die fueling him. If he already spilled blood, what was it to take it one step further?

Penn's hands trembled as he gripped his sword. But his inexperience did not move him from his spot.

Nicholai saw them. He removed the shield from his back.

Vadim and Penn clashed blades.

The Southeastern Time Father ran to Umbriel and Aggi, charging into Vadim with the full force of his shield.

Vadim stumbled but caught himself before he fell over. "Give it up, Nicholai! Your weapon's been stilled!"

Nicholai matched Vadim's angered look. He knew he referred to Kazuaki. They were down without the immortal, but they were not out. "You have the power to end this now, Vadim. Unfreeze your division before this gets worse!"

An explosion erupted near the battling armies. Instinct urged Nicholai to turn, but he knew he couldn't take his focus off Vadim. Shrieks sounded from dying men in the distance as they burned in the unforgiving fire. Chaos surrounded them.

Vadim showed no intention of bending to Nicholai's pleas. He lunged at the Southeastern Time Father, swinging his sword like a mad man.

Nicholai kept him at bay with the shield. Each slam of Vadim's blade bounced off the oval armor. The man's wild swings were relentless. It was all Nicholai had to continue blocking them.

Granite turned from Nordjan, watching as the two men sparred.

Umbriel cradled Aggi in her arms on the ground. Even with Penn's help, Nicholai could not keep him at arm's length forever.

Granite abandoned his fight with Nordjan and crossed the distance with a swiftness others did not know he possessed. Granite knew he couldn't kill him, but he could render him harmless. He approached from behind and drove his blade through the back of the Time Father's knee. It entered the soft flesh and sank into the patella before he pulled it out.

Vadim crinkled under his weight.

Before Granite pierced the other leg, Nordjan fired a round into his back.

"Nordjan!" Nicholai stepped back from the fallen Vadim. "What are you doing? Stop this nonsense!"

Granite turned, glowering at Nordjan. He stepped toward him.

Nordjan, terrified, fired again. The bullet sank into Granite's shoulder.

He continued to advance.

"Granite, stop!" Nicholai ran to the man, but a panicking Nordjan fired again.

The third bullet found Granite's side, and he showed his first signs of pain.

Penn charged the Northern Time Father.

Nordjan readying to shoot again, but Granite's dog beat Penn to the punch and bit hard onto his wrist. The gun fired into the rocks. The beast's teeth sank deep into his opponent's skin, tearing flesh and muscle as he jerked his head to the side. Nordjan cried out. He dropped his gun and tried to shove off the animal, but its attack was without mercy.

Penn tackled him, his hands around the man's Chronometer as he tried to rip it from its chain.

Granite took two more steps toward Nordjan before he fell to his knee.

Nicholai witnessed his labored breathing from behind.

Umbriel abandoned Aggi; though he lingered outside a full recovery, he was free from the dark woods of death. She rushed to assist Granite.

"Edvard!" Nordjan shouted as he battled with Penn and the mongrel. "Your Chronometer!"

Edvard saw Nordjan standing in Western with his assailants; Granite and Umbriel were in the division too. It became clear what Nordjan had screamed about. He wanted him to stop Western's time.

"Edvard!"

Nicholai watched his father battle a large, mental monster.

He hesitated. The man had never sullied his title before. What came easy to the others in their alarm did not come easy to the elder Addihein. His eyes found Nordjan as the beast pulled him to the ground. It attacked his forearms as Nordjan protected his neck.

"Edvard! Now!"

The Western Time Father shook. He looked to Nicholai and saw it in his son's pleading eyes not to do it. With a hesitating resentment, Edvard looked once more to Nordjan as Penn and the dog clawed him. A trembling hand removed his Chronometer from his breast pocket and pulled the crown.

That was the last. Nicholai looked at Aggi, who pulled himself to his feet. Umbriel had stopped the bleeding, but the wound still felt fresh.

Nordjan scowled as he pushed himself to his feet, crawling from beneath Penn and the dog. He glared at Nicholai and approached him. He opened his mouth to speak, but another buck from the earth below knocked everyone off their feet.

More large chunks of land crumbled into the giant chasm. It swallowed the rubble whole. Nordjan's wrath consumed his mind too much for him to pay it any mind. With his gun frozen in time, he approached Avital's body and plucked the dead man's weapon from his hands. "I believed you would be Panagea's salvation," Nordjan said as he advanced toward Nicholai, his fury surrounding him like violent flames.

Nicholai stepped backward but was running out of space. His boot touched the edge of the canyon, and debris fell into the darkness. "I still could be, if you'd listen to reason."

Nordjan shook his head. "You don't even know the darkness you're trying to invite back into the world, Nicholai. I can't let that happen." He raised Avital's gun and aimed at Nicholai's head.

"Nordjan ..." Nicholai gripped his shield, ready to use it if need be. "Darkness is already upon us. Look around. How much worse could it get?"

"You have no idea." Before he fired, Nicholai lunged forward, ramming into Nordjan with his shield. The man fell backward but caught himself before he hit the earth.

Aggi watched the men wrestle and stepped forward to help, but his chest still felt as though its contents would spill out. The pain split across his entire torso, from arm to arm. It sent his body back to its knees.

Nicholai blocked a series of Nordjan's efforts.

The Northern Time Father could not get a clean shot with Nicholai's shield in the way. He seized Nicholai's arm, but a swift headbutt from the Southeastern Time Father sent the man stumbling backward. He growled, staring down Nicholai from his position near the canyon wall. "You can't win," he said, exasperated and out of breath. "I won't let you destroy the world, Nicholai."

"Look around us, Nordjan." Nicholai outspread his arms, gripping the shield. "The world is already dead. I'm trying to save what's left."

"You don't—" Nordjan lost his footing as the piece of land where he stood gave way beneath him.

Nicholai abandoned his shield, lunging to grab Nordjan's arm before the abyss swallowed him. He grunted, his stomach flat against the jagged earth as he clung to the vulnerable man.

Nordjan's face showed terror. He dropped his gun into the shadows below. His boots tried to scrape into the wall, but it only gave way from the pressure of his feet. Another eruption sounded in the background. The fires spread so far he witnessed a soft orange glow glisten in the sweat on Nicholai's face. Soft pieces of ash fell from the deadened sky. It was a surreal experience, being surrounded by four division's frozen in time. The world seemed only half alive as Nicholai summoned all his energy to pull Nordjan from the edge.

The Northern Time Father felt relieved to find solid ground again. He crawled forward, panting as he distanced himself from Nicholai. Edvard's heart pounded. His son had saved Nordjan's life. The wind blew his hair as he watched, paralyzed like half the world around him.

"Are you okay?" Nicholai leaned forward as he rested his palms on his knees.

Nordjan curled his fingers into the hard rocks. His gun belonged to the underworld now, but he still had his machete. "Never better." He panted as he unsheathed the weapon from his side and drove it upward to Nicholai in a surprise attack.

Nicholai raised his arms in defense, an instinct to protect his face guiding him. The blade ate through his forearm, severing it at the elbow. Nicholai's face whitened as he fell to his knees. Blood turned cold in his veins. His brain tried to process what had happened to his body, but it was so quick. He gripped his arm and tried in vain to tourniquet the wound, but his condition didn't grant him much success.

Nordjan towered over him, casting a shadow over the fallen man's form. "It had to be this way, Nicholai." His breath spilled out in large gasps. "You stay the course. There is no unknown to fear if you keep the unknown at bay. I'm sorry. Your ideals are just too grand."

Nicholai's blood pooled around his knees. "Are my ideals too grand?" he whispered, his hand shaking as he clutched his elbow, "or are yours too small?"

"I'm sorry, Nicholai." He raised his weapon to finish the job.

Nicholai felt every beat of his heart. Despite the surge of adrenaline, the organ seemed to slow. He felt the surrounding earth. Panagea. Her desperate howls of agony at her unnatural state. He heard her in his head, screaming. But the screams sounded angelic as he waited for the blade to come. He wasn't sure if it was the blood loss that caused him to watch Nordjan collapse to his knees, but soon the Northern Time Father's body was on the ground with his; his machete dropped from his hands. Nicholai looked up.

Edvard towered over him, his blade wet with blood from the back of Nordjan's knees.

The screams of Panagea died out from Nicholai's ears, replaced by the haggard cries emanating from Nordjan.

Edvard reached down and pulled his son to his feet and away from the fallen man. He set him down a safe distance away as half the world burned in flames.

Nicholai found his father's gaze, his confused eyes darting around the elder Addihein's face.

"I'm so sorry, Nicholai." Edvard exhaled heavily, spying his son's missing arm. "I'm so sorry."

Nicholai reached a quivering hand to his elbow. He laid the palm on the gash and closed his eyes. It was a nerve-racking gamble, but he had no other choice—roll the dice or risk bleeding out. Concentrating with an effort he hadn't attempted since he killed had Darjal in Avadon, Nicholai isolated the time on his injury.

Damaged veins healed. Torn muscle fused. Skin regrew over the wound, and he dropped his hand, exhausted.

Edvard almost dropped him from the startling display. "H-How did you ...?"

"Restart your time." Nicholai coerced his legs to work as he got to his feet. The world around them shook. They didn't have much time. He put one desperate hand on his father's shoulder to steady himself. "Please."

Edvard tightened his jaw and nodded. He pushed his Chronometer's crown, releasing Western from its frozen state.

Umbriel shook her head as soon as she could and found Granite's body before her. Without delay, she went to work, desperate to spare his life.

Nicholai dragged himself to Vadim and fell to his knees.

Aggi joined his side. The Northwestern Time Father felt weak from his blood loss, but he still gripped his leg with vigor.

"Restart your division," Nicholai ordered, "and I will heal your leg."

Vadim noticed Nicholai's detached. He thought the Southeastern Time Father was as good as dead. The man held a magic Vadim did not know he possessed. Though he didn't show it on his face, the unknown potential terrified him into submission. He looked to Avital's body then to the writhing, powerless Nordjan, and, at last, to Edvard Addihein, who had betrayed their trust. He scowled, but, despite his hesitation, he gripped his Chronometer and pushed the crown.

As soon as Western and Northwestern restarted, the shaking decreased. The violent rumbles slowed. A man of his word, Nicholai placed his hands on Vadim's leg and healed the injury, pleased he had enough volition to keep his efforts contained to the wound.

Revi, Brack, Rennington, and Elowyn stumbled on their feet as the division returned to life. They all gazed around, trying to make sense of what had happened while they sat immobilized.

Edvard watched his son for a moment before he tore his gaze away and advanced toward Nordjan. He knelt.

Nordjan peered at him with malice. Another low rumble of thunder occurred, but this time, from the gathering storm clouds. Rain fell on his disappointed face. "What have you done, Edvard?"

Drops of water from the heavens slithered down the Western Time Father's cheeks. "Enita's ideals live on through my son, Nordjan. I won't watch her vision die twice." He wore his guilt on his face. His beloved wife. He had wronged her so terribly. He was unsure which gutted him more: that his ignorance had driven Enita to her fate or that he had almost led Nicholai to the same predetermined course. "It's over, Nordjan. You're either with us or you're against us."

The Northern Time Father stiffened, and he winced as the pain in his leg spread throughout his body. "You know where this path leads. You'll regret this one day, Edvard Addihein. Mark my words."

Edvard tightened his lips. He drew a deep breath and looked over his shoulder at Nicholai. Nordjan was right. Perhaps one day he would regret his decision. But not today. "Restart your division, Nordjan, or I'll find someone who will."

His opponents outnumbered him. Vadim had relented. Edvard had betrayed him. Avital was dead. Nordjan was not an unintelligent man. His blood-caked hands slid to his Chronometer, and he pressed the crown, freeing Kazuaki and Bermuda from their prison.

The individuals reacquainted themselves with movement again. They seemed confused but were quick to catch up to the goings-on.

Kazuaki gripped Bermuda's arm, relieved she was still alive.

She found his eyes and flashed an exasperated smile. Though the world around them burned, they took solace in the safety of the other.

"Call off your armies," Nicholai instructed Vadim, Edvard, and Nordjan.

The men looked across the expanse to the battling militias. The split in the earth separated them. It would take time to reach them, and he had none to spare.

The Southeastern Time Father looked to Kazuaki. "Captain, I have to go to Southeastern."

Kazuaki noticed Nicholai's missing arm. He wanted to address it but stopped himself. "Take the flying machine. We'll finish up here."

Nicholai beheld the chaos that surrounded them. The rain tempered the flames, but their surroundings still appeared ravaged. Vadim and Nordjan had relented, but a chance existed that they might buck. Umbriel loomed over Granite, still trying to heal the man's bullet wounds. His dog licked his face. Avital was dead. They needed a new Time Father for Eastern before the day's end. There were so many uncertainties. "Are you sure?"

"We got this, Nico. Go."

Nicholai hesitated but only for a moment. Duty drove him forward. He climbed into the flying machine and booted it up, his heart pounding as he rose farther away from the people who had become his closest comrades. He trusted they could handle it. What he was less sure of was himself. But he couldn't delay it any longer. After witnessing the aftermath of four frozen divisions and what it did to Panagea, after hearing her screams burn inside his brain, he knew he could stall no longer.

It was time to restart Southeastern. It was time to say goodbye to Lilac Finn.

Chapter Twenty-Seven

The journey to Southeastern bathed Nicholai in surrealism. With nothing but his thoughts to keep him company, he should have gone insane. His final months had hardened him. His resolve grew countless callouses. The flying machine floated over the war-torn land of Panagea for only a moment until it followed through Southeastern's stillness. He felt illusory as he left behind the chaos and noise of Panagea's center, where the soldiers still battled, unaware the war had ended in icy neutrality on all sides.

The quiet of Southeastern issued a madness. Nicholai felt fortunate to operate the flying machine, for the squeaks of old gears saved him from the insanity of complete and total silence. It took almost a full day to arrive at his home. He departed Panagea's center in darkness and watched the sun rise and fall again with many sleepless hours of internal contemplation before he neared his hometown. A part of him felt thankful for the long trip. They were additional hours Lilac got to live.

Nicholai landed the machine when the familiar sight of Nenada came into view. He experienced a strangeness entering the land again. He felt uninvited. Nicholai dragged his resistant feet from the flying machine and stepped onto the cobblestones of his home for the first time in what seemed like years. It felt like a foreign land. Free from the crippling aftermath of months' worth of disasters, Nenada remained as he had left it, down to the last spec of dirt.

He saw his house. He saw Lilac. Rodgie. Though he tried to prepare himself for this moment, no amount of time could have made it any easier. Seeing her again just as he'd left her gutted him in a far more critical way than Nordjan had when he stole his lower arm. He wanted to run, to jump back in the flying machine and restart his quest to save her. But he couldn't. He had traversed the world, searching for a certainty, but he only found one.

He could not save Lilac Finn from her fate.

Nicholai took a deep breath and coerced his legs to cross the distance to her. She reflected perfection still, more stunning than any goddess from the tales of old. He reached to touch her face, though the action left him with more sorrow than comfort. Her skin still felt warm, her body not allowed to deteriorate. Her hair, the red curls he fell in love with, still framed her horror-stricken expression.

"I am so sorry, Lilac," Nicholai whispered. Though his words were soft, they felt loud in the stillness. "I really let you down."

He had promised her when he had left he would find a solution. But promises and pipedreams lived in the same category. This was one ideal even the idealist could not trick himself into believing anymore. He freed his Chronometer from its hiding place beneath his clothing and stared at the clock face—5:15. That time had lived on the Chronometer for months now. He would never forget that sequence of numbers.

Nicholai's thumb crept to the crown. "You would have been proud of where the world's going," he said to her as he tried to catch his breath. "It's everything you ever wanted for this place."

It hurt that she couldn't respond, but he hoped on some cosmic level she heard him. His head told him it was impossible, that she couldn't absorb his words, but his heart let him believe a small shred of possibility existed. Nicholai leaned forward. He gave her a final, tender kiss on the cheek and took several steps backward.

"Goodbye, Lilac." He clutched the cold metal of his Chronometer. "I'll always love you."

For Panagea. For her people. Summoning every ounce of willpower he possessed, Nicholai rubbed his thumb over the exterior of his Chronometer and locked eyes with the woman he loved. Then he pressed the crown.

SIX MONTHS HAD PASSED since the decennial. Panagea was slow to heal, but her progress breathed relief into everyone's lungs. Edvard sat at his desk, finishing a letter he intended to send to Nicholai. The Western Time Father discovered contentment in keeping the doors of communication with his son open. Though their responsibility to their divisions kept them from seeing one another in person, the written word carried their sentiments well.

Their relationship had grown one step beyond neutrality. With each passing month, Nicholai abandoned slivers of his caution toward Edvard. It was understandable why he clung to it. Edvard did not blame his son for his skepticism. His behavior, while Nicholai was on the run, would leave a bitter taste in any man's mouth. Not a day passed when Edvard did not count his blessings that Nicholai spoke to him at all.

He folded the parchment with care and placed it in an envelope. A wax seal bearing the Western insignia secured the letter inside. Edvard frowned as he picked at a small trace of red wax that tainted his near-perfect circle. He sighed, sitting back in his chair with the letter in his hands. So much had changed in the last six months.

Trees grew. Plants. Things the people of Panagea had never witnessed in their lifetimes. Some were slower to embrace the change than others. Edvard worried about Nicholai's safety more than he'd like. While the majority relished in the new opportunities, Panagea's society of elites despised Nicholai's efforts—the factory owners who had to shut down production to make way for reforestation efforts, the blue bloods who no longer enjoyed the constant filter of finances the poor folk of Panagea hurled into their bank accounts, the citizens of Southern who still believed Darjal was a god; even a handful of men and women who lost their industrial jobs expressed a clear dislike for the man who had changed the world.

But the voices of those who had witnessed the daily horrors of Panagea's state rejoiced. And those voices were the majority. Only a few lived in denial, sheltered from the bucking world's brutality. Unfortunately, they were also the most influential. It earned Nicholai several assassination attempts. With Kazuaki Hidataka and the crew still living in Southeastern territory, none of the attempts were successful, but still, he worried.

His concern for Nicholai replaced his previous concerns for Western. What was once a daily routine of sending aid to ravaged lands and finding suitable shelter for those whose homes had disintegrated from the disasters slowed. Months passed since Edvard heard any word about a natural disaster. Panagea responded well to nature's reintroduction. The ecosystems appeared to soothe the crumbling land. No longer did whole chunks of earth break off into the sea. Though the terrain was healing, it still showcased its scars. The split that bisected the world center remained the most devastating. A huge canyon that sliced through the land, it had taken many homes and even more lives, forever a marker of what had occurred at the previous decennial.

Rebuilding in all the divisions took time. Resources were hard to come by. It was clear several territories blossomed sooner than others. Bartholomew of Southern put great effort into turning his division into a learned land. Scholars and eager young minds flocked to the Southern division's learning institution to gain skills beyond general labor. Bartholomew promised one institution would become many as soon as they rebuilt the rest of Southern and insured the people's safety.

Emont of Southwestern fared well. Though he did not have a strong political background, he harbored a natural resolve to ensure his people lived well. Once a castaway himself, much of his efforts poured into humanitarianism. Southwestern sprawled with farmland as he encouraged others to grow edible foods and medicines in the hopes his people never went hungry or lingered in sickness again.

The biggest change Edvard and many other Time Fathers needed to get used to, however, was Elowyn of Eastern. Never had a woman taken a position of power. Confusion existed as to her title, but, after initial hesitation, she and the rest of Panagea settled on Time Mother. A handful of revolts followed. Some men were not ready to admit women harbored leadership potential. Eastern's footmen handled their outbursts humanely. Though Elowyn stood as a firm leader, she remained fair. She always let the voices of her people rise, even when the words were less than flattering.

Eastern still suffered from the aftermath of its many facilities. The surrounding air stayed thick with pollutants and chemicals that plagued the constituents. But Elowyn's medical degree benefitted the failing health of Eastern's people. She had established several new hospitals within the six short months she ruled her division. She threw an invisible net over the whole of Panagea, summoning its most talented doctors to flock to her cities with offers they couldn't refuse. There weren't many, as the medical profession remained undervalued, but Elowyn Saveign worked without rest to change that.

Watching the people take piles of rubble and turn them into something better was incredible. It seemed more of Panagea was salvageable than Edvard had first thought. He looked at the letter in his hands. With any luck, his blossoming relationship with

Nicholai would be as salvageable as the whole of Panagea. Edvard sighed once more. So long as his son never discovered the truth about his mother, Enita, he hoped they could mend those fences again.

"COME NOW, I'VE SOMETHING to show you." Umbriel led Malcolm Finn toward his modest backyard. With one hand guiding his and another covering his eyes, she ushered the man outside.

Malcolm chuckled, trying not to stumble in his current state. "I haven't seen you this excited since you first laid eyes on the greenhouse."

"Yes, well ..." Umbriel smiled as she positioned him in the right spot. "I think you'll find this surprise quite special."

Malcolm caught its scent before she removed her hand. His eyes welled beneath her palm. When Umbriel unveiled her gift, he nodded, raising his hands to his face to cover his mouth. The fragrant blossoms were unmistakable. Though fifty years had passed since he last inhaled the once-extinct shrub's distinguishable scent, the brain never forgot. Scent remained the strongest tie linked to memory. "Umbriel ... it's perfect."

The delicate purple splashes of tiny flowers greeted him. The lilac bush waved in a soft breeze. With a tender hand, Malcolm touched the tips of the buds yet to spring to life. A tear slid down his cheek. "She would have loved it."

Umbriel smiled again, her hands behind her back. "It's the least I could do. You and Nicholai have been most accommodating while we rebuild Southeastern's ecosystems."

Malcolm tore his gaze from the bush to face the Earth Mother. "You two have started something incredible." He wiped an impending tear from his eye. "Lilac would have absolutely adored you, my dear."

A blush swept across the woman's cheeks. "I suspect I would have adored her as well. I'll see you tomorrow, Malcolm. I assured Nicholai I would handle some responses to the letters he's gotten."

"Ahh ..." Malcolm nodded in understanding. "Off to visit her grave again, is he?"

"Third time so far this week," Umbriel replied with a gentleness. "But a healing heart takes time."

"Indeed, it does," Malcolm faced his lilac bush again. "This will certainly help mine. Thank you, Umbriel. Take care. I'll see you on the morrow."

The Earth Mother bowed out of respect and sauntered from Malcolm Finn's greenhouse toward Nicholai's homestead. She took up residence in his modest home, though he ensured she maintained utmost privacy. It was an arrangement of convenience. Often, the pair went to reforest different parts of Southeastern. She planted the seeds, he expedited the growth, she replenished his life. Long nights had been spent away from Nicholai's home in Nenada. It was a tandem effort that only made her feelings for Nicholai flourish, but she possessed enough respect to keep her heart in check. She'd suffered hundreds of years to come to terms with losing the love of her life. Nicholai had only endured six short months.

The Earth Mother arrived at the Addihein homestead and seized the overwhelming number of letters from the satchel left on the porch. A series of penned words flooded Nicholai's doorstep since word spread and the revolution had ended. Most of the letters exuded gratitude. Others were death threats. They answered as many as they could, sure to address any of Panagea's citizens' concerns.

Just as Umbriel sat and spilled the satchel's contents onto the tabletop, she heard a knock. With a curious tilt of her head, Umbriel abandoned her task and opened the door.

A young woman stood before her, barely an adult. She looked to be a strong thing. Short, unkempt hair the color of rust framed her thin face. She looked the part of a traveler who had come a long way; her old clothes showed clear evidence of repairs. Her skin went unwashed, but her eyes shined with eagerness at Umbriel's appearance.

"Pardon me, miss." The youth adjusted the traveling pack she held over her shoulder. "I'm looking for the Southeastern Time Father. Is this his residence?"

"It is," Umbriel replied with a smile. "He's out at the moment but should be back in about an hour. You're more than welcome to rest here while you wait for his return." The Earth Mother stepped aside, allowing the teenager to enter.

Cautious steps carried her forward, and she loitered awkwardly in the hallway. "I appreciate your kind gesture, ma'am. Thank you."

"Of course." Umbriel disappeared into the kitchen to fetch food. Her visitor appeared as though she needed a good meal. "May I ask what your business is with Nicholai?"

The young woman cleared her throat. "Well, I'd like to ask him about the revolution. I understand he had some help in the matter."

"Oh, very much so." Umbriel placed sliced apples on a plate and returned to her guest. "It was a grand effort on everyone's part. Help came from all around us."

"So I've heard." She accepted an offered apple slice and took a bite.

Though she tried to restrain herself, Umbriel saw she inhaled the food with expedience. "Have as many as you'd like." She set the plate on a table beside her visitor. "Can I ask your name, young lady?"

She swallowed the apple and grabbed another. With her mouth half full, she nodded, trying to finish the bite before she spoke again. "Avigail. Avigail Houton."

NORDJAN PACED HIS GRAND room with impatience. It had taken weeks to find the right man for this job. When he heard Jernal had survived the slaughter at sea on Darjal's ironclad, he knew he was the soldier for the task. Darjal spoke of him well. Prying the man from his family and escorting him to Northern territory had been a feat. Jernal had resisted slightly, contemplating retirement from the militia, but Nordjan was desperate. He made him an offer he couldn't refuse.

The door creaked open, and a footman stuck his head inside. "Jernal is here to see you, sir."

Nordjan sat up straighter. "Send him in."

Panagea's finest soldier slipped through the towering doors and into Nordjan's presence. He did not seem eager to be there, but he donned an obedient face. "You wished to see me, My Lord."

"You can drop the semantics, Jernal. My ego is not as large as the late Darjal Wessex. Call me *Nordjan*."

The footman's shoulders eased but only a little. "Can I inquire what this is about, Nordjan? I've only gotten several months with my family since ... since the decennial," he forced himself to say, unsure how else to describe the end of the revolution. "I would very much like to return to them if we're through with the war."

His words were bold, but Nordjan resisted expressing a show of irritation as he paced before the soldier. "The war is far from over, Jernal. I'm afraid it's just beginning."

Jernal arched a brow. He held fast to the secret that he was pleased things had ended. Restoration efforts had dominated the last six months. He did not have to worry about the deaths of men under his command anymore. He did not have to send letters to spouses and children detailing their husbands' and fathers' funerals. "I don't follow."

"That damnable Kazuaki Hidataka eliminated every assassin I've sent to Southeastern. So long as that immortal is in his back pocket, he's untouchable."

"Yes." Jernal remembered Kazuaki Hidataka's power well. Darjal had lied to him. His immortality was not the fabrication the late Time Father had claimed. He still counted his blessings Nicholai had instructed the captain to leave him on the ironclad that fateful day. "I'm well aware of his ... abilities."

"As word spreads of their uprising, more tales come to light about the company he keeps. Biographers and wordsmiths from across Panagea flocked to Southeastern. They've pulled details of those peoples' lives from the darkest crevices of the earth. An obscure rumor has surfaced about our legendary captain, Jernal."

The soldier narrowed his eyes. Dealing with Nordjan was unfamiliar to him. Hope existed he led with a different perspective than the late Darjal Wessex, but Jernal realized the two were more similar than he thought. He suspected he knew where Nordjan was headed with his monologue. "With all due respect, sir, I have a hard time putting lives on the line for rumors. Especially when that rumor involves a cutthroat immortal."

"Yes, an immortal." Nordjan laced his hands together behind his back. "But an immortal whose soul belongs to the lesser god Mimir."

Jernal blinked. Not only did Nordjan show a similarity to Darjal in his quest for revenge, but he also showed a similarity in his level of insanity. "The lesser god Mimir is a fairytale, sir."

"No, no." Nordjan craned his neck to look at his ceiling. "As the old world returns, so will its gods. I tried to stop it, but the life that breathes into Panagea will soon ignite them as well. My fight to save Panagea continues, but, if they're coming, I will use them to my benefit. I dedicated the last several months trying to find that well, Jernal. I hired historians, poets, analysts, anyone who could decipher the texts of old who have long hidden from the public eye. I have narrowed it down to several places. You will lead a band of men there to free Mimir from his prison."

The man's plan lived in insanity. Jernal looked down and clenched his jaw. No matter how crazy he thought Nordjan, as long as he donned the uniform, he remained duty-bound to follow his orders. "And what if I do manage to find Mimir and free him? What then?"

Nordjan scowled. It was small but present. "I'm just trying to do the right thing, Jernal. We'll let him claim what is rightfully his."

"ALMOST THERE," KAZUAKI said. What remained of his crew followed close behind as he approached the large storage building.

Revi, Brack, Granite, Bermuda, Penn, and the mongrel stopped near Kazuaki's side as they beheld the tall facility with questioning eyes. The captain appeared eager to show them whatever prize hid inside. A huge build up had existed during the last several months. Kazuaki seemed to know something they didn't, but the time flew by. Many things had occurred, which made the wait quick to pass.

Elowyn had accepted the leadership of Eastern. Bartholomew thrived as Southern's Time Father. Rennington had issued his retirement from hunting legends and reinstated his old title as a soldier to Southern now that it operated under a man worth fighting for. His farewell had held a heaviness, but he said Iani's ghost had called to him, pushing him to finish what they had started together in Southern many years ago: protecting the land they called home. The crew missed him with a fierceness, but they were delighted he remained close to Bartholomew as he climbed his way to becoming an immaculate division leader.

Though their small group felt smaller, Bermuda did not feel the absence as much as she had anticipated. They had found their homes. For that, she felt grateful. It felt like less of a loss and more of a victory.

Kazuaki faced them all with a smirk. "Ready?"

Without waiting for a response, he opened the door. The team entered. The stunning sight of the airship filled their vision. It looked reminiscent of Kazuaki's ship but outfitted with everything it needed to conquer the skies instead of the seas.

"She's a beauty, Cappy," Brack said with a grin.

"Like the phoenix that rises from the ash," Revi added, smirking.

The men approached the airship to admire it closer.

Kazuaki directed his words to Bermuda, though he did not turn to look at her. "I got a real taste for it, flying that machine into Panagea's center. Nico hired some of the best engineers he could find. He told me the most talented went to restructuring Southeastern, but the leftovers were still capable."

She smirked at his joke, though truth lived in his statement. No longer did Nicholai blindly favor those he preferred. He had blossomed into a fair leader and took the collective's well-being into his thoughts first. She suspected that was why Kazuaki's surprise took so long to unveil itself; repairing homes and businesses were far more vital than crafting the airship. "It's amazing, Kazuaki. Truly."

The closeness of her body reminded him of their time spent in Aggi Normandy's residence. He thought of that moment a lot. Much more than he should have allowed himself to. They never discussed that day. Perhaps it was for the best.

The strong possibility existed he might never fall victim to Mimir's well. Without the ability to cleanse his soul, Kazuaki's tainted existence remained too much for Mimir to pull into his underworld. He felt he had returned to square one—an immortal man in love with an earthly woman, a woman he loved too much to allow himself to have. "Bartholomew sent me a letter," he said, tearing himself from his torturous thoughts. "He says his libraries grow by the day. He's taken on a lot of old texts, unearthed from many of Darjal's churches."

"Oh?" She arched a curious brow. She, too, noticed his proximity. Though Bermuda never discussed it, she did not forget the moment they shared in Northeastern, where only a sliver of air separated their lips. The memory made her stomach rise, but a pang of guilt in her chest always stopped her. It was hard to lose her heart to the captain when Ty still haunted it. "Anything of interest?" she asked, trying, as Kazuaki did, to redirect her mind's focus.

"A few. I know Nicholai isn't out of harm's way, but I feel his footmen can protect him and Umbriel during our departure." He peered at her from the corner of his eye, and his face shifted into a confident smirk. "How about it, Bermuda? Can you promise me the excitement of one more adventure?"

The quartermaster matched his grin. "Promise?" She nodded. "Cross my heart and hope to die."

FOR AN INTIMATE CEMETERY, it looked like a beautiful thing. In the stillness of a freshly grown forest on the outskirts of Nenada, Nicholai stared at the ornate statue that served as Lilac's headstone. She rested alone out here, but he did not consider her afterlife an isolated one. Life surrounded her. It just happened to be the life of plants, flowers, and trees.

He came here often. She called to him like a siren from beyond the grave. Though many months separated him from her when he had tried to find her salvation, she still felt like part of his existence, right until the moment he had restarted Southeastern. Since then, Lilac felt far away. Untouchable. And she was.

Nicholai spotted a vine of buds that tried to crawl up Lilac's statue. He reached his hand before him. A metal creation had restored his severed forearm; his steel fingers stretched as he gave time to the vine. He watched as it slithered up the marble and embraced it, twisting and curling until it engulfed it in its touch. Delicate white flowers opened in seconds and gave light to the statue. He lowered his mechanical arm to his side. He missed her.

"Mr. Addihein?"

Nicholai spun around, not at all surprised to see young Evvy standing behind him. She followed him out here often. Rodgie's daughter stood short at the tender age of eight and approached him with tiny steps.

"Good afternoon, Miss Evvy." Nicholai issued the child a quick bow. "How are you today?"

"Um, I'm good," she started, always skittish in her conversations, though she shared many with the Southeastern Time Father. "I wanted to tell you that my papa sends his sincerest apologies."

Nicholai nodded. It was the same speech Evvy gave him every time she followed him into the forest. After Nicholai had administered the black lung treatment he had secured from Aggi, the little girl responded well. While Rodgie had gone to Nenada's jail for his crimes against Lilac, Evvy had fallen into the capable hands of her aunt and uncle. She visited her father in jail often, and every time, he sent her to Nicholai with the same message. He mourned for what he'd done. "I know he does, Evvy. Thank you."

"Do you think he'll get out of jail soon?" she asked, the picture of innocence as the sunlight from the treetops filtered over her face.

Nicholai clenched his jaw. He remained slow to forgive Rodgie for what he'd done. Unlike Umbriel and her limitless heart, he just wasn't there yet. But he did not wish to sully the little girl's ideal of her father. "Evvy, when we do something wrong, we have to accept the consequences of our actions. It's what saves us from making the same mistakes twice. But no cage can keep his love from you, no matter how long he's there. If I know one thing about your father, it's he would do *anything* for you."

Evvy nodded and lowered her gaze to the grass. Nicholai gave her the same answer every time. "Thank you, Mr. Addihein." She turned to head back to her homestead.

Nicholai watched her go. His heart went out to her, but he could do nothing for Rodgie. He had made his bed. The Southeastern Time Father redirected his attention to Lilac's grave. It would be her home forever. Just as Rodgie's cell would be his.

He closed his eyes and tried to let the negative thoughts melt away from him. Some deep breaths in this peaceful place helped. Nicholai opened his eyes again, staring at the marble statue. Bright, colorful flowers flanked it on all sides. Much more fitting than the metal abominations she had put in that vase at their bedside. Not unlike the flowers Panagea blossomed—Lilac's vision of utopia.

A bird chirped from overhead. Nicholai looked up. It was the first sign of wildlife he witnessed since their reforestation efforts began. The winged creature landed on a branch, sounded several cheerful tweets then spread its wings and flew away. A genuine smile spread across Nicholai's face for the first time since he had restarted Southeastern.

The flowers, the trees, the birds—Lilac would have loved it.

A Note from the Author

From the bottom of my strange heart, thank you for picking up this book and giving your time to read it. I hope the characters crawled into your minds and live with you as they live with me. I would love to hear your thoughts if you wished to leave an honest review of your experience.

The Panagea Tales series by McKenzie Austin:

The Panagea Tales series:

The Tree That Grew Through Iron: Book One of the Panagea Tales

The Gods Who Harvested Men: Book Two of the Panagea Tales

The Serpent That Swallowed Its Tail: Book Three of the Panagea Tales

The Canary That Sang to the World: Book Four of the Panagea Tales

Other books in *The Panagea Tales* universe by McKenzie Austin:

From Steam to Salt: A Collection of Short Stories Featuring the Panagea Tales Crew

9 798201 652005